Praise for Graham Hurley

'A pleasurably intricate plot leads to a satisfying grotesque resolution, further enhancing the reputation of one of Britain's best-ever police procedural writers'
Morning Star

'Hurley never disappoints and here proves his standing as one of the UK's finest crime novelists'
Independent on Sunday

'There is no one writing better police procedurals today'
Sunday Telegraph

'Hurley's decent, persistent cop is cementing his reputation as one of Britain's most credible official sleuths, crisscrossing the mean streets of a city that is a brilliantly depicted microcosm of contemporary Britain'
Guardian

'There is no doubt that his series of police procedural novels is one of the best since the genre was invented more than half a century ago'
Literary Review

'Hurley writes inch-perfect, matter-of-fact police procedurals, but he peoples them with an almost Dickensian cast that set the books way above most of his peers'
Crime Review

'It is a very cleverly manipulated whodunnit, with a trickle-down conclusion that contains one final twist'
Crime Fiction Lover

Graham Hurley is the author of sixteen highly acclaimed crime novels, including the Faraday and Winter series. Adapted for TV in France, they proved a massive hit. Twice shortlisted for the Theakston's Crime Award, Graham now writes full time. He lives in Exmouth with his wife Lin.

Find out more at www.grahamhurley.co.uk or follow him on Twitter @Seasidepicture

By Graham Hurley

FICTION

Rules of Engagement • Reaper
The Devil's Breath • Thunder in the Blood
Sabbathman • The Perfect Soldier
Heaven's Light • Nocturne
Permissible Limits • The Chop
The Ghosts of 2012

DI JOE FARADAY INVESTIGATIONS

Turnstone • The Take
Angels Passing • Deadlight
Cut to Black • Blood and Honey
One Under • The Price of Darkness
No Lovelier Death • Beyond Reach
Borrowed Light • Happy Days

DS JIMMY SUTTLE INVESTIGATIONS

Western Approaches • Touching Distance
Sins of the Father

NON-FICTION

Lucky Break? • Airshow
Estuary • Backstory

THE ORDER
OF THINGS

Graham Hurley

An Orion paperback

First published in Great Britain in 2015
by Orion Books
This paperback edition published in 2016
by Orion Books,
an imprint of The Orion Publishing Group Ltd,
Carmelite House, 50 Victoria Embankment
London EC4Y 0DZ

An Hachette UK company

1 3 5 7 9 10 8 6 4 2

A CIP catalogue record for this book
is available from the British Library.

ISBN 978 1 4091 5343 6

Typeset by Deltatype Ltd, Birkenhead, Merseyside

Printed and bound in Great Britain
by Clays Ltd, St Ives plc

www.orionbooks.co.uk

For Daisy and Dylan
and
Mother Earth

Prelude

People talked about the jet stream all winter. They said it was too far south and way too violent. Bentner, especially when he was drunk, likened it to a conveyor belt totally out of control, bringing storm after storm crashing in from the Atlantic. People – strangers especially – were a little wary of him but they couldn't argue with the evidence.

Beachside cafés on the coast reduced to matchwood. Whole streets underwater. Yachts dragged from their moorings and tossed miles upriver. The main line to Cornwall left dangling over a huge breach in the Dawlish sea wall. In nearby Exmouth, storm watchers gathered in the windy darkness as wave after wave burst over the promenade, bringing more ruin. The sea had become an animal, they agreed. Voracious. All-powerful. Terrifying.

Then, in late spring, a big fat bubble of high pressure settled gently over the estuary, consigning a nightmare winter to the history books. The temperatures climbed. Kids paddled. Bird-watchers queued at Exmouth Quay for the morning cruise up-river. There were godwits, oyster catchers and an especially fine gathering of avocets. Nature, after a savage blip, had reset itself. No one, at first, seemed to notice the absence of the salmon.

They'd arrived at this moment in the cycle of the seasons ever since anyone could remember, near exhausted after their long migration from the depths of the Atlantic. A pair of grey seals patrolled the narrows where the river met the sea. Poachers prepared their nets a mile or so further inland. Local restaurateurs made a quiet call or two, reserving the first of the catch. But nothing happened.

The local pubs – in Exmouth, Lympstone, Topsham – were full of speculation. Fishermen blamed the farmers upcountry. Too many nitrates. Too much cow shit. A devout Baptist writing to the *Journal* suspected the hand of God. Only Bentner knew better.

From his precious patch of garden, down by the harbour in the village of Lympstone, he watched the river, listened to his neighbours and brooded. Earlier in the week those same neighbours had noticed the candles he used in his study still burning way past midnight. Then came the morning of his disappearance. It happened to be a Monday.

His line manager at the Hadley Centre, a woman called Sheila, phoned around midday. No reply. His mobile likewise was switched off. Late that afternoon she drove down from Exeter. Lympstone was a small waterside village which she barely knew: picturesque, intimate, not cheap. With the aid of a map, she found the street down by the harbour where Bentner lived.

Bentner's address had long been a joke at the Centre. *Two Degrees*. Was there any other climatologist who took his work that seriously? Who'd nailed a prediction about global warming on his front gate? For the benefit of the postman – and anyone else who might be interested in the future of the human race? Sheila, parking her car, thought not.

The house lay at one end of a small terrace. She paused by the gate, realising that the house name had been changed. The sign on the gate looked new, hand-lettered black script against a white background. *Five Degrees*, it read. She lingered, taking it in. She knew about this stuff. Everyone at the Hadley Centre knew about this stuff. A five-degree Celsius increase in global temperatures would be endgame. Over. Finished. Cooked. Gone.

Sheila knocked at the door. Waited. Knocked again. Nothing. She tried the door. It was unlocked. She wondered about going inside, then had second thoughts.

A path around the side of the terrace led to a scrap of pebble beach. The tiny back gardens of the terrace of houses ended in a brick wall that overlooked the beach. She paused for a moment, gazing out at the view. It was high tide, not a whisper of wind. The sun was still warm in a cloudless sky. Boats sat idly at their moorings. From way out across the water came the liquid cry of a curlew. Beautiful.

Five degrees? Hard to imagine.

On the beach she turned and studied the back of Bentner's house. A weathered wooden table sat on a scruffy oblong of paving stones. Two ancient camping chairs, the canvas seats bleached and frayed, were arranged for the view. A pair of unwashed plastic plates lay on the table. A wicker basket beside the door brimmed with empty cans and bottles. In the garden next door a line of flags hung motionless.

She eyed the wall, wondering whether she might be able to clamber over, but knew there was no point. If she wanted to get into the house, the door at the front was open.

Sheila retraced her footsteps, knocked a couple more times, then stepped in. A minute hall gave way to the sitting room. Through the window at the far end she could see the table in the garden and the water beyond. The sitting room was narrow and cluttered: threadbare carpet, piles of books, two battered armchairs, a card table with more books, a small TV, plus a couple of house plants that badly needed watering.

'Alois?' She called Bentner's name. No response.

The kitchen lay beside the sitting room. At first she put the flies down to rotting food – the smell too – but on closer inspection there was nothing edible to be seen. A four-ring electric stove blackly caked with ancient spills. A couple of days' washing-up in the sink. A lopsided fridge with a very noisy motor. Cupboards painted institutional green. She found herself smiling. To no one's surprise, least of all hers, the world of fitted kitchens had passed the legendary curmudgeon by.

She retreated to the hall, peering up the narrow wooden stairs, wondering just how far her responsibilities extended. Was it her business to check the whole place? Or was this the moment to head back out into the sunshine and phone for help?

Sheila tussled with the decision a moment longer, then came a movement in the darkness at the head of the stairs. Her blood iced. A cat stepped down into the light. It was a tabby. It looked at her and then turned and headed upstairs again.

She followed it, one step at a time, one hand extended, feeling for the scabby plaster on the walls. At the top of the stairs was a narrow landing. She counted three doors. The cat had disappeared but the smell, and the insistent buzzing, was stronger.

'Alois?' Almost a whisper this time. 'Are you there?'

She knew he wasn't. She knew something terrible had happened to him. Over the past couple of months his drinking and his temper had become an open secret. Alois Bentner was brilliant – everyone who knew him agreed on that – but the man had become his own worst enemy: ungovernable, erratic, given to wild explosions of something she could only describe as rage. Last weekend, at a barbecue at a canalside pub, he'd been physically restrained after a younger colleague had made a joke about the Siberian tundra farting methane. In Bentner's world, superheated or otherwise, there was no longer any room for jokes.

The first door opened on to a bathroom – cramped, dirty, with a dripping tap. The second door belonged to a room empty except for a pile of cardboard boxes and an air bed, semi-deflated, on the bare wooden floorboards. Through the grubbiness of the window she could see her own parked Astra. Was now the time to go downstairs, close the door and leave? She thought not. The least she owed Alois Bentner was to try the third door, to pursue the smell and the flies to their source. To do anything less would be a betrayal.

Sheila pushed at the door, felt it give under the pressure, let it open. For a second she couldn't believe what lay beyond. Then she backed away, gasping.

And fled.

One

It was Oona who took the call. Jimmy Suttle, in the shower after a day's recreational stoning of the force riot squad, saw her outstretched hand through the steam.

'Carole,' she mouthed.

DI Carole Houghton was Suttle's boss on the Major Crimes Investigation Team. Thanks to a riotous curry in an Exeter restaurant only weeks ago, the two women had become friends.

'Boss?' Suttle was already reaching for a towel.

'Lympstone, Jimmy. Soon as.'

'Why?'

'Murder. Ghastly scene. Truly horrible. If you're planning dinner ...' She broke off to talk to someone else, then she was back again. The job had been called in by a woman from the Met Office. Scenes of Crime had just turned up and were debating what to do. Det-Supt Malcolm Nandy, meanwhile, was driving over from another job in Brixham.

'Address, boss?'

'Down by the harbour. Terrace of little houses. You can't miss us. Quick time, yeah?' The phone went dead.

Suttle padded into the bedroom. Oona had retreated beneath the duvet, only her face visible. She'd arrived an hour earlier, bearing gifts, a routine she and Suttle adopted when their shift patterns offered the chance for an evening together.

Now she was watching Suttle as he threw on a shirt and tie. She'd already started on the first bottle of Rioja and was halfway

5

through a bowl of hummus and olives. Suttle eyed her in the mirror. One of the many things he loved about this woman was her talent for hiding disappointment.

Dressed, he stood beside the bed. She extended a hand, gestured him lower, ran her fingertips across his ruined face.

'Later, my lovely?'

'Later,' he agreed.

Lympstone was ten minutes away. Mid-evening, the light was dying over the soft ridge lines of the Haldon Hills as Suttle drove down into the village. Mention of the terrace of houses beside the water took him back a couple of years. Eamon Lenahan, a key witness on another job a couple of years ago, had lived in one of these houses, and Suttle remembered his first sight of the view before he'd rung the bell and brought the little man to the door: the water lapping at the footings of the garden, the way the boats flirted with the tide on their moorings beyond the tiny bay, the broad reach of the river as it gathered and fell back, day after day, year after year.

Wee Eamon had let this rhythm seep into his life. No TV. None of the me-me crap that passed for real life these days. A wandering doctor fresh out of Africa, he'd embraced the silence and the ever-changing fall of light through his window, and now – with a similar view from his rented Exmouth flat – Suttle knew exactly how important that could be.

'Skip?' Luke Golding was bent to the driver's window. He was wearing a grey one-piece forensic suit a size too big.

Suttle wound the window down. Golding was still one of the youngest DCs on the squad. He'd just returned from a week in Turkey, and it showed in the peeling skin across his forehead.

'Good time?'

'Crap, skip.' He nodded back towards the end house. 'You're not going to believe this one.'

Suttle got out of the car and limped towards the Crime Scene Manager, who was standing beside the front gate. The CSM was on the phone. He had a pile of bagged forensic suits at his feet and he tossed one to Suttle as he approached. Golding wanted to know why Suttle was limping.

'Day out with the Public Order lot.' He was tearing at the polythene around the suit. 'I did OK with the baton rounds, and the petrol bombs worked a treat. Then a bunch of them caught me. My own fault.'

'And?'

'I'm limping. As you noticed.'

'This was a jolly, right?' Golding took care of the polythene as Suttle clambered awkwardly into the suit.

'Right.'

'You go out to some forlorn bloody place and pretend to be the EDL, yes?'

'Yes.'

'So the hooligans in the ninja gear can beat the shit out of you? Am I wrong?'

'Not at all. It seemed a good idea at the time. In fact I was flattered to be asked.'

'Sure. So can anyone volunteer? Or do you have to be *really* mental?'

Shaking his head, Golding led the way to the open door. A line of treading plates disappeared into the house. A CSI was already at work on the ground floor. Suttle, aware of the smell, wanted to know what Serafin had made of Marmaris.

'Loved it, skip. Big time. Brought the Asian out in her. Couldn't get enough of the heat.'

They were climbing the stairs now. Serafin was Golding's latest trophy acquisition, a tribute to Internet dating. She had a degree in metallurgy and wonderful legs. Suttle had only met her once but knew she had the measure of Luke Golding.

'This one, skip. The pathologist's due within the hour. Deep breath now.' Golding had stopped beside one of the upstairs doors. He had a couple of paper face masks in his pocket. He handed one to Suttle. Suttle put it on, then took it off again.

'Who's been wearing this?'

'Me.'

'Since when did you smoke?'

'Last week, skip. I'm blaming Serafin. She drove me nuts, if you want the truth. Never stopped bloody talking. Yak, yak, yak. You need to stop drinking so much. We need to commit to each other. We need to take this thing seriously.'

'Thing?'

'Her. Me. Us. Here ...' He pushed the door open with his foot. 'Help yourself.'

Suttle, on the point of stepping into the room, stopped. A woman's body lay on the bed. She was naked, her legs splayed, her stomach ripped open. She looked late thirties, early forties. Coils of intestine spilled onto the blood-pinked duvet.

Suttle eased himself into the room. The stench – heavy, viscous, cloying – made him put the mask back on. The woman's face was battered and swollen, the bruises already yellowing. She was wearing a single gold ring on the third finger of her right hand, and a thin silver chain with a Celtic cross was looped around her left breast. Like Golding, she must have been away recently. Her skin was golden, and beneath the wreckage of her belly Suttle could see the outline of a bikini-bottom tan line.

'We've got an ID?'

'Yeah.'

'So who is she?'

'Her name's Harriet Reilly.'

'She lives here?'

'No. She's got another place in the village.'

Suttle was circling the body, trying to commit every detail to memory. The sightless eyes. The artfully permed hair. The silver piercings in one ear.

'Weapon?'

'Just the knife. There. Look.' Golding pointed at the floor on the other side of the bed. It looked like a kitchen knife. Serrated blade. Black plastic handle.

'It was lying there?'

'That's the assumption. No one's touched a thing.'

'So who owns the house?'

'Guy called Bentner. Alois Bentner.'

'So where is he?'

'No one knows.'

Suttle's mobile began to ring. It was DI Houghton. She needed a word. Suttle met her out in the street. It was starting to get dark now, and lights were on in the neighbouring properties. Twitching curtains. Faces at windows.

'Boss?' Suttle loosened the drawstring at the neck of the suit. He felt sullied, dirty. The fresh air tasted indescribably sweet.

Houghton tallied the actions she wanted him to take care of. Suttle knew the list by heart. Build the intel file on the victim and on the missing Alois Bentner. The latter, for the time being, was prime suspect. Talk to his friends, to his workmates, to anyone who might have crossed his path over the last few days and weeks. Same for Harriet Reilly. According to a woman across the road, she'd been a regular visitor at Bentner's place. Explore the relationship. Build the bigger picture. Why her? Why here? Why now?

'So who is she, exactly, boss?'

'We believe she's a GP. Word is, she works in an Exeter practice.'

'Any other leads, boss?'

'Nothing specific, but Bentner seems to be in some kind of trouble. Drinks too much. Thinks too hard.'

'Ugly combination.'

'Exactly. You need to start with the woman who called the job in. Her name's Sheila Forshaw. She's his boss. Bentner works at the Met Office. Heads up some kind of unit at the Hadley Centre. Bit of a star, the way we're hearing it.'

'Hadley Centre?'

'They deal in climate change. Ask Forshaw.'

'Where do I find her?'

'Heavitree nick. She's waiting for you. Operation *Buzzard*, by the way. Make a note.'

Houghton's phone rang. She was a big woman in every respect, but lately a crash diet had taken its toll. Her eyes were pouched in darkness, and in a certain light, like now, she looked ill. She answered the call, the frown on her face deepening by the second. The pathologist had been held up for some reason. Nandy was demanding yet another update. There were staffing problems with setting up the Major Incident Room for Operation *Buzzard*. All the usual gotchas.

'Take it easy, boss.' Suttle stepped out of the suit, remembering some advice she'd given him only months ago. 'Just another job, yeah?'

Two

Taking the train down to Exeter for a long weekend had been Lizzie's idea. She'd met him at the station, driven him back to her new house and shown him the wilderness that passed as the garden in the last of the light before they'd spent the rest of the evening in bed. Billy McTierney, she was pleased to discover, still did it for her. The months apart while she attended to all the post-publication rituals had, if anything, sharpened her appetite for his presence, and his body, and for the moments in the middle of the night when she jerked awake to find him propped on one elbow, a smile on his face, just looking at her.

Kissing him goodbye at the station, she'd told him to come back soon. Next weekend. The weekend after. For ever, if he fancied it. He held her for a long moment, told her she was fantasising, promised to stay in touch, and then – with a smile and a wave – he and the train were gone.

Driving back to the white stucco Victorian ruin which had relaunched her life, she felt warm, and wanted, and unaccountably lucky. The house lay close to the city centre, yet retained its privacy. The tall sash windows, golden in the last of the sunset. The huge front door, badly in need of a little TLC. The quarter-acre of garden with its encircling wall, mellow red brick dripping with honeysuckle and clematis.

She'd fallen in love with the property at first sight, undaunted by the years of work it would need to restore any kind of decorative order. The huge kitchen hadn't been touched for

11

decades, the central heating was a liability, and finding a use for five bedrooms would be a serious challenge. Yet the place had a presence and a quirkiness with which she felt immediately at home. Lizzie Hodson. The author of *Mine*. Praised in the broadsheets. Feted on local television. Already on the must-invite lists of countless literary festivals. And now the proud owner and sole inhabitant of The Plantation. Perfect.

Later that same evening, making the bed she and Billy had abandoned only hours earlier, Lizzie found the note he'd left her. It was tucked under the pillow, sealed in an envelope. She began to rip it open then had second thoughts. Another glass of wine, she thought. Give yourself time. Savour the moment.

Now, curled in front of an electric fire in the draughty sitting room, she laid the envelope on the rug and looked at it. In truth she'd been nervous about the weekend. Billy had helped her through the nightmare months after Grace's abduction and death. She'd been in pieces, incoherent with grief, but somehow he'd managed to bring her solace and comfort and the kind of undramatic but solid advice that had finally persuaded her that life was worth another shot.

In some kind of vague and wholly desperate way she'd always had a book in mind, but it had been Billy's idea to write it through the eyes of Claire herself. Claire Dillon had always been the monster in all this. It was Claire who had taken Grace, Claire who had hidden the little girl away, Claire who had silenced her crying with the overdose that had killed her, and Claire who had finally jumped from the seventh-floor balcony with Grace's limp little body in her arms.

If you were looking for blame then it had Claire Dillon's name in marquee letters all over it, yet a couple of months of exploring every bend in this girl's journey had taught Lizzie that life was never as simple as pain and retribution demanded. The woman had become a stranger to herself. Not only that, but as the weeks of writing sped by, and the pile of printed-out pages grew higher, Lizzie had concluded that – one way or another – we all had a bit of Claire Dillon in us.

She'd shared this thought with Billy over the weekend. That could have been me, she said. Given certain circumstances, I might have appointed myself Grace's guardian, Grace's best friend, the one good person in a bad, bad world to truly understand why this little girl had to be saved.

Billy had been unconvinced.

'That doesn't work,' he had said. 'You *were* Grace's guardian. You *were* her best friend. You were also her mother. And that makes a difference.'

'But you don't understand. We're all closer to the edge than we think we are. And you, of all people, must know that.'

Billy dealt with mentally ill people every day of his working life. He was an expert in the field. In a previous life he'd also been a professional climber, paid well for it, a man on intimate terms with gravity, the science of belays, karabiners and chockstones, the whole shtick. He knew about mountains, about keeping your balance – your sanity – on near-vertical faces of ice and slate, never admitting that there might ever be a problem that guts, and experience, and sheer nerve couldn't resolve. Billy McTierney had always been his own man, and that was one of the many reasons she'd quietly fallen in love with him. Nothing urgent. Nothing must-have. Simply the comforting knowledge that they were already, in countless unannounced ways, together.

She reached for the envelope. Then came the summons of an arriving email. She got up and settled herself behind her PC, the portal that had taken her to *Mine* and everything that had followed. She owed the PC her new home, her peace of mind and the weekend that had turned out to be such a success.

The email came from one of the handful of local contacts who'd signed up to the investigative website she'd launched. *Bespoken* had grand ambitions, not least to free itself from the tyranny of print media, but these were early days and she wasn't at all sure where this new adventure – funded on the proceeds of *Mine* – might lead. Were there really enough stories out there to attract a significant readership? And if so, did she have the financial resources and the sheer nerve to bet her investigative instincts against an army of litigious so-called victims? To both questions, on a cosy Monday night, she had no answer, but she bent to the screen, eager to know who might have touched base.

The message was both enticing and blunt. 'A local GP,' it read, 'is supposed to be in deep shit. It seems the woman plays God. Post-Shipman, this shouldn't be happening. Are we interested?'

Lizzie studied the screen for a long moment. Were we talking mercy killings? Something more sinister? Or what? She didn't know, couldn't make up her mind. What was the strength of the evidence? Where might an investigation like this lead? She shook her head. Exeter was a city for the young. So was Portsmouth. But there were places down on the coast that had become warehouses for the elderly.

The last time she'd been down to Exmouth to see her estranged husband, to tell him that the scars they both carried would one day heal, she'd been astonished at the sheer numbers of old folk around. They were everywhere: in the street, queuing at the bus stops, wandering uncertainly through the town-centre supermarket. With budgets squeezed and life getting tougher by the month, might people like these welcome the attentions of a rogue GP?

Back beside the electric fire, still uncertain, she at last opened the envelope. To her surprise, the note inside was typed. Billy hadn't arrived with a laptop and he'd never asked to borrow her PC. He must have composed it in Portsmouth, she thought. Even before he took the train west.

The note was short, written in the kind of carefully measured prose that clogged the arteries of corporate organisations. He was really glad about the success that the book had brought her. He'd hoped something like this might be on the cards but he'd never expected it to happen so fast. Getting her first book into the *Sunday Times* top ten was a real achievement. She nodded to herself, only too aware that this was the good news. He'd said something very similar on Friday night. What next?

'You're free now. You've really done it. You're home safe. You don't need me any more. It's been a real pleasure and a real privilege but for both our sakes I suspect we've come to the end of the road. Your book will open a million doors. I'll be thinking of you when I next open a copy of the *Sunday Times*. My fingers are crossed. Go well.'

She sat on the rug, staring at the note. 'Pleasure'? 'Privilege'? 'End of the road'? 'Go well'? Where did words like these belong in the relationship she thought they'd had? He must have carried this news in his head throughout the weekend. He must have known that every smile, every touch, every lingering kiss would end with this.

For a moment she toyed with phoning him. He'd be on the train. He'd probably be deep in a book. She wanted to know whether he was sitting there in an agony of guilt wanting to change his mind. She wanted to be told that everything she'd thought they had was real and true and *meant*.

She was crying now but she was angry too. Angry that she'd lulled herself into believing in something that would never happen. Angry because – in ways she couldn't yet voice – he'd taken advantage of her. *Bastard*, she thought, struggling to her feet.

At her PC she reread the email about the rogue GP. Then she reached for the keyboard.

'Yes,' she typed. 'Let's do it.'

Three

Sheila Forshaw was struggling to put her feelings into words.

'I expected it to be him ...' she said. 'Alois. That's what shocked me.'

'Alois Bentner?'

'Of course. It was his house. He lived there. If something bad had happened, something awful ... it had to be him on the bed ... didn't it?'

Suttle had met her downstairs, in the Custody Suite at Heavitree police station, where she was nursing a mug of stewed tea. Now they were sharing one of the adjoining interview rooms.

Sheila Forshaw was in her late forties, trim figure, office suit, barely any make-up. The image of the woman's body in the bedroom, she said, would stay with her for a very long time. On field trips abroad she'd seen plenty of bodies, often bloated in the heat. In Africa she'd watched what a lion could do to an antelope it had just run down. But nothing could compare to this. So raw. So savage. So ugly. So *still*.

Suttle wanted to know more about Bentner. Was she close to the man?

'No one's close to him. He's a loner, always was. Apparently there was a wife some while back, but I don't know anyone who ever met her.'

'Is she still around? The wife?'

'I don't know. You could check with HR, but they don't always keep that kind of information. Maybe she died. Or maybe she just left him and moved on. I know it sounds harsh, but I'm not sure I'd blame her.'

'So no real friends at work? Is that what you're saying?'

She nodded. Bentner, she said, had been at the Hadley Centre since it moved down from Bracknell in 2003. He was German by birth but had spent most of his childhood and early adult years in the States. She knew he'd landed a big job at NCAR at a very young age and had subsequently produced the string of papers that had finally brought him to the Hadley Centre.

'NCAR?'

'National Centre for Atmospheric Research. It's the top institute for climate research in the States. Boulder, Colorado. Up among the ski slopes. Lucky Alois.'

'And the Hadley Centre? How do you rate?'

'We're good, as good as NCAR. In fact in some respects we're probably better. World class, whichever way you cut it.'

'Is that why Bentner came on board?'

'Partly, I guess so. The other reason was much simpler. The States had started to piss him off. These are his words, not mine. He thought it was a country full of kids. Press the right button and he'd bang on about them for hours. How greedy they were, how wasteful they were, how they never spared a thought for tomorrow. Huge cars, vast fridges, everyone grossly overweight. Before the drinking got out of hand, some of this stuff could be quite amusing, though we had to be careful about who was listening.'

The Met Office, she said, attracted climatologists from every corner of the planet. Many of them were visiting Americans, aware of the Hadley Centre's reputation and wanting to find out more. In the early days on the new Exeter site, Bentner would never pass up an opportunity to berate his ex-colleagues. As a nation, he was convinced they'd converted a crisis into a disaster, partly by hogging way more than their fair share of resources and partly by frustrating other countries' attempts to rein in global warming.

'He was right, of course,' she said, 'but that wasn't the point.

There was always something very biblical about Alois. He wasn't just a climatologist, he was a prophet. One day, when he was being particularly obnoxious, I told him he belonged in the Old Testament. He loved that. It was one of the few times I heard him laugh.'

'So what does this guy actually *do*?'

'He analyses climate impacts. His big speciality has always been trees. Forest ecosystems are often where you look first if you want to figure out what we're doing to the planet. Every tree tells you a story, and I guess Alois made a friend of the trees pretty early on. He certainly prefers them to people.'

Suttle smiled. He liked this woman. He liked her easy intelligence, her candour about Alois Bentner and the way the jargon of her trade, lightly Americanised, sat so sweetly on her lips.

'But Bentner's good?'

'The best. That's partly an issue of standards. He never puts up with bullshit. He can smell a half-baked theory within seconds. He's truly rigorous, and in our business that matters. In the end we're scientists not tree-huggers, though Alois always lays claim to both.'

It was a neat phrase. Suttle wondered how many other times she'd used it.

'And you're his boss? Have I got that right?'

'I run his team. Though Alois is a bit of a stranger to the team idea.'

'So you indulge him?'

'I cut him lots of slack. Always have done. There aren't too many Alois Bentners in the world, and that's maybe a good thing, but we'd struggle to replace him.'

'And he knows that?'

'Of course he does. In fact he was probably the first to tell me.'

'A bully, then?'

'Without question. With people like Alois you fight or flee. The ones who flee are off his radar. He likes the ones who fight.'

'And you?'

'I'm his boss. That's supposed to make a difference.'

'But you stand up to him?'

'When it truly matters. Because that's the only option. Otherwise I'd be the punchbag.'

Suttle was thinking about the body on the bed.

'Does he ever talk to you about his private life?'

'Never. There'd be no point. In his view it wouldn't be relevant.'

'He never mentioned a girlfriend?'

'Never.'

'A woman called Harriet? Harriet Reilly?'

A shake of the head this time. And then something close to a frown.

'This is the woman I saw at his place?'

'Yes.'

'And you're telling me they were friends?'

'I'm asking you whether he ever mentioned her.'

'Then the answer's no, but that means nothing. They could have been married for years and we still wouldn't know. This is a man who walls off bits of his life. Maybe it's a German thing. I've no idea.' She paused. Something else even more troubling had occurred to her. 'You're suggesting Alois did that? To the woman on the bed?'

'It's a possibility. Of course it is. According to the neighbours, she was a regular visitor. She knew the house. She died in his bedroom. And now we can't find him.' He held her gaze. 'In my trade we call that a clue.'

'Christ.' She sat back, shocked. '*Alois?* Are you serious?'

The Major Incident Room, Operation *Buzzard*'s home for the coming days and weeks, lay in the Devon and Cornwall operational headquarters at Middlemoor, in Exeter. Suttle logged himself in at 21.57.

Det-Supt Nandy had arrived and was in conference with DI Houghton when Suttle rapped on their office door. Nandy, he thought, looked as knackered as Houghton. In a world of ever-deepening budget cuts, keeping the serious crime machine in working order was a constant battle, and a drug-related kidnapping in Brixham hadn't helped.

'Son?' Nandy, sat behind a desk, wanted an update.

Suttle told him about Bentner's workplace reputation. Brilliant climatologist. Crap human being.

'Crap how?'

'Classic Mr Grumpy. Zero people skills. Hated the rest of the human race and told them so.'

'Should be here then, with this lot. Sounds very ACPO.' Nandy barked with laughter. His ongoing feud with the bosses upstairs was common knowledge.

'Are we thinking he did it, Jimmy?' This from Houghton.

'I've no idea, boss. He's obviously in the frame. What's the scene telling us?'

'Dodman thinks she was killed in situ. There's no blood anywhere else.'

'None at all?'

'Not that the guys have found so far. She had a key to the house in her bag so access wouldn't have been a problem.'

'Prints on the knife?'

'Two sets. One of them hers.'

'*Hers?*'

'Yes. It means nothing, Jimmy. She could have been using the knife downstairs. We think it came from the kitchen.'

'And the other set?'

'We're thinking Bentner. They match with other prints elsewhere. But again it proves nothing.'

'Except it might rule out a third party?'

'Sure, son.' Nandy was studying his mobile. 'Unless they were wearing gloves.'

Nandy glanced up. He'd been talking to the CSM. Scenes of Crime had recovered a stash of empty bottles – chiefly wine and spirits – plus a handful of receipts from the convenience store down the road. This was a guy who seemed to be putting away industrial quantities of alcohol. He wanted to know about Bentner's drinking.

Suttle nodded. He'd asked Sheila Forshaw the same question. 'He's always had a thirst on him, sir. That's the impression I'm getting from his line manager. But lately it got out of hand.'

'How out of hand?'

'He'd turn up reeking of booze in the mornings. His boss got worried because he was driving, but there was nothing she could say that would make much difference.'

'Was he drinking at work?'

'She says not.'

'Just at home, then?'

'That's the assumption.'

'But a lot?'

'Yes.'

Suttle explained about a recent barbecue. Bentner had evidently lost it completely. Threatened to punch a younger colleague.

'Over what?'

'Methane emissions. In Siberia.'

'What?'

'Methane, sir. It's a greenhouse gas. You find it in cow farts. I gather that was part of the joke.'

'Shit.' Nandy's eyes rolled.

'Exactly. These people are a breed apart. Seriously bright. And in Bentner's case seriously damaged.'

'That's a big word, Jimmy.' Houghton, behind the other desk, was tapping out an email.

'That's the line manager's take, boss. Not mine. I got the impression that she thinks Bentner is a breakdown waiting to happen. The way I read it, most climatologists stick to the science and avoid thinking too hard about the consequences. Bentner doesn't see it that way, never has done. He thinks the two go together. We pump all this shit into the atmosphere, the world heats up, and we all die. I think that's the way it goes. That's certainly Bentner's line.'

'He changed his address recently, sir.' Houghton was looking at Nandy. 'The place used to be called Two Degrees. Since last week, according to the neighbours, he's been living at Five Degrees.'

'Meaning what?'

'We're all doomed, sir.' This from Suttle. 'Five degrees is where Bentner thinks we're headed. A temperature rise that big would kebab us all.'

'And is he right?'

'I asked that.'

'And?'

'No one knows. These people are scientists. They're into evidence.'

'Sure. Just like we should be. So where is Mr Bentner?'

Houghton shook her head, said she hadn't a clue. His ID photo from the Met Office had been circulated force-wide and would be going national tomorrow, along with details of his ancient Skoda. The media department were organising a press conference for late morning at which Nandy would be making a personal appeal to find the missing man. In the meantime local uniforms were scouring empty properties and other likely hidey-holes within a three-mile radius in case Bentner had gone to ground.

Suttle wanted to know about Harriet Reilly. Houghton gave him the headlines. Local address, a sweet little cottage on the outskirts of the village. Worked as a GP partner in a big Exeter practice. Allegedly lived alone after the collapse of her marriage years back. DC Luke Golding had already talked to a neighbour up the lane, and tomorrow, after the first *Buzzard* squad meet, Houghton wanted him and Suttle to pay the GP practice manager a visit.

'Her name's Gloria, Jimmy.'

'And she knows what's happened?'

'She does.'

Houghton scribbled a couple of lines and passed them across. The practice address plus a phone number.

Suttle looked up. 'Anything else I should know, boss?'

'Yes.' She gestured at her PC screen. 'I just had the pathologist on. He's finishing up at Lympstone, and whether it's germane or not, he thought we ought to know.'

'Know what?'

'Our victim was pregnant.'

Oona was asleep when Suttle got home. It was nearly midnight. He checked in the bedroom then helped himself to a can of Stella from the fridge. She'd left him half a saucepan of chilli con carne and the remains of some rice left over from a takeout they'd bought over the weekend. Also, a note.

Suttle sat in the window. 'My beautiful one,' she'd written. 'What's a girl supposed to do without you? The porn channels are useless and masturbation's a wank. Wake me up and tell me you love me. Special prize if you mean it. XXXX'

The big loopy letters brought a smile to Suttle's face. In the view of many in the Job he'd nicked this amazing woman from Luke Golding. Luke and Oona had been living together for the best part of six months when she transferred her affections to Suttle. It was true that Golding couldn't keep his hands off other women, and it was equally true that her departure hadn't surprised him in the least. There'd been some awkwardness between the two detectives for a while, but nowadays Golding was the first to admit that Oona deserved a great deal more than his serial excursions into Exeter's clubland, expeditions that frequently ended in sex with his latest conquest.

Only last month, for the first time since the break-up, the three of them had risked an evening in the pub together and a curry afterwards. Serafin had promised to show but never turned up, a gesture Oona attributed to more than a lapse of memory. 'She's probably shagging someone else,' she'd told Golding with a smile. 'Long live the sisterhood.'

Later, close to one o'clock, Suttle went to bed. Oona stirred and reached for him and then went to sleep again. Suttle lay in the darkness, his hand in hers. He loved the simplicity of the relationship. He loved that they still had separate addresses. He loved the space she allowed him and the way she seemed able to muffle the noises in his head.

Losing his daughter had triggered a nightmare that had threatened to engulf him. He had blamed her disappearance entirely on himself, but after months of talking it through with Oona, the pressing weight of guilt had begun to ease. It helped that he'd later had his own brush with death, a savage attack by a prime suspect that had nearly killed him, and whether she believed it or not, Oona had agreed that he should view the incident as payback. In the Almighty's scheme of things, she told him, he'd now paid his debt in full. More to the point, if anyone in heaven wanted to check up, he had some magnificent scars to prove it. It was moments like these, little spasms of gleeful madness, that made him love this woman. She was whole, she was full of appetite, and she knew exactly what made him tick. After a period of the most intense darkness, she'd taught him how to laugh again.

Four

The first *Buzzard* squad meet took place at the Middlemoor Major Incident Room at 08.30 next morning. Nandy had managed to lay hands on seventeen DCs, most of them seasoned detectives, and was determined to carpet-bomb the investigation over the next forty-eight hours. Photographs from the bedroom were passing from hand to hand, sparking little comment beyond an acknowledgement that the attack on Harriet Reilly had been especially savage.

Despite the overnight search, the whereabouts of Alois Bentner remained a mystery. His house beside the harbour was still a crime scene, protected throughout the night, and the SOC team had already resumed work on the remaining rooms. Harriet Reilly's cottage had also been sealed off, pending a full search.

The medical evidence indicated that Reilly had been attacked at some point over the weekend. Nandy was pushing the pathologist for a tighter time frame but so far, on the balance of probabilities, he'd go no further than agreeing a window between Saturday evening and Sunday morning. This, said Nandy, tallied with other findings. The last time Reilly's phone had been used was 23.47 on Saturday, when she'd called Alois Bentner's mobile. Three incoming calls after that had gone to divert. Flash analysis of a laptop and a PC recovered from her cottage had likewise revealed no activity or outgoing traffic after 15.34 the same day.

'What about Bentner, sir?' This from Jimmy Suttle. 'Do we know where he was when he took the call from Reilly?'

'To the east of Exmouth. Cell site analysis won't give us anything closer than that. After taking the call the phone was switched off. Nothing since Saturday night.'

Another hand went up. It was a female DC who'd just arrived from Plymouth. She understood Bentner's house was at the end of a terrace. Thin walls. Poor sound insulation. She wanted to know about the people next door.

Nandy glanced at Carole Houghton. She was studying her notepad.

'We understand the property belongs to a woman called Gemma Caton. It's unclear whether she lives there full time but we're still trying to find her.'

'Was she around over the weekend?'

'We don't think so. We have contact details and an address in London but she's not answering either. There's a retired guy in the next house down the terrace and he confirms a sighting of Reilly on Saturday afternoon. Apparently she was in the garden at the back. That seems to be the last time anyone saw her.'

'And Bentner?'

'His car wasn't there all weekend. That means nothing, of course. Parking down by the water is a nightmare. He could have stashed the car anywhere.'

Inquiries about Bentner's Skoda, she said, were ongoing. Officers on house-to-house were carrying photos of a similar vehicle.

Nandy wanted to move the meeting on. *Buzzard*'s prime suspect, he confirmed, was Alois Bentner. He appeared to have had a relationship with the victim, and the baby she was carrying may well have been his. Workplace inquiries indicated that they were dealing with a guy on the verge of some kind of breakdown. He had a serious drink problem and was known to be occasionally violent. By all accounts, Bentner was a solitary, a loner, and at this point in time Harriet Reilly seemed to have been the only person in his life. Quite why he'd attack her with such violence was still a mystery, though the fact that she'd been disembowelled might offer a clue or two.

The same DC wanted to know more about the fetus. How long had Reilly been pregnant?

'Between three and four months.'

'Do we have any DNA from Bentner?'

'We've got hair samples from the bed and we've seized a couple of toothbrushes, but we need to find him to be sure.'

The DC had yet to see the photos. One was passed to her. It was a close-up. She glanced at the tiny comma of a life to come. Then she looked up.

'It hasn't got a head,' she said. 'Why's that?'

Luke Golding, an hour later, voiced the same question. He and Suttle were en route into Exeter to talk to the practice manager at the family health centre where Reilly had worked as a GP.

'Has to be seriously weird, doesn't it, skip? Beheading something that tiny?'

Suttle nodded. First thing this morning, still groggy after consuming the entire bottle of Rioja, Oona had pressed him for details of the latest job. He'd yet to see the photos, but the pathologist had described the state of the fetus, a detail he hadn't shared with her. Oona was currently working as a scrub nurse in one of the operating theatres at the Royal Devon and Exeter Hospital, and she was no stranger to hacked-about bodies, but the last couple of months she'd been dropping heavy hints about the wasted space that was her own womb, and this particular image, he knew, would seriously upset her.

'Weird,' he agreed.

'So what does that make Bentner?'

'Invisible, for the time being.'

'Sure, skip, but you're not suggesting we should be looking for someone else?'

Suttle said nothing. Golding repeated the question. Suttle slowed behind a couple of kids on bikes. His years in Major Crime teams, both here and in Pompey, had taught him the merits of keeping an open mind. Life, he wanted to remind Golding, had a habit of taking you by surprise.

Golding hadn't finished. He took out his wallet and put a ten-pound note on the dashboard.

'This says Bentner's our guy.'

Suttle spared him a glance, then pulled out to overtake.

'Make it twenty,' he said. 'Unless you want to go higher.'

Gloria Bellamy managed the Pinhoe GP practice from a cubbyhole of an office behind the main reception area. She was a big woman, middle-aged, and wore a pair of rimless glasses on a chain around her neck.

'Here OK for you?' She gestured around. There was room for one spare chair and the door wouldn't shut.

Suttle shook his head. They needed privacy. Was there anywhere else they could go? Otherwise he'd have to conduct the interview at a police station.

The word interview appeared to alarm her.

'I thought this was a chat. About Harriet. Awful, what happened. Terrible.'

'I'm afraid we need somewhere quiet, Mrs Bellamy.' Suttle was still standing in the open doorway. Already the waiting area beyond the reception desk was packed, a sea of faces staring into nowhere. 'What about Dr Reilly's consulting room?'

'We're expecting a locum.'

'When?'

'Later this morning.' She looked at her watch, then frowned and struggled to her feet. 'Follow me.'

Harriet Reilly's consulting room was much bigger. Suttle let Mrs Bellamy take the chair behind the desk. For some reason the PC was live. Suttle could see a list of names on the screen, presumably patients. Mrs Bellamy reached for the mouse and closed the program. Harriet Reilly's desktop background featured a range of wooded slopes rolling away into a soft blue haze. On the far horizon a jagged line of mountains was capped with snow.

Mrs Bellamy was looking at her watch again. Tuesdays were always mad, she said. The practice was under huge pressure but

Tuesdays, for some reason, were especially difficult. They had half an hour of her time. Max.

Suttle didn't comment. He wanted to know about Harriet Reilly. How long had she been with the practice?

'Eight years, give or take.'

'Does that make her a partner?'

'Yes.'

'And you knew her well?'

'Yes. To a degree.'

'What does that mean?'

The question prompted a frown. Already Suttle sensed that this women resented their presence. They were unwelcome here. He could feel it.

'Harriet was always her own person.' Her eyes had strayed to the PC screen. 'One of our other partners had a word for it. Unclubbable? Few social skills? Does that make sense?'

'Not really. She was a doctor. She must have met dozens of people a day. Surely—'

'No, Mr Suttle ...' An emphatic shake of the head. 'You've got me wrong. With her patients she was wonderful. We know she was. They all speak highly of her. She had the knack. That's less common in our business than you might think.'

'Knack?'

'Of getting through to them. Of becoming their friend. Of looking out for them. You know how much time we have to allot to each patient? Ten minutes. That's all you've got. You're sitting behind this desk and someone you've never seen in your life comes in through that door and they might be vague about what's wrong with them because what they really want is a chat, someone to talk to. Harriet? She was brilliant at that. Real empathy. Like I say, her patients loved her.'

'And you?'

'Me? I'm a manager.'

'So was she easy to manage?'

'Not always, no.'

'Did you get on? Did you like her?'

29

'I admired her. As you've probably gathered.'

'That wasn't my question.'

'I know, Mr Suttle, but it's the best I can do. Harriet was a woman of fixed views. She was an excellent doctor. Beyond that, I'm afraid I can't help you.'

A woman of fixed views. In some respects, thought Suttle, Harriet Reilly was beginning to resemble Bentner: difficult, perhaps a little antisocial, doubtless impatient of people who might stand in her way.

Luke Golding wanted to know whether Mrs Bellamy knew anything about Reilly's private life.

'Do you ever go out together? Socially? As a practice?'

'Of course we do. Not often, but for special occasions, yes.'

'And did Harriet come?'

'Never.'

'Was there a man in her life? To your knowledge?'

'There had to be. She was pregnant.'

'But you didn't know who?'

'She mentioned a friend a couple of times.'

'What's his name? This friend?'

'She called him Ali.'

'Did you ever meet him?'

'Never. Harriet was a woman who kept herself to herself. We only knew she was pregnant because she warned me she'd be needing maternity leave.'

'Was she excited by the prospect of a child?' This from Suttle.

'We never discussed it. You need two to make a conversation, Mr Suttle.'

'Had she been married before? Kids?'

'Not to my knowledge. She never mentioned any family, but who knows ... ?' She shrugged and checked her watch again. The message was plain.

Suttle smiled. He felt like a patient sitting in this airless room with his allotted ration of precious NHS time.

'I believe you've been told about the circumstances of Harriet's death.'

'I have, Mr Suttle. Not in great detail but enough. Horrible. Ghastly.'

'Can you think of anyone she'd upset? Anyone who might want to hurt her?'

'Absolutely not.'

'Can you think of anyone we might need to talk to? Someone close to her? Apart from this Ali?'

'I'm afraid not.'

'A friend, maybe? A relative? Someone she might have mentioned?'

'No.'

'Do you have a next of kin on your records?'

'Yes. I checked this morning. It was her father.'

'And?'

'He died last year. Prostate cancer. Harriet insisted on being with him at the end. I remember giving her compassionate leave.' She offered him a chilly smile and then struggled to her feet. 'Will that suffice, Mr Suttle? Because I have a practice to run.'

Outside in the sunshine Suttle and Golding strolled across the car park. Golding was already on the phone to the MIR, talking to the D/S in charge of Outside Enquiries. DI Houghton wanted them to drive back to Lympstone. Reilly's closest neighbours had been briefly questioned by uniforms and were happy to submit to a longer interview. Mr and Mrs Weatherall. Retired. Both ex-teachers. Beside the car, Golding ended the conversation and pocketed the phone. Then he glanced across at Suttle.

'Over there, skip. Brand-new Audi. Classy.'

Suttle followed his pointing finger. 'What about it?'

'The lady behind the wheel. Ring any bells?'

Suttle looked harder. It was Lizzie. She was easing the car into a tightish space beside the surgery entrance. He walked across, waited for her to kill the engine, then bent to the lowered window.

'Hi.' He did his best to muster a smile. 'Nice motor.'

'Thank you.'

'How are things?'

'Fine. You?'

'Fine. You're registered here?'

'No.'

'Social visit?'

'Hardly.' She got out of the car and locked the door. 'Are we up for the full interview or is that it?'

Suttle toyed with apologising but thought better of it. Since her move down from Portsmouth, he'd steered well clear of his estranged wife. For one thing, he had precious little to say to her. For another, he didn't want to upset Oona. If a marriage has crashed and burned, she'd once told him, leave the embers well alone. Good advice.

Lizzie wanted to know whether Suttle was on the Lympstone job.

'I am.'

'I understand the victim was a GP.'

'That's right.'

'She worked here?'

'That would be an assumption on your part.'

'Sure.' She shot him a sudden grin. 'And that would be cop-speak on yours. Have a nice day, Mr Policeman.'

She reached forward and gave his arm a squeeze. Moments later, she'd disappeared into the surgery.

Golding was waiting in the car.

'What was she after, skip?'

Suttle was reaching for his seat belt, his eyes still on the Audi beside the practice entrance.

'Very good question,' he said.

Five

Lizzie took advantage of the queue waiting patiently at the reception desk and slipped past into the waiting area. She'd caught the Lympstone murder first thing on the BBC local news and put a check call through to a journalist she'd befriended on the Exeter *Express and Echo*. The police at Middlemoor had yet to release the name of the victim, but word from one of the civvy inputters in the MIR suggested it had been a female GP from the Pinhoe practice.

Now, sitting quietly behind her copy of *Devon Life*, Lizzie was eyeing the list of practice doctors. There were nine in all. Five of them were men; that left four candidates for last night's murder. Two of them were listed as present in the building, calling their patients one by one. The remaining two were Dr Alison Bell and Dr Harriet Reilly. Lizzie waited for the queue at the reception desk to clear and then approached the woman behind the counter.

She said she was new to the area. She said friends had spoken well of the practice. If possible she'd prefer a woman GP, either Dr Bell or Dr Reilly. Both had come highly recommended. Might there be room for her on either's list?

'I'm very healthy,' she added. 'Definitely low maintenance.'

The receptionist said it would have to be Dr Bell. She consulted her computer then produced a sheaf of forms from a drawer. 'If you wouldn't mind filling in these and letting us have them back. It's Ms ...?'

33

'Hodson,' Lizzie said. 'I guess Dr Reilly must be run ragged.'

'Far from it, I'm afraid.' The receptionist was making a note of her name. 'We'll need your NI number.'

Lizzie thanked her, collected the forms and left. In her car she scrolled down the directory in her mobile. Journalists, like policemen, routinely discount the power of coincidence.

The number answered in seconds. A male voice.

'Anton? Lizzie. Your place or mine?'

Anton Schiller lived in a basement flat in the depths of Heavitree, a red-brick suburb to the east of Exeter city centre. Lizzie had known him now for a couple of months. He'd left his native Vienna with a doctorate in literature and sizeable gambling debts. His father had paid off the gambling debts on condition that he move to the UK, perfect his English, find himself a job and keep away from the casino and the gaming machines.

With the exception of an occasional tussle with the slots, Anton had kept his side of the bargain. He taught conversational German to a variety of age groups and was about to embark on a series of lectures at the university on the novels of Thomas Mann. Lizzie had run into him at a function at the local Picturehouse and liked him a great deal, not least because he loved the idea of *Bespoken*, her investigative website, and was keen to contribute.

Last night's email had come from him. Now she wanted to know more.

'We're talking mercy killings?' she asked.

'Yes.'

'How do you know?'

'I had a friend. A good friend.' He frowned. 'This is difficult.'

'Just tell me, Anton. Don't fuck around.'

Under pressure, Schiller was good at doing coy. When they'd first met, Lizzie had known at once that he was far too interesting and flirty to be anything but gay. Now, his long body curled on the sofa, he gazed into his herbal tea. He had a number of boyfriends but his regular date was a Tunisian student at the medical school.

34

'Was it Ghassan?'

'No.'

'Who, then?'

'An older man. Jeff. You don't know him.'

'And?'

'Jeff had a partner. They lived together for years. His name was Alec. He was an American like Jeff but even older and he'd been here a long time. He had Aids. Full blown. No coming back. He was dying and Jeff was nursing him. Tough stuff.'

'You were there too?'

'No. But I know Jeff. I know Jeff well. He's a sweet guy. The sweetest. No bullshit with Jeff. He tells it the way it is.' He frowned. 'Or was.'

Lizzie knelt on the floor beside him. The best stories, she told herself, come from moments like these, guys like these, the yeast in life's rich brew.

'So what happened?'

'Alec was suffering. And he was frightened. No one wants to die. He didn't want to die. Jeff didn't want him to die. But he didn't want to see him the way he was either. Skin and bone? You say that?'

'We do. Alec had a doctor?'

'Of course. Jeff said she was wonderful. Nothing too much trouble. She set up nursing support. She made sure there were always plenty of drugs. She spent time with them both. This woman was an angel.'

'Sure.' Lizzie was thinking about last night's email. 'Who told you about Harold Shipman?'

'Jeff did. A famous GP? Killed hundreds of patients?'

'That's right. So what happened with Alec?'

'He'd had enough. He wanted it to end. And so it did.'

'Thanks to the doctor?'

'Thanks to the angel. Just an injection. Jeff was there. Jeff held him in his arms, watched him go. So peaceful. So perfect.'

'And her name? This doctor?'

'Harriet Reilly.'

Lizzie was back home within the hour. Anton had given her other names. Some of these people were from the gay community. Others for whatever reason had hit rock bottom. Several were simply old and tired, and wanted out. But the link between them all, according to Anton, was Harriet Reilly.

No one had a bad word to say about her. There wasn't the least suggestion that she'd helped people on their way for any other reason than simple compassion. But word of the service she offered had slowly spread. If you wanted a good death for yourself or a close friend, then Harriet Reilly would spare you the one-way trip to Zurich. Get yourself on her list, and your troubles would be over.

Lizzie looked at the names Anton had supplied, all of whom were now dead. Including Alec, there were three. After Harold Shipman had been found guilty, Lizzie knew that there'd been a full inquiry. That, she presumed, must have led to changes in the law around GPs and the certification of death. Ten minutes on the Internet told her the rest of the story. Patients who die and go for burial are released on the death certificate signature of a single GP. For cremations, on the other hand, the process is more complex. Another form is involved, which must be countersigned by a second GP, plus a nurse or carer or even relative who was close to the deceased towards the end of their life.

Lizzie leaned back from the screen and made herself a note. Three people to certify a death, she thought, one of them probably a fellow GP from the same practice. The makings of a conspiracy? She didn't know. The seed of a decent story? Again she was uncertain. It was common knowledge that many doctors hastened nature on its way when it came to terminal disease, and as long as these gentle killings spoke of nothing but compassion then she saw no point in pursuing Harriet Reilly any further. But the fact that this same GP had herself been killed told her to keep looking, keep pushing the story on.

In Pompey her address book had been full of contacts in

every conceivable field. She fetched it out of her desk drawer, a name already in mind, and reached for the phone. She had the woman's mobile number. She liked to think they'd been good friends. Moments later came a voice she recognised.

'Coroner's office. How can I help you?'

'It's Lizzie, Dawn. Lizzie Hodson.'

Six

Suttle and Luke Golding were back in Lympstone by late morning. Harriet Reilly's cottage lay up a lane that climbed away from the river. Suttle parked behind the Scenes of Crime van and got out. The front door of the cottage, half-open, was guarded by a uniformed PC.

'How are they doing in there?'

'Fine.' The PC turned and yelled a name. There was a muffled response and then Suttle heard the clump of heavy footsteps coming down the stairs.

The Crime Scene Investigator was an overweight Brummie who'd recently joined the force. Gordon Wallace had already won himself a reputation for painstaking attention to detail, and he had a nose for the story that every scene can tell. Suttle had worked with him on a dodgy suicide on a hill farm near Bodmin earlier in the year, and on the evidence of that single job he had considerable respect for the man.

'Well?'

Wallace pushed back the hood of his protective suit, peeled off a glove and shook hands. He was sweating in the hot sun and he gestured Suttle into the shade of a nearby tree.

So far they'd boshed the downstairs and had just made a start on the bedrooms. The place was small and, as far as they could judge, the woman seemed to have lived alone. A handful of riding gear – jodhpurs, recently muddied boots – suggested an interest in horses, and Wallace had been through a photograph album

38

he'd found in the living room. What had taken his fancy was the fact that Reilly had bothered to print out photos and stick them in the album. These days, given hard disks and Facebook, he didn't know anyone who did that.

'These are recent shots?'

'Yeah. She put the date and place under each one. Very anal.'

'So what do they tell us?'

'She's travelled a bit, especially recently.'

'Like where?'

'The States, earlier this year. March they were in Oregon. Nothing but bloody trees.'

'They?'

'Reilly and Bentner.'

'You're sure it's him?'

'Positive. She calls him Ali in the captions. Same face we saw on the ID. Lots of selfies, just the pair of them, mainly in the same diner.'

'Close? Affectionate?'

'Very. And often Bentner looks pissed. He obviously liked a drink.'

'We can't do him for that.'

The thought made Wallace laugh. He said he'd found a stack of wine at the back of the cupboard that served as Reilly's cellar. Spirits too. Mainly gin.

Golding reminded Suttle about the image on Reilly's desktop at the practice.

'What about it?'

'There were lots of trees. That could be Oregon too. Plus there were mountains in the background, with snow on the peaks. The Rockies go through the state.'

'Right.' Suttle was still looking at Wallace. 'So where else did they go?'

'Brazil last year. The Amazon basin. They seemed to have started in Manaus and headed upriver. If you're thinking some kind of recce for the World Cup, you'd be wrong. This is serious travel. Dugout canoes. Blokes with bamboo through their noses.

Women with dangly tits. Not a pool or a beach to be seen.'

'And Bentner?'

'In pretty much every shot. Remember what you were telling us this morning? At the brief? About the guy being a solitary? A loner? She obviously saw another side of him. Good-looking woman too. Lucky old Ali, eh?'

'Letters?'

'No. But she kept a diary on these trips. I haven't had a chance to read the thing properly but it's bagged and ready. You want to take it now? Only you'll need to sign the log.'

Suttle nodded, and Wallace stepped back into the house, reappearing with the diary. Through the plastic bag, it looked like an A4 ring binder, travel-stained.

'Anything else?'

'Not yet.' Wallace was putting his gloves back on. 'But you'll be the first to know.'

The Weatheralls, Reilly's closest neighbours, lived two hundred metres up the lane, a modern bungalow with carefully tended flower beds and a square of newly mown lawn. A woman in her early sixties was bent over a rose bush beside the garden gate, carefully pruning the lower stems.

'Darcey Bussell,' Golding said softly.

'How did you know that?' Suttle was staring at him. Golding's breadth of knowledge never failed to amaze him.

'My mum's got some. If you can keep the blackfly off they go on for ever.'

'Greenfly's worse.' The woman was smiling. 'My name's Molly.'

She shook hands and said she was appalled by what had happened to Harriet. She used 'unthinkable' twice, and when Suttle told her that so far the inquiry had drawn a blank she looked briefly despairing.

'This should never have happened,' she said, 'especially in this neck of the woods.'

She took them into the bungalow. A man of similar age was

watching a DIY programme on the TV. The way he struggled to his feet spoke of a lower back problem, and the sag of his face on one side told Suttle he'd probably had a stroke. A thin trickle of saliva leaked from a corner of his mouth, and he kept dabbing at it with a tissue from the pocket of his cardigan. There were more tissues in the basket beside the armchair.

'My husband, Gerald.'

Gerald extended a hand. He seemed confused by Suttle's sudden appearance in his life.

'The policemen, darling. About poor Harriet.'

'Ah ... yes, of course.' He sank back into the armchair. A spaniel had appeared from the garden. It jumped into his lap and tried to lick his face as he fondled it. 'Poor Harriet,' he said. 'Poor bloody woman.'

Molly disappeared to make a pot of tea. Suttle asked whether he might put the sound down on the TV. Weatherall gestured towards the set. Help yourself.

Golding turned the set off. Suttle asked how long the couple had been living in the bungalow.

'A couple of years ...' he frowned '... I think.'

'First time in Lympstone?'

'Yes. Definitely. We were in Plymouth before, working. Teachers. All that bloody pressure. One step from the grave. Occupational hazard, *quoi*?'

Just the use of this single French word put a smile on his face. Suttle had noticed the camper van on the hardstanding that served as a drive.

'You're retired now?'

'We are. We are.'

'And do you travel much? Abroad maybe?'

'Of course. The ferry goes from Plymouth. All good, all good. *La belle France*. Can't beat it. My wife does the driving now. Brittany? You know Brittany?'

'I'm afraid not.'

'You should. Very nice people. Give you the time of day. Helps to speak the language, of course, but when it comes to ...

41

you know …' he touched his face lightly and lowered his voice '… this.'

'This?' Suttle was lost.

'God's imperfections. Mine I can't help. Yours neither, I expect. But the French don't seem to care about that kind of thing. After the Great War, of course, men lived without a face at all. Terrible business.' The smile again, uncertain. 'Do you use creams at all? My wife rubs some in every morning.'

It dawned on Suttle that this man was talking about the scars on his face. He couldn't remember when they'd last been any kind of issue.

Golding came to the rescue. He wanted to know how well Weatherall and his wife had known Harriet Reilly.

'Well, very well. Fantastic woman, if I may say so.'

'You knew her socially?'

'Er …' He frowned, a sudden panic in his eyes. The spaniel stiffened and jumped off his lap. Then Molly was back with a tray of tea. Her husband gazed up at her. Adoring. At peace again.

'Socially doesn't quite do it justice, Mr Golding.' She must have been listening from the kitchen. 'We were neighbours. We'd bump into each other most days. We'd help each other out when we could. She'd look after Fleur sometimes when we were away.'

'Fleur?'

'The dog. She'd had a Lab once but I gather it died. She was good with dogs. Fleur adored her. Milk? Sugar?'

Golding helped with the tea. Suttle wanted to know who else might have been in Harriet Reilly's life.

'Her love life, you mean?'

'Not necessarily, but if that's where you want to start, then yes.'

'She had a man. Would he have been her partner? I'm not sure. But she certainly saw a lot of him. He was a scientist. Worked at the Met Office. She was very proud of him, if that makes sense.'

'Was this the man?' Suttle produced the photo the media department were using.

Molly glanced at it, bobbed her head. 'Yes.'

'Did you ever talk to him?'

'No. I tried a couple of times when I ran into them both in the lane or down in the village, but he wasn't very ...' she frowned '... giving.'

'Bloody rude, if you're asking me.' This from her husband. The spaniel was back in his lap.

'Rude how?' Golding asked.

'Wouldn't give you the time of day. Especially men. Hated men. You could see it.'

'But they were definitely a couple?' Suttle was back with Molly.

'Yes and no. She was very fond of him. I know she was. Harriet was no slouch intellectually. She was a wonderful doctor – she's been more than kind to us, and she had hinterland, she really did. She knew lots about lots, and I'm not talking medicine. She was curious about things. She never took things on trust. She always had to find out for herself. I always got the sense that most people bored her. Not this one. Not her Mr Bentner.'

'She called him that?'

'She called him Ali most of the time. Mr Bentner when he amused her, or when she was angry.'

'She was angry a lot? He made her angry?'

'Only once that I can remember. Harriet had very low blood pressure. It took a lot to rattle her.'

'So what happened?'

Suttle saw a flicker of alarm in her eyes. Golding was making notes, and she wanted to know whether any of this would get Bentner into trouble.

'I've no idea, Mrs Weatherall. Why don't you just tell us what happened?'

She gazed at Suttle a moment and then shrugged.

'Harriet had been riding with a friend,' she said. 'It was a weekend. The friend had brought a couple of horses over. The two women had just come back and they were preparing the horses before getting them back in the box. Mr Bentner turned up. He was very drunk. God knows what he was doing behind the wheel of a car. Anyway, he frightened the horses, one of them badly. It went off into the field out the back there. It took them for ever to catch the poor thing.'

'And Harriet?'

'Very calm. Very measured. First she took his car keys. Then she told him to fuck off home and find someone else to upset.'

'She *said* that?' Suttle blinked.

'Yes. If you want the truth, I got the tiniest feeling this wasn't just about the horse.'

'I'm not with you.'

'I think there may have been someone else in his life.'

'You mean another woman?'

'I imagine so. I simply don't know. To be honest, this is a wild presumption on my part and probably very unfair. But Harriet was extremely choosy about who she spent time with and who she didn't. I think she really liked her Mr Bentner. In fact I think it was probably stronger than that. Was she jealous that day? Is that what I heard? Hand on heart, I can't be sure.'

Golding scribbled himself another note. Suttle wanted to know more about the relationship. How long had they known each other? How had they met?

'Met?' Molly laughed. 'As it happens, I can help you there. Most days Harriet would cycle into work. There's a new path opened, down by the river. It's a real success. One day, one evening I think, she got a puncture, and Bentner was the good Samaritan who helped her out.'

'He cycled too?'

'Every day, according to Harriet. That's got to be a fair old hike, all the way to the Met Office and back. She said it was the one thing that kept him alive.'

'Meaning?'

'The amount he drank. She liked a drop too, but recently she seemed to have stopped completely.'

She exchanged looks with her husband then went across and helped him to his feet. Unsupported, he made it to the hall. Then came the sound of a door opening and closing.

'Did Harriet offer to help with your husband at all?' Suttle's gaze returned to Molly.

'Yes, of course. Harriet was a GP. That was her job. Gerald had a stroke around Christmas time. It didn't look at all good for a couple of weeks but, touch wood, he seems to be on the mend now.'

'And Harriet?'

'She offered to help in whatever way she could, especially when things were really grim. I thought that was generous of her. These days GPs are rushed off their feet. He wasn't even her patient.'

'Of course. Did she have family at all? That you know about?'

'She had a husband some time back, but I don't think there were any children.'

'Was he a local man?'

'Not to my knowledge. I believe he was in the navy. They lived in Portsmouth for a while. She hated it.'

'But he's not around any more?'

'Not that I'm aware of, no. I think his name was Tony.'

'Tony Reilly?'

'No. Reilly was her maiden name. She never mentioned her married name.'

'But no kids?'

'I don't think so.'

'I see.' Suttle hesitated. From the hall came the sound of a lavatory flushing. 'Did you know she was pregnant?'

'Harriet?'

'Yes.'

'Not at all. Are you sure? How much pregnant?'

'Between three and four months.'

'I'm astonished.'

'She never mentioned it?'

'Never.' She frowned. 'We're talking Mr Bentner?'

'We don't know yet. Not for sure. Not until we get the DNA results.' Suttle paused. 'You think it might have been anyone else's?'

'I've no idea. Bentner is certainly the only man I ever saw in her life, but these days that doesn't mean anything. Like I say, she was really, really fond of him. A *baby*?' She shook her head. 'Good God.'

Seven

Lizzie spent the afternoon at a caravan site on the outskirts of Dawlish, a seaside town south of the estuary. Jeff Okenek occupied a mobile home tucked into a corner of the top field. A line of washing blew in the wind off the sea, and he'd created a small herb garden, carefully netted from pests, on the sunny side of the nearby hedge.

The mobile home was spotless. Sepia prints of San Francisco in the 1930s hung on the few available stretches of wall, and a fold-up double bed beneath the window at the end served as a sofa. Jeff had a cat he called Ferlinghetti in memory of a beat poet Lizzie had never heard of and a huge long-haired tabby of uncertain age that he treated with something close to reverence.

Lizzie had knocked on his door an hour or so after a catch-up on the phone with her friend from the Portsmouth Coroner's office. Dawn had confirmed Lizzie's Internet findings about death certification post-Shipman. She'd agreed it should now be impossible for any working GP to dispatch his or her more vulnerable patients without raising suspicions among fellow medics – GPs or otherwise – but half a lifetime straddling the no-man's-land between medicine and law had taught her that legislation in this field was far from perfect.

Life and death decisions at the end of somebody's life, she'd pointed out, were famously difficult. If someone was truly suffering, and you had the means to bring all that to an end, wouldn't it be kinder to put the poor bastard out of his misery?

In the world of pets no one raised a peep if Tootsie had to be put to sleep. So how come human beings had to hang on and on because no one had the guts to do anything about it? This was strong stuff, but Dawn made Lizzie laugh when she added a thought about the eighty-pound payment made to a GP for completing the cremation form. This, she said, was known in the trade as 'ash cash'.

Lizzie had wondered about sharing this with Jeff, but fifteen minutes' conversation convinced her it would be deeply inappropriate. Jeff was a serious man, intense, the gauntness of his face hollowed out by an energy you could almost touch. He spoke with a light American accent. He was barefoot. He wore black jeans and a grey vest that hung baggily on his thin shoulders. He must have been at least fifty, but his eyes glittered with the passion and focus of a much younger man. Once he knew she was a friend of Anton Schiller – a fact he took the trouble to check by making a phone call – he was very happy to tell her about Alec, about the way it had been between them, and about what had happened at the end.

'This was a guy you'd give your life for. Me? I was happy to do that, and he knew it. We first met in LA. He was living down the street. Every day I used to watch this guy going off to work. He used to carry a bag, like a sports bag, and I so wanted to know what was in that bag. Then one day I met him coming home. It was in the afternoon. We'd never met, never talked, but right there in the street I asked him about the bag. That was a pretty hot move, right? I mean the guy could have said anything.'

'So what happened?'

'He said to come up to his place. Then he'd show me.'

'And you went?'

'Of course I fucking did. And you know what was in the bag? Ballet tights and a kind of jerkin thing. Turned out the guy was a dancer. He performed with a company downtown. He had the build for it. He was slim but so, so strong. And he had balance like you wouldn't believe. This was a guy who never walked, this was a guy who *glided*. No way you wouldn't fall in love with a man like that.'

'And you did?'

'Big time. And it turned out he felt the exact same way. Me? I'm no ballet dancer, but a body like Alec's isn't hard to please. My pleasure, I used to tell him. And you know something? I meant it.'

They moved in together. They became a couple. They left LA and went upstate to San Francisco. They lived in Haight-Ashbury, hung out with the art crowd and got on with their lives. Jeff worked in IT. Alec taught dance in a local performance centre. Weekends they'd use a particular bathhouse until Alec woke up one morning with swollen glands, a raging fever and a mysterious rash. HIV had ravaged a generation of gay men by now. Antiretrovirals could slow down the progress of the disease, but Alec was careless with his meds, and very slowly his body's immune system began to collapse. He was dying and they both knew it.

'We were over here by now. I'd been in England before. I loved it. Man, we were so, so frank with each other. I said there was no better place to die, and Alec believed me. We had a little money. Enough to meet the rental on this place and maybe travel a little. I bought a car from a guy up in Exeter, a big old Jaguar, seven hundred bucks, drank gas. I polished it up real nice, looked after it. A ride fit for a king, I told him. Alec loved that car. He loved the leather seats, loved the way you never heard the engine, loved the way people looked at us from the sidewalk. I drove my adorable man everywhere in that car. There isn't a beach, a cove, a bay we didn't visit. But most he loved Cornwall, the north coast, the light especially. When the sun shone, he'd say it was a trailer for heaven. When the wind blew and the gales came, it was a trailer for hell. Either way, he couldn't care less. We'd had a fine life. We'd had each other. Towards the end he was so, so thin. Nights he would sweat so much. I'd try and hold him but he'd push me away. Then the sores came, places you didn't need them, and his glands blew up, and then it even got tough to breathe. That man's whole life had been his body, and it was like – hey – you've betrayed me. I can't tell you how pissed he felt. And he hurt too. He hurt bad. And that was hard for both of us.'

He swung off the sofa and fetched a photo from a drawer. The face in the photo could have belonged to a man in his eighties: the dullness in his eyes, the sagging flesh, the thinning hair, the purple blotches around his mouth.

'This is Alec?'

'Yep.'

'Sad.'

'Yep.'

Lizzie took another look. Jeff was right. This thing of beauty, key to a precious relationship, had become a husk of a man. She wanted to know whether Jeff had been registered with a doctor.

'Sure. A guy right here in Dawlish.'

'And what did he say?'

'He said Alec would need care. Maybe a hospital. Maybe a hospice. Neither of us wanted that.'

'So what was the alternative?'

'Alec needed to die at home.'

'You mean here?'

'Sure. With me. On our own terms.'

'Not easy.'

'No.'

'You talked about it?'

'You bet we talked about it. Heroin was one answer. That's not hard to find, but you never really know what you're buying out on the street and quality can be an issue. Plus there's all the drama afterwards. A death like that, you can guarantee an autopsy. They're gonna find this stuff in his system. And they're gonna be asking questions.'

'So there had to be another way? Is that what you're telling me?'

'Sure. And there was.'

'Harriet Reilly?'

'Yeah.'

'Care to tell me how?'

For the first time he hesitated. He wanted to know what Lizzie was going to do with all this stuff. He wanted to know where this story of his might be headed next.

'It's background,' Lizzie said.

'Background for what?'

'Background for an investigation I'm running.'

'Investigation? I don't want any part of some bullshit investigation. You told me on the phone this conversation would stay private.'

'That's true.'

'So how come we're suddenly talking investigation?'

Lizzie explained about *Bespoken*. Jeff wanted to see it. He was angry now. He fetched over a laptop and fired it up. Lizzie sat beside him while he scrolled through the last three months of stories she'd uploaded. A developer trashing the planning rules on a waterside site in Exmouth. A care home deep in East Devon where patients were mercilessly bullied. A Torquay garage specialising in dodgy MOT certificates. Rules bent. People hurt. Customers ripped off.

'Like this is some kind of Robin Hood thing?'

The phrase brought a smile to Lizzie's face. She didn't deny it. Jeff hadn't finished.

'So where does Harriet belong? This is a woman who took a big fucking risk. I asked her to kill my favourite human being, and that's what she did. Not for money. Not for gain. Just because she understood. Does that make her a bad person? No fucking way. Does that make me grateful? And just a little protective? Sure it does. So let me ask you the question again. What do you plan to do with all this?'

'I don't know.'

'*You don't know?* Baby, this conversation is going nowhere. Like nowhere. I invited you along because of Anton. Anton's a sweet guy. I trust him. I like him. And if he tells me you're OK then that's cool with me. Except you're not what Anton said you were.'

'What did he say?'

'He said you were a friend.'

'That's true.'

'He also said you'd done some book. Have I got that right?'

Lizzie explained about *Mine*. Last year her daughter had been abducted and killed. In a bid to find some kind of closure, Lizzie had tried to get inside the head of the woman who'd done it.

Jeff had heard of the book. Some of his anger seemed to melt away.

'You say she died? Your daughter?'

'She did.'

'Not the little girl they filmed in the woman's arms? Jumped off a balcony? Last year? Maybe the year before?'

'The same.'

'Shit.'

Jeff got up to make coffee. He said he was sorry. Living alone did strange things to a man.

'Tell me about it.'

'You live alone?'

'I do. And no matter what happens I probably always will. In here –' Lizzie touched her head '– where it matters.'

'Cool ...' He was looking for the coffee. 'Cool. Just one thing, though. Does any of this ever get back to her?'

'To Harriet?'

'Sure.'

'I doubt it, Jeff. Someone killed her last night. If you don't believe me ...' she nodded at the TV on the kitchen table '... check it out.'

'*Killed* her?'

'Killed her.'

'That's bad shit.'

'Exactly.'

Eight

Suttle was back at the MIR by mid-afternoon. He found DI Carole Houghton alone in the SIO's office. Nandy had returned to Plymouth, sorting reinforcements for a domestic that had got out of hand. Partner and one kid dead. The other in Derriford Hospital fighting for her young life.

Houghton looked up. 'Some days I know I'm on the wrong planet,' she said. 'Tell me something to cheer me up.'

'Bentner?'

'Still missing.'

'*Nothing?*'

'Nothing.'

'That's not supposed to happen.'

'I know. Nandy thinks he's probably topped himself. Should we have our fingers crossed? Hope and pray it's true?'

'I doubt it.' Suttle slipped into the spare chair. 'Luke's been talking to the CSM. He's taken a look at the scene analysis at Bentner's place. We dropped by there on the way back.'

'And?'

'The SOC guys boshing Reilly's cottage seized a couple of items they released to us.'

Suttle explained about the photo album and Reilly's journal. Analysis of the latter would have to wait until later, but Golding had been through the shots of the winter holiday in the States that Reilly had shared with Bentner, making detailed notes of what the guy had been wearing. These notes he'd shared with the CSM.

'We're missing this stuff, boss.' Suttle handed over a list. 'No sign of the gear at Bentner's place. He may have left it in the States or got rid of it since, but I'd say that's unlikely.'

Houghton ran quickly through the list. It included a blue anorak, a sleeping bag, lace-up boots and a sizeable rucksack.

'You're telling me they went to the States during the winter?'

'Early March, boss. Oregon. Still bloody cold.'

'And you're suggesting he might be using all this gear now?'

'Yes.'

'But it's June, Jimmy.'

'Sure. But he may be living rough. Nights can be tricky, even in high summer.'

Houghton gave the proposition some thought. 'Devon's a big place,' she said at last. 'So where do you suggest we start?'

It was raining by the time Suttle and Golding got down to Exmouth. The CSM had also shown Golding receipts from the Co-op in the town's Magnolia Centre, where Bentner evidently did his weekly shop, and Suttle was on nodding terms with the handful of street people who sat cross-legged outside the store and begged for spare change. A couple of them, Suttle suspected, were ex-squaddies, adrift on Civvy Street with a big drink problem and absolutely zero prospects. They both had dogs and disappeared late afternoon with their rucksacks and their sleeping bags in the general direction of the seafront. Quite where they kipped was anyone's guess, but now was a very good time to find out.

Neither of them, as it happened, was around. Enquiries at the shop next door revealed that they hadn't been seen all day. Maybe Suttle might check further up the precinct. Geordie John had been around earlier.

Suttle had never heard of Geordie John. He turned out to be a scruffy forty-something with a sizeable gut barely contained by a US Army combat jacket that had seen better days. His jeans had gone at the knees and he badly needed a shave, but he had a face made for laughter and definitely wasn't drunk. He'd spread himself on a tartan blanket outside Boots. Two puppies nestled between his thighs, and his upturned forage cap was brimming with small change.

'Gentlemen?' he peered up and gestured them in from the rain.

Suttle squatted beside him in the shelter of the overhang. The army-issue rucksack was full to bursting, and there were tins of dog food in the Iceland bag beside it.

Geordie John was amused by Suttle's interest.

'If you get a choice next time, come back as a puppy. The women in this town? Never bloody fails.'

Suttle offered his warrant card. Golding, still on his feet, didn't move. Geordie John was staring up at him.

'What's this about then?'

Suttle wanted to know where he slept at night.

'Depends who's asking, my friend.'

'I am.'

'Why do you want to know?'

Suttle didn't answer. Not at first. Then he asked whether other people slept at the same place, wherever it was.

'Always. You can get rolled otherwise.'

'The same people every night? People you know?'

'Yeah. If you're after names I've got a shit memory.'

'Do strangers ever turn up?'

'I'm not with you.'

'People you don't know.'

'Yeah. Sometimes.'

'And what happens then?'

'Depends. Blonde? Nice tits? Good attitude?' He threw his head back and laughed. No teeth.

Suttle let him settle again. Then he produced Bentner's passport photo. 'How about this guy?'

Geordie John spared it a glance, and Suttle knew at once that Golding had been right: Bentner was out there somewhere, not that far away, living rough.

'Well?'

Geordie John shook his head, rubbed his eyes, stifled a yawn, then extended a filthy finger for one of the puppies to lick.

'You're telling me you've seen this guy?' Suttle still had the photo.

'I'm telling you nothing. Don't get me wrong, but a man can't live on dog food.'

Catching Golding's eye, Suttle nodded in the direction of a butcher's shop across the precinct that sold burgers and sausage baps. Golding shrugged and then departed.

Geordie John watched him go. He seemed, if anything, amused.

'It'll take more than that, my friend.'

Suttle sorted a couple of twenty-pound notes from his wallet. He folded them carefully into Geordie John's fist. 'I need a location,' he said. 'I need to know where you people live.'

'I bet you do. There's another sixty in that stash of yours. I saw.'

'You have to be joking.'

'Never.' He struggled to his feet 'That mate of yours ... what's his name?'

'Luke.'

'Tell him no onions, yeah?' He bent to gather up his puppies. 'These little buggers can't stand them.'

Twenty minutes later, Suttle and Golding parked at the far end of the seafront where the long curl of beach collided with the looming mass of Orcombe Point. A zigzag path took them to the top of the cliff. From here another path led out towards the monument that marked the beginning of the Jurassic Coast.

'Where did he say, skip?' Golding was a stranger to Exmouth.

'The wooded area off to the right. We're nearly there.'

The path suddenly opened out. Golding followed Suttle towards the trees that blocked the view from the cliff top. The scrub and brush was thicker than Suttle had expected but some of the vegetation had been flattened, an indication that people had been here recently. Suttle could hear the rasp of surf on the beach below. It was still raining, the trees overhead drip-dripping onto the sodden ground.

'There, skip.' Golding was pointing to the left. A tarpaulin had been stretched between two saplings. Nearby was a smaller tent, zipped up against the wind that funnelled over the edge of the cliff. Beneath the tarpaulin two figures were huddled in sleeping bags, only their beanies visible. Suttle counted more than two dozen discarded cans of Special Brew, all crushed. He nodded towards the tent. More cans plus an empty two-litre bottle of White Lightning. No wonder these guys were wrecked.

Golding circled the tent. No way would anyone escape. Suttle knelt by the entrance and slowly unzipped the front flap. The stench of unwashed bodies gusted out. He put his head inside, let his eyes accustom themselves to the gloom. Two more bodies, curled under a couple of blankets. He could smell the booze now. He gave the nearest body a shake. A head emerged. It was a woman, grubby face, piercings, few teeth, totally befuddled.

'Who's your friend?' Suttle looked at the other body.

'Who the fuck are you?'

Suttle produced his warrant card, held it to her face.

'Filth?'

'Yes.'

She rolled her eyes then licked her lips. She needed something to drink. Badly.

Suttle found what might have been water in a bottle nearby. She sucked greedily at it. Her partner farted, then raised his head.

'What the fuck ...?'

Suttle didn't bother answering. No way was this Alois Bentner. He wanted to know where the money came from for the booze.

'My pension, sweetheart.' It was the woman again. London accent, thickened by roll-ups.

'I'm serious.'

'Then I don't know. Ask the guys outside. Party time last night. You free at all?'

Suttle withdrew from the tent, grateful for the fresh air. Golding was bent over the nearer of the bodies beneath the tarpaulin. Suttle joined him. The guy had done his best to roll over. He lay on his back, still trapped in his sleeping bag, blinking into the sudden daylight. Scarlet-faced, unshaven, he might have been a cartoon insect emerging from his chrysalis. Definitely not Bentner.

Suttle held the photo inches from his face. A flicker of recognition.

'You've seen this person?'

'Never.'

'Stay there.'

Suttle helped Golding roll over the fourth body. Another woman – younger, out for the count. In the bushes nearby more discarded Special Brew tins.

Suttle retrieved one of the tins and returned to the first sleeping bag and knelt beside the face.

'You did this lot last night?'

'Yeah.'

'Who paid?'

'Dunno.'

'Don't fuck around. Just tell me.'

'What is this?'

'I'm going to ask the question one more time, OK? Who paid for all this booze?'

The face stared up at him. Then came a shake of the head. Suttle glanced up at Golding and nodded. Golding checked around and then took a step backwards. The first kick was enough. The face grunted. Winced. Then two hands appeared. A gesture of surrender.

'Big bloke. Beard. Well pissed.'

'Is this him?'

The face gazed at the photo of Bentner.

'Yeah.'

'How long was he here?'

'Saturday night. Last night. Fuck knows. Can't remember.

Nice tent though. Good gear.' He nodded towards a rectangle of flattened grass.

'Is he coming back?'

'No idea.'

'Did he *say* he was coming back?'

'He had a car. That's all I know.'

'What sort of state was he in?'

'Pissed. Like us.' His eyes returned to the same patch of yellowing grass. 'Shame. He must have gone.'

At the Major Incident Room Suttle shared the news with DI Houghton. Nandy, back from Plymouth, was on the phone. The conversation over, Houghton briefed him quickly. Alois Bentner had evidently spent Saturday night partying with a bunch of vagrants on a cliff top outside Exmouth. This would tally with cell site analysis of the call he'd taken from Reilly's mobile. In Houghton's view they should declare the site a crime scene, full bosh.

Nandy didn't believe it. Time was short. He was due for a live BBC interview down in Lympstone. *Buzzard* was suddenly news.

'You think Bentner was in Exmouth?' Nandy was already on his feet. 'Total bollocks. You're telling me he goes to an offie? You're telling me he spends the night dossing with these people? You're telling me he leaves his car out in the open on some street or other? After doing something like that?'

Nandy, to Suttle's intense pleasure, had nailed it in one go.

'Totally right, sir. Unless it wasn't him who killed her.'

Nine

The Lympstone murder was the lead story on the BBC's local magazine programme. Lizzie, still making notes at home on her conversation with Jeff Okenek, lifted her head from the laptop to watch. The reporter was live from the slipway. He gestured towards the nearby terrace of houses. Over there, he said, a woman had died at the hands of an unknown assailant. The killing was so brutal that investigating officers were refusing to release details.

The shot cut to a man in a dark green anorak. Introduced as Senior Investigating Officer Det-Supt Malcolm Nandy, he was slim, early fifties, receding grey hair cut short, his eyes pouched in darkness. He shifted from one foot to another like a boxer pre-fight, and he'd clearly anticipated the reporter's question. Lizzie recognised him at once. Jimmy's boss, she thought. She'd met him twice. Nice man if he liked you, but aggression on legs if he didn't.

'Progress, Simon?' Nandy was talking to the reporter. 'These are early days. We have leads, of course we do, but our priority just now is trying to find a particular person of interest.'

Nandy changed his eye line, addressing the camera direct. Lizzie had no idea whether this was his idea or the reporter's but it certainly worked.

'If you see this man,' he said, 'please get in touch with us. His name is Alois Bentner. And since the weekend, he seems to have disappeared.'

Lizzie found herself looking at a photo of a forty-something white male. A tangle of greying hair. Full beard. And an expression she could only describe as forbidding. The photograph might have come from a passport booth, she thought, but even so she guessed he rarely smiled.

Back with Nandy, the reporter was wrapping up. A national manhunt was under way for Alois Bentner. His photo was all over Facebook and Twitter. If there was a moment to be thankful for social media then this was surely it. Nandy offered a grim nod and added a final health and safety warning. If you see this man, don't approach him. Just give us a ring.

Lizzie returned to her laptop. A couple of keystrokes took her into the Devon and Cornwall Police Facebook page. There, on the home page, she found the same face but a different photo. She was wrong about the smile. Alois Bentner was pictured on a beach she recognised as Copacabana, sitting cross-legged on the white sand. His jeans were rolled up to his knees and he was wearing a red singlet and a back-to-front baseball cap. He was lightly tanned, and either the sunshine or the face behind the camera had brightened his mood. He looked relaxed, even radiant. By no means the monster Det-Supt Nandy was so keen to nail.

Lizzie's phone rang. It was Anton. He needed to sort out his evening. Were they still going to see Ralph Woodman?

Woodman lived in a beautiful Georgian house at the end of a gravel drive near the airport. Anton had rung ahead, and Woodman must have been waiting inside because he stepped out of the front door the moment Lizzie pulled her Audi to a halt. He was a tall man with a slight stoop. Lizzie guessed his age at past seventy. He wore needlecord trousers over polished brogues and a green quilted gilet against the strengthening wind.

The lounge was at the back of the house, a big handsome room, exquisitely furnished. An acre or so of garden filled the view from the big sash windows: freshly mown lawn, flower beds bursting with a palette of colours, a wooden gazebo occupying the far corner. One day, Lizzie thought, my garden might look like this.

'May I?'

Lizzie turned to find herself offered a glass of sherry. Fino. Dry. Nice. She was trying to work out whether anyone else lived in this glorious house. A view like that was made for sharing.

'I'm sorry about your wife,' she said. 'I understand it was motor neurone disease.'

'It was, my dear. I've been a Christian all my life. We both were. But we were sorely tested, believe you me.'

The merest nod directed Lizzie's attention to a row of framed photos on the marble mantelpiece.

'Do you mind?' Lizzie wanted to look at the photos.

'Not at all. I understand that's why you're here.'

In the car Anton had explained that Ralph Woodman had recently become a major supporter of an organisation called Dignity in Dying and believed that Lizzie was in a position to offer publicity and perhaps PR advice. In his view she needed to understand in some detail the blessings conferred by assisted dying. Hence the invitation to The Old Rectory.

Lizzie was looking at the photos. One pictured Ralph's wife as a child, sitting on her mother's knee. Another was more recent. A lifetime later, even in a wheelchair, Julia Woodman had retained a beauty and a presence that Lizzie could only describe as luminous. She sat erect, if a little lopsidedly. Her face was turned to the camera, strong features, a full mouth, a melting smile. She must have been the sunshine in this man's life, she thought. To lose a woman like that would close the curtains on years of warmth and laughter.

'You know anything about MND?' Ralph had joined her at the mantelpiece.

Lizzie shook her head. Mercifully not, she said.

'Then you're lucky. It's the stranger that comes ghosting into your life. For months you don't realise it's there. A little stiffness in the legs after a decent walk? Difficulty getting the odd word out? Looking back, you realise what these things meant, but at the time you dismiss it. In the army I'd have called it collateral damage. None of us is getting any younger.'

Julia, he said, had been nearly sixty before the medics could put their finger on what was wrong.

'That was how many years ago?'

'Four. She's always been the younger woman in my life, the one I nabbed when she was silly enough to say yes. I always worshipped her. Nothing ever changed in that respect. Even at the end.'

'I understand she died recently.'

'Nearly nine months ago. To tell you the truth it feels like yesterday.' He took Lizzie lightly by the arm and guided her across to the window. 'She's down there by the gazebo.'

'You buried her in the garden?'

'I did. In a wicker coffin she designed herself. My daughters wove flowers into it for the celebration. *Very* hippy.' He smiled at the memory. 'I visit her every morning. Take little gifts. We talk to each other. I find it helps immensely.'

To be frank, he said, the Church had been a disappointment, and the same was true of their GP. After countless tests, Julia had been diagnosed with a variant of the disease called progressive bulbar palsy. PBP, he said, was something you wouldn't wish on your worst enemy. It attacked the nerves in your face and throat. You started to drool. You couldn't swallow properly. You had difficulty breathing. And as it got worse, you lived every day in terror of not being able to breathe at all.

'Then there was the crying,' he said. 'Julia was always the strong one. She could stand pain, disappointment, despair, everything that life throws at you. In that department she always put me to shame. But towards the end she simply couldn't cope. She'd cry and cry, and that, of course, only made it worse. My poor, poor love. You've no idea what that does to a man. There's a sense of utter helplessness. You're together day and night. You do your best, of course, but deep down you both know there's absolutely nothing you can do.'

He turned away from the window, shaking his head.

'Your GP ...?' Lizzie asked.

'Absolutely useless. Nice enough man but wouldn't begin to entertain what we both had in mind.'

'Which was?'

'Ending it. May I call you Lizzie?'

'Of course.'

'It wears you down, Lizzie. It wore me down, and dear God it certainly wore my darling wife down. There's help out there if you want it. Physiotherapists. Reflexologists. Dieticians. You name it. But after a while you realise you're at a place from which there's no coming back. The only absolute certainty, the only thing you can rely on, is that this disease, this hideous stranger, is here for keeps. Until one morning he decides to end it all. His decision. Not ours. That's the moment when you start getting angry, the moment when you realise that both your life and your death are beyond your control.'

'So what did you do?'

'I'd met this young man.' His eyes settled on Anton. 'One of my daughters teaches at the university. She bumped into Anton one day and they started talking. Normally she wouldn't dream of sharing these kinds of confidences, but it turned out that Anton was something of an expert in the field. His mother had elected to die in Switzerland. You're aware of the Dignitas people?'

'Of course.' Lizzie was looking at Anton. 'You never told me.'

'You never asked.'

'Your mother was ill?'

'She had pancreatic cancer,' Anton said. ' She was very brave but sometimes courage isn't enough.'

'Precisely.' Ralph reached across and patted his arm. 'Absolutely right. And so young Anton here became part of our little family for a while, which was wonderful because he started to teach Julia German. Me too, when I could get my brain into gear.'

Lizzie shook her head. Another surprise. 'And learning German helped?'

'Anything helped. Anything that could take Julia's mind off it. I'd use the term therapy but that would be misleading. Therapy implies cure, and with MND there's no such thing. At that stage we were thinking about Zurich, about Dignitas. That's why learning German made so much sense. But the worse things became the more we agreed that it had to happen here, in a place we both loved so much.'

Anton, he said, had mentioned a GP he'd heard of through a friend, someone who'd be prepared, at the very least, to visit and to talk to them both, and to listen. Listening, he said, was absolutely key. Very few professionals, very few people, did that any more. They nodded and they smiled and sometimes they even agreed. But they seldom *listened*.

'This was Harriet Reilly?'

'It was.'

'And?'

'She listened.'

She came for dinner, he said. They decided to treat her like an old friend. He cooked quail that night, with a very thin pasta that Julia could manage. Harriet stayed for most of the evening, and by the time she left they had a plan.

'We ex-army people love a plan, my dear,' he said. 'To be honest it was a huge relief. It meant we could take a little time, do it properly. This hideous thing wasn't going to push us around any more. With Harriet's help, it would be our decision, on a day of our choosing.'

By now they'd joined Harriet's practice. It was early September. The garden had never looked so full, so alive, so wonderful. He'd employed a gardener for a week. He was an older man, working under Julia's direction, and Ralph was absolutely certain that he knew what was going on.

'Not only that, Lizzie. I think he *approved*.'

'Did he come to the funeral?'

'The celebration? Of course he did. I made sure his wife came too. And I made sure he took a bow.' He paused. 'I understand you're a supporter of the Dignity in Dying people.'

'That's right.'

'Then I need to tell you about the way it ended. May I do that?'

'You mean Julia? Going?'

'Of course.'

Lizzie accepted an invitation to sit down. Part of her was wishing she could record this stuff, get it down on disk, but she knew there was no way she'd ever forget a single phrase. In the nightmare months after Grace had died, she'd lost all faith in redemption. Now this.

'We chose the season first. That was tricky. In the view of the consultant, Julia had between six months to a year left. A year would have been an eternity. Autumn was already upon us. And so September seemed something of a blessing.'

Harriet, he said, insisted that only Ralph be present at the moment of Julia's death. Until that moment they'd been thinking in terms of a family gathering – certainly their two daughters – but under the circumstances they respected Harriet's wishes. She, after all, was the one running the legal risk. Proof that she'd killed Julia Woodman could land her in prison.

'Weather?' Lizzie was beginning to get the drift.

'Sunny, of course. Had to be. There's a very good chap on the local BBC, David someone, and of course you can look at all sorts of websites.'

For days he and Julia scanned the weather forecasts. As well as sunshine, they wanted as little wind as possible.

'It was Julia who spotted it first.' He was smiling now. 'A huge area of high pressure drifting north from the Azores. It was due over the UK in a couple of days' time. She said it had her name on it. Sweet, sweet thing.'

He had baked her a special cake, a recipe he'd acquired in one of their excursions across the Channel. He bought a bottle of Krug and another of Armagnac for afterwards. They spent an entire evening mulling over music and finally settled on Ravel's G major Piano Concerto.

'Do you know it at all?'

'I'm afraid not.'

'Sublime. Utterly wonderful. Upbeat, mysterious, challenging, full of surprises, not a whisper of regret.'

Not a whisper of regret. Lizzie wanted to hear this music. Share this departure, this take-off, this release.

'Do you have a copy?'

'Of the music? Ravel?'

'Yes.'

'Of course.'

He was on his feet in a second. He looked delighted. He went across to the oak cabinet where he kept his player and CDs. He loaded the machine and then disappeared. When he came back he was carrying three glasses and a bottle of what looked like champagne.

'It's not Krug, I'm afraid, but it's not bad.'

Lizzie drained her sherry while he uncorked the bottle. The champagne fizzed and danced in her glass. Then came the music.

'Martha Argerich,' Ralph whispered. 'The Krug of performances.'

Lizzie sat in silence, listening to the first movement while Ralph described the way it had been back in September. The best view of the garden was from their bedroom upstairs. With the help of Harriet, he'd already positioned Julia's favourite couch in the window with a thick nest of pillows to support her back. The weather, he said, had been perfect since dawn. They'd been up at four, waiting for sunrise, and hadn't been disappointed. Not a cloud in the sky. Not a breath of wind. Harriet had arrived mid-morning. Julia wanted to die once the sun had come round the side of the house and hit the gazebo. That's where she planned to rest. That's where she'd spend the rest of her days.

'So what time was that?'

'Any time after twelve. Harriet set up a cannula. I've no idea what she was using and she never told me, but she assured us that it would be painless and pretty much instantaneous. That was important because Julia wanted to judge the moment perfectly.'

'The moment of her death?'

'Of course.'

The first movement of the concerto, much of it scored for piano and trumpet, was coming to an end. The adagio was next. This, said Ralph, was the music that Julia wanted to take with her.

Lizzie settled back and closed her eyes. She'd seen the frail courage in the last photograph, the smile for the camera, the tissue balled in one thin hand. It wasn't hard to imagine this woman on her couch, waiting for the sunshine to kiss the gazebo, waiting for the music to happen, waiting to give Harriet Reilly that final nod of her head, the signal that it was nearly over.

Ralph was right. The music was truly divine, the theme picked out on the piano, then gathered up by the soaring strings and warmed by an oboe and a flute. It surged on, music to fly by, music for seagulls, music with no respect for either gravity or pain. Then came a particularly poignant passage and Lizzie opened her eyes to find Ralph's gaze locked on hers.

'Here?' she whispered.

'Yes.'

'She didn't want to listen to the rest of the movement?'

'No. She said she wanted something to listen to on the other side.'

'And the gazebo?'

'Full sunshine. Absolutely perfect.'

He raised his glass and closed his eyes until his head went down and he started to sob. Anton was first to his side. He wanted to know about the music. Should they turn it off? Might that help?

'God, no.' His head came up again, tears streaming down his face. 'Leave it on. That's the whole point.'

Ten

The flat was empty when Jimmy Suttle finally made it home. Among the messages on his answerphone was one from Oona. 'The Fureys are playing at the Corn Exchange on Friday.' She was laughing. 'Lucky old you.' He stood in the big window while he listened to the rest of his messages. The view across the water, especially at this time in the evening, never failed to speak to him. The rain had cleared, and seagulls hung in the remains of the sunset. Below them a lone sculler was pushing hard against the rising tide, and further away lights pricked the dark mass of Torbay.

He stood for a moment, savouring the peace. It had taken him a while to get used to living up here on his own, but now he knew that nothing would shift him. Not the temptations of moving somewhere bigger and more practical. Not the nightmare parking. Not even Oona. Lately she'd started dropping hints about getting a place together or maybe moving in, but he'd kissed her, and held her, and told her that now wasn't the time. Life would never be perfect, he'd said, but this was bloody close.

He left the room. A couple of Stellas from the fridge and the remains of last night's chilli con carne was more than he needed. He readied the chilli for the microwave and then returned to the front room. Harriet Reilly's travel notes were in his briefcase.

The notes related to two trips. She was scrupulous about dates and locations. The first trip, back last year, had been to Brazil,

Bentner's idea. In a full page of jottings, evidently done on the flight over, she admitted that she'd had mixed feelings about the trip. Ali wanted to take her to the tropical rainforest, wanted her to see for herself what uncontrolled logging was doing to the planet and its people, wanted to put flesh on the evenings back home when they sank a decent bottle of wine, and he banged on about arboreal respiration rates and the miracles of the carbon cycle. 'This stuff obviously matters hugely to A.,' she'd written, 'so I'm guessing it must matter to me.'

To Suttle this sounded more like duty than conviction, but the moment they hit Brazil her feelings changed. They'd landed in Rio, where their three-week journey would begin and end, and the city blew her away. The energy. The colour. The beach. The beauty of the people. Even the grimmest of the favelas. 'These people seem to make light of poverty,' she wrote. 'Is that a state of mind? Or should we be looking for a Brazilian gene? A. tells me that these people play football to die for, and judging by the kids on the beach that has to be true. Viva Brazil!'

Three days later they flew up to Manaus. Here the journey was to start in earnest, and once again Suttle detected a hint of foreboding. 'Hot!' she recorded. 'The sweat's pouring off me. If I was some horrible virus, then this is where I'd live.' The following morning they took a riverboat upstream. The sheer breadth of the Amazon she found hard to cope with. Not a river at all. More like a big brown sea pleated with submerged currents that frightened her. Huge freshwater turtles. Crocodiles. Dugout canoes. Indians. A script written in Hollywood, except it was true. 'A. talks about the lungs of the planet and here they are. Back home you can have no conception of the vastness of this place, which probably makes A. more right than even he knows. Rip this lot out and we're talking global post-mortem. RIP. Flowers lashed to railings. God help us all.'

They made a landing at a riverside settlement called Tefe. To Reilly this was the Wild West. Bars full of native loggers, American oil men and local hookers. Much drinking. Noise in the small hours like you wouldn't believe. A little violence, possibly recreational but scary nonetheless. Not a place you'd necessarily choose for peace and quiet.

These entries in the diary married with photos in her album, which Suttle had also brought home. As they pushed deeper into the interior of the country, he paused from time to time, trying to read from their faces in the album more than Reilly's journal might be prepared to admit.

The first real clue came towards the end of the second week. They seemed to have hired a local guide to take them into an area where logging had yet to start. This was virgin forest. The side trip was scheduled to last a couple of days, and they'd be living under canvas on the forest floor. 'Normally I'd have run a mile,' Reilly had written, 'but camping and A. are made for each other. He's really really good at it and a total genius at improvisation. He never complains, never despairs, just gets on with it. Even our guide is impressed. Practice, I suppose, plus A.'s usual contempt for the easy way.'

A.'s usual contempt for the easy way. It was a telling phrase, and Suttle sat back, reaching for the remains of his first Stella, trying to picture Bentner camped out in some secluded spot, living on his wits and maybe fuelled by the knowledge that the days of this wilderness were probably numbered. Was this man really on the run? Was he really aware of the way the manhunt was developing? Or was the real story behind Reilly's death more complex than the guiding lights on *Buzzard* were prepared to admit?

Suttle didn't know. Back in the text, back in the rainforest, another entry caught his eye. 'A. bad this morning. D & V plus a determination not to talk to me any more. As a doctor, not good. As his mate and favourite bedfellow, deeply worrying. Am I right about ND? Is she as mad as I think she is?'

ND? Suttle scribbled the two letters down, then read the entry again. The word 'worrying' was key. Was there someone else in Bentner's life, as Molly Weatherall had suspected? Was this thing more complicated than it looked?

He read on, alert now for fresh signs of discord, but within

71

a day everything seemed normal again. 'Back in civilisation,' wrote Reilly. 'No hot water and an army of cockroaches but heaven after the fire ants. Where was God in the jungle when I needed him most?'

Suttle paused again. For the first time it occurred to him that Harriet Reilly might be Catholic. Reilly, after all, was an Irish name. Quite where this possibility might take him, Suttle didn't know but he wrote himself a note to check it out with Oona. What was the papal line on dealing with competition in your love life? And how might Reilly have felt about getting herself pregnant with nothing as comforting as marriage in the offing?

Suttle turned the page. For some reason, the last week of the trip shrank to a mere handful of entries, most of them disappointingly factual. They'd taken a battered old car ferry downriver. They'd been lightly mugged in a Manaus backstreet, two urchins with nimble fingers and a knack of vanishing into the night. They'd taken a flight to Belem, then another to João Pessoa, and ended up back in Rio, waiting for the plane home. For the first time in this final week a blush of emotion. 'Magical night,' Reilly had written. 'Why not say yes?'

Suttle gazed at the question. Yes to what? To a proposal of marriage? Or to something more immediate? Like doing away with birth control? Like binning her pills and giving all those trillions of little Alois Bentners a fighting chance? If so, it hadn't worked. Not then. Not in Brazil.

The second expedition started a page or two later. It was March this year. This time they were in Oregon, via a flight to San Francisco, seemingly another busy chapter in Harriet's crash course on why trees held the key to global warming. In the bitter fag end of an American winter, the contrast in temperatures couldn't have been starker. From San Francisco, Reilly and Bentner sped north in a hired Ford Mustang, an interesting choice, thought Suttle, for a man worrying about the future of the planet. For a brief mile, on US 5, they had the top down. 'Christ,' Reilly wrote. 'Wind chill factor minus 100? We have to be crazy.'

After a visit to a clinic in Portland, about which she wrote nothing, they turned inland. Whether or not Bentner had planned a definite itinerary was unclear, but this time there was no mistaking Reilly's tone of voice. She was in love with this man. She really was. On 9 March, in a rented log cabin beside the Columbia River, she wrote of his warmth and support and his ceaseless assurances that 'things will work out just fine'. None of this stuff sat easily with either the grimness of his ID photo or Nandy's conviction that Bentner was squarely in the frame for what had happened later, but the fact that Reilly – a hard sell by all accounts – was besotted with her wild climatologist sounded an important alarm in Suttle's head.

Rushing to judgement, as he'd learned on countless occasions, had no place in any detective's manual. Real life was a trickier proposition as he, above all, knew to his cost. The following week in the diary, the source of Reilly's passion became abruptly clear. She'd been into the local town. She'd bought herself a test kit. And she was very definitely pregnant. 'A. *over the moon*,' she wrote in bigger script than usual. 'Me too. ND? Who bloody cares?'

ND again. Who was this person? And where did she figure in Harriet's story? He read on, aware that the pace of travel had slowed for Bentner and his newly pregnant partner. 'He cossets me. It's lovely. It's like a hot bath. A. said it would happen and it has. Something new in my life. More, please.' Then this from a motel stop in Goldendale several days later. 'A. nervous about penetrative sex. I tell him it will make no difference. The fetus is always tougher than you think. But he won't have it and so we look for alternatives. No bad thing as it turns out. Who'd have thought?'

Suttle sat back again, staring out of the window. It was dark by now, and the wind was beginning to stir in the trees across the road. He got to his feet and drained the second can. The Oregon trip was within sight of the return flight. Once again the entries became sparsely factual. Back down US 5. A couple of nights in San Francisco. A trip out to Alcatraz, which Bentner likened to

73

the moon. And then home. Somewhere over the Atlantic Reilly had written, 'Why do I feel so happy? And so loved?'

Good questions. En route to the kitchen, Suttle phoned Oona. She couldn't believe he was saying yes to the Fureys.

'Blame the Stella.' Suttle turned the microwave on. 'Front row, please.'

Eleven

Lizzie woke early. Automatically she reached for the bedside radio, then changed her mind. At this time in the morning, way before the rush hour brought the roar of traffic into the city, it was deliciously quiet. She lay back, enjoying the spill of sunshine through the half-curtained window.

After yesterday, for some reason, she felt strangely liberated. She'd been able to share someone else's grief, someone else's loss, and the realisation that death could be softened, maybe even tamed, came as both a surprise and a comfort. She'd now listened to two men bearing witness. For both Jeff Okenek and Ralph Woodman, Harriet Reilly had been able to offer a rare and precious service. A death not to be feared but celebrated. A departure all the more memorable for its sweet grace. So why would a woman who'd brought such relief meet such an ugly end? Was this death's way of getting even? A smack in the face for daring to interfere?

Lizzie thought yet again about Grace. Her daughter had died in the ugliest of circumstances. For months afterwards, still in shock, Lizzie had barely been able to function. Anything that triggered a memory – a girl in the street of Grace's age, even the sound of kids' laughter from a playground – she had found impossible to cope with. Moments like these had made her feel physically ill. She trembled. She panicked. She ran away. It was during this time that she'd systematically wiped her life clean of any reminder, any memory, of her daughter. She deleted hundreds of photos from her computer. She hauled bags of dresses and toys to the charity shop round the corner. Not for her the web campaign to raise awareness about the mentally ill, the stony comforts of coloured ribbons and tearful anniversaries, the post-midnight phone conversations with long-suffering friends, the same old questions rehashed a thousand times: why Grace? Why this? Why *me*?

No, for Lizzie, strong brave Lizzie, the past had become a locked room, neither shrine nor sepulchre, simply a cold dark space she never wanted to inhabit again. From now on, she told herself, she would live exclusively in the present tense, following each new moment to wherever it might lead, obeying no rules but her own. Then had come the invitation to write a book about what had happened.

Months of research had taken her inside the head of the woman who'd killed her daughter. Understanding wasn't forgiveness but it came very close. Then followed more months of writing, of trying to catch Claire's tone of voice, of trying to live in Claire's fevered imagination, of trying to picture the world through the eyes of a woman hopelessly adrift in a nightmare of her own creation. And at the end of it all – the completed first draft of the book dispatched to her editor – she'd found a kind of release.

She thought again about Ralph Woodman and then got out of bed and padded downstairs to the living room. Her laptop was still on from last night. She googled 'Ravel', then 'piano concerto', and thanks to YouTube she was looking at a choice of performances. She remembered Martha Argerich. Twelve hours ago the name had meant nothing; now she couldn't wait to see what this woman looked like. She was bulky. She seemed to be wearing a homespun grey dress. She had a long fall of greying hair, big hands. She hung over the keyboard, awaiting the rise of the conductor's baton, then the music began.

Lizzie was mesmerised. Three movements came and went. After the book she'd so recently written she was good at getting into other people's heads, and it wasn't hard to kid herself that she was Julia Woodman just minutes away from looking Harriet Reilly in the eye and maybe nodding to signal that the moment had arrived for her own death. After years of pain, frustration and possibly disgust at the betrayals her body had inflicted upon her, this would have been a release. So briefly in charge again, this music – maybe this very performance – would have borne her away. From either point of view – Julia's, Ralph's – Lizzie could think of nothing sweeter, of nothing more fitting.

The concerto came to an end. Lizzie pasted the link into a new email and then added a note: 'This is amazing. We need to talk.' She gazed at the screen a moment longer, then hit send. Whether her estranged husband would even open the link was anyone's guess. But she hoped, at the very least, that he'd read the message.

Four hours later, Suttle and Golding were sitting in the reception area at the Met Office in Exeter. The building felt huge, a soaring atrium galleried on three sides. Golding thought it looked like an airport and Suttle agreed. Terminal Four, he thought. Book in for the ride to a nightmare future.

A live multi-screen satellite map beside the reception desk displayed a vast curl of cloud about to sweep in from the Atlantic. Towards the centre of this depression, where the isobars tightened, was a furious swirl of winds which would hit south-west England towards the end of the day. Suttle had lived with weather like this for more than a year now. The winter storms had been the worst in living memory. For night after night, in the dead weeks after Christmas, he'd stood at the window of his flat watching wave after wave exploding against the sea wall.

A couple of times, with Oona, he'd gone down to the seafront for a closer look, bent against the roaring wind, hanging on to each other, their faces turned against the sting of the driving spray. They'd gone no closer than twenty metres to the sea wall, but even so the bigger waves threatened to engulf them, rolling in from the darkness, bursting like shellfire. One in particular had nearly washed them away. Belly deep in brown water, Suttle remembered the suck of the backwash tugging them towards the sea, Oona screaming beside him. Fear, that night, had been laden with the taste of salt.

'Mr Suttle? Mr Golding?'

It was Sheila Forshaw. Suttle had phoned her earlier from the MIR, asking for another meet. My pleasure, she'd said.

Suttle and Golding followed her upstairs. The Hadley Centre for Climate Prediction and Research occupied a big open-plan office on the second floor. There were small meeting rooms along one wall. Forshaw had booked the one with the open door, six chairs around a circular table.

'Skip?' Golding drew Suttle's attention to a quote on the wall. It came from Paul Cezanne. 'We live in a rainbow of chaos.' Too right, Suttle thought, accepting Forshaw's offer of coffee.

Suttle was still looking out at the nests of desks, T-shirted figures bent over PC keyboards, pretty women on the phone. For an organisation tasked with exploring the likelihood of catastrophe, it felt very relaxed. A Scenes of Crime team had already been here, arriving yesterday morning, seizing Bentner's PC and searching his desk and locker. Even their visit, according to the CSI at this morning's *Buzzard* meet, had barely made a ripple.

Forshaw was back with the coffees. She wanted to know how the investigation was going.

'Slowly, I'm afraid. You start in the middle and work out.'

'So where are you?'

'Still in the middle.'

'And Alois?'

'Still AWOL.'

'Strange.' She was frowning.

'That's what we think.'

'So did he do it? Only we'd all find that hard to believe.'

'Why?' The question came from Golding. 'Why do you say that?'

Forshaw was looking uncomfortable. Suttle had the impression that already the conversation had run away with her.

'He's simply not the type. I know that sounds wishy-washy but that's the best I can do. You work in a team long enough and you start to get a feeling for who people really are. We all know that Alois can be difficult, even aggressive sometimes, but that ... you know ... up there in the bedroom ...' She shook her head. 'No way. Deep down the man's a puppy.'

'Really?'

'Yes. You have to dig a bit, and he loves to play the curmudgeon, but he's not like that at all.'

Suttle and Golding swapped glances, then Suttle shrugged. Everything he'd read in Reilly's diary last night confirmed what this woman was saying, but now wasn't the time to agree.

'People can be a mystery, I'm afraid.' It was the best Suttle could offer. 'For the time being we just have to keep an open mind.'

'That's not the way it sounded last night. On *Spotlight*. I don't know exactly who that man was – the detective – but he might as well have announced that Alois is the man you're after.'

'You're right. He *is* the man we're after. It was his house. She was his partner. At the very least, he might have a view.'

'That's not what I meant.'

'I know it's not.'

Suttle held her gaze. Then he asked how much of an outdoors person Bentner was.

'Very,' she said at once. 'He's always off at weekends.'

'He takes a tent? Camps overnight?'

'Yes. Famous for it. Alois is the go-to man in that respect. Anything to do with camping gear, he's got the answer.'

'Does he have favourite places? To your knowledge?'

'I'm sure he does, though I don't know precisely where. You're spoiled for choice round here. The coast? Upcountry? Out on the moor?' She reeled off a list of places Bentner had mentioned over the years. Golding wrote them down. Then she stopped, struck by another thought.

'Letterboxing,' she said. 'You know anything about that?'

Golding again. He said it had to do with leaving trails of clues

79

across Dartmoor. One clue led to another. You hid the clues in a box with a rubber stamp inside. Whoever found the box would leave their own mark in the visitors' book before moving on to hunt for the next one.

'Bit like us, skip.' He was looking at Suttle. 'Except it rains all the time.'

Suttle wanted to know why Forshaw had raised letterboxing.

'Because of Alois,' she said at once. 'He got quite keen over the spring, and I had the impression he might have taken his partner along.'

'You think he might be out there on Dartmoor?'

'It's possible. He certainly knows it well. I imagine there must be umpteen places to –' she shrugged '– hide.'

'But why would he want to do that? When it's so obvious we'd like to talk to him?'

'He may not know. Alois never has much time for the media, Facebook, all that stuff. He lives in a bubble. He rations himself. He does what he wants to do. He's not interested in tuning in, unlike the rest of us.'

There was a long silence. Golding was thinking what Suttle was thinking. The foreplay was over. They'd established a rapport with this woman. Now for the question that really mattered.

'He's been in touch with you, hasn't he?'

The silence stretched and stretched. She held their gaze. At length she nodded. 'Yes.'

'When?'

'Last night.'

'What time?'

'Around one in the morning. I thought it must have been some kind of emergency. Maybe for him it was.'

'What did he say?'

'He wanted to tell me that he didn't do it. Didn't kill her. Just that.'

'And did you believe him?'

'Yes.'

'Did he say anything else?'

'Yes. He asked me to pass on a message.'

'Who to?'

'You lot. He wanted me to tell you you're wasting your time.'

'Because he didn't do it?'

'Because you'll never find him. Unless he decides otherwise.'

Suttle checked his watch.

Golding wanted to know whether Bentner had made the call on his mobile.

'No. He told me he was ringing from a box.'

'Did you 1471? Check out the number?'

'No. I thought I'd leave that to you.'

'So why didn't you phone us at once? Share the information? Tell us about the call?'

'I thought I'd leave it until this morning. Then you saved me the trouble.'

'But you never mentioned it on the phone.'

'You're right. But I'm mentioning it now, aren't I?'

Suttle wondered about arresting her, then decided against it. They'd take her home, check out Bentner's call, at least get a fix on where he was in the small hours of the morning. He'd read her the riot act, tell her she was lucky to avoid a Perverting the Course of Justice charge and pressurise her into acting as a go-between. If Bentner had pulled this trick once, he'd do it again. And this time Sheila Forshaw would be on the phone to Suttle within minutes.

'There's something else I need to check out,' he said.

'Please do.'

'You owe me this time, right?'

'If you say so.'

'I have a couple of initials for you. We think it may be a name. And we think this person may work here.'

He produced a slip of paper and passed it across the table. Forshaw glanced at it. 'ND?'

Twelve

Lizzie took Anton to lunch. She knew an Arab café near Exeter Central station was a favourite of his, and he'd already commandeered a table by the window by the time Lizzie arrived. Two toddlers were playing on the floor beside the door. Lizzie picked her way between them, spared their mothers a nod and settled herself in the chair across from Anton.

'I wanted to say a proper thank you for last night.' She nodded at the menu. 'And for Jeff too.'

'*Kein Problem*. You want more of these people?'

'Yes, please.'

'So ... OK.' He bent forward across the table, lowered his voice. 'So far, no complaints. Am I right?'

'From me?'

'From the ones left behind. But this time maybe something a bit different.'

'Like what?'

'Like the third person on that list I gave you. Like someone not at all pleased with Dr Reilly.'

He explained that Ralph had taken a call from a man called Dean. His mother – Betty – had breast cancer, and Anton understood that a friend of hers had been in touch with Ralph after reading a piece he'd written for the Dignity in Dying website.

'This was about Julia? About how she went?' This was news to Lizzie.

'Of course not. This was much earlier. The article was about

82

how his wife was suffering so much. About why the law should be changed.'

Dean, he explained, had been a Royal Marine. Now he was working in maritime security in the Gulf, a job that kept him away a lot. He knew his mother wasn't well, and he knew the cancer had spread to her liver, but she didn't much like the carers he'd sorted out for her and preferred to be looked after by a friend her own age.

'This was a woman called Frances,' Anton said. 'She was the one who read Ralph's piece on the website and got in touch with him. This was much more recently. Ralph drove across to meet them both. He said it was obvious that Betty was in pain. He said she was really distressed. Because of her liver failing, she'd gone yellow. She hated taking drugs and refused to go into hospital but she didn't want to live alone any more. She felt there was nothing left for her.'

'Ralph mentioned Harriet Reilly?'

'He did. He talked to her first, of course. Then she came to meet Betty.'

'And?'

'Harriet was happy to do what she could.'

'When was this?'

'Six weeks ago. Betty died at the beginning of this month.'

'Thanks to Harriet?'

'Yes.'

'Natural burial?'

'Yes.'

This was becoming Harriet Reilly's trademark, her way of avoiding the extra checks and paperwork that went with cremations. First Alec. Then Julia. And now – it seemed – Betty.

'So where did this woman live?' She'd abandoned the menu.

'Lympstone.'

Nandy, on a short fuse already, exploded. Suttle had just reported back on Sheila Forshaw.

'She did *what*?'

83

Suttle repeated the story's headline. They'd taken Forshaw back to her Exeter house. Luckily, her phone hadn't been active since Bentner had been in touch and 1471 had delivered the number of a call box. Suttle had dialled the number there and then to save the hassle of going through BT, and after a minute or two a passer-by had lifted the receiver. The call box was on the northern edges of Ivybridge. Which, in Suttle's view, probably meant that Bentner was hiding out on Dartmoor. He was describing Bentner's recent passion for letterboxing when Nandy interrupted.

'He'll have moved on after making the call. That time in the morning he'll have the roads to himself. We need to ANPR him.' Automatic number plate recognition was a vital tool for operations like *Buzzard*. If Bentner stuck to the major roads, they could track him from camera to camera.

Houghton reached for a phone but Nandy hadn't finished. He wanted to know why Forshaw hadn't reported the call.

'I've no idea, sir. My best guess is that she likes him and was trying to protect him.'

'By giving him a head start? After what he'd done?'

'That's a supposition, sir, if I may say so. Remember she has a vested interest in this. It was Forshaw who found the body. That was a horrible scene. She doesn't believe he could have done it. That's what she said. That's what she told us.'

'Brilliant. Top work, son. You think she's implicated some-how? An affair, maybe? You think they might have been at it? Should we pull her in? Bosh her house? See how she takes a conspiracy charge? This is beyond belief, son. We've just spent twenty-four hours putting that man's face in every house in the kingdom and we end up with dick all. He phones this woman in the middle of the night and it takes her another eight hours to let us know. What are we looking at here? Just give me something to go on.'

Suttle glanced at Houghton for help. The DI was deep in the latest email. Oddly enough, it came from the Met Office.

'ND?' she queried.

Suttle explained about the entries in Harriet Reilly's travel journal. Nandy had at last begun to calm down. Suttle wanted to know more about the email.

'It's come from their HR department. They're giving us three names.' Houghton bent towards the screen. 'Nadine Drexler. Nathalie Dorman. Nikki Drew.'

'Addresses?'

'No.' She shook her head. 'If you want more, they're suggesting you talk to Sheila Forshaw again. She's his line manager, as you know.'

'Perfect.' Suttle couldn't resist a smile. 'Just as well I didn't arrest her, boss. She might have gone No Comment by now.'

With Nandy's blessing, Suttle left the office to make the call. On the phone Sheila Forshaw sounded almost cheerful. The knowledge that Bentner was still free, still out of reach, must have made her day.

Suttle wanted to know whether she'd seen the email from HR.

'I was copied in. Like your DI.'

'So what's the strength?'

'Strength?'

'Do you know any of these people?'

'Only Nikki Drew.'

'And Bentner?'

'He knows her too. She's part of the same team.'

'So you manage her?'

'I do.'

'And?'

There was a brief silence. Then Forshaw was back on the line.

'What is it you want to know, Mr Suttle? Let's not waste each other's time.'

'I want to know whether she and Bentner might be close.'

'You mean sexually? Emotionally?'

'Yes.'

'That I doubt. Nikki is already in a relationship.'

'With another guy?'

'I didn't say that.'

'I see.' Suttle made a note. 'So where does she live? Ms Drew?'

'Topsham.'

'You have the address? Contact details?'

'Of course.' Suttle heard a sigh. 'I'll put them in an email.'

The conversation came to an end. Golding had drifted across the MIR and perched himself on Suttle's desk. The force helicopter had been criss-crossing Dartmoor for the last hour. It had an infrared camera aboard, and if Bentner was still out there somewhere, there was just a chance that body heat might give him away. Nandy had also put in a bid to use Royal Navy and coastguard assets if another search area presented itself, but so far there'd been no response to either request.

Houghton, intrigued by Bentner's recent interest in letterboxing, had also tasked a team of officers to start scouring likely sites on the southern fringes of the moor. Maybe *Buzzard*'s fugitive may have left some kind of message. Maybe this was another back passage to the wanted man.

Suttle wanted to know whether any other leads had emerged.

'The guys boshing Reilly's cottage called in. They've just finished.'

'And?'

'They've found bits of glass and wine stains around the living room. They're thinking someone tried to clear it all up but didn't do a great job. The pattern suggests some kind of fracas.'

Suttle nodded. This latest news fitted the picture of Reilly and Bentner that was beginning to develop: their volatility, their passion for each other, Bentner's fondness for strong drink. Then he had another thought. *Stupid*, he thought. *I'm so, so stupid.*

'The scene at Bentner's place,' he said. 'Reilly on the bed.'

'And?'

'She had a tan. She'd been somewhere hot.'

'Like the back garden?'

'Not a tan like that. No way. We need to check it out. Try the practice. Or maybe those neighbours of hers. Find out whether she took a break over the last couple of weeks. Then cross-check with Sheila Forshaw.'

'I'm not with you, skip.'

'See if Bentner went too.'

Golding headed for his own desk, then paused. He wanted to know whether it might be safe to bank on having the evening free. Serafin had scored a couple of tickets to a stand-up gig in Taunton and Golding fancied going along.

'Stand-up?' Suttle could use a few laughs himself.

'Yeah.' He named a couple of broadcast comedians Suttle had never heard of. Golding's nod covered the entire room. 'This inquiry's nearly through, skip. All we have to do is wait for Bentner to show up. A few beers won't do us any harm.'

Suttle smiled. His PC signalled an incoming email. It was Sheila Forshaw with Nikki Drew's contact details. She'd just talked to Nikki, and she was happy to have a conversation with Suttle this evening if that might help.

Suttle responded, accepting the invitation, then sat back. Golding was still waiting for an answer.

'You go.' Suttle nodded at the screen. 'I'll sort this.'

Thirteen

Frances Bevan lived on an estate on the edges of Lympstone. Its sturdy properties had been built as council houses and later sold to their tenants on very favourable terms. Over the last couple of decades the village had become a trophy postcode and prices had gone through the roof. Frances Bevan was one of the original tenants who'd stayed on. And so, as it turned out, was her friend across the road.

On the phone Lizzie had explained her interest in euthanasia. At Ralph Woodman's request, she was spreading her net as wide as possible to try and understand why an organisation called Dignity in Dying was becoming so popular. Initially dubious about any kind of conversation, mention of Ralph Woodman had opened Frances Bevan's door. Such a gentle man. So well intentioned. And such a blessing as far as Betty was concerned.

'So you'd been neighbours for ever? You and Betty?'

'That's right. Neighbours and best friends. To be honest, we've both had our little problems but life's like that, isn't it?'

Lizzie nodded. Frances Bevan was a small, neat, busy little person with freshly permed hair and a lapful of knitting. Her sitting room, spotlessly clean, was deeply retro – a tribute to 50s decor – and Lizzie could imagine her fending off countless suggestions from friends or well-wishers pointing out the benefits of a thorough makeover. Her husband, it turned out, had died more than a decade ago, and she'd been living alone ever since. A crucifix hung on the wall over the brown-tiled fireplace.

Lizzie wanted to know more about Betty. Had she also been living alone?

'Good Lord, yes. That's one of the reasons we saw so much of each other. As I say, Betty was just across the road, there. Number 13.'

'And her husband died?'

'He's dead now, yes. But that was only a couple of years ago. Long before that – years and years ago – he walked out on her, took up with another woman in the village. It turned out they'd been seeing each other for months and months. Everyone knew except Betty. And me, of course.'

'Lucky she had you, then.'

'I like to think so. We can always get through these things, that's what I used to tell her. The Lord is listening, and all we have to do is open our hearts.'

'Betty was religious? A believer?'

'Not then. But later, just a bit, yes.'

'Just a bit' made Lizzie smile. Exactly which bit would you believe in? Given a shock like that? She didn't know.

'You took Betty to church?'

'I did. I told her it was important to keep going out. She had to hold her head high. She had to be bigger than that grubby little man.'

'And Dean? He was their only child?'

'He was. I watched that little boy grow up and I knew he was troubled. Maybe it's true what they say about children. We never had any of our own so I can't speak personally, but people say the little ones can sense when a marriage isn't working. That must have been true with Dean.'

As he got older, she said, he began to go off the rails. Silly little things at first – riding his bike without lights, smashing panes of glass in a neighbour's greenhouse with his football. But then came the shoplifting and getting drunk when he was much, much too young, and fighting on the bus with boys much older than himself.

'That's why Harry pushed him into the Marines. Looking back, maybe it wasn't such a bad idea.'

Harry was Betty's feckless husband. By now he was living with his girlfriend in a flat above one of the village pubs. Dean would drop by from time to time but never really accepted the new woman in his father's life. Neither did he get on with his mum.

'I think he blamed her for the break-up. Betty was always a stickler for discipline, and that must make for tension within a family. In some ways Dean became a bit of an orphan. I know he had problems with women ... you know ... with relationships ...'

Problems with women? Lizzie bent forward, pushed a little harder.

'Did he marry? Dean?'

'Not as far as I know. I think a couple of times he moved in with women he'd met, just to see whether it would work, but it must have been difficult, being away so much. I know it broke Betty's heart. She wanted him to be normal. She wanted a daughter-in-law, grandchildren, and who can blame her? Her own marriage had turned out to be a bit of a mess, and I suppose she was looking to her son to put all that right.'

'But he didn't?'

'Not at all. And he was hopeless with money too. When you come out of the Marines you get a lump sum and a nice pension on top. Betty told me that. She said Dean had lots and lots of money but no idea what to do with it. In the end he tried to set up this company. He met a man who'd invented some security gadget and needed backing. Dean gave him everything he asked for, but it never worked. That's why he ended up being a guard on all those ships. I don't think it was what he wanted to do but he had no choice.'

'This was recently?'

'A couple of years ago. Betty was ill by that time but Dean never seemed to take much notice. He was away for months on end. Then he'd come back and because he had nowhere of his own he'd end up living across the road. You'd think he'd help out with Betty but he never did.'

'So who did she have?'

'Me. Betty was in bed most of the time by then, but she was a big woman and she took a bit of lifting. Dean would help with that when he had a mind to, but sometimes I had to phone and get him out of the pub if it was an emergency. That didn't go down well, believe you me.'

'With Betty?'

'With Dean. He'd met someone. A terrible, terrible woman, a real Gypsy. No one has a good word to say for her. Good-looking, mind, if you like that sort of thing.'

'I'm not with you.'

'Dark, my dear.'

'You mean black?'

'No, swarthy. Spanish-looking. Gypsy blood. Drinks like a fish. No pride. Never minds her manners.'

'And he's still with this woman?'

'As far as I know. She's got a place down in Exmouth. That's why he wasn't around towards the end. When he was back from being away, he lived with her.'

Lizzie was trying to picture the way it must have been in the end, with Betty bed-bound, riddled with a cancer she knew was killing her. Lizzie asked whether hospital had ever been an option.

'Of course it was, my dear, but it wasn't what Betty *wanted*. She didn't want any fuss, any bother, and she had a real fear of hospitals. She was a very private person, Betty. She just wanted to be left alone.'

'Which was out of the question.'

'Of course it was.'

'Which is where you came in.'

'Happily, yes.'

She described the final weeks. Betty was in pain most of the time. She had arthritis as well as cancer, and some days the pain was bad enough to make her cry.

'I'd never seen that,' Frances said. 'She'd always been such a strong woman. That came as a real shock.'

The doctor, she said, would call when needed, and there were a couple of weeks when Dean got back from abroad and organised a team of carers, but Betty didn't like any of them and cancelled the contract.

'Leaving just you?'

'Yes. Not that I minded. Betty had nice neighbours, new people, a young family, and the father was happy to come in for the heavy stuff. Between us we managed. More or less.'

Lizzie nodded. The next question voiced itself: 'And Harriet Reilly? How did she come into the story?'

'Harriet?' Frances frowned, taking her time. 'That was Betty's idea. The one thing Dean *had* done for her was get hold of one of those iPad things. I gather he brought it back from Dubai. Betty was on it a lot. I think it was a bit of a lifesaver.'

Lifesaver, under the circumstances, was a strange choice of word. Lizzie wanted to know more.

'Betty started finding out about … you know … assisted dying. She'd had enough. I knew that. I'm a believer, my dear. I believe that life is a precious gift from our Maker and that we have no right to end it on our own terms, not before it's taken from us. So Betty's choice of websites began to disturb me. Not disturb. Upset would be a better term.'

A favourite site, she said, was Dignity in Dying. Betty would show it to her. There was no secret about it.

'There were lots of personal stories,' Frances said. 'People in the same situation as Betty, maybe different cancers, different conditions, but the same pain.'

'And the same frustration?'

'Exactly.'

'So what did you say?'

'I'm afraid I wasn't much use. If you want the truth, I told her to grin and bear it. By now we were all finding it a bit of a struggle.'

'And Dean?'

'He'd stopped coming. In his defence, I think he found the whole thing difficult. I don't think he could cope. Whatever the truth, I know it broke his mother's heart.'

'That he wasn't there for her?'

'Yes.'

'So what did she do?'

'One of the stories came from Mr Woodman. The man you mentioned on the phone.'

'And what did he say?'

'He said he might be able to help. He'd lost his own wife to motor neurone. He didn't say how but both of us, Betty and I, sort of guessed that there'd been some kind of ... I don't know ...'

'Assistance?'

'Yes. A helping hand.'

'Which turned out to be Harriet Reilly?'

'Yes. I met her too. A very nice woman, a very nice woman indeed.'

'Nice how?'

'Sincere. Serious. You could feel her commitment. Betty felt it too.'

'Commitment to what?'

'To helping. It was a terrible situation, my dear. Even now I have nightmares about it, and that's because I feel so guilty. We should never have done what we did. Speaking to you like this makes it easier, funnily enough. I need to get it off my chest.'

'But it was what Betty wanted. Wasn't it?'

'Of course it was. But it was *wrong*, my dear. And nothing can change that. Only God. And he never will.'

Harriet, she said, had said that burial would be essential because with a cremation it might be difficult.

'I was all for a Christian burial, of course, but the more I thought about it, the more it seemed wrong. If Betty went through with this thing then she was breaking one of God's laws. She wasn't really a churchgoer, either, hadn't been to church for years and years, and getting a plot these days isn't easy. Harriet said she knew a lovely site they use for natural burials over on the Haldon Hills, and she found the website for Betty on her iPad. Betty loved it. So green. The views. The trees. Wonderful. Harriet asked whether she'd like to meet the man whose idea it had been. He was nice too. So gentle.'

'They met?'

'Yes. And she signed up on the spot.'

'How much did it cost?'

'Three thousand something. You design your own celebration, choose your own readings. This was last month. The weather was lovely. I know it sounds silly, and as I expect you can imagine I didn't approve at all, but I believe she was actually looking forward to it.'

'Dying?'

'Yes. Having the pain stop.'

Poor Betty, she said, had a couple more weeks to get through. She had to sign up for Harriet's practice, which meant all kinds of forms to fill in, and she'd also decided to change her will.

'Why was that?'

'Because of Dean. That woman of his was the last straw. Betty was upset about him never being around, and she was angry too, almost ashamed of him. She thought the woman was a slut. That's very strong language coming from Betty, but she knew her like we all knew her. She had a terrible reputation in the village. A truly awful woman.'

'What was her name?'

'Tania. Horrible name. Cheap. The thought of some of her money ending up with someone like that was more than she could bear.'

'We're talking lots of money?'

'Yes.'

'Do you know how much?'

'Yes.' Frances was beady-eyed now. 'Do you want me to tell you?'

'Yes, please.'

'Just over half a million pounds. The house was hers, all hers.

94

She'd had it valued recently. It's got a garage and a lovely garden at the back. It needs a bit of TLC but it's all there. Around £340,000.'

'And the rest?'

'She had savings. And a legacy from her own mother that she'd never touched. Betty was like me. Why spend good money when you don't have to?'

Lizzie needed to check that Dean really was the only child. He was.

'And all that money was going to him?'

'Yes.'

'He knew that?'

'Yes. Betty had told him when things between them were less difficult. I expect that woman knew too. He's bound to have told her.'

'So what did Betty do?'

'She phoned her solicitor. He drove down from Exeter. I witnessed the new will.'

'So where did the money go?'

'Betty divided it in two. Half went to the Dignity in Dying people. She thought they were providing a wonderful resource.'

'And the rest?'

'The Woodland Trust. She thought at first about the man who ran the natural burial site but she wasn't really sure. The Woodland Trust was on his website. He encouraged donations. If you want the truth, I was rather proud of her.'

Lizzie asked about the day Betty died but knew at once that this was pushing Frances too far. She'd been there, of course she had, and she'd held poor Betty's hand and said a prayer as she drifted off. Afterwards she'd left for a little weep while the doctor tidied up.

'What about Dean?'

'I had to phone him. That was Betty's last request, practically the last thing she said. Wait until tomorrow and tell him I've gone. See whether he remembers who I am.'

'And?'

'He was really upset.'

'Genuinely?'

'Yes, I think so.'

'He came over?'

'Yes.'

'With his girlfriend?'

'No. By himself. Betty had gone by then. The undertakers had called to collect her. All that remained was the burial. Out in the hills.'

'Was Dean surprised?'

'Very.'

'Did he go?'

'Yes.'

'Alone?'

'No. That Tania came too. Horrible. It spoiled everything.'

'And the will? When Dean found out?'

Frances gazed at her, then fumbled in her bag for a pen and paper. With some care she wrote what looked like an address.

She looked up. 'I'm afraid you'll have to find that out for yourself, my dear. I don't want to get involved any more, not really.' She handed over the slip of paper. The address was in Exmouth. 'That's where you'll find Dean. Might I ask you a favour?'

'Of course.'

'The address didn't come from me.'

Minutes later, having said no to tea, Lizzie sat around the corner in her car staring at her laptop. She'd been on the Dignity in Dying website a couple of times already, briefing herself on the background. The board of the charity was led by Sir Graeme Catto, Emeritus Professor of Medicine at Aberdeen University and President of the College of Medicine. The Vice Chair had been a leading psychiatrist at the Hospital for Sick Children in Great Ormond Street. The Treasurer was an MP. This wasn't some bunch of tree-huggers. Far from it.

A keystroke led to a series of personal stories, individuals whose lives had been touched – and often ended – by terminal disease, a chorus of voices begging for a change in the law to permit assisted dying. Whether you were a loved one at the bedside or someone approaching death, nothing seemed more cruel than having to wait for mortality – and pain – to take its time. Lizzie had read some of these stories before, but like the best websites, this one was constantly replenished with new uploads and there was fresh testimony, some of it barely twenty-four hours old.

Half an hour later Lizzie lifted her head, convinced that the world needed more people like Harriet Reilly, GPs compassionate and brave enough to risk their careers and their liberty to spare people an ugly death. One day, she thought, Harriet Reilly's contribution to the cause would somehow be recognised. Maybe some kind of citation. Maybe even a medal. The irony, of course, was that the recognition would be posthumous. Because the woman who'd decided to cheat death of its winnings had herself been killed.

Lizzie checked her watch. Nearly six o'clock. She was thinking about Dean. About Tania. About Harriet Reilly. She produced her mobile and composed a text. 'I'd like to buy you a drink,' she wrote. 'I wouldn't ask if it wasn't important.'

She read it through, went to her directory and found Jimmy's number. She checked the text one last time, then hit Send.

Gone.

Fourteen

Nikki Drew lived in one of a row of red-brick terraced houses overlooking Topsham station. Suttle had called earlier to confirm that she was happy to talk. Her partner was away until Thursday and even on the phone Suttle had the feeling she'd welcome the company.

Suttle parked in the health centre down the road. As he was about to get out of the car his mobile signalled an incoming text. Lizzie. He glanced at it, then read it properly before slipping the phone back in his pocket. Seconds later, the phone rang. It was Golding.

'I checked out the holiday thing, skip. It turns out Reilly went to Tenerife for eight days.'

'When?'

'A couple of weeks ago.'

'Alone?'

'Yes.'

'Good work.'

Suttle ended the call and sat back for a moment behind the wheel. An hour ago he'd had a conversation with DI Houghton. Bentner's Skoda had been found on an industrial estate in Bodmin. Bodmin was in Cornwall, an hour's drive west of Dartmoor. The car had been declared a crime scene and would shortly be brought back to Exeter. Bentner, according to Houghton, would now be driving a fresh pair of wheels, making the prospect of finding him even bleaker.

Suttle frowned, trying to tease a little sense from these latest developments. Nowadays, every purchase left a trace, so how come there'd been no movements on Bentner's various accounts? And why, more to the point, hadn't he accompanied his pregnant partner to Tenerife?

Minutes later Suttle was knocking on Nikki Drew's door.

She was a good-looking woman, late thirties, early forties, with a strong face and good eyes. She was wearing Lycra shorts and a grey T-shirt and must have been running because the T-shirt was dark with sweat. She apologised for being a tad disorganised, told him to make coffee if he fancied it and disappeared. Moments later Suttle caught the fall of water in a shower and a blast of Stevie Wonder. Nice.

Waiting for Drew to reappear, Suttle found the kitchen and filled the kettle. Either Nikki or whoever else lived here did a lot of cooking. Italian recipe books. Thai. Nepalese. Classic French. By the time she was out of the shower, Suttle was back in the living room with two mugs of coffee.

'No biscuits?' This woman had a sense of humour. She settled down and unwound the towel from her head. Her hair fell around her shoulders, black threaded lightly with grey. She was wearing a tracksuit now, with CORNELL UNIVERSITY on the back. Her feet were bare, perfect nails painted a deep blue dusted with tiny stars.

'You want to know about Alois?'

'Yes.'

'So why ask me?'

Suttle had been anticipating the question. Under the circumstances he saw no point in hiding the truth.

'Bentner had a partner,' he said, 'as you may or may not know. She's the woman who was killed in Lympstone. They went away together a couple of times over the last year and she kept a kind of diary. She refers from time to time to someone she calls ND. This is a murder inquiry. We action every lead.'

'And you think that's me?'

'I think it might be.'

'Why?'

'Because you work in the same office. And because I therefore assume you knew him. Does that sound reasonable?'

'Perfectly. So how can I help you?'

It was a good question. Suttle asked her what she'd been doing on Saturday night.

'I was here with Connie.'

'Your partner?'

'Yes.'

'Anyone else around?'

'You mean corroboration?' She shook her head. 'No.'

'And you were here all night?'

'Sure. Together. Upstairs. If I'd have popped out to murder someone, Connie would have been the first to know. She's a light sleeper. And I'm lousy at keeping secrets. Something like that? Shit, I'd have told her the moment I stepped back inside the house.'

Suttle was warming to this exchange.

'So tell me about Alois Bentner,' he said. 'What kind of guy was he?'

'Was? You think he's dead?'

'I think he's gone missing. In fact I know he's gone missing.'

'That's not the same as dead, though.' For the first time she smiled.

'Of course not.' Suttle smiled back. 'So what kind of guy is he?'

'He's canny. He's sharp. He can be mega-difficult. He's probably a genius. What else do you want to know?'

'Genius? How?'

She gave the question some thought.

'We're all scientists where we work,' she said at last. 'Scientists speak the language of data. We're cautious by nature. It comes with the territory. You think you're looking at a 98-per-cent chance of catastrophic global warming, you want to know about that remaining 2 per cent. Not our Mr Bentner He's a probabilities man. He calculates the odds, sees what's coming down the road and goes into battle. That makes him a warrior as well as a scientist, which is a lot less common than you might think. On some days I think we need more Bentners at the Centre. On other days he can be a pain in the arse.'

Suttle nodded. Sheila Forshaw, the first time he'd interviewed her, had said much the same. Suttle remembered her story about Bentner losing it at the pub barbecue beside the canal. *A breakdown waiting to happen*, she'd said.

'I understand he could be violent,' Suttle suggested. 'Especially recently.'

'Violent?' Drew shook her head. 'More frustrated. Alois was an early believer. He'd done the sums. He could figure out the implications. He was proud to be a warmist. He thought the rest of us had the same responsibility.'

'And now?'

'Now's no different. In fact now's worse. I had a conversation with him only last week. He'd just got hold of a paper from a guy called Merrilees. It was about increasing shrub abundance in the Arctic. It was published in *Nature*. If you're familiar with the data set this stuff makes for scary reading.'

'And Bentner? What did he say?'

'He always wants to take the battle to the enemy. You're talking Big Oil, Big Gas, Big Coal, Big Everything, plus all the neocons that want to keep cranking up the boiler and stuff the consequences. These are the guys who think people like Alois are trying to turn their world upside down, and of course they're right. Alois says they're evil. He talks about disaster capitalism. He thinks they're the devil's spawn. If you've got the time to listen, a lot of this stuff is fascinating. God knows, he's probably right, but I'm not sure it does much for his blood pressure.'

'So what do *you* think?'

'About global warming? Some days I'm glad it keeps me in a job. Other times it scares me shitless. Thank Christ I haven't got a child.'

'I meant Bentner. Here's a guy on top of the data. He thinks he knows what's coming down the track. I get the impression that he thinks no one is listening to him. Even where he works, even with people who are tuned in, there's no real appetite to get out there and beat the drum. Am I right? Am I being fair?'

'No. That's way too simplistic. Of course we care. We just happen not to take it to extremes.'

'And Bentner did? Does?'

She didn't answer. She was cautious now, recognising the trap that Suttle was baiting. He tried it a different way.

'He just changed the name on the front of his house. Two Degrees to Five Degrees. Did you know that?'

'Yes.'

'And?'

'That's simplistic too. Five degrees is off the map. If we get to five degrees we're all poached.'

'But that's his point, isn't it?'

'Of course. But it's highly unlikely.'

'You mean extreme.'

'Yes.'

'So you think he believes it? Believes it enough to change the name of his house?'

'It's a warning, not a prediction. Even Alois can't be that certain. But that's the way he works. Maybe it starts with the postman. Alois hopes the guy has a think about the name change. Hopes he has a chat with his buddies. Hopes his buddies pass the word on. Assumes that pretty soon the whole world is sitting up and taking notice. That's the way Alois would see it.'

'Chinese whispers?'

'Not far off. Certainly propaganda.'

'Rather than science?'

'Rather than something we could – in all conscience – prove. Some of us had a chat to Alois about five degrees. He couldn't stand it up. No way.'

'So what did that make you lot?'

'In his eyes?'

'Yes.'

'Denialists. Big time.'

'And was he angry?'

'No. He just told us we were wrong. He thinks we're at the point of no return. He thinks we're all fucked. Not only that but he thinks we *deserve* to be fucked. Some of this stuff doesn't make for a jolly conversation, believe me. That's why people started to avoid him.'

'He drinks a lot. Do you think that helps?'

'Probably not. But the guy's in a bad place. Inside his head I'd probably do the same thing.'

'Did you know his partner was pregnant?'

'Really?' For the first time genuine surprise. 'Ali? Putting out for a *baby*?'

'That's right. Sadly it won't happen, but she was definitely pregnant.'

'And it was definitely his?'

'Subject to confirmation –' Suttle nodded '– yes. So how does that sit with five degrees? With disaster capitalism?'

'I've no idea. Maybe he was drunk at the time. Maybe his partner was a Catholic. Nixed the abortion.'

'By all accounts he was pleased.'

'I'm astonished. *Alois?* You're sure?'

'Yes. As sure as I can be.'

'That makes no sense.' She shook her head. 'None.'

She reached for her mug again. Then she folded her legs beneath her, thinking hard.

'There's a word Ali loves to use,' she said at last. 'Overburden. It comes from the oil industry. It means all the useless stuff on top like trees and grasses and meadows these oil people have to shift before they go after the black stuff locked up below. Trees are Alois' business. As a climatologist, that's where he made his name. What they've done to Alberta seriously upsets him. He's been out there for a look. The Athabasca tar sands. He says it's beyond belief. Press him just a little bit, not much, and you get to the heart of it. The way Alois sees it, the overburden, the real overburden, isn't nature at all. It's us. He thinks we're the parasites. He thinks we're the takers. Once he told me that when it came to the planet we were death on legs. So why would he ever bring a child into a world like that?'

Suttle shrugged. Said he didn't know. *Death on legs*. A distillation of everything this man believed about the human condition. A phrase to remember.

'So how far did Bentner take all this?'

'All what?'

'His campaigning? Five degrees? All that?'

'I've no idea. If you're asking me whether he was the kind of guy to go on marches, I'd say not. He wasn't much of a joiner so that probably rules out Greenpeace and Save the Planet and all the rest of them. He certainly wrote articles, and he had the academic clout to get them published. He has profile, if that's what you're asking. He likes to get in the face of these people. He likes to upset them. Maybe that's his role in life. Maybe that's what he's best at. Give these guys a big shake. Make them fall out of their tree.'

'Enemies?'

'You mean serious enemies? Big business? Big Oil? People who might want to hurt him? Steal into his house? Kill his partner?'

'Yes.'

'I suppose it's possible. If these people ever bother to listen.'

'You think they might?'

'I doubt it. Money always has the loudest voice and the deafest ears. Always.'

'That sounds like something Bentner might say.'

'You're right. It was his phrase. But I suspect it happens to be true.'

'Suspect?'

'I know it happens to be true. We're lucky at the Centre. We're well funded, well led, and there are lots of people in the world who are starting to wake up and take notice. Especially after winters like the last one. But Alois is right. Nothing's going to happen until we sort out the guys with the real money. And maybe there isn't enough science in the world to do that.'

'Shame.'

'Yeah. And probably terminal.' She paused. 'Do you mind me asking you a personal question?'

'Not at all.'

'What happened to your face?'

'I got attacked.'

'What happened?'

'It doesn't matter.'

'Was it recently?'

'Last year. They tell me the scarring will soften in the end.'

'So how do you cope?'

'I avoid mirrors.'

'I don't believe you. No one avoids mirrors.'

'That's true. Maybe I just shut my eyes.'

'That's worse. That puts you alongside the denialists.'

'Thanks.' Suttle swallowed the last of his coffee and stood up. 'Is it that bad?'

'Not at all.' She made no effort to move. 'Quite the reverse.'

Suttle retrieved his car. Sitting behind the wheel, the keys still in his hand, he fought the temptation to check his face in the rear-view mirror. Very few people had ever been as direct as Nikki Drew, but in a way he took it as a compliment. In his trade the best interviews happened on a level of semi-intimacy. The closer you got to someone, the more truthful they tended to be. She'd been relaxed enough to ask him the bluntest of questions, which shed an interesting light on her view of Alois Bentner. No way would this man have butchered his partner like that, she'd told him. None.

Suttle glanced at his watch. Gone seven. He fetched out his mobile, read the text from Lizzie again, then tapped out an answer: 'Where and when? Your call.'

Fifteen

Suttle had already arrived by the time Lizzie made it to the pub. She'd never been here before but a couple who were near-neighbours raved about the ambience and it was easily walkable. She'd been tempted to wear a scarlet halter top she knew Jimmy had always loved, but after trying it on she'd decided to stick to designer jeans and the new soft leather jacket she'd bought as a present to herself only last week. She knew how important the next hour or so might turn out to be, and she knew as well that she should feel at ease about her new life. Lizzie Hodson. Best-selling author. Mother of none. And now – to her surprise and delight – apprentice sleuth.

He was sitting at a table in the corner, nursing the last of a pint. She thought he looked even more exhausted than usual. He got to his feet, asking what she'd like to drink, but she waved him back down.

'Stella? Or is that a silly question?'

Without waiting for an answer, she went to the bar, returning with a fresh pint of lager and a spritzer. Tonight was open-mike night. At the moment they were between acts but she knew it wasn't going to last.

'You're going to hate this,' she said at once, 'but I can't think of any other way of putting it.'

She told him about her investigative website and the modest network of co-journos she'd put together to nail down stories and see where they might lead. It turned out that Suttle had googled *Bespoken* a couple of times, prompted by ex-CID colleagues in Pompey who remembered Lizzie's maiden name and were intrigued by what she was up to after the success of *Mine*. He'd been impressed: nice home page, punchy writing, a reminder of the young investigative reporter who'd caught his attention all those years ago.

'So where's all this going?' he said. The question sounded aggressive and clumsy, but he didn't apologise.

'To assisted dying.'

'Assisted what?' The next act was up on the rostrum that served as a stage, testing the mike.

'Dying.'

'*Dying?* Can't leave it alone, can you?'

For a moment he thought she was going to leave. He leaned forward over the table and apologised. She looked at his hand on her arm, said nothing.

'Sorry,' he muttered again. 'That was unnecessary.'

'You're right. There might be something in this for you. In fact for both of us.'

'I'm not with you.'

She told him about Alec, about Ralph Woodman's wife, about Betty, but left out their names. All three, she said, had been helped on their way by a local GP.

'That's illegal. Technically, we'd call it manslaughter.'

'I know. But it goes on all the time. This woman happens to be killing more than most. No one has a bad word to say about her. In my book she's providing a service.'

'Sure. So why expose it?'

'I'm not going to.'

'Then what's this all about?'

'Her name's Harriet Reilly. Or it was.'

Thin laughter had greeted the latest stand-up's opening joke. Suttle was staring at her. He asked her to repeat the name.

'Harriet Reilly.'

'You know who she is?'

'Yes.'

'We're talking about the same woman?'

'We are.'

He sat back, reached for his pint, then had second thoughts. The laughter was getting louder. The novice was on a roll.

'You hungry?'

'Is that an invitation?

'Yes.'

They went to an Indian restaurant a couple of hundred yards away. The place was nearly empty and there was a wall-mounted TV playing a Bollywood movie behind the tiny bar. Suttle chose a table in the far corner. Perfect.

On the walk from the pub they'd barely exchanged a word. Now Suttle wanted to know more.

Lizzie shook her head. 'You first,' she said. 'How's it going?'

'You mean the Reilly job?'

'Yes.'

'Slowly.'

'Have you found the man yet? The partner? Bentner?'

'No.'

'Why not?'

It was a good question. Suttle had ordered drinks at the bar and he watched the waiter approaching with a pint of Kingfisher. Turn the clock back, and this could have been any number of Indian restaurants in Pompey or Southsea, the pair of them catching up while Lizzie's mum minded Grace. Strange.

'He's gone to ground,' he said. 'That's the assumption.'

'You think he did it?'

'That's very blunt.'

'Would you like it some other way? Half the nation seems to have decided yes.'

'That's unfortunate. No one can possibly know.'

'So he didn't do it? Is that what you're telling me?'

'I'm telling you we don't know.'

'But what do you *think*, Jimmy? You used to be good at this.'

'I am good at it. In fact I'm probably better than I was. Wiser, certainly.'

'And?'

'No way did he do it.'

'Thank you.'

There was something in her smile that stirred Suttle. It wasn't the small victory she'd just scored. It wasn't the admission she'd wrung out of him. It was something else. She could have been a stranger, he decided. She could have been someone who'd walked in off the street and sat herself down and taken control. She'd had some kind of makeover and it had worked. This woman wasn't the morose depressive he'd lived with out in Colaton Raleigh. Nor was she the howling mum who'd just lost her daughter. This was someone new and faintly exciting.

'So what else are you going to tell me?' For the first time he was smiling.

'There's a guy you ought to check out. This time you get a name. Here's why.'

She told him about Betty's death in her house in Lympstone, about her last-minute change of will and about the likely reaction of her only son, who'd just lost his inheritance.

'His name's Dean Russell,' she said. 'He's an ex-Marine. He's working on maritime protection in the Gulf.'

'And the inheritance? How much are we talking?'

'Half a million.'

'Shit.'

'Exactly. I get the impression he's one angry man, but it gets better. He's living with a woman called Tania. I don't think she's a hooker but we're not talking choirgirl. In fact she was one of the reasons Betty had second thoughts about her will.'

'Tania's surname?' Suttle had produced a pen.

'I've no idea. Tania might not even be her Christian name. Just a name she goes by. Here ...' Lizzie reached across the table and borrowed Suttle's pad. 'This is the reg number of the car she drives. Betty's best friend took it down because she came round with Dean one evening and backed into another car when she was parking.'

'What sort of car?'

'It was red. That's all Betty remembers. Red with that plate.'

Suttle nodded. If she owned the vehicle, DVLA would have her details.

'You think she's got previous?'

'Highly likely. The way I heard it, she's a bad, bad girl. Drinks like a fish. Reputation for kicking off when she doesn't get her way. Half a million pounds is a great deal of money. What wouldn't you do if it suddenly wasn't yours?'

Suttle nodded. A call to DVLA and a check on the Police National Computer would be his next stop. Then a knock on Tania's door.

'Is Dean around at the moment? Or has he gone back to work?'

'I've no idea, but please leave my contact out of this. Promise?'

Suttle nodded again and felt her hand close over his. He'd never seen the ring before. He studied it more closely.

'Where did you get that?'

'From a hippy shop in Gandy Street. I bought it myself. Sad or what?'

'No one on the radar?'

'Used to be. Until a couple of days ago. I got that wrong as well, didn't I? Still ...' she sat back and shrugged '... it was nice while it lasted. How about you? Still shacked up with the nurse?'

'Yes. Her name's Oona. She's Lenahan in a skirt.'

Lizzie had known Eamon Lenahan, Suttle's tenant at Chantry Cottage, the wee medical registrar who had brought so much laughter into his life.

'Eamon was lovely,' she said. 'You should have married him.'

'That's what he thought.'

'So maybe that makes Oona perfect. Should I be jealous? Are you going to marry her?'

'No.'

'Why not? I wouldn't be difficult about a divorce. I promise.'

'That's not the point.'

'So what *is* the point?'

'The point is we're very happy. We live apart. We have our separate spaces. We see each other lots. It works. That's rare.'

'Great. Until she wants a baby.'

'Funny you should say that.'

'It's not rocket science, my love. It's the way we're programmed. How old is she?'

'Thirty-four.'

'I'll give it six months. Max.'

'She's on the pill.'

'That's what we all say. Until we're not.'

'What is all this?' Suttle was laughing now. 'Should I ask for a lawyer? Go No Comment? What do you think?'

'Is that a serious question?'

'Are there other sorts?'

'Never, Jimmy. Not in your world.' She leaned forward. 'Listen to me for a moment, yeah? We have another drink. Something to eat. Not too much. Then you walk me home. How does that sound?'

Suttle considered the proposition. To his shame, he didn't say no.

'You're telling me I owe you?' Her hand was still on his.

'That's offensive, Mr Detective. I'm asking you to walk me home.'

The house was ten minutes away. By now it was dusk. Suttle stood in the wilderness of the front garden staring up at the peeling white stucco, at the rotting window frames, at the bubbles of moss on the roof where the water was getting in.

'It's a wreck,' he said. 'You hate wrecks, leaks, draughts. That's partly what did for us.'

'That was Colaton Raleigh. That was different. This place gives me everything. Including peace of mind.'

'You mean solitude?'

'Yes.'

'But you hated that as well. I think you called it loneliness.'

'Then maybe I've changed. Come inside. It gets worse.'

It did. She pushed the front door open and then led him from room to room. She knew that her months in residence had made precious little impact on the bareness of the place but she didn't care.

'It's huge,' Suttle said. 'It must have cost a fortune.'

'Just under four hundred. That's cheap for round here.'

'How many bedrooms?'

'Five. Four I won't even show you. Too shameful.'

'And the other one?'

'Follow me.'

Suttle watched her disappearing up the strip of threadbare carpet that covered the stairs. So far, on the ground floor, he hadn't seen anything he recognised: no photos, no scraps of furniture, no rugs, no bits of bric-a-brac, not a single indication that they'd once shared a life and – all too briefly – a daughter. She'd wiped out every trace of her former life and started again. Odd.

She was waiting for him on the top landing. He sensed she had readied herself for a kiss but he was careful to preserve the distance between them.

'You got a mortgage?' he asked.

'What kind of question is that?'

'I'm just curious.'

'Then the answer's no.'

'You *paid* for all this? Cash?'

'I did. I tried offering glass beads but they weren't interested.'

'Four hundred grand? The lot?' Suttle shook his head. The last time they'd lived together, especially towards the end of the month, he'd been pushed to put petrol in his car. Without Lizzie's job, they were facing mounting bills on his salary alone. Now this.

'I got lucky,' she said simply. 'And I'm not just talking money.'

She took him into the bedroom. At last he spotted something

112

he recognised, a 30s dressing table Lizzie had bought at an antique fair on Southsea Common. The big mirror was dotted with yellow stick-on reminders, and half a dozen postcards were tucked beneath the wooden frame, another habit she hadn't abandoned. On the right-hand side was an obvious gap.

Suttle stepped across. There were more postcards in the waste-paper basket beside the stool, all of them ripped to shreds. Suttle could see Lizzie's face in the mirror. She seemed amused.

'You're thinking crime scene,' she said. 'I know you are.'

'You're telling me I'm wrong?'

'Not at all. On the contrary.'

'Anyone I might know?'

'I'm afraid not. One cop at a time's more than enough.'

'What's that supposed to mean?'

'Whatever you want it to mean.'

'So who was he?'

'A guy from Pompey. I thought I knew him. It turns out I was wrong.'

'He rolled you?'

'Big time.'

'Your fault?'

'Undoubtedly. And you know something else that happens in a situation like this?'

'Tell me.'

'A girl needs a little TLC. No strings. No recriminations. No commitment. Nothing heavy.' She nodded down at the unmade bed. 'So what do you think?'

Suttle left at three in the morning. He could still smell the scent of new leather on his clothes, on his skin. She'd worn the new jacket in bed, just the jacket. Another first. He drove back to Exmouth, knowing he had to shut the door on the episode but aware as well that it might not be easy. What had really surprised him was the way they'd slipped back together again. So effortless. So simple. So little baggage.

Saying goodbye downstairs, still wearing nothing but the

softness of the leather jacket, she'd made him promise to keep her in the loop. They both knew exactly what she meant – not simply *Buzzard* but each other as well – and again he hadn't said no.

Crazy, he told himself. Totally bonkers.

Sixteen

Lizzie woke up before seven. Through the blur of the window she sensed a grey morning with drizzle in the air. She rolled over, her hand outstretched, and then remembered Suttle leaving. She lay there a moment, smiling to herself, glad it had happened. *What next?* she wondered.

She knew that *Buzzard* would crank into action with a full squad meet first thing because Suttle had told her, one of the reasons he'd declined to stay the night. Her estranged husband's windfall intelligence about the change in Betty's will and its likely impact on her only son would form part of that meeting, and there was no way detectives wouldn't be descending on Tania's address once the meeting was over.

Lizzie was in Exmouth by half past eight. She had the address from Frances Bevan, and her Tom-Tom took her to an area called the Colonies, wedged between the town centre and the railway line. Chapel Road turned out to be a long terrace of red-brick houses, the pavement choked with wheelie bins. She drove slowly past number 49. The curtains were still closed top and bottom, and the recycling box was brimming with empty bottles. She got to the top of the street and parked up. From here she could monitor comings and goings in her rear-view mirror. Her years as a journalist, and now a writer, had taught her the value of getting ahead of a story.

She switched off the radio and settled down behind a copy of last Saturday's *Independent*. At weekends they ran decent-length book reviews, and her agent, a pushy fifty-something called Muriel, believed that *Mine* was in with a shout. Muriel was a savage negotiator and fought tooth and nail for her hand-picked stable of writers. To be taken on by Muriel, as she was fast realising, was to be lashed to the wheel of best-sellerdom. Muriel had been on the phone again only days ago. What did Lizzie have planned for a follow-up now that *Mine* had broken her out? Where next for the surprise success of 2014's new titles?

In truth Lizzie hadn't a clue. *Mine*, although written through the eyes of Claire Dillon, had been the most personal of stories. How many other traumas did she have to share with her ever-swelling readership? What if she'd mercifully run out of the kind of near-death experiences that seemed to badge the best-seller lists? She'd put both points to Muriel on the phone, incurring her agent's wrath.

The only thing that mattered, it seemed, was the numbers. *Mine* was still selling thousands a month. The paperback was yet to come, and the TV development deal was showing every sign of making it to broadcast. Maybe Lizzie should be looking for other people's stories. Maybe she could turn her back on real life and step into fiction. Either way her window of opportunity – what Muriel called 'that fucking chance to make yourself even richer' – was fast closing. The reading public, she reminded Lizzie, had the memory of a pebble. In a year's time she'd be history. So get out there and weave the Lizzie Hodson magic again.

It was a tempting thought. *Mine* had brought Lizzie serious money, more than she'd ever imagined possible, but just now she was enjoying her new life too much to face the slog of another 100,000 words. It had always been her dream to have a platform for the kind of journalism and feature writing she loved best, and thanks to the Internet she could now make that happen. *Bespoken* was one of a rash of new investigative websites that had appeared – the idea was too obvious and tempting not to be pursued by others – but she knew from reader feedback and hit stats that her precious baby was in rude health. People were reading her stuff. People were sitting up and taking notice. And each fresh lead opened a new door in her life.

Like now. She sank a little lower in the driving seat. Number 49 was sixty metres away. An Impreza she recognised only too well had just turned in at the top of the street. Jimmy Suttle, she thought. With Golding for back-up.

Suttle was still trying to fend off Luke Golding.

'I don't get it, skip. All this stuff just falls into your lap? Reilly knocking her patients off? The Angel of Death? Issues over some will or other? Trust me, skip, it's a tasty lead but where the fuck did it come from?'

'A journalist.'

'And this guy just phoned you up? Out of the blue?'

'He doesn't want to be named. Otherwise there'd have been no conversation.'

'You knew him before? He had your number?'

'Yeah.'

'And you think he's on the money? You trust him?'

DI Houghton had asked exactly the same questions less than half an hour ago. Nandy, mercifully, hadn't been at the squad meet. Suttle had told Houghton that the information seemed too detailed not to be kosher, and when she'd asked what was in it for the source, he'd said he didn't know. Maybe the guy was an outraged Christian. Maybe he was settling some personal debt or other. Either way it was worth a shot, if only to shift the log jam that had become Operation *Buzzard*.

Suttle reversed down the street and wedged the Impreza into the tightest of spaces. Wooden panels on the door of 49 showed signs of recent splintering and there were gouge marks around the lock. So far so good, he thought. These were clearly people who'd resisted the temptations of a quiet life.

He knocked twice. Then again. Then a fourth time. Finally he heard the flush of a lavatory from deep inside the house and footsteps on the stairs. When the door opened he was looking at a woman in her forties. She was wearing a Plymouth Argyle football top and not very much else. Her eyes were puffy and there were signs of recent bruising under one eye. Both ankles were tattooed, one with barbed wire, one with a thin blue chain. Once, Suttle thought, this woman would have been a stunner. Now she was wrecked.

'What's this about?' She was trying to make sense of Suttle's warrant card.

'Police. Are you Tania Maguire?' He'd got the surname from DVLA.

'Yeah.'

'We need to talk to you.' Suttle nodded at the gloom of the narrow hall behind her.

'I don't want to talk.'

'I'm afraid that's not an option. Unless you want to be arrested.'

'What for?'

'That's why we need to talk.'

Her gaze went from one face to the other. She was scratching herself now and Suttle noticed the redness on her forearms. Finally she shrugged and stepped unsteadily backwards.

They went through to the tiny kitchen/diner. The house smelled of chip fat with a thin top dressing of dog shit. Takeout containers were piled on the draining board, and the broken swing bin was full of empty bottles of sherry. There was a dog in the yard and it was barking fit to bust. Suttle went to the window for a look. It was a pit bull, squat and angry, chained to a ring in the wall, and the moment it saw a strange face at the window it went berserk. Suttle shot Golding a look. Golding hated dogs.

'We need to talk about your weekend, Ms Maguire.' Suttle saw no point in trying to establish any rapport. 'So where were you?'

'Why?'

'Just answer the question.'

'Here, like always.'

'Alone?'

'No.'

'Who was with you?'

'That's my business.'

'Fine.' Suttle glanced at his watch. 'Five minutes to put some clothes on. Then we take you into Exeter and book you in.'

'Book me in where?'

'The Custody Centre. Don't tell me you've never been there.'

Suttle had checked her out on the PNC first thing. Among a string of drunk and disorderly offences were two charges of aggravated assault.

Tania stared at him, slowly beginning to understand. She reached uncertainly for the stool beside the table and sat down. The dog was hurling himself at the door now. Tania yelled at it, telling it to shut the fuck up.

She turned back to Suttle. 'What do you guys want? This is totally out of order.'

Suttle asked her again about the weekend. He needed to know exactly where she'd been and when.

'I just told you. Here. We're skint. OK, we go out sometimes. Take the dog. But that's it. Life in the fucking fast lane. Enjoy, eh?'

There was a spark of life in her eyes. Her head was up. She was fighting back.

'We?'

'Yeah. Me and my partner. Lovely fella. Manners too. Unlike you lot.'

'Does he have a name?'

'Yeah. Deano. Big guy. Trained killer. Scare the shit out of you.'

'So where is he?'

'No idea.'

'Upstairs?'

'Not when I last looked. Don't fucking believe me, help yourself.'

Suttle glanced at Golding, who left the room. The dog was going mental. Suttle tried to ignore it.

'So you're telling me you were here all weekend? Saturday, Saturday night, Sunday, Sunday night, you never left the house?'

'Yeah. More or less. Just the dog. There's grass and stuff at the end of the road.'

'And Deano?'

'Yeah.'

'Yeah what?'

'He was here too.'

'Do you ever eat at all, drink, buy food?'

'Of course we do.'

'So you did leave the house?'

'Yeah but not properly.'

'What does "properly" mean?'

'Like for a trip. We can get pissed here as easy as anywhere else.'

Golding had returned. He beckoned Suttle into the hall. Golding was holding a slip of paper by one corner. It looked like it had been ripped from a pad.

'On the floor by the bed, skip.'

There were two lines scrawled in biro: *Sunrise Cottage, Miller's Lane*. Harriet Reilly's Lympstone address.

Suttle stared at it a moment. Then he heard the back door open and a cackle of laughter before the dog was upon them. It lunged at Golding. He tried to fight it off. Suttle kicked it hard in the backside and it turned on him, snarling. Suttle felt the teeth sink into his calf. Golding had retreated briefly, folding the scrap of paper into his pocket. Beside the front door, propped against the wall, was a baseball bat. He grabbed it, circled the dog briefly, waiting for his moment, then brought it crashing down on the pit bull's skull. The dog yelped, let go of Suttle's leg, and collapsed on the bare boards. Golding hit it twice more, studied it a moment, then stamped on its head. It twitched briefly, then lay still.

'Cunts.' The woman had appeared. She knelt beside the dog. 'You've fucking killed it. You fucking have.'

She looked up. Suttle was bent over his leg, trying to staunch

120

the flow of blood. Golding was on the phone, summoning help. An ambulance. Police back-up. Man down. The woman grabbed at the baseball bat dangling from Golding's other hand. Taken by surprise, Golding let it go, raising his other arm as she tried to smash it against his face. The force of the blow, taking him on the elbow, sent the mobile skidding across the floor.

Suttle abandoned his leg, grabbed the woman and pinned her against the wall. Their faces were inches apart. She spat at him and tried to knee him in the groin. He told her to calm down, but when she did it a second time he headbutted her, feeling her nose pulp beneath the blow. She screamed in pain and dropped the baseball bat. Golding's phone was still live. The voice on the other end wanted an address.

Suttle picked the mobile up. He was trying to remember the address.

'Number 49, skip.' Golding was rubbing his arm. 'Soon would be good.'

Lizzie watched the ambulance arrive. The door opened to the paramedic's first knock and he disappeared inside. Minutes later Luke Golding emerged. He was handcuffed to a woman wearing a pink dressing gown. She'd covered her face and appeared to be crying. Then came Jimmy Suttle. He was hopping on one leg. The trouser leg on the other had been scissored at the knee and a crepe bandage, already pinked with blood, was wound around his calf.

By now a police car had turned up. Two officers, one male, one female. Suttle stopped to talk to the woman before he climbed into the back of the ambulance, nodding towards the open door. The woman checked her watch then began to talk into her radio as she entered the house. Moments later the ambulance was driving away. For a second or two Lizzie debated whether to follow it then decided to stay put. She knew this wasn't the end of it, and she was right.

The ambulance and the police car gone, the female uniform was standing guard outside the house. Lizzie knew what Scenes of Crime vans looked like. This one was a white Peugeot. Two guys got out, both carrying holdalls. They paused at the door, exchanged a word or two with the officer, then returned to the van to fetch treading plates. A moment later Lizzie saw a red car turn in at the top of the road. It drove slowly towards the house. Lizzie had memorised the first two letters and first two numbers of the reg plate Frances Bevan had noted down. GV 38. This was Tania's car, had to be. And the man at the wheel would be Dean.

He drove past the SOC van. By now the red car filled Lizzie's rear-view mirror. She reached for the key, started the engine, let Dean get to the top of the street. He was indicating left. She pulled out. This man had never seen her in his life. Lizzie was just a stranger in the street, paying a visit, looking for a parking space, whatever.

She was behind Dean's car now. It was a battered Fiat, rusting around the edges. He was on the phone. At the main road he indicated right, heading for the middle of town. Lizzie was still behind him, sensing the importance of the call. Maybe he was passing on the news that the Filth had arrived. Maybe he was setting up some kind of meet, driving over to someone's house. Maybe.

Wrong. In the middle of town, behind the main shopping precinct, he found a space in the car park. To Lizzie's slight surprise he bought a ticket from the machine. She did the same, using the other machine. Then he headed towards the precinct itself. She followed him, glad of the mid-morning swirl of shoppers. Beyond the Co-op supermarket a short cut took him to the back entrance of a Wetherspoons pub called the Powder Monkey. He disappeared inside.

Moments later, Lizzie followed him.

The pub was filling up. Dean had found a cubicle in the corner and was shedding his denim jacket. He was a big man, tall, starting to run to fat. He was wearing jeans and a pair of Adidas trainers and he badly needed a shave.

She went straight to the bar and ordered herself a coffee. She hadn't been to a Wetherspoons for years. £2.89 for an English breakfast? No wonder people were mobbing the place.

She took the coffee to a table from where she could watch Dean. He was at the bar now, ordering a couple of beers. Carrying them back, he spared her a nod and the hint of a smile. He had reddish curly hair lapping the collar of his jacket, and the backs of both hands were heavily tattooed. By no means out of the question, she thought, if you'd arrived at the end of the line and you were looking for remaindered goods.

Dean was back on the phone. His date arrived minutes later, another man, similar age but smartly turned out: suit, carefully cropped hair, military bearing. He scarcely touched his beer, commanding the conversation with brisk stabs of his finger. Dean listened, nodded a couple of times, then emptied his pint. The other man had a briefcase. He extracted an A4 Manila envelope and emptied the contents onto the table. Dean flicked through the document page by page, pausing from time to time to ask a question. Tired of looking at the document upside down, the other man slipped round the table to join him. Perfect, Lizzie thought.

She took out her mobile, pretended to read through an incoming text, then carefully composed a reply, the phone held in front of her, the camera lens pointing at the cubicle. The lighting wasn't great but there was no way she was going to risk the flash. She took three shots, and then finished the text. The text was real. 'Thinking of you,' she'd written. 'And don't forget we're still legal. xxx'

Seventeen

Suttle was waiting in A & E when he got the text. His leg was throbbing and he felt hopelessly exposed with only half a pair of trousers. Golding had delivered Tania to the Custody Sergeant at Heavitree police station and was now waiting in a spare office for instructions from the MIR. He'd already given DI Houghton a full account of exactly what had happened over the phone. Houghton, in turn, had alerted Nandy. There were signs, she told him, that *Buzzard* had begun to flap its wings.

Suttle opened his phone and read the text. By 'legal' he assumed that Lizzie meant married. For a split second he toyed with replying but decided against it. Then he deleted the text and pocketed the phone.

'Mr Suttle?'

A nurse Suttle knew by sight had appeared at the door that led to the treatment bays. Suttle limped across. Her face brightened. She was a good mate of Oona's.

'You're Jimmy.'

'That's right.'

'What happened?' She nodded at his bare leg.

'Dog.'

'Line of duty?'

'Yeah.'

'You brave man. This way.'

She led him to an empty bay and examined the wound. The bite was deep and the pit bull's teeth marks were clearly visible, but under the circumstances she thought he'd got off lightly. The flesh was only lightly torn. She'd seen far worse.

'Thanks.'

'Pleasure. Shall I get Oona down?'

'God, no.'

After the Registrar had stopped by and decided against stitches, she cleaned the wound and then dressed it. A couple of injections and Suttle was ready to leave.

'Do you have a spare pair of trousers, by any chance?'

She found him some orange trackie bottoms and then gave him the top as well. She wanted them back in the end but there was no great hurry. Maybe Oona could oblige.

Suttle thanked her, stepping out into the fresh air. On foot, Heavitree police station was ten minutes away. He walked as fast as he could, trying to ignore the pain in his calf. At the Custody Centre the Sergeant led him through to the office where Luke Golding was still waiting for word from the MIR. It arrived in the shape of both Houghton and Nandy. Only Houghton asked about the state of Suttle's leg. Nandy wanted to know the strength of the case against the woman banged up in a cell along the corridor.

'Tania Maguire? Have I got that right?'

'Yes, sir.' Suttle explained about finding Reilly's address on the floor beside the bed.

'Where is it?'

'I left it with the CSI at the property. He's bagged and tagged it.'

'Anything else?'

'No, sir.'

'Why not?'

Golding and Suttle exchanged glances.

Houghton came to the rescue. 'I'm assuming that's when the dog appeared.' She was looking at Suttle. 'Am I right?'

'Yes, boss. We can do her for that, if nothing else.'

Nandy nodded. The Custody Sergeant had called in the police doctor to attend to her facial wounds. An obligatory photo accompanied the booking-in procedure, and Nandy had paused by the desk to give it a glance.

'So who did her face?'

'Me, sir.' Suttle tapped his forehead. 'I'm claiming self-defence.'

'I hope it helps, son.'

Suttle said nothing. Back in Pompey, officers routinely met violence with violence. Down here in Devon life was a little more sedate. How many more scars was he supposed to collect in the line of duty? Or was he just accident-prone?

'And Dean Russell? The boyfriend?' Nandy had turned to Golding.

'I've no idea, sir. He wasn't in the property. I checked.'

'Does he have previous? Do we have a photo?'

'Only as a kid, sir.' Suttle this time. 'He was in trouble a couple of times. He was fourteen at the time. After that he went to the Marines. They'll have photos. Bound to.'

'Right.' Nandy was looking at Houghton. 'Get on it, Carole. Find the man. Pull him in. There's no way Suttle and Golding can do the business with the woman, but they should brief the interviewing team and monitor what follows. You'll make that happen?'

'Of course, sir.' Houghton had produced her mobile and was already on her feet. Seconds later only Suttle and Golding remained in the office.

Suttle's mobile was signalling an incoming text. He opened the phone. Lizzie again. Attached to the text was a photo of two men in what looked like a bar. He returned to the text.

'The guy on the left is Dean Russell. He's in the Powder Monkey in Exmouth on his third pint. Table under the TV. All yours ... with my compliments. XXX PS The other guy's gone.'

Suttle was still sitting down. Golding had circled the office and was reading the text over Suttle's shoulder.

'Who sent that?'

Suttle didn't answer. He was trying to work out how Lizzie could have got a photo like this. Had she been following Dean? Had he been living somewhere else?

'You think it's kosher, skip?' Golding asked. 'Or are we getting dicked around?'

'Good question.' Suttle was scrolling through his directory. Seconds later he was talking to a mate in the Exmouth CID room.

'Kenny? There's a guy called Dean in the Powder Monkey. Table by the telly.'

'Would that be Dean Russell?'

'It would. Do us a favour? Nip down and nick him?'

'What for? Just give us a clue.'

'Conspiracy to murder.'

'Murder?' Kenny was laughing. 'You're telling me he's become a *serious* criminal?'

Suttle said nothing. The conversation over, he glanced up to find Golding still gazing at the phone.

Dean Russell was arrested eighteen minutes later and driven to Exmouth police station. Suttle relayed the news to Houghton, who was back in the MIR. A surprised if pleased Nandy ordered Russell to be taken to Torquay police station and booked into the Custody Suite. He wanted separate interview teams for Russell and Tania Maguire, and he needed Suttle to brief the detectives dealing with each. The booking-in procedures, plus disclosure sessions with attending solicitors, would push the interviews into the afternoon. He suggested Suttle find himself a suit from somewhere; *Buzzard* had no room for orange trackie bottoms.

Eighteen

Lizzie left the Powder Monkey and retrieved her Audi from the town centre car park. The sight of two uniformed officers escorting an outraged Dean Russell from the pub had seriously impressed her, not least because without her input the arrest would never have happened. As a working journalist she'd often been struck by the similarity between her job and Jimmy's. Same mindset. Same determination to check out every lead. Same reluctance ever to take life at face value. Do the job properly, she thought, and you might as well be carrying a warrant card.

She was about to take the road back to Exeter when she had second thoughts. She'd never seen Jimmy's new home. Maybe now was the time to check it out. She had the address from her mother, who still forwarded Jimmy's stray mail from time to time.

The Beacon turned out to be a long terrace of tall Regency houses straddling the bluff overlooking Exmouth seafront. She drove slowly up the hill, looking for a parking space, finding one almost opposite Shelley House. Jimmy's flat was number 3. She peered up at the white stucco frontage, at the big windows, at the once-grand entrance, trying to imagine the view across the estuary towards the distant smudge of Torbay. No wonder Jimmy preferred this to the gloom of Chantry Cottage. After the living death of Colaton Raleigh, where their marriage had finally collapsed, it must have felt deeply liberating to be suddenly in a working town again: kids, chatter, busy pubs, decent restaurants, proper shops. She got out of the car and gazed up at the third-floor window. *I could almost live here myself*, she thought.

The front door opened, and a young woman stepped out wrestling a buggy down the flight of steps to the pavement. The rain had gone now and the wind was stiffening from the south-west. Racing clouds. Broken sunshine. Sudden bubbles of warmth. Nice. The woman parked the buggy and went back into the house, returning moments later with a baby. Lizzie judged it to be one, maybe one and a half, suddenly realising that this must be the Polish girl who lived in the flat above Jimmy's. It was her partner, a huge guy called Tadeusz, who'd saved Jimmy's life last year when he'd been ambushed by a prime suspect determined to settle a debt or two.

The woman was having trouble with the buggy, trying to open it while juggling the baby from arm to arm. Lizzie crossed the road and offered to help. The mother was pretty, a big open face, jeans and T-shirt, good English. Lizzie held the baby while she set up the buggy. The baby gazed up at her as Lizzie rocked it in her arms.

'What's Polish for "You're beautiful"?' she asked.

'You know we're from Poland?' The girl was staring at her, surprised.

'I do, yes.' Lizzie nodded up at the third-floor flat. 'I'm Jimmy's wife. My name's Lizzie.'

'Really?'

'Yes. We're not together, of course. You'd know that.'

The girl said nothing. She took the baby and strapped it into the buggy. Then she stood upright again and extended a hand.

'My name's Klaudia,' she said.

'And the baby?'

'Kasia.' She smiled. 'Jimmy's a good man, a good friend. Kasia loves him. They take her for walks at the weekend sometimes. To give us a little time together.'

'They?'

'Jimmy . . .' she laughed and then touched Lizzie lightly on the arm, a gesture of apology '. . . and his girlfriend.'

'Sure.' Lizzie returned the smile. 'You're going for a walk now?'

'Yes. Not long, but yes.'

'Mind if I come?'

'Of course.' Klaudia bumped the buggy off the pavement and pointed towards a path beyond the greensward. 'The beach is down there.'

Golding drove Suttle back to Exmouth to pick up his Impreza. He pressed Suttle again on the source of the information that had taken them to Tania Maguire, but Suttle didn't budge. Old media contact. Solid as a rock. Wanted to return a favour.

'Call it karma,' he said to Golding. 'Call it what you like. Either way it's turning out just fine.'

'You think they did Reilly?'

'I think they've got a lot of questions to answer.'

Back in Chapel Road Suttle stepped out of the car. He'd pick up a suit at home and then drive straight back to the MIR. It was just gone midday. Houghton had called the interview teams dealing with Russell and Maguire for a full brief at two o'clock. She wanted Suttle and Golding in Torquay to monitor the interview with Russell. Based on what little she knew, her money was on Russell to break first.

Golding nodded and drove on down the road. Suttle walked to his Impreza, passing number 49. The SOC van was still parked outside and there was a uniformed officer on the door, but so far he'd heard no word from the CSM. He was tempted to look in but knew that time was tight.

On the Beacon he parked at the back and limped slowly up the stairs. His leg had stiffened now and the throbbing was worse. Getting out of the trackie bottoms was awkward, and he had to sit on the bed to shake them off. He doused his face in the bathroom, avoiding the mirror, and then sorted himself another suit. In the big living room, knotting his tie, he paused for a moment by the window. Nailing Russell so quickly had been a big win, but the implications made him feel deeply uncomfortable. He'd never liked being in debt to anyone, least of all his estranged wife.

He thought about last night, about the texts she'd sent since, about the weird YouTube clip with the piano concerto, about the photo of Dean Russell in the pub. He knew he had to get a statement from the witness Lizzie had cornered, Frances Bevan. He knew he had to regularise the file, tidy up the audit trail, try somehow to airbrush Lizzie out of the inquiry. And he knew as well that no way could any of this ever get back to Oona. Last night had been a huge mistake. It would never happen again. He wanted to wind his life back twenty-four hours and start all over. What a twat.

He gazed out at the view then became aware of two figures bumping a buggy across the grass towards the house. One of them was Klaudia from upstairs. The other was Lizzie. She was looking up at him, framed in the window. She was waving.

He checked his watch: 12.26. He headed for the door, took the stairs faster than his leg wanted to allow him.

Lizzie met him on the pavement. 'How bad is it?' She was looking at his leg.

'It's OK. It's fine.'

'It didn't look that way.'

'When?'

'When they put you in the ambulance.'

'You were there?'

'Yeah. How else would I have ended up in the pub?'

Of course she was there, Suttle thought. Russell must have turned up afterwards, cruised on by, led her straight to the Powder Monkey.

He tried to shoot Klaudia a smile. 'Give us a moment?'

He took Lizzie by the arm and walked her down the pavement.

'This is getting out of control,' he said.

'Do I hear the words thank you?'

'You do. Of course you do. But I need a favour.'

'Another one?'

'Don't fuck about. This Frances Bevan, where does she live?'

'You don't believe the stuff I gave you?'

'I have to statement her. You know that.'

'Of course. She lives in Lympstone.'

'House? Street? Number?'

Lizzie looked away. She was smiling. 'The scene of the crime,' she said. 'The place where it happened. Bentner's place.'

'What about it?'

'I'd like the address.'

'Why would you want that?'

'None of your business.'

'You can find it yourself. He's in the phone book.'

'So is Frances Bevan.'

'Wrong. I just checked. This is urgent, Lizzie. I haven't got much fucking time.'

'Sure.' The smile was wider. 'It's a small village. Do the reporter thing. Ask around.'

He held her gaze for a long moment. In spite of everything he had a sneaking regard for this new woman in his life. The leather jacket, he thought. And the sheer height of the ceiling above them when she'd straddled him last night.

'The terrace on the Strand,' he said. 'End house. Number 4.'

'Thank you.' She reached up and kissed him on the lips. 'Number 35 Edinburgh Crescent. Give her my regards.'

Suttle was at Lympstone within ten minutes. He knocked three times on Frances Bevan's door and was on the point of giving up when it finally opened. She examined his warrant card with visible misgivings and finally let him in. He explained that he was a friend of Ms Hodson's as well as a policeman, and the mention of Lizzie's name warmed the atmosphere a degree or two. She'd been thinking a great deal about the conversation she'd had with the young lady and on reflection she rather thought she'd said too much. Would any of this ever get back to Betty?

The question startled Suttle.

'I was under the impression that Betty was dead.'

'She is. But that's not the point. One has an obligation to the dead as well as to the living. I'd like to think we'll stay friends.'

Suttle assured her this was more than possible. He led her briskly through the headlines he'd plucked from Lizzie's account of their conversation: how much Betty had been suffering, how she'd got in touch with Harriet Reilly, how she'd been abandoned by her only child, and how she'd changed her will before Harriet brought her suffering to an end. The account filled a page and a half. Suttle left the statement undated, and with a degree of obvious reluctance Frances signed it.

Back in the Impreza Suttle checked his watch: 13.35. He'd make the briefing meet with the interview teams. Just.

Parking in Lympstone was a nightmare. Lizzie finally settled for a vehicle bay at the halt that served as a station and walked back down the hill to the village centre. Past the pub, a lane took her down to the slip that gave access to the tiny harbour.

It was high tide, the water lapping against the footings of the riverside houses. Gulls and terns soared on the strengthening wind, and the hills across the estuary were mottled with the racing clouds. Dinghies and bigger yachts bobbed at their moorings, and further out, beyond the buoyed channel, she could just make out five stick figures in a rowing quad, sculling downstream on the first of the ebb. The splash of the red hull against the brownness of the water told her that the quad had come from Exmouth. *That was me once*, she thought.

She turned to study the terrace of houses that looked out across the water. Bentner's was the one at the end. Next door a line of coloured flags stirred in the wind, reds and yellows and blues. There was no way she could access the properties from here at high tide and so she walked back, skirting the water. There was no sign of any kind of police presence at Bentner's property, and she imagined the SOC team would have gone by now. It was a small house, and a couple of days should have been ample time to give it the full treatment. The front door badly needed a coat of paint.

She rang the bell. Waited. Rang it again. Stooped to the letter box, pushing it open. At once she could smell the chemicals the SOC guys had used. She called Bentner's name, just in case. She had no idea what made this man tick, but disappearing from the face of the earth for nearly a week had won her respect. Maybe he'd come back under cover of darkness. Maybe, even now, he was upstairs in bed, a fugitive in the one place no one would ever bother looking.

Nothing. She stepped back, wondering about the next-door neighbour. These were old houses, probably thrown up for fishermen. The sound insulation would be rubbish. She knocked on the door. Knocked a second time. Again no response. The letter box was bigger, wider, deeper. She pushed it open and peered inside. The hall was dark but the light through the letter-box slot fell on a pile of letters scattered on the rug inside the door. Dr Gemma Caton, BA, MA, PhD. Two of the letters came from the University of Exeter.

'Where you to?' Rough voice. Male. Very Devon.

Lizzie stood up, shading her eyes against the sun. He was in his fifties, maybe older, stooped, nut-brown face, greying stubble. Dark blue beanie, jeans and a baggy old sweater. Splashes of white paint on the jeans and a hole in the sweater where an elbow had gone through. A riverside life fraying at the edges.

'I'm a reporter,' Lizzie said. 'Maybe you can help?'

'Yeah, and maybe I can't. What gives you the right to poke around other people's business?'

'I'm trying to find a man called Alois Bentner.'

'So's half the bloody world. What's he to you?'

'Nothing. Yet.'

'Come to help him out, have you? Only that man's in the shit.'

'So everyone says.'

'And you know different? Is that it?'

'I know nothing. Which is why I'm here.'

The answer seemed to pacify him. He shuffled back, wiped his face with the back of his hand.

'Do you know Mr Bentner?' Lizzie asked.

'Met him a couple of times, just like everyone else. Know him? No one knows him. Least of all now.' He glanced at Bentner's house. 'Talk to my son. He kept that place together.'

'What's your son's name?'

'Gerry.'

'Gerry what?'

'Just Gerry.'

'So what does he do? Gerry?'

'What *doesn't* he do, more like.' A wheezy bark of laughter. 'Carpentry, plumbing, electrics. No certificates, mind, but Gerry always does his best by Mr Bentner. Cheap too, which is just as well. That man counts his pennies, believe me.'

He talked about Bentner for a while, telling Lizzie how mean he was, except when it came to his bar bills.

'You mean the pub?'

'The shop down the road. Hundreds of quid across the counter for booze since he came down here. Must be. Talk to them. Talk to Doris.'

'Doris?'

'Runs the place.'

'Thanks.' Lizzie nodded down at the letter box. 'And what about Gemma Caton?'

'Nuts.'

'Nuts?'

'Talk to Gerry. He knows.'

Nineteen

The interview briefing at Middlemoor started late. The abortive hunt for Alois Bentner seemed to have taken the wind out of Det-Supt Nandy's sails. DI Houghton had launched a search of all letter boxes on Dartmoor, but so far the teams had found nothing. She'd also secured RIPA warrants on two phone lines – Sheila Forshaw's and Nikki Drew's – but since Bentner had been in touch with Forshaw there'd been no word from him on either.

Buzzard had also checked out the other two Met Office employees with the initials ND but had drawn a blank on both names. Neither had known Alois Bentner and both had cast-iron alibis for the weekend of Reilly's death.

Not good. As the days went by Nandy had become more and more convinced that Bentner had either gone abroad using a false passport, or that the man was dead. His ancient Skoda, meanwhile, had been trucked back to Exeter and forensically searched, yielding nothing worthwhile.

Suttle wanted to know about the SOC take on Bentner's premises. What had the scene told them?

Nandy looked at Carole Houghton. The SOC file had arrived this morning and she'd had time to go through it.

'We're looking at two key issues,' she said. 'Getting in and getting out. There's no sign of forced entry. Reilly may have been in the property already with whoever killed her. She may have opened the door to them, or they may have had a key.

Putting this report together with the post-mortem we're thinking she was probably killed late Saturday night or early Sunday morning. We also think the disembowelling happened after she was clinically dead.'

This was news to Suttle. So how did the woman die?

'She was beaten around the face and head and then suffocated. We're also thinking she was killed in situ. Probably smothered with one of the pillows. There was less blood from the disembowelling than you might expect because she was dead before it happened. Whoever did it wouldn't have been covered in the stuff. Which made getting out all the easier.'

'No blood on the stairs?' This from Golding.

'None.'

'Downstairs?'

'Nothing.'

They were talking in a briefing room attached to the MIR. Nandy had been canny in his choice of detectives for the Dean Russell interviews. Rosie Tremayne was a seasoned interviewer with a memory schooled for retaining the smallest details. Face to face she could be disarmingly sympathetic, but Suttle always remembered one rueful suspect down for a manslaughter charge. 'I trusted that Tremayne woman,' he said, 'and she turned me over.'

Rosie's partner was a newcomer to Major Crimes, a DC from Penzance called Colin Myers, even younger than Golding. He had the face of an eighteen-year-old and the voice of a choirboy, and there was no way a man like Dean Russell wouldn't regard him as a pushover. Underestimate either of these detectives, thought Suttle, and you'd be in serious trouble.

Nandy asked Suttle to deliver the intelligence that had led to this morning's arrests. Suttle told them about Dean's mother, Betty, and the circumstances surrounding her death. The news that she'd opted for assisted dying brought a frown to Tremayne's face. She was the wife of a Church of England vicar. Assisted dying, as far as she was concerned, was within touching distance of suicide. In her world this stuff mattered.

'It's too late to do her for that, Rosie.' This from Nandy. 'She's home free.'

'That wasn't my point, sir, with respect. I'm just wondering how much pressure she was under.'

Nandy shot Suttle a look.

Suttle remembered Lizzie in the restaurant describing Betty's final weeks. 'She was in great pain, Rosie,' he said. 'The initiative came from her.'

'We're sure about that?'

'According to her best friend, yes. It's down there in the statement. There's a photocopy in your file.' Suttle wondered whether to talk about Ralph and Jeff, two other witnesses to Reilly's work at the bedside of the dying, but decided against it. The less that Lizzie's work figured in *Buzzard*, the better.

Myers wanted to know more about Frances Bevan. Was she to any degree a benefactor from the change of wills?

'No.'

'She was left nothing at all?'

'Not that I know of. I've got a call in to Betty's solicitor. She's yet to come back.' It was a lie but a small one; Suttle had yet to make contact.

'So how did you find this witness?' The question came from Rosie Tremayne.

'Through a journalist I know. He's working up a piece on assisted dying.'

'But why come to us? To you?'

'Because he was worried about Bevan. Russell frightens her. She thinks he's dangerous. In fact she thinks he's off his head. She doesn't want him knocking on her door. Ever.'

'So she talked to the journalist?'

'Yes.'

'And he talked to you?'

'Of course. We go back a while. It's a trust thing.'

'Are we allowed to know who he is?'

'I'm afraid not.'

The bluntness of Suttle's answer raised eyebrows around the

room. Suttle was aware of Golding watching his every move. He knows, he thought. He's bloody sussed it.

Nandy, to Suttle's relief, came to the rescue.

'Your call, son,' he grunted, 'but don't make a habit of it.'

The briefing continued. Both Nandy and Houghton recognised that the two interviewing detectives would be facing an uphill battle with Tania Maguire. According to the Custody Sergeant at Heavitree she was going to press assault charges against Suttle and wanted a further million quid for the loss of her precious dog. The woman was clearly out of her tree, and whatever she said had to be treated with a great deal of caution, but there might be the odd evidential nugget in among all the rubbish. Key to everything, Nandy insisted, was the timeline. Russell and Maguire were offering mirror alibis, relying on each other's words, but a couple this volatile might be easy to wind up.

'We need to drop the odd hint about Russell. Suggest he might have been getting it elsewhere. No harm in making the woman wonder.'

It was a common tactic, cheap as you like, and most lawyers would jump on it at once, but *Buzzard* – as Nandy was the first to point out – was badly in need of a little TLC and in his view it was certainly conceivable that both of them might have made threats against Reilly, if only to make themselves feel better.

'That's not the same as killing her, sir,' Suttle pointed out.

'You're right, son. We'll have to wait for Bentner before we bottom this bloody thing out.'

Gerry turned out to live in Polsloe Bridge, a down-at-heel suburb of Exeter. Lizzie had wrung the address from his father in Lympstone. His second name was Piercy and he shared a downstairs flat with a woman called Gwendoline who had two young children. Lizzie had no idea whether the kids belonged to Gerry but it was obvious at once that this family needed more room.

The kids were three and four, pre-school, hyperactive. They tore from room to room, the little girl doing most of the chasing, her brother shouting fit to bust. Living on top of a floor show like this would require either earplugs or a great deal of patience. Gerry sought shelter in the front room, which was full of cardboard boxes. He seemed to believe that there was money waiting for him if he was able to give Lizzie what she was after, and to some degree he was right. She'd stopped off at an ATM on the drive up from Lympstone and withdrawn £200.

'Tell me about Bentner,' she said.

'What do you want to know?'

'You worked for him, right?'

'Yeah. Bits and pieces when he needed me.'

'You saw him often?'

'Enough.'

'Enough for what?'

'Enough to know the kind of bloke he is.'

'And?'

'He's all right. An all-right guy. My dad thinks he's an arse-hole. He's not.'

As far as the property was concerned, he said, Mr Bentner had no interest in keeping the place up. He treated the house like a tent. He'd once told Gerry that if he could fold it up and cart it off, he'd do just that. Bentner enjoyed the situation, liked living with the view, but in his head he was as free as the air.

'A Gypsy, right? That's what he believed.'

Lizzie nodded. Gerry's use of 'Mr' was significant. It meant he respected this man and probably liked him.

'You knew his girlfriend? Harriet?'

'Of course. Nice lady.'

'Was she there a lot?'

'I dunno. She may have been. When I was there it was always during the day unless there was an emergency, so I only met her a couple of times. You could tell though.'

'Tell what?'

'That they were … you know … tight.'

The kids were beating at the door. Any minute now they'd wrench the handle off. Gerry seemed impervious.

'Your dad says Bentner drank a lot.'

'That's true.' He shrugged. 'If you've got the money, why not? Any port in a storm.' His eyes at last flicked to the door. 'If you're asking me whether he killed her, the answer has to be no.'

'That's what you believe?'

'That's what anyone believes who ever took the time to give the guy a fair hearing. People like my dad? Excuse me saying so, but they never bother to listen. Like I say, the guy's OK. If he chooses to disappear, that's his business. Some days I wouldn't blame him.'

He at last got to his feet and unlocked the door, shooing the kids back down the hall. Lizzie heard his partner complaining that she had no more tokens for the electric. Another hour and they wouldn't have a kettle to boil water for tea.

Gerry returned, locking the door behind him. Lizzie sensed that time was tight.

'The next-door neighbour,' she said. 'Gemma Caton. Your dad says you think she's nuts.'

'He's right.'

'Why nuts?'

'She's just a crazy woman. Bright, mind. Works at the university. Some kind of scientist? I don't really know. But she plays this weird music, Balinese I think it is. I could hear it through the wall when I was working there.'

'Does that make her nuts? Balinese music?'

'It's not just that. Mr Bentner says she's got a thing about allergies, about what you do eat and what you don't. Like no proper milk. No nuts. No cheese. I went in her house once. She had a leak in her boiler. All these weird carvings. African they looked like. Witch-doctor stuff. Creepy.'

'You asked her about them?'

'I couldn't. She wasn't there.'

'So how did you get in?'

'Mr Bentner has a key.'

'Does he?'

'Yeah. He says she's away a lot. Field trips? I dunno. Anyway, he's supposed to keep an eye on the place. In fact it was Mr Bentner who spotted the leak. That has to be a first for him.'

Lizzie felt a tiny prickle of excitement. Did Jimmy Suttle know this? Had Operation *Buzzard* bothered to swoop on Gemma Caton's nest? Have a poke about? Ask a question or two?

There was a knock on the door, sterner this time. Gwendoline, Lizzie thought. With an ultimatum about the electricity meter.

Gerry was on his feet again. Lizzie joined him. Was he certain that she worked at the university?

'Yeah.'

'Department?'

'Dunno.'

Lizzie thanked him for his time. The fold of notes from the ATM lay in her shoulder bag. She gave him the lot and wished him luck.

He stared down at the notes, and then counted them.

'Fuck.' He looked up. 'Are you serious?'

Twenty

The interview with Dean Russell started late. His solicitor had been stuck in traffic at Kingskerswell, and it took another forty minutes before she was satisfied that her client had told her the whole story.

Rosie Tremayne and Colin Myers had been waiting in the interview room for nearly an hour. Tremayne opened by offering Russell her condolences on his mother's death. When he didn't respond, she asked him how close they'd been. This time he was more forthcoming.

'Not at all close. Not ever.'

'Why was that?'

'My dad went off when I was a nipper. She was always rubbishing him. It got so bad I could see why he'd gone. Didn't help me none, though.'

'You blamed her?'

'I did. She wound me up. Never failed. I'd go off, like, get hammered on cider or lighter fuel or whatever, get in trouble, get in a fight, and there'd she be on the doorstep when they took me home.'

'Who took you home?'

'The police. You lot. Tell you the truth I preferred you lot to her.'

'But she was dying, Dean.'

'Yeah, and ...?'

'You couldn't be with her? Couldn't help out?'

'I did. A bit. But ... you know ... not a lot.'

Rosie asked about his mother's will. He admitted at once that he knew the money was coming to him because years back she'd told him.

'And you had plans for that money?'

'Of course I did.'

'What were you going to do with it?'

'Get a decent place. Maybe abroad. Tania likes abroad.'

'And did your mother like Tania?'

'She never knew her. Not properly.'

'Did she ever say anything about her?'

'Not to me. I never gave her the chance. I knew she'd say she was a slag. That's one of the reasons I was never around at the end.'

Colin Myers picked up on Tania's role in Russell's life. When he suggested that she might have made a big difference, Russell nodded. 'All the difference in the world.'

'Why?'

'Because she loves me. That woman's as straight as you like. She says she'll take care of you and she does. Honest. That's what she is, honest.'

'And she knew about the money as well?'

'Of course she did. No secrets, me and Tan.'

Tremayne introduced Harriet Reilly. Was Russell aware that his mother was contemplating assisted suicide?

'Of course not.'

'Would it have made any difference if she'd have told you?'

'Yeah.'

'Why?'

'Because it's wrong.'

'Who says?'

'Tan. And I agree. In God's good time you go. Not before.'

'Is that what your mother did? Mess with the schedule?'

'Yeah. Too right.'

'OK.' Tremayne was trying to nail down a timeline. 'Your mother's friend phones you. Frances Bevan. She tells you your mother's died. I understand you asked about the will. She told you your mother had changed her will. You want to speak to someone about that, so you phone your mother's solicitor.'

'Yeah.'

'And?'

'She said it was true. About the will. Nothing for me, nothing for Tan. It all went to some charity. Half a million quid down the khazi.'

'How did you feel?'

'Gopping. I was hanging out.'

'What does that mean?'

'It's Marine-speak. I couldn't believe it.'

'Did you blame your mum?'

'Yeah. And that new doctor she had.'

'How did you know about her?'

'My mum left me a note. That's how I knew she'd gone the way she'd gone. She said the doctor was one of the few friends she had left. Her and that woman across the road.'

'So you blamed the doctor as well?'

'Yeah. We went to see her, Tan and me.'

'Where?'

'At her place. Where she lived.'

'How did you find the address?'

'Tan knew already. She drinks in Lympstone when she's got the money. She'd heard about this woman. She was shacked up with that bloke who's gone missing.'

'And what did she say when you went round? This Dr Reilly?'

'She refused to discuss it.'

'And you? How did you react?'

'I told her she was a disgrace. Doctors are supposed to save lives, not end them. I said something else too. She'd been away for a holiday. It was obvious, the look of her. My mum paid for that, I said. I bet she did.'

'And Tania?'

'Tania was off her head.'

'What does that mean?'

'Don't ask.'

'I am asking, Dean. You say she was off her head. What exactly does that mean?'

Russell hesitated. For a moment, watching this exchange, Suttle thought he was going to hide behind his solicitor, but he was wrong.

'Tan can get a bit emotional,' he said carefully. 'Sometimes she drinks a bit too much.'

'She was drunk? Is that what you're telling me?'

'Yeah.'

'So are you surprised Dr Reilly didn't want to take the conversation any further?'

'No.'

'When was this?'

'Last week. Thursday, I think. Maybe Friday.'

'Right.' Tremayne scribbled herself a note. Myers took over.

'So Saturday comes. You've been to see Dr Reilly. You've got nowhere. What happens next?'

'Tan spent the day in bed. She wasn't well.'

'And the evening?'

'I went out.'

'By yourself?'

'Yeah.'

'Where?'

'Local. Exmouth. Tell you the truth, Tan was driving me nuts. Wanted to come with me. Kept phoning once I'd gone. Wouldn't leave me alone.'

'Where did you go?'

'All sorts.' Russell named several pubs.

'You were alone?'

'No way. I got lots of mates around town. We all got hammered. Ended up in a big fight. Me and two other guys.'

'And?'

For the first time he smiled. He looked from one face to the other. 'You're telling me you don't know?'

'Know what?'

146

'You lot arrested me. Three in the morning. Outside the Q Club. I never got bailed until Monday.'

Suttle reported back to Houghton by phone; Nandy was nowhere to be seen. The news that Dean Russell had the perfect alibi raised a mirthless chuckle. *Buzzard* was turning into a car crash.

'Why didn't we know this before?'

'I never checked, boss. I belled a mate at Exmouth and told him he was on a nicking, but I never went into any detail. My fault,' said Suttle.

'You're right.'

Houghton wanted to know who Russell had met in the pub in Exmouth.

'Guy called Wilson, boss. He runs a maritime security company. Russell says he's on a contract for Wilson's next job.'

'Have you checked him out?'

'No, but I will.' He frowned, then glanced at his watch. 'How are they doing at Heavitree?'

'They're not. The lady's gone No Comment.'

'*No Comment?*'

'Yes.'

'I don't believe it.'

'It gets worse. The only time she opened her mouth was to confirm she's going to do you for assault.'

'And the brief?'

'Appears to confirm it.'

'Great.' Suttle paused. 'This is a woman without an alibi. She told me they'd both been there on Saturday night. That's obviously bollocks. He was out on the lash. What if she went up to Lympstone? Talked her way into Bentner's place? Say Bentner's not there? Say Reilly's been drinking? This is a woman with previous for assault. She's no stranger to violence. She's got half a million quid's worth of motive. She's got the opportunity. The kitchen's full of knives. She's got a debt to settle. She's not the

147

forgiving kind. She may be off her head herself. Am I getting warm here?'

Houghton admitted he had a case. 'But we need more,' she said. 'A lot more.'

'Forensics?'

'They're still boshing their property.'

'And?'

'Nothing so far.'

'Shame.'

Suttle rang off. The interview room was already empty, Russell en route back to Heavitree with Tremayne and Myers to sign the release forms.

Golding checked his watch. Nearly half five. 'Drink, skip? I'll drive.'

Twenty-One

They settled for a pub in Exeter, the Angel, just across from the Exeter Central station. Suttle's leg was beginning to aggravate him. The constant throb-throb had become a burning sensation that made him irritable as well as faintly anxious. Oona, he thought, as soon as I get home. I'll give her a ring. She'll know what's wrong. She'll know what to do.

Golding bought the drinks. Suttle lifted the top off his Stella and then half-drained the pint. Within seconds he was starting to feel better.

'Bad sign, skip. And you're talking to an expert.'

'Thanks, and I mean that.'

He put his hand on Golding's arm and gave it a squeeze. But for the baseball bat he might not have a leg at all. 'I owe you, mate. I do.'

Golding told him it was nothing. All his life he'd wanted to kill a dog, and now he'd done it. A pleasure and a privilege. The stuff of dreams.

He gave Suttle a look. The pub was filling up nicely, mainly students.

'Mind if I ask you something, skip?'

'Help yourself.'

'Who did that text really come from?'

'The one in the pub?'

'Yeah. And the lead on the dead woman.'

Suttle reached for his glass, avoiding his gaze. *He knows*, he thought. *What now?*

149

'Lizzie,' he said. 'She's always fancied being a cop.'

'Yeah? And what else?'

'Fuck knows.'

'Be honest, skip. Think motive. She wants you back.'

'No way. She's got a sweet life. Why ruin it?'

'And you?'

'I've got your ex-partner. And she makes me very happy.'

'I'm glad.'

'Truly? You mean that?'

'I do. And I happen to know she feels the same way.' He sat back a moment, then leaned forward again. 'Spot of advice?'

'Go on.'

'Don't fuck it up. She loves you. You know she does.'

Suttle stared at him. He knew it was true. He also knew that Golding still had the ear of Oona. One word from her wayward ex-lover and Suttle was looking at a car crash all of his own.

He drained his pint, looked at his watch. His Impreza was still at Middlemoor but he didn't fancy driving. Trains left for Exmouth every half-hour.

'I'm off.' He got to his feet, his hand on Golding's shoulder. 'Thanks for the pint.'

Ten minutes later, waiting for the train, Suttle took a call from DI Houghton. She had a team working house-to-house enquiries in Tania Maguire's street. One of the DCs had just phoned to report that Saturday night a neighbour had found Maguire passed out on the pavement below her bedroom window at one in the morning. She'd gone down to help. Maguire, as pissed as ever, had set out to try and find Dean but had never made it.

'So what happened, boss?'

'The neighbour walked her back home. Put her to bed. Sunday morning she went round to check up on her but Maguire couldn't remember a thing. Dean wasn't around either but she didn't seem to have noticed.' Houghton permitted herself a dry laugh. 'Does that sound like someone who could have done the job on Harriet Reilly?'

*

Lizzie phoned Anton the moment she got home. When he volunteered more of Harriet Reilly's patients, she told him the story had moved on. She had the name of a scientist at the uni, some kind of environmentalist. Her name was Gemma Caton. Might Anton find out a little more?

'What do you want to know?'

'Everything you can lay your hands on. Married? Partnered? Age? Reputation? Strengths? Weaknesses? Whatever ...'

Anton said he'd do his best and rang off. He was back within the hour. Lizzie was in the kitchen, trying to conjure something interesting from what little she could find in the fridge. She wedged the phone against her ear.

'Any luck?'

'Of course.'

Dr Caton, he said, was an American anthropologist with a big following among the watermelons.

'The what?'

'Watermelons.' Anton was laughing. 'Green on the outside, red on the inside. Activists. Warmists. Socialists. Maybe even communists if we have them any more. She's very political, this woman. Her colleagues are maybe not so keen. I get the impression she can be an embarrassment. But she's very popular with some of the students. Go to her lectures and they're packed. Apparently she says things no one else will say.'

'About what?'

'About society. About the way we are.'

Lizzie was making notes on the back of an envelope. Anthropology, as far as she understood it, had to do with the study of human evolution.

'Does she have a speciality? Something in particular?'

'Native Americans in the Pacific Northwest.'

'You mean Indians?'

'Yes. I think she's written a book. That's what I'm told. Oregon. British Columbia. Foothills of the Rockies. Are you writing all this down?'

'Yes.'

'Why?'

Lizzie didn't answer. She wanted to know about this woman's private life.

'Is she married?'

'I don't know. I don't think so.'

'Age?'

'Forty-something. You want me to keep asking? You want more?'

'Yes, please.'

'What are you after?'

'I need to know who she's close to. Who matters to her.' For the first time Lizzie mentioned Bentner.

Anton interrupted at once.

'The climate scientist? The one who's gone missing?'

'Yes.'

'He was here last week. Up on the campus. Dr Caton runs evening meetings sometimes. Bentner came to talk.'

'How do you know?'

'I saw the posters. They were everywhere.'

'What was the talk about?'

'Global warming. Four degrees? Five degrees? I can't remember exactly but that was the title.'

Suttle was home by half past seven. His leg, if anything, was worse. He fetched a Stella from the fridge, popped a couple of ibuprofen and then sat in the window with his leg propped up on another chair. He felt about a hundred. The leg was bad enough after all his other injuries, but there was something else even more menacing, a feeling that he'd somehow lost control of events.

He brooded for a while, trying to concentrate on *Buzzard*, tallying the various leads, weighing one against another, trying to silence the voices in his head, but even here, on home turf, he couldn't rid himself of the thought of Lizzie. She was everywhere: on his mobile, in his ear, on the strip of grass outside his window. She'd found herself a perch in *Buzzard*, fed him information he didn't know existed, led him from the restaurant and bedded him.

What followed had taken him by surprise in all kinds of ways. Who'd taught her to be so playful? So deft? So light-fingered? And what – exactly – had she meant by asking him to keep her in the loop? Was this Lizzie the journalist? Or Lizzie the hot near-divorcee wanting to cash in on her independence and her new-found celebrity? She could have any man she wanted, so what had brought her back to her ruined ex-husband?

To all these questions Suttle had no answer, and that knowledge, that degree of helplessness, simply made things worse. Look at the last twenty-four hours from one perspective, and Lizzie couldn't seem to keep her hands off his life, professional or otherwise. She was everywhere. She was staking out her territory. She was in his face. But take a tiny step back, try and be as honest as he could, and it was hard not to accept that he too was a player in this game. Had he enjoyed last night? Yes. Did it feel like having sex with a stranger? Yes. And was there a tiny voice in his head that suggested there might come more leads from Lizzie? Again, yes.

Crap, he told himself. Nonsense. Excuses. Forget it.

He took a long pull from the can, tipped back his head against the chair, closed his eyes. Guilt was a feeling he didn't much like. Oona, he told himself. Think Oona.

He phoned her within the hour. She listened for maybe ten seconds.

'You're pissed, my lovely.'

'You're right.'

'It's Thursday, for fuck's sake. You're ahead of the game. You've got a day in hand. That makes you either wicked or lucky. Your call, big man.'

He explained about the dog, about Luke rising to the occasion, about the throbbing pressure in his calf. She said she knew about it already. Her mate in A & E.

'She said you were very brave. I said you were a great actor. I'd settle for either just now but I've got a mate coming round

153

and she'll slaughter me if I'm gone.' Tiny pause. 'Do you want me to give her a ring? Put her off?'

'No.'

'What's the matter?'

'Nothing. The leg. That's all.'

'You lie, my lovely. What else has happened?'

'Nothing.'

'So why won't you tell me?'

'Nothing to tell.'

'So now you're worrying me. Stay there. We'll both come down.'

'No, please don't.'

'Shit.'

'What?'

'I think you mean it.'

Suttle did. He did his best to mumble an apology, to tell her he was knackered. He was off to bed. *Buzzard* was driving him mental. He'd give her a ring in the morning.

'You mean that?'

'I do.'

'Be good, big man. Two things.'

'What?'

'Number one, the Fureys. Number two, me. Not necessarily in that order. Deal?'

'Always.'

'Thank fuck for that. You know what, my lovely? You're starting to sound human again.'

She blew him a kiss on the phone and rang off, leaving him staring into nowhere. He reached for the can on the table. It was empty. He scrolled back through his recent texts until he found the message from Lizzie with the link to the YouTube clip. This was the first of the texts she'd sent and he'd yet to take a proper look at the clip. Now he did so. Martha Argerich playing Ravel's Piano Concerto in G major.

The moment the music started, he knew he needed a bigger screen. He hoisted his laptop onto the table and tapped the link into his browser. Until he'd met Eamon Lenahan, he'd been a stranger to classical music, but the wee Irishman, passionate about opera, had waved away his reservations and swamped the cottage with composer after composer. Verdi. Puccini. Wagner. Blown away was a big phrase, but there had come moments – many moments – when Suttle had wondered how he'd ever let this stuff pass him by. So rich. So passionate. So overwhelming.

Ravel was the same, as was the pianist. The second movement, for reasons that Suttle could only guess at, reduced him to tears. The music soared, swooped, soared again. He thought of Grace, his daughter, the times they'd shared together, the memories embedded in what passed for his soul. Lizzie had been part of that, and here she was again, his warrior queen, her bow raised, her aim unerring, the impact of the music she'd chosen pinning him to the laptop. He couldn't tear his eyes away, nor did he want to.

The concerto over, Argerich taking her bow, Suttle reached for his mobile. Lizzie answered within seconds.

'You,' she said.

'Me,' he agreed.

She was down within the hour. He met her at the door. He had a list of things to say – conditions really – but she stepped around him, extending a hand, leading him into the bedroom, pushing him softly backwards, loosening the belt of his jeans, slipping them off, then bending to inspect the bandage.

'You want me to undo it?'

'Whatever.'

'I don't think it's bleeding. Do you have another one?'

'No.'

'Then maybe we ought to leave it. What do you think?'

'I think it's fine.' Suttle was trying not to grin. The leather jacket, he thought. So soft. So new.

'You're telling me it still hurts?'

'I'm telling you the reverse.'

'Really?' She was sitting on the bed. She took his hand, lifted it to her lips, kissed it. 'You're a good man, Jimmy Suttle. You know that?'

'I'm crap. I lost my daughter. And then she died. How clever was that?'

'We lost her, Jimmy. You and me. And you know something else? We've never really talked about it.'

'That's true.'

'You think we should?'

'No.'

'You're right. Life goes on. You turn the page. Thank Christ for clichés. Any port in a storm, eh?'

She smiled down at him, asked how much he'd had to drink. He shook his head, refusing to answer.

'There's red wine in the kitchen,' he said, 'if you fancy it.'

She left the room. Within a minute she was back. Empty-handed.

'So who drinks Rioja?'

'Guess.'

'Good taste.'

'Have a glass. Help yourself. Drink the lot.'

'It's not mine, Jimmy. And neither are you.'

'Is this some kind of negotiation?' Suttle propped himself up against the pillows. 'Only you're right. I'm pissed.'

The smile widened. She was dancing her fingers up his leg. Then she stopped.

'This might become a habit,' she said. 'Could you handle that?'

'Could you?'

'I'm not the one with anything to lose. You've got a relationship. You love the woman. And in case you're wondering, the answer is yes.'

'Yes to what?'

'Yes, I'm jealous. And yes, I'd like to fuck you again.' She stood up and slipped out of her jeans. 'How does that sound?'

Twenty-Two

Buzzard's first week limped to a close. Nationwide there were no sightings of Alois Bentner, and he made no more bids to contact any of his work colleagues at the Hadley Centre. After two further interviews, during which she refused to answer any questions, Tania Maguire was released on police bail. The SOC search of her flat in Exmouth had revealed nothing to link her to the murder scene in Lympstone, and the neighbour who had rescued her in the small hours of Sunday morning had been only too happy to supply a full statement.

Under these circumstances even Nandy was obliged to admit that Maguire had probably stayed at home all weekend, blitzed. The Chief Constable, meanwhile, was demanding regular up-dates on *Buzzard*'s progress, not least because the nation had begun to take the missing climatologist to its heart.

This, as it turned out, was largely his neighbour's doing. The first time Suttle set eyes on Gemma Caton was Friday morning. Lizzie had gone, disappearing before Suttle had even woken up. As soon as she got home, she'd sent him a YouTube clip from an eco website called Terra Sancta. Half dressed, he found himself watching a bulky forty-something with a wild frizz of greying hair being interviewed on the subject of climate change.

Gemma Caton was forceful, with an American accent and a turn of phrase that helpfully skewered an otherwise complex debate. The extractive industries, she said, had long treated nature as a bottomless vending machine. Put money in one end, and out came all the goodies – oil, gas, coal – that were threatening to cook us alive at the other. Chief villain in this global tragedy was the sheer muscle of the money markets, juiced by the performance of the oil and gas giants.

These guys, she said, were in turn keeping their stock prices buoyant by loading the value of their unexploited reserves onto their balance sheets. In total, these reservoirs of untapped oil and gas amounted to 2795 gigatons. The existing capacity of the planet to deal with carbon emissions without risking meltdown? Just 565 gigatons, one fifth of that sum. Suttle blinked. Even this early in the morning it wasn't hard to do the sums and draw the inevitable conclusion: that the survival of capitalism relied on the world cooking itself to death.

The clip moved on. Up came a shot of Bentner, one he hadn't seen before. He was standing in a garden that Suttle recognised as Bentner's own. In the background was the tight curl of the bay, the ochre-red bluffs and the broadness of the river beyond. Bentner had a half-empty glass in his hand and was toasting the camera.

Gemma Caton's voice-over introduced him as a fellow activist and a good friend. She knew him well. He cared about stuff. About the planet. About our place in the scheme of things. Bentner began to talk. He had a faint but perceptible American accent. He eyeballed the camera with an intensity that mirrored Caton's as he mused about the wild distortions in global weather patterns. These he blamed on Big Business and Extreme Energy. This, he growled, was a marriage made in hell. It was another arresting phrase, and Suttle was reaching for a pen when his phone rang.

'Did you get the clip?' It was Lizzie.

'I'm watching it.'

'Incredible, isn't it? Have you talked to this woman?'

'Not yet.'

'Why not?'

'She hasn't been around.'

'Neither has Bentner. How hard are you guys looking?'

'That's unnecessary.'

'Not from where I'm sitting. Listen ...'

She gave him an address in Polsloe Bridge where *Buzzard* would find the handyman who kept Bentner's life in working order. This guy had some interesting things to say about him. And about the woman next door.

'You mean Caton?'

'The very same. She's an anthropologist, by the way. With a big reputation.'

'You've *met* her?'

'No, but it's amazing how much you can put together if you find the right people and ask the right questions.'

'Thanks. So why didn't you mention any of this last night?'

'You weren't in the mood.' She laughed. 'And neither was I.'

Buzzard's end-of-week squad meet started at just gone nine. Suttle had shown the YouTube clip to DI Houghton and arrangements were in hand to interview Gemma Caton later in the morning. It turned out she'd spent the last seven days in London, catching up with a number of friends and colleagues, and had been too busy to attend to texts and emails. She was perfectly happy to present herself at Heavitree police station once she'd got down to Exeter but warned *Buzzard* that her schedule was impossibly tight. She'd help out all she could, but time was precious. Because time was running out.

Houghton had already put Suttle and Golding on standby for the interview. Now she had another piece of breaking news to impart.

'This came into our possession this morning,' she said. She was holding up a neatly folded square of paper. Inside was a message dated 10 June.

'This was handed in yesterday evening,' she said. 'It comes from a letter box we never searched on Dartmoor.' She adjusted her glasses and read the message: '"*Step one for getting out of the hole? Stop digging.*" It appears that this comes from Bentner.'

'How do we know, boss?' The question came from Luke Golding.

'Because he left a fingerprint. We think he used dirt from the ground. He'd know we've boshed his house so we'd have a match.'

'And?'

'Definitely Bentner.'

Suttle was putting together the timeline. Tuesday was the night Bentner had phoned Sheila Forshaw. The letter box, according to Houghton, was three miles north of Ivybridge, where the call had come from. After which he'd driven west, sensibly dumped the Skoda and disappeared.

The D/S in charge of Outside Enquiries wanted to know about Bentner's transport options.

Houghton fielded the query. 'We're thinking he's using another vehicle. A rental car's unlikely. We're sitting on his credit cards. No movement there, either. So it has to be a colleague, a friend, a mate, whatever.'

'But this guy doesn't do mates.'

'Exactly.' A wan smile from Houghton. 'The mystery deepens.'

The interview with Gemma Caton at Heavitree police station started at 14.21. By the time she arrived, bustling into the Custody Centre, Suttle and Golding had been waiting for nearly an hour. She was even bigger in the flesh than she'd seemed on the YouTube clip. She wore a pair of glasses with thick red frames and cloaked her bulk in a tent-like olive-green dress that stopped just short of her boots. These had nothing to do with fashion or style. They were Gore-tex, heavily used, caked with mud. Had Bentner been a woman, Suttle thought, he'd have looked just like this.

Half-expecting an apology for being so late, Suttle found himself listening to a breathless account of what the rest of this woman's day would be holding. A faculty meet up at the university at four o'clock. A seminar on Balinese *hyang* spirits at five. A peer review session with a couple of fellow academics at six. Followed by a function up at the Hadley Centre at seven.

'So go for it, guys.' She beamed at them both. 'Time and this little lady were never best friends.'

Suttle and Golding exchanged glances. The Hadley Centre seemed a sensible place to start.

'We need to talk about Alois Bentner,' he said. 'Did you meet him at the centre?'

'Nope. Next-door neighbours. Happenstance. Serendipity. Sometimes life is on your side. You ever get that feeling?'

They'd been friends, she said, from the moment she'd moved in a couple of years ago. Used to the inane small talk she took to be the English default conversational setting – all shit television and Z-list celebs – she'd found herself living beside a world-class recluse.

'The man was a honey, a real specimen, a true original. I loved him from the start. A bear of a guy. Grumpy as hell but sunshine underneath if you knew where to look.'

By her own admission, she'd known where to look. They quickly became friends. They shared the same despair, the same busy pessimism, the same conviction that mankind was stumbling blindly towards oblivion. Not because people were unaware of the dangers or even the science, but because they simply didn't know what to do about it, which buttons to press, how to raise their empty little heads above the parapet.

Suttle wanted to know whether they socialised.

'You mean get wasted?' She shook her head. 'Alois needs booze. That's his only failing. I used to kid him that his personal emissions would double the UK output. Me? I don't need the stuff. I'd love to tell you I run on empty but it ain't true. As long as it's sweet, as long as it's toothsome, it keeps me going. Alois? Couldn't abide the stuff. Me? I live on it.'

'Stuff?'

'Coke.' She grinned. 'And pasta.'

The unlikely news that a climate warrior and fervent anti-capitalist relied on industrial quantities of Coca-Cola to get through her day put a smile on Suttle's face. He wanted to know more about her relationship with Bentner.

'I just told you guys. Brother love. Comrades-in-arms love. Marching-to-the-barricades love. If there's a prize for best neighbour ever, no contest. I live in the shadow of eco history. My man next door may save the planet. You wanna write that down?'

My man, Suttle thought. Interesting. 'So where is he?' he asked.

'Doing his thing. Biding his time.'

'Hiding from us?'

'I doubt it. Alois doesn't do hiding. This is a guy who goes to ground from time to time. He needs time to think, to sort stuff out, to come up with new questions, new answers. When he's ready, I'm sure he'll be in touch. But he ain't hiding.'

'Have you talked to him?'

'When?'

'Since he disappeared.'

'Which would be …?'

'Last weekend.'

'No way.' An abrupt shake of the head. 'You have to get this thing right, and I guess I'm the one to help you here. Alois and I don't live in each other's pockets. We have a meeting of minds. We share time together when we're both around and we're both in the mood. I guess it's respect. Respect and stimulation and maybe just a scintilla of relief.'

'Relief?'

'That we're not alone. Climate change is no big secret, don't get this girl wrong, but you'd be amazed how many people have just switched off. Is the science complex? Of course it is. Is there any real doubt about what we're about to be facing? None at all. So are folks out in the street making life tough for the guys with the money and the influence to make things happen? You bet your sweet fanny they're not. Now why is that? Serious question. Either of you care to give me a clue?'

In the space of less than a minute this interview had turned into a seminar. Golding was looking deeply uncomfortable. Suttle felt the first stirrings of anger. This is a tactic, he told himself. This woman knows a great deal more than she's letting on.

'Tell me about Harriet Reilly,' he said softly. 'How well did you know her?'

'Barely at all.'

'But you knew that she and Bentner were close?'

'I guess so.'

'What does that mean? You did or you didn't?'

'I knew she came round from time to time. Does that make them close? You tell me.'

'Did you know they went on holiday together? Brazil? The US?'

'Sort of. Alois showed me some photos one time. Rio. Manaus. She was in those pictures. I guess you might call that a clue.'

'But he never talked about her?'

'Never. Alois lives in separate silos. I guess I belong in the one with FELLOW SPIRIT on the door. We think alike. We ask the same hard questions. We ain't prepared to compromise. What's left of the future is staring us in the face, and if we're brave enough to keep our eyes open we've got all the evidence we need. Global warming is telescoping the time frame. We tell ourselves we have a century to get on top of this thing but that's way off the reservation. In short, Mr Suttle, we're probably fucked.'

She'd done it again. Neat.

Suttle held her gaze. 'So you never socialised? You and Harriet and Alois? Shared a meal, maybe? Fellow spirits around the table?'

'Never. Why would we? What would we talk about? Like I say, Alois rations himself out. Maybe he had a real thing going with Harriet, I've no idea, and I guess it's too late to ask the woman herself, but whichever way you cut it I get the juicy bits.'

'Juicy bits?'

'The essence of the man. Who he really is. This is something you can't really put into words. It's a fingertip thing, a soul thing. Bonded? Is that too big a word? I guess not.'

'And Harriet? Which bit of him did she have?'

'I've no idea. You could maybe ask her but I guess it's too late. Shame.'

She pushed herself gently back from the table, her eyes glittering, and then checked her watch. Suttle had touched a nerve, he knew he had.

'Where were you on Saturday night, Ms Caton?' This from Golding.

'Saturday night?' She frowned, leafing back through her mental diary. 'I guess that would be London.'

'Whereabouts in London?'

'You want an address?'

'Yes, please.'

'So you can check me out?'

'We call it elimination. Basically it's the same thing.'

'Elimination from what? Killing that woman?'

Golding let the question hang in the air. Suttle didn't say a word. Eventually Caton plunged a meaty hand into her bag and extracted an address book bulging with receipts. One of them was for what she called 'accommodation' in Whitechapel.

'We're talking serviced rooms,' she said briskly. 'Over a halal restaurant.'

'And you stayed there?' Still Golding.

'Six nights. Starting on Friday, 6 June.' She was squinting at the receipt. 'Forty-eight pounds a night. Three bus stops and you're in the City of London. Fortress Greed. In my little place you get the sheets changed daily, wall-mounted TV, kettle, fridge, the lot. They even have Wi-Fi. Where I come from, we call that good value.'

'You were there alone?'

'Of course.'

'But we understand this was a catch-up time. Friends? Colleagues?'

'Sure. All of that. But I don't sleep with these people. No way.'

Suttle wanted to know who she might have been with on the

Saturday night. Caton gave the question some thought.

'Saturday? That would be Michala. A colleague. Beautiful person.'

She said they'd met at Michala's new flat. She had a place on Streatham Hill.

'You went out for a meal?'

'We stayed in. Michala cooks like an angel.'

'And then you went back to Whitechapel?'

'As a matter of fact, no.'

'So what happened?'

'I stayed over with Michala. I'm not a drinker. You know that. But – hey – once in a while a girl earns herself a hangover.'

'Wine? Spirits?'

'Wine. Red. Tasty. Then aquavit. Water of life.' Big smile. 'If you want the full picture, I bought chocolates, lots of chocolates. You want me to walk you through the evening? Belgian truffles? Profiteroles?'

Suttle let her finish. Then he asked for Michala's contact details.

Caton looked astonished. Then hurt. 'You're gonna talk to her too? You think we *both* did it?'

Suttle said nothing. At length her hand dived back inside her bag. She scribbled a mobile number from memory, big loopy script, then tossed it across the table.

'You guys done?' she said. 'Only this girl has to move on.'

Suttle thanked her for her time, noted her contact details and promised to keep in touch.

'Why would you want to do that?'

'Because one day we'll find Mr Bentner. And maybe you'd like to know.'

'Sure ...' She picked up her bag. 'You gentlemen take care.'

Suttle escorted her back to the custody desk. When he offered to get her a taxi, she said that wouldn't be necessary. She had a car outside. LPG. A million miles on a single tank.

'Pray for the planet, Mr Suttle.' She wasn't smiling. 'It's the only one we've got.'

Back in the interview room Golding was studying his notes. At length he looked up.

'Remember that journal of Harriet Reilly's, skip?'

'Yeah.'

'ND?'

'Yeah.'

'You know what it stands for?'

'Tell me.'

'Next door.'

Twenty-Three

Anton phoned just before midday. Lizzie took the call at her desk, rereading yet another terse email from Muriel that demanded a response. Her agent was under siege from publishers needing more from Lizzie Hodson. A follow-up to *Mine*. More teasing insights into what it was like to be young and good-looking, with a rare talent for turning heartbreak into best-sellerdom. That was all well and good, but so far Lizzie hadn't got beyond a rather limp apology for taking time out and enjoying herself. Thank Christ for Anton.

'What have you got?' she asked.

He told her to get a pen and something to write on.

'You asked me about this woman's private life,' he said. 'She's very close to a mature student called Michala. Different department. Environmental Science.'

'Are we talking partners? Is this some kind of gay thing?'

'I don't know. It may be. But they're both on the same page when it comes to global warming.'

Lizzie smiled. Anton's command of English was growing by the hour. He must be bedding a management consultant, she thought.

'She lives locally? This Michala?'

'London. I've no idea where. She's from Denmark originally.'

'And down here? When she's at uni?'

'Lympstone. She's got a room at Caton's place.' He gave Lizzie a mobile number.

167

'You've met her?'

'Yes.'

'So what's she like?'

'Small. Bright. Perfectly formed. Ambitious.'

'Did you mention me?'

'Of course. That was the whole point. I said you were doing a big piece on global warming.'

'Did you mention Gemma Caton?'

'No. But I told her you were a huge fan of wind power. The Danes love wind power.'

'Thanks.'

'My pleasure. She'd love to meet you.'

DI Carole Houghton, for once, was close to losing her temper. *Buzzard*, after a hectic start, was fast running out of manpower. On Nandy's orders, half a dozen detectives had been extracted to blitz a particularly nasty double murder in a village outside Barnstaple. For now the finger of suspicion was pointing at a couple of Romanian fruit-pickers with addresses in Bristol, and the top corridor was keen to limit the damage to community relations. UKIP were beginning to matter in the sleepy politics of the south-west, and a swift result would limit the inevitable headlines.

Houghton looked up from her PC screen. Her face was pale with exhaustion and her waste bin full of discarded coffee cups.

'Well?'

Suttle had just returned from the Custody Centre at Heavitree. He offered a brief account of the interview with Gemma Caton.

'So where does this take us, Jimmy?'

'I think she's probably in touch with Bentner. She denies it, but then she would. She's a very strange woman.'

'Strange how?'

'Dominating, for sure. Clever? Yes. But not as clever as she thinks she is. The weekend puts her in London. She's got the makings of an alibi. We need to check it out.'

Houghton nodded. Her phone rang. She checked caller ID,

then put the mobile to her ear. Even from the other side of the desk Suttle could hear Nandy. He was bossing the double murder from Barnstaple nick. He was close to a result. He needed three more *Buzzard* DCs on the road and up to Barnstaple within the hour.

Houghton rolled her eyes. She had no option but to say yes. Nandy's assurances about having the guys back in harness within a couple of days were wildly optimistic. *Buzzard* was running on empty.

She put the phone down and left the office without a word. Through the open door Suttle could see her conferring with the D/S in charge of Outside Enquiries. When the guy stared up at her, his hands spread wide in a gesture of resignation, she simply shrugged. Then he called her back and offered her a slip of paper. She scanned it quickly. Seconds later, she was back with Suttle.

'This is mad,' she muttered. 'Give me a couple of minutes.'

She keyed a phone number from memory and waited for the call to connect. Then she bent to the phone and reached for her notepad.

'Thanks,' she said, 'I'm grateful.'

The call over, she stared down at the pad. Suttle was beginning to feel sorry for her.

'Boss? You OK?'

'No.'

'What's the matter?'

'That was the CSM. He's just got the results of the DNA test on the fetus.'

'You mean Harriet Reilly's baby?'

'Yes.'

'And there's a problem?'

'Yes.' Her head came up at last. 'It wasn't hers.'

'But it had to be hers.'

'No. Not if she was carrying it for someone else.'

'Like who?'

'Good question.'

Suttle asked about Bentner. Without a sample of his DNA there was no way of establishing paternity. Houghton nodded. She pushed her pad across the desk. 'That's the name of Reilly's own GP. This is going to be tricky but we need to bottom this thing out. Take Luke. Tell him to be charming. See what you can do.'

Lizzie found Michala on a pontoon beside the Exeter Ship Canal. She'd phoned earlier, asking for an interview, and Michala had said it would have to be this afternoon, preferably around three, after she came back from coxing a university eight on a training row down the canal. After that was hopeless because she'd be on the road to Bristol for an early-evening flight to Copenhagen.

Now, parked up in her Audi beside the university boathouse, Lizzie was watching the all-girl crew lifting the sleek racing shell from the water. They stepped from the pontoon onto the river-bank, a complex little dance conducted by the waif-like figure Lizzie assumed to be Michala. She was a child compared to the rest of the rowers: thin, pale, long blonde hair tucked under a baseball cap.

As the crew walked the long white shell into the boathouse, Lizzie stepped from her car.

'Michala?'

'That's me.'

Lizzie fell into step beside her, introduced herself.

'You're the journalist, right? Friend of Anton's?' Michala's English was perfect.

'Right. You must be freezing. You want to talk in my car? Or go somewhere else?'

A moment's hesitation. A glance at her watch. Then a nod.

'Your car would be fine. But not too long, yeah?'

They talked for half an hour, Lizzie carefully seeding the conversation with what little she knew about state-of-the-art turbine windmills, offshore energy farms and the likelihood that a barrage across the Severn Estuary might offer the answer to a gluttonous nation's prayer.

'Gluttonous?' For once Michala's English let her down.

'Greedy,' Lizzie explained.

'Ah.' She had a fetching grin. 'You mean power-hungry?'

'Exactly. That's perfect. Is that your phrase?'

'If only. No. It comes from a friend. She knows so much more than me.'

'She's in the same field?'

'Not really. She's an anthropologist. But that's the thing about global warming. It doesn't matter where you're coming from, as long as we all end up at the same destination.'

Lizzie smiled. *As long as we all end up at the same destination.* Another phrase borrowed from Michala's friend.

'I heard exactly that on a YouTube clip. Terra Sancta. An American woman.'

'That's my colleague. Gemma. I know the clip.'

'Really?'

'Sure, small world, eh?'

'Absolutely.' Lizzie was doing her best to sound excited. And surprised. 'So this is Gemma Caton, right?'

'Yes.'

'And you really know her?'

'I know her well. In fact I have a room in her place.'

'How strange.'

'Not at all. I met her a couple of years back. Now I'm doing a doctorate here.' She paused. 'You've met this woman? Listened to one of her lectures, maybe?'

'Never.'

'You should. You want me to fix it? Maybe introduce her?' She nodded down at Lizzie's notepad. 'She's the one who should be doing this interview, not me. She's big. Really big. And she deserves to be.'

Lizzie had been watching Michala's hands. They were delicate and expressive, just like the rest of her. She wore a thin gold ring on the index finger of her right hand, another on her left thumb and a man's watch on her left wrist. The face of the watch was on the inside of her wrist, and when she checked the time Lizzie noticed a small blue tattoo against the whiteness of her forearm.

'That's lovely. Do you mind?' Lizzie reached across and touched the tattoo. It was beautifully done: a horse caught in mid-gallop, neck arched, tail flying, no rider.

Michala's head came up. There was a different smile on her face now.

'You like it?'

'Very much. What is it?

'It's a wind horse. It comes from Tibet. It's a symbol of peace and harmony. You see them on flags as well. The horse carries your prayers to heaven.'

Lizzie nodded. Flags, she thought. Fluttering in the wind outside Gemma Caton's waterfront home.

'You've been to Tibet?'

'Never. One day, maybe. But not yet.'

'So why the horse?'

'It's for a friend. Someone I knew.'

'A memento?'

'A prayer.' She held Lizzie's gaze. 'The wind horse was Gemma's idea. You should meet her. I mean it.'

'I'd like that.'

'You would?'

'Yes.'

Lizzie wrote down her email address and handed it across. Michala studied it a moment and then looked up. The smile again and a softness in her eyes.

'Gemma might invite you to supper,' she said. 'Would you like that?'

Harriet Reilly's GP worked out of a practice in Topsham. Her name was Amelia Bishop. On the phone she'd been extremely guarded about her late patient. Yes, she'd been as horrified as everyone else by what had happened to poor Harriet. And yes, she'd be prepared to meet to discuss her pregnancy, but only in the broadest terms. She reserved the right not to answer questions she deemed intrusive or otherwise inappropriate. If those conditions were understood and fully accepted then yes, they were welcome to call by.

It was late afternoon. Dr Bishop's last patient had just departed. To Suttle's surprise, she was a tall blonde with a ready smile and a warm handshake. Stepping into her consulting room, Suttle wondered whether he'd been talking to someone else on the phone. Golding's reaction was altogether simpler. He loved this woman on sight.

'We're really sorry,' he said at once. 'You guys must live in a madder world than even we do. You don't need us, you really don't.'

Bishop offered them juice from a fridge. Golding went for the remains of a carton of Tropicana, asked whether she had any peanuts. Suttle declined the offer. He was looking at the line of photos over Bishop's desk. She had at least two young kids. No sign of a father.

'You wanted to ask me about Harriet,' she said.

'We do.' Golding again. 'How come you're her GP?'

'Rather than someone from her own practice, you mean?'

'Yes.'

'I've no idea. Some GPs prefer it that way. You're working with colleagues every day. You don't always want to share your haemorrhoids with them.'

'What about you?'

'Is that relevant?'

'Probably not.'

'Then ask me another question.'

'About Harriet ...' Suttle this time. 'Did you know her for a long time?'

'Thirteen years. Just under.'

'And did you know her as a friend?'

'No. She wasn't that kind of woman. And, to be frank, that can be a relief. Work and pleasure?' She gestured towards the line of family photos. 'Best kept separate.'

Suttle asked about Harriet's previous status.

'I'm not with you.'

'We understand she was married.'

'That's true.'

'And no kids.'

'That's also true. Have you talked to her ex?'

'Not yet. He's in Australia. Was she married when you first met her?'

'Yes.'

'And was getting pregnant ever an issue?'

'I don't understand.'

'Did she want to get pregnant? *Try* to get pregnant?'

'Ah ...' her gaze moved from face to face '... that's a question you should be asking her ex. His name is Tony. I expect you know that.'

'But you won't tell us?'

'No.'

Suttle nodded. This was going to be difficult. A production order would release certain data, but Houghton had been right to put her faith in a face-to-face meet.

Golding sensed it, too. 'We don't need to dwell on this,' he said softly, 'but the scene was horrible. She was butchered. We need to find who did that, and motive is one of the ways we can move the inquiry along. It turns out she was pregnant. It also turns out that whoever did it removed the baby's head.'

'You mean the fetus' head?'

'Yes.'

'I didn't know that.'

Golding nodded, said nothing. Bishop gazed at him for a moment, visibly shocked, then opened a drawer and took out a yellow file.

'There are two ways of doing this,' she said. 'I can give you the name of the surrogacy clinic Harriet attended or I can tell you myself. If I give you the name of the clinic, that may take a while. These people have commercial interests to protect. It also happens to be in America. That can be doubly tiresome.'

'But she was your patient,' Golding pointed out. 'Your responsibility.'

'That's true.'

'So is there anything you're prepared to tell us?'

Bishop looked from one face to the other. Finally she frowned.

'Harriet had been depressed for a while,' she said. 'Her father died, and it hit her badly. That can be something no amount of medication can take away. In situations like that you sometimes look for a change of direction.'

'That's why she got pregnant?'

'That's why she tried. We're talking *in vitro* fertilisation. That means conception outside the body. The science is moving on all the time but IVF isn't easy. Especially for someone of Harriet's age.'

'She had several attempts?'

Bishop consulted a bundle of notes in the file. 'She had a couple of miscarriages in this country, then a third try in the States. Bingo.'

'How did she feel?'

'Over the moon. Totally. It was the first time I ever saw her smile.'

Suttle nodded. He'd never met Harriet Reilly when she was alive but slowly she was beginning to swim into focus: stubborn, determined, hard to reach yet oddly vulnerable.

'There's something we need here,' he said. 'We're assuming the sperm came from her partner, Alois Bentner. Where did the eggs come from?'

'You're telling me you don't know?'

'No.'

'Then I'm afraid I can't tell you.'

'So how do we find out? Short of going round the houses with the IVF people?'

'I suggest you ask Mr Bentner.'

'He's still missing.'

'So I understand.'

She looked down at the file again and sorted through the notes inside until she found what she was after. Then she got to her feet, leaving the file open on the desk.

'There's something I have to do,' she said. 'I'll be gone a couple of minutes.'

She left the office. Golding was already reading the file. The document on the top had come from an IVF clinic in Portland, Oregon. Suttle remembered the entry in Harriet's travel diary, She and Bentner had been in Portland in early March. By the time she died the baby had been between three and four months old. The dates worked perfectly.

'The eggs came from a woman called Marianne Hausner, skip.' Golding was deep in the file. 'An address in Colorado.'

He passed the document across. Suttle made a note of the details. By the time Bishop returned, the key document was back in the file.

She stood over them and then asked Suttle to look up. Suttle did her bidding. He felt her fingers pass lightly over the scars on his face. For the first time he spotted the tube of cream in her other hand.

'Mind if I ask you a personal question?'

'Not at all.'

'Are you under any particular stress at the moment?'

Suttle shook his head. Then he caught Golding's eye. 'Maybe,' he said. 'Just a bit.'

'Are you drinking a lot?'

'No more than usual.'

'What's usual? A lot?'

She took Suttle's shrug as a yes. She gave him the tube of ointment. She told him the scars were way too inflamed.

'Go easy on the booze,' she said. 'And whatever else isn't agreeing with you.'

Suttle didn't know what to say. She escorted them both to the door, where Golding thanked her for her time. She nodded, said it was OK. Then she looked at Suttle.

'So why on earth would someone do that?'

'Do what?'

'Cut the fetus' head off?'

Twenty-Four

Lizzie had no problem getting a ticket for the Fureys concert. Prowling around Suttle's flat in the small hours of the morning, she'd browsed a handful of texts on his mobile. One of them had come from Oona. 'Half seven, my lovely,' she'd written. 'Usual place? The Fureys await.' Now she was looking at the band's website. Tonight they were at the Exeter Corn Exchange. Eight o'clock.

She hit Google, looking for a clue to the kind of music these people played, and found herself on YouTube listening to a soupy version of 'When You Were Sweet Sixteen' scored for ukulele, strings and what sounded like a stage Irishman determined to squeeze every last ounce of Celtic tearfulness from the lyrics. This was a trillion miles from Jimmy's usual faves. What was this woman doing to her man? What had happened to Neil Young and the Pretenders?

She scrolled on down the website. Online, tickets were twenty pounds. She looked at the seating plan and chose a perch beside the right-hand aisle towards the front. Arrive early, she thought, and lurk in the bar. That way she might lay eyes on this woman who'd slipped so guilefully into Jimmy's bed, into Jimmy's life. Tall? Petite? Thin? Full figure? She'd no idea. Her cursor hovered over Seat 23.

Done.

*

Suttle had already found a table in the pub by the time Oona turned up. The Fat Pig lay in a sidestreet within a couple of minutes of the venue. Oona had texted earlier, warning that she might be late: '*Carnage in A & E. Are we at war?*'

Suttle fetched her a large glass of Côtes-du-Rhône. She toyed with it a moment then put it down. She looked exhausted.

'Another shift like that and I'm a walk-in myself,' she said. 'How's my wounded soldier?'

'Fine.'

'You lie. You were limping just now. I'm an expert, remember. Trained to spot the clues. *Slainte*.' She reached for her glass. 'May the angels protect you.'

Suttle drained the remains of his lager.

'You mind if I have another?'

Without waiting for an answer, he made his way to the bar. By the time he got back to the table, Oona's glass was nearly empty.

'You never kissed me.' She patted the bench beside her. 'A girl likes to be kissed.'

Suttle eased himself in beside her and gave her a peck on the cheek. She studied him a moment, surprised.

'I'm your aunt now?'

'Of course not.'

He kissed her again, this time on the lips.

'That's better,' she said. 'But only just. The name's Oona, by the way. And I'm pleased to meet you.'

She extended a playful hand, let it drop to his thigh, gave it a stroke.

'It's the other one.'

'I know that, you eejit. This is a little something to keep you going. If the Fureys get too much I'll take you home and make it all better again. That's nursey talking, by the way. Tell me you missed me.'

'I missed you.'

'Really?'

She meant it. Suttle knew she meant it. She'd sensed a change in him. Something had happened, and she hadn't a clue what it was. Not a good start.

He asked her about the Fureys. How come she'd never mentioned them before? When did this passion of hers begin?

'Don't change the subject, my lovely. I'm your friend. Tell me what's wrong.'

'I got bitten.'

'Sure. I know. And Golden Bollocks nailed the little bastard.'

'How do you know?'

'He told me.'

'You've talked to him?'

'I have. Twice. He's very proud of himself. A whole lifetime hiding from them and at last he's home safe. Baseball bat? Am I getting warm here? Isn't Mr Bollocks just the Man of the Hour?'

Mr Bollocks was Luke Golding. Suttle wondered what else he'd told her.

'I'm grateful,' he muttered. 'I bloody owe him.'

'That's what he says.'

'It's true.' He reached for his pint. 'And the answer's yes.'

'Yes to what?'

'I've missed you.'

Lizzie had found herself a seat in the corner of the upstairs bar at the Corn Exchange. By ten to eight the place was packed, a scrum of middle-aged couples besieging the bar. By now she'd discovered that the Fureys never opened on time. Maybe they're waiting for that third pint to work, she thought. Maybe this whole gig floated on an ocean of Guinness and beery goodwill.

She'd begun to wonder whether Suttle and Oona had decided to bin the evening when she spotted him pushing past a knot of drinkers by the door. Beside him, enfolded by one arm, was a woman her own age – taller, milky complexion, lovely figure, auburn curls, face full of mischief. She was wearing jeans and a tight-fitting T-shirt with a whorl of blues on the front. Bare feet in sandals. Black nail varnish. They headed for the bar then got caught in the crush. Her head nuzzled Suttle's shoulder. Then she reached up and kissed him.

Lizzie turned away. To her surprise she couldn't handle this. She felt insanely jealous, a sensation close to physical pain, and she felt angry too. This man was her husband, the father of the child they'd cherished and lost. They'd been through a great deal together. They'd made huge mistakes, both of them, and they could have been kinder and more patient with each other. But none of that gave this woman the right to make her estranged husband so obviously happy.

They were waiting at the bar now. Suttle had checked his watch. Oona had shrugged and grinned. A ten-pound note bought the drinks. They turned and made their way towards the door that led to the auditorium. Suttle was juggling the drinks, trying to avoid spills. Oona had her finger hooked into the waistband of his jeans. Then he paused to avoid a couple of women coming out of the hall and half-turned to protect the brimming glasses. This was the moment Suttle saw her. For a second he froze. Then, after a tiny nod of recognition, he was on his way again. Lizzie settled back, satisfied. She told herself she knew this man. She'd read the expression on his face, the fleeting grin. She was back in his life.

After the concert Oona took Suttle home. She was still living on a soulless new estate ribboned by arterial roads on the southern edge of the city. It was a reasonable rent, handy for work, and everything in the house worked, but she knew Suttle didn't like the place.

They'd bought a couple of bottles of Rioja from a Londis in the city centre, and Suttle had also splashed out on a copy of the Fureys' latest CD. They'd watched the gig from seats towards the back, immediately behind a bunch of fans seriously in love with the music. There were five of them, middle-aged, and they swayed with the lilt of the music, their arms in the air one moment, interlinked the next. They were word-perfect on the lyrics and, towards the end, when the band launched into

'Red Rose Café', they were out in the aisle, doing an impromptu jig that brought others to their feet.

Oona had joined them, tugging Suttle behind her, and Suttle took advantage of the next five minutes to scan the audience, looking for Lizzie. He finally found her, way off on the other side of the hall. She was sitting watching him, and when she knew he'd spotted her raised her hand, the briefest salute. Afterwards, with the crowd streaming away into the night, he'd looked for her again but she'd disappeared.

Now Oona was uncorking the first bottle. She'd made a salad earlier and a sauce for the pasta. Soon they'd eat. But first a little more of the Fureys. Suttle took the hint and slipped the CD into the audio stack.

'You want to dance with me? Look silly? Fool around? Fall over?' She was in the middle of the carpet, her hands outstretched.

Suttle shook his head. He was eyeing the bottle. The walking wounded deserved another drink.

'Were they that bad?'

'They were great.'

'Is it me, then?'

She was still on her feet. Suttle had opted for the tiny sofa. He looked away, not knowing what to say.

'It hurts,' he said.

'How about the leg?'

He stared up at her. Luke Golding, he thought. They've had the conversation. He's told her. Bastard.

'I don't know what you mean,' he said.

'Something's happened. I know it has. You can't fool a girl from Killarney. Ever.'

'Nothing's happened. Except I've had a couple of shit days.'

'Like the rest of us don't? Like life's a peach? Talk to me, Jimmy Suttle. Can't you even do that?'

She was on her knees now, beside the sofa. Suttle could see the bewilderment in her eyes. *Why am I doing this?* he asked himself. *How can this be happening?*

He took her hand, told her he loved her.

'Shit,' she said. 'This is worse than I thought.'

'What do you mean?'

'This isn't you at all, my lovely. Wrong script. Crap lines. What do you really want to say to me? Be honest.'

'I just told you.'

'Tell me again.'

'I love you.'

'I think you do. I've no quarrel with that. And I think you probably mean it. I love you too. But where are we? Where is this heading? What happens next?'

For the first time Suttle began to relax. Maybe he was wrong about Golding. He and Oona had been this way before. Often drink did it. She wanted more of him, all of him, a lifetime together. She wanted them to share a house, any house, maybe even this little hutch. She wanted a baby. She wanted to roll all over him. She wanted to engulf him in laughter and good sex and fine cooking, and one day she wanted to take him home to Ireland and buy an acre or two out on the west coast and let the cycle of the seasons shape the rest of their lives.

He knew all this because she'd told him – no secrets, no hidden surprises – and every time it happened he'd loved her a little more. She was wild, and guileful, and reckless as fuck. She'd been a physical turn-on from the moment they'd met, back when she was still with Golden Bollocks, and he'd known at once that she felt exactly the same way. So here they were, on a mild summer's evening, with wine on the table and the Fureys roaring away, and if he got drunk enough he knew exactly where this evening would lead.

'You want to make babies, right?' He touched her face.

She gazed at him. First surprise. Then delight. 'You mean that?'

'I do.'

'Now?' She nodded at the rug on the carpet. 'Here?'

'In a bit. When we've done the bottle.'

'Wrong, my angel. Life is precious. Seize the moment.' She reached up for him, kissed his face. '*Carpe* fucking *diem*, right?'

Twenty-Five

Suttle and Oona spent the weekend together. *Buzzard* paused for breath while Nandy and Houghton took stock. Suttle was grateful for the break. He'd given Houghton a full account of the interview with Harriet Reilly's GP, and when he and Golding returned to the MIR on Monday they'd pursue the lead they'd lifted from the IVF file. In the meantime, in Oona's favourite phrase, they were home safe.

Saturday morning they woke up late, made love again and then drifted back to sleep until midday. They shared a lazy brunch in a bar on Exeter Quay and afterwards strolled down the towpath as far as a pub beside a pair of lock gates. A real ale called Full Bore looked too good to miss. Suttle sank a couple of pints while Oona fed the swans with the remains of an abandoned baguette. When he asked her why she wasn't drinking, she simply patted her stomach.

'Last night was great,' she said. 'Babies need a fighting chance.'

Late afternoon she drove him down to Exmouth. Early rain had cleared, and the remaining wisps of cloud over the Haldon Hills promised a glorious sunset. Oona bought veggies and salad from the farm shop in the precinct while Suttle managed to corner the last sea bass on the fishmonger's slab. He had no idea about cooking fish and knew that Oona was the same but guessed they'd muddle through. Muddling through had been the essence of their relationship from the start. No plans, nothing grown-up. Simply a weather eye for the next passing opportunity and a mutual agreement that life was there for the taking.

The fish turned out to be a triumph. Oona swallowed her reservations about descaling the thing, raided the Internet for recipes, propped her iPhone on the kitchen worktop and produced a meal that Suttle knew he'd never forget. Delicate hints of fennel and chicory. Lightly boiled Cornish new potatoes. A side salad of watercress and beetroot. Plus a velvet sauce Oona dribbled artfully around the side of the plates.

'Food porn,' she said. 'How come a good Catholic girl knows tricks like these?'

How come, indeed. The meal over, Oona succumbed to the TV: a preview documentary about the forthcoming World Cup. Suttle, passionate about football, talked her through the teams he believed were in with a shout. The Spanish. The Germans. The Brazilians of course. And one of the outsiders, an African team, maybe Ghana.

They were both sprawled on the floor, backs against the sofa.

'What about you lot?'

'Us lot?'

'The Brits. The English. Wayne Thingo. Doesn't he figure?'

'Fat boy. Too rich. No incentive. Footballers used to be hungry. Winning mattered then.'

'And now?'

'Now is about money. Whatever happens you still get paid.'

She nodded. The room was warm. She'd stripped off to the thinnest of T-shirts. She wanted to know what he'd do if he wasn't a cop.

'This.' Suttle was watching a sequence featuring Lionel Messi. So far he'd beaten five defenders. The goal that followed was the merest formality.

'You're too old.' Oona was stroking the scars on his face. 'And too lovely.'

'You say.'

'I say. Come to bed with me. I'll let you score. Promise.'

They made love again, then lay entwined as they drifted off to sleep. After the turmoil of the last few days Suttle had rarely felt so happy, so secure. Oona always did it for him. She knew where he kept the key, and when it mattered she always found it. No tensions. No drama. No me-me-me. With her wit, her looks and her readiness for anything, his friends often took her for a lightweight, but they were so, so wrong. Oona, in all the important respects, was one of the wisest women he'd ever met.

Sunday morning they took the baby from upstairs for a walk along the seafront. It was a glorious day. They pushed the buggy the length of the promenade, pausing to watch the local rowing club launch one of their big quads. Oona hoisted Kasia out of the buggy and cradled her in her arms while the rowers wrestled the quad into the waves.

Years back, when Suttle had first come down from Pompey, he'd encouraged Lizzie to join this club. He'd done it because life in rural Devon, surrounded by the old and the infirm, had begun to depress her, and rowing had offered – at the very least – the promise of company her own age. Lizzie had fallen in love with the opportunity in more than one way, and their marriage had hit the rocks shortly afterwards. The sight of these boats, blood red, had haunted Suttle for years afterwards, but now they belonged to another life.

'Ever fancy it?' Oona too was looking at the boats.

'Never.' Suttle nodded towards the distant jut of Orcombe Point. 'Onwards.'

That afternoon, having returned the baby, Oona announced an attack of spring fever. Suttle's flat was a pit. It needed a good sorting. Her shout. A little prezzie for her lovely man. Suttle protested. No way was he wasting half a precious Sunday on the Hoover.

'Then we'll split it,' she said. 'I'll do the front room. You do the bedroom. Then we'll fight over the kitchen. An hour. Tops. Arse in gear, Mr Messi.'

Suttle complied with as much grace as he could muster. In truth she was right. He hadn't given the flat a proper sort-out since way before Christmas. He retired to the bedroom, opened the window, turned on the radio and set to work. After stripping the bed, he tossed the sheets into the hall and found some new ones – still in their packaging – he'd bought only recently. He left them on the bed and got to work on his knees with a dustpan and a stiff brush. Next door, over the whine of the Hoover, he could hear Oona singing. Nice.

The carpet in the bedroom was furred with little balls of fluff. Painstakingly, working slowly towards the head of the bed, he used his fingers to pick up stuff the brush had missed. Then his fingers snagged on something hard, and he found himself looking at a silver earring. It was on the side where Lizzie had slept. It was hers. He recognised the bird shape. He stared at it, his blood icing, knowing that Oona would have found it too. Nurses were meticulous. The earring would have given him away. What would he have said? How would he have explained it?

He got slowly to his feet, ever the cop, struck by another thought. What if Lizzie had left it down there on purpose? Knowing that Oona also slept in this bed? What if this was yet another move on the chessboard that had become her life? An opportunity to wreck a relationship she found deeply threatening?

He went to the open window, unaware of the door opening behind him, paused for a moment, and then tossed the earring into the void.

'What was that?' It was Oona.

Suttle stepped back and turned to face her.

'Fluff.' He held her gaze. 'Who needs it?'

Twenty-Six

By the time Suttle got to the Major Incident Room on Monday morning Luke Golding was already at his desk. Friday night, to Suttle's surprise, he'd stayed on late. A call to Sheila Forshaw at the Met Office had already confirmed that Bentner had worked at the National Centre for Atmospheric Research in Boulder, Colorado. Armed with an in-house contact she'd supplied, he'd phoned NCAR for more details, ending up with a helpful executive in Human Resources.

There was no way she was going into any kind of detail on the phone, but she confirmed that Bentner had been married to a woman called Marianne Hausner who had sadly died after several years from a form of leukaemia. Marianne had been a fellow scientist at NCAR, maybe not the most conversational person you'd ever meet but a fine climatologist. Beyond that she knew very little, and Mr Golding would be well advised to put any further questions in writing.

'And?'

'Here, skip ...' Golding passed a draft letter to Suttle. Among the issues Golding was keen to resolve was whether or not Ms Hausner had indeed donated eggs for freezing and storage.

'Her DNA would nail it, skip. But she's been dead a while.'

'Like when?'

'Fifteen years – 1999.'

Suttle handed the letter back. The information in Harriet Reilly's file had been unambiguous. The fertilised egg had come from Marianne Hausner. The fact that she turned out to be Bentner's late wife should come as no surprise.

'So what does that tell us about Reilly, skip?'

It was a good question. Reilly, according to her own GP, was on the old side for gestational surrogacy. Three attempts had failed. To persevere like that told its own story.

'She must have loved him,' Suttle said. 'It's there in the travel journals I read, and this confirms it.'

'So why didn't they have their own child?'

'No idea.' Suttle shrugged. They'd asked Reilly's GP exactly the same question but she'd refused to comment. 'I'll talk to her ex, the guy in Australia.' He glanced at his watch. 'Now would be a good time.'

He left Golding's desk and checked in with DI Houghton. She confirmed that it had been her who'd broken the news about the murder to Reilly's ex-husband. His name was Tony Velder.

'How did he take it, boss?'

'Hard to judge. He's a man of few words. He was surprised, obviously, but if you're asking me whether it hit him hard I'd have to say no. I'm not sure there was much love there.'

'How long did the marriage last?'

'Four years. Almost to the day. That's the one thing he did tell me.'

'Anything else?'

'No.'

'Is he coming across for the funeral?'

'I think not.'

'He said that?'

'More or less, yes. I said it would be good to meet him. He said he thought that was unlikely. Unless I was planning on a trip down under.'

Suttle nodded. Houghton wanted to know how Golding had got on with the people in Colorado. Suttle gave her the details about Marianne Hausner.

'The egg had to be hers, then.'

'That would be the assumption.'

'So why didn't Bentner and Reilly have a baby of their own?'

'That's exactly what we're asking.'

Houghton scribbled herself a note. Then her eyes strayed to an incoming email on her PC screen. After a while she looked up. 'Good luck with Mr Velder,' she said. 'Give him my best.'

Lizzie had spent most of the weekend trying to get in touch with Gemma Caton. Michala had given her a mobile number before they'd said goodbye on the towpath, but every time she dialled the phone was on divert. She left a number of messages, inviting Caton to get back to her, but nothing happened. Then she added that Caton's number had come from Michala and the phone rang within minutes.

It was Monday morning. Wet. Nearly ten.

'Who is this, please?' American accent. Gravelly voice. Lizzie scribbled a note: '*Butch or what?*'

Lizzie introduced herself. She was a published author and a freelance journalist. She was lucky enough to be running a well-resourced website of her own and she had a lifetime passion for issues around global warming. Thanks to the presence of the Met Office and the Hadley Centre, Exeter was fast becoming a magnet for people wanting to make a difference in this field. Ms Caton's reputation spoke for itself. Might she be interested in an interview?

'How did you find little Michala?'

'Through a contact.'

'That wasn't my question. How did you *find* her? As in how was she to you?'

'Very pleasant.' Lizzie at last understood the thrust of this conversation. 'In fact extremely helpful.'

'How?'

'All sorts of ways. Some of the science in this area is tough. At least to me. She—'

'Where do you live?'

'Here. In Exeter.'

'You want to meet this morning? I can do that. I have a window. Is 11.20 good for you?'

Tony Velder was slow in answering the phone. Suttle eased his chair back from his desk, hoping the man was in. This was a landline number in Melbourne. According to Suttle's calculations, it would be mid-evening in Oz.

Finally the call connected. A man's voice, sounding older than Suttle had expected and slightly out of breath. Scottish accent.

Suttle introduced himself. Was he talking to Tony Velder?

'You are. I thought I'd finished with you people.'

'Sadly not, Mr Velder. My sympathies over the loss of Harriet. It can't have been easy.'

'Nothing's easy. You'd be a fool to think otherwise. How can I help you?'

Suttle explained about the baby Harriet had been carrying. Evidently this news hadn't featured in his exchange with DI Houghton.

'You're telling me she was pregnant?'

'Yes.'

'How? She hated sex. Wouldn't entertain it.'

Suttle pulled himself into the desk and reached for his pad. This, he sensed, might be the beginnings of a breakthrough. For a man of few words, Velder was remarkably upfront.

'You didn't ...? She didn't ...?' Suttle was waiting for Velder to fill in the gaps.

'Not once. Never. A gentleman waits. You put it down to their upbringing or their religion, or any of that tosh. First-class mind. Shame about the rest of her.'

The sound of laughter struck Suttle as odd. Then came a pause and a slurp. Suttle could picture the wine bottle at his side. *The man's pissed*, he thought. How lucky am I?

'You never had sex? As husband and wife?'

'Never. I'm starting to repeat myself, laddie. Maybe you should take notes. S-E-X. Very definitely off the menu.'

'That must have been difficult.'

'So-so. I was in the navy. You spend a lot of time banged up aboard. There are ways and means, Mr Simple.'

'Suttle.'

'Mr Suttle. You know what I used to say to my chums after a week or two back home? Life with my darling wife was just like the navy without the travel and the views. Better food too, once you got afloat again.'

'Meaning what?'

'Thin pickings back on the ranch. We were living in Portsmouth, if that means anything to you. Not a pretty place, to be frank, and not a lot of compensations once you've closed the front door. Gruel and hard tack, Mr Suttle. With Harriet I learned to keep my hands to myself.'

'She didn't want a baby?'

'She didn't want my baby. In fact she didn't want my anything. A chap can take that personally. And you know what? I did.'

After three and a half years at sea, he said, he came home for good. This time there was no escape. What was left of the marriage lasted three and a half months.

'You were counting?'

'Every bloody day. My fault, I'm sure. One hint that I had a todger, and that was it. Early night. Lights out. Sleep well.'

'Was she a doctor at this point? A practising GP?'

'Very much so. That made it worse. She must have seen more of her male patients than she ever saw of me.'

'And now?'

'Now? I'm a lonely old bastard living on a decent pension and drinking far too much. Every man has a best friend, and mine comes out of the Barossa Valley. Treat yourself to a bottle of the 2004 Kaesler Shiraz. It's worth staying alive for.'

'That's good to know, Mr Velder.'

'You're right, Mr Suttle. And it's Commander Velder if you're ever down this way. Goodnight.' He laughed again. 'And God bless, eh?'

The line went dead. Suttle stared at the phone, shaking his head, aware of Golding at his elbow.

'Well, skip?'

'Bonkers. Out of his tree. No wonder she wouldn't let him fuck her.'

Gemma Caton arrived a minute early. Lizzie was standing in the window of her living room, watching her struggle out of her car. She was a big woman, verging on huge, and she seemed to do everything by instalments.

Lizzie had the coffee on. She went through to the hall. Caton was making her way along the line of broken paving stones through the ankle-high grass that served as a path to the front door.

She didn't bother with a formal greeting.

'Hellava place you've got here.' She gestured up at the building. 'Lots of potential.'

Lizzie extended a hand. Apologised for the mess. Work in progress, she said. Fire risk, according to a surveyor friend. Caton ignored her. She wanted to get out of the rain. She loved England but couldn't abide the weather. She clumped into the hall and shook herself like a dog. Lizzie wondered whether to switch on the central heating but decided against it. This woman would probably steam, like some giant Labrador.

'You mind?' Caton gestured at her boots. Lizzie, thinking she was about to take them off, nodded. Caton shed her anorak instead, handing it across.

'Which room?'

'The one with the open door. Would you like coffee?'

No reply. Lizzie watched her ignore the open door, disappearing instead into the chaos of the kitchen. This too met with her full approval. 'You live like a tramp. We like that.'

'We?'

'Me. I like that. God made tidiness for the also-rans. Sure sign of a second-rate mind. You ever find that?'

She was gazing around. She spotted a door in the far wall, bolted top and bottom.

'What's that?'

Lizzie explained it went through to next door. The adjoining house was empty at the moment, after the death of the old lady who'd had the place for years.

'You been through? Had a look-see?'

'Of course.'

'And?'

'It's a mess. Just like this place.'

'Wonderful. Better and better.' She had a final look in a couple of cupboards and then strode through to the living room.

Minutes later Lizzie followed her with a tray of coffee and a plate heaped with biscuits. Caton had spread herself on the sofa. She managed the coffee cup with surprising delicacy. Thick fingers, heavy rings but a deftness of touch. Muddy footprints tracked across the scatter of rugs from the kitchen door.

'Is Michala back from Copenhagen?' Lizzie asked.

'She will be. Mid-afternoon. You're in luck. She likes you. Otherwise I'd never be here.'

'She's your secretary?'

'My buddy. And my colleague. In our neck of the woods the buzzword is collaboration. If you're lucky you get to build a critical mass. That makes life easier, believe you me.'

'Safety in numbers?'

'Hell, no. *Excitement* in numbers. *Momentum* in numbers. Safety's for the birds. No one got anywhere by thinking safety.'

'And Alois Bentner? He's part of this thing? This critical mass?'

'Alois? Who said anything about Alois?' She was slumped on the sofa now, a mountain of a woman, but her eyes were ablaze. Lizzie seemed to have touched a nerve.

'I got the name from Michala.' It was an easy lie. 'She said you two were close. She told me you were next door neighbours.'

'Were?'

'I understand he's gone missing.'

'Sure. And on his own terms. Like always.'

'Some people think he's dead.'

'*Dead?* Alois? Not true.'

193

'You know that?'

'Of course I know that.'

'How?'

She wouldn't answer. Instead she asked Lizzie whether she was familiar with her work.

Lizzie nodded. A couple of hours on the Internet over the weekend had taken her deep into this woman's academic career.

'*Native Indian Rituals on the Pacific Coast*,' she said. 'And your book was shortlisted for the Ralph Waldo Emerson Award.'

'That's right. Proudest day of my life. I never made it to the prize itself but I was in the best of company. Get that far and important doors start to open.' She brushed crumbs from the shelf of her bosom. 'You get to read the book at all?'

'It's on order. Amazon.'

'Good girl. Bring it along and I'll sign it for you.'

'Along where?'

'My place. Lympstone.' For the first time she smiled. The smile transformed her face. She looked suddenly feminine, a far less aggressive woman struggling to get out.

Lizzie asked for an address. Now wasn't the moment to admit that she knew it already.

Caton plunged a fat hand into her bag. She sorted through a clutch of cards, then handed one over.

'I thought Michala would have made contact,' she said. 'The invitation's for 7.30. Bring a bottle. Just the three of us. Stay over if you want. I'm cooking.' She reached for the last of the biscuits. 'Salmon OK with you?'

Houghton convened a meet in her office. Nandy had arrived from Barnstaple. To his immense satisfaction, his team had just drawn a cough from the two Romanians. They'd encountered the elderly couple while pulling early spuds in the field behind their bungalow. They'd clocked the new Volvo and the paid gardener and concluded there was money to be made. They'd broken in at night, hauled the couple from their beds and demanded everything they had. The old boy's big mistake was keeping his money in the bank. When he told them he couldn't remember his PIN number, they battered him to death. His wife was killed for watching.

'Lovely.'

Houghton's sarcasm was wasted on Nandy. He beamed at Suttle, at Golding.

'Full confession.' He looked at his watch. 'Forty-seven hours from start to finish. Textbook. A classic.'

The contrast with *Buzzard* was all too obvious. Nandy wanted to know the latest.

Houghton summarised what few leads they had. The SOC team had finished with the property in Exmouth. They'd also boshed Tania's car, just in case. Both scenes had yielded nothing except ample evidence of two lives in chaos. Russell, she said, was about to embark on another eight-week posting to the Gulf. How he managed to pull contracts like these was beyond her.

'Look on the bright side, boss.' This from Golding. 'He probably frightens the pirates to death.'

'So where's Mr Bentner?' Nandy wasn't amused.

Houghton said she hadn't a clue. Short of turning the country upside down and giving it a good shake, she'd run out of options. Media interest in the story was fast disappearing, and Bentner's details had been distributed nationwide to no obvious effect. Her working assumption was that he'd either reappear at a time of his own choosing or make a silly mistake. The latter was a tempting proposition, but the longer this thing went on the unlikelier it seemed. This guy was a pro. He knew how to hide. He was world class at going to ground.

'He kipped on the cliff top with a bunch of drunks,' Nandy pointed out. 'How world class was that?'

'With respect, sir, that tells us a great deal.' This from Suttle.

'You still think he's innocent?'

'I still think he didn't know she was dead. Not on the Saturday night. Not when he was in Exmouth. You're right. That would have been an insane thing to do.'

'So maybe that's it. Maybe you've nailed it.'

'He's insane?'

'Yeah. Or dead. That's another option. The guy phones the woman from the Met Office. He heads on west. He has to dump his car. He's run out of options and he knows it. Even buying booze is off limits. Food. The lot. He's depressed because he's a drunk. He's out of his tree because the world is disappearing up its own arse. Plus he's just killed the one human being who seems to matter to him and cut the baby's head off. Cornwall's full of mineshafts. You can't move for them. He'd know that. He'd take his pick. Shut your eyes. Step into the darkness. Gravity does the rest. Easy.' He looked round, hands outstretched. 'Am I wrong?'

It was Houghton who broke the silence. She sounded weary.

'So what do you suggest, sir? We search every mineshaft west of the Tamar? Or we wait for something to happen? Or we call it a day?'

'For the time being we wait,' he said. 'I was going to reassign the officers I nicked for the Barnstaple job, but if there's nothing to action I can use them elsewhere. It's Monday. We'll give it until the end of the week. We need leads. Are you really telling me there's *nothing*?'

Suttle raised a hand. He told Nandy about Gemma Caton.

'This is the next-door neighbour, sir.'

'I understood she was in London.'

'That's right. She's alibied herself. But we still need to check it out.'

He explained about her friend with the flat in Streatham Hill. He'd put in two more calls today but still no response.

'Has the flat been checked?'

'A Met guy went round at the weekend.'

'And?'

'No answer. He checked with a neighbour, and the woman turns out to be Danish. He thought she might have gone to Copenhagen for a bit.'

'Handy.'

'Exactly.'

Houghton had had enough. She had files to go through from her last job and a meeting with one of the ACCs about the state of her overtime budget. After that she was thinking about a canter across Dartmoor followed by a couple of hours in a spa hotel.

Her gaze went from face to face.

'That's a joke, guys, in case anyone's wondering.'

Twenty-Seven

Lizzie went to the convenience store in Lympstone for her bottle of wine. Dallying between a Chilean Merlot and a decent bottle of white, she remembered that salmon was on the menu and settled for the Chablis. Still too early to knock on Gemma Caton's door, she wandered through the village until she found a bench that overlooked the water.

At half-tide the exposed mud that fringed the tiny bay was gleaming as the sun sank towards the low swell of the hills beyond the water. The flags in Gemma Caton's back garden had disappeared, but dinghies from the sailing club were queuing on the slip, readying for launch, and an orange safety tender was already busying around offshore. Junior night, she thought, watching a couple of kids pushing the first of the dinghies into the water. One of the girls sank calf-deep in mud, and the laughter of her mates carried in the wind. How come a village this tight, this intimate, had managed to breed an act of such savagery? And how come dozens of detectives still had no clue where to look for the culprit?

She sat back, the sun full on her face. It was still warm, and she thought about treating herself to a glass of wine from the nearby pub before knocking on Gemma Caton's door but decided against it. The next few hours, she told herself, might put her ahead of Jimmy's precious investigation. Already, to her surprise, she seemed to have established that *Buzzard*'s prime suspect was alive and well. That much had been implicit in Caton's silence about his whereabouts. She knew, Lizzie thought, and more important still, she seemed happy to have Lizzie – a total stranger – share that knowledge. Whether Lizzie believed this woman was another matter, but she sensed that there might be a great deal more to come, precious leads she could use to her own advantage when it came to her next encounter with her estranged husband.

She thought of him now, tussling with this latest development in his love life. She hadn't a moment's doubt that she could bed him again. What she'd become over the last year or so excited him. She'd seen it in his eyes, in the urgency of his love-making. He wanted to get to know her all over again. He wanted to check her out, to convince himself that she – that they – were for real. And afterwards? Once he'd found some kind of answer to his questions? What then? She didn't know, and for once she didn't care. Success, she realised, had brought not just money and profile but a sense of independence she could practically taste. She belonged to no one, and that realisation was the biggest turn-on of all.

It was Michala who opened the door of Caton's house. She leaned forward and kissed Lizzie on the lips before leading her inside. The house was bigger than it looked from the street. Lizzie could see Caton bent over the stove in the galley kitchen, mopping her face with a tea towel. She was wearing an apron over a pair of baggy jeans, and when she turned towards the open door Lizzie saw the figure of a leaping fish thrusting upwards over her huge chest. A salmon? Lizzie had no idea.

'Welcome.' Caton was chewing gum. 'Fix the lady a drink.'

The smells were delicious. Fennel. Mint. Rosemary. Michala took Lizzie through to the living room. French doors at the far end were open, and beyond the scruffiness of the garden Lizzie could see the kids in their dinghies out on the water. They were racing now, jockeying for space as they rounded a buoy, and Lizzie watched as one teetered on the edge of a capsize.

'You want wine? A beer? Something else?' It was Michala.

Lizzie settled for a glass of wine. The room – bare boards,

antique furniture – might have belonged in an art gallery. There were artefacts everywhere – spears, a shield, a crude-looking net and a hand-carved face in a wood that might have been mahogany. The walls of the room had been painted a soft sea-green, and there wasn't a space that wasn't occupied by photographs. These were old prints, many of them sepia, and Lizzie moved from image to image.

This must be Gemma's book come to life, she told herself: carefully posed snapshots of Indian life out on the Pacific coast. In one photo two naked children were struggling with a dead-looking fish. In another a family group was standing in front of a huge drying rack. The rack was the size of a house, the timber framework hung with the splayed carcasses of yet more fish. There must have been hundreds of them.

'You like the pictures?' Michala was back with the wine.

'Very much.' Lizzie's eye had gone to a third shot, high up on the wall. A biggish group of Indians, all men, was gathered round a circular booth made of wooden poles. A couple of the men were carrying what looked like spears, and there were more of these weapons inside the booth.

'You know about this stuff?' Lizzie hadn't heard Caton coming in from the kitchen. For a big woman she moved with surprising lightness. She stood beside Michala, wiping her hands on the apron.

'Tell me.' Lizzie turned back to the picture.

'Those poles must be taken from the highest mountain. And you know why? Because otherwise the salmon will see them. Something else too. Every year you have to use new poles. Else the old salmon will tell the young salmon about them.'

'This is way back?'

'Nineteenth century. These are Californian Indians from the Karuk tribe. See here?' Her finger stabbed at another picture lower down, three children struggling to carry a huge fish up the beach. 'This is the first salmon of the run. The elders say prayers before the flesh is cut. That way the tribe honours the fish. And afterwards? You know what happens afterwards? You protect the bones. You make sure they never touch the ground. And then they go back to the river or maybe the sea. That way you keep the spirits sweet. And – hey – the bones come back next year inside a new fish.'

Lizzie nodded, returning to the booth that held the spears. 'You're telling me these fish are sacred?'

'Always. You're looking at the gods of the river. They have souls. They alone decide whether to return or not. You're looking at a big slug of marine protein, sure, but you're also looking at the power of life and death. If the salmon don't show, then the tribe starves. Honour the fish. Propitiate the spirits. Otherwise, no kidding, you die.'

'And is this why you've chosen to live here? Beside a river?'

'Sure. But you know the irony?'

'Tell me.'

'I can't swim. Not that it matters. The river's in here.' One hand half-covered an enormous breast. 'That's the way the Indians figured it too. Live life right, and you *are* the river. That's where it starts and that's where it all ends.'

Lizzie nodded. It seemed a simple proposition. One thing though.

'There are salmon out there?' She nodded towards the window. 'In the river?'

Caton's smile split her face. She was looking at Michala.

'Great question,' she said. 'I guess we ought to eat.'

Michala laid the table beneath the wall of photos. Lizzie fetched more wine from the fridge in the kitchen. When the food was ready, Caton beckoned Michala out of the room. They returned with a big wooden platter. Steam curled from the fish on top. The salmon, resting on a bed of samphire, was huge. Caton laid the dish in the middle of the table then, with a glance at the view beyond the French doors, aligned it carefully towards the river before gesturing Lizzie to her feet.

'Face the water,' she whispered.

'Why?'

'Just do it.'

'For the spirits?'

'Sure. And for each other. Gimme your hand.'

She stood in the middle, flanked by Lizzie and Michala. To Lizzie the palm of Caton's hand felt warm and fleshy.

'You close your eyes, right?'

Lizzie nodded, cheated, peeped through the tiny crack between her eyelids. Caton was intoning something in a language Lizzie didn't understand. It sounded like a prayer, the same phrase repeated and repeated. She was swaying now, her body rocking back and forth, her hand urging Lizzie to do the same. Then, without warning, it was over.

'The spirits have spoken.' She nodded at the table. 'Sit.'

Lizzie did as she was told. Caton was still on her feet, bent over the fish, cutting a thin line down the backbone, parting the pinkness of the flesh. Another glimpse of a delicacy, a deftness, Lizzie hadn't expected.

'Plate?'

Lizzie got the first slice of the fish. Michala helped her to potatoes, French beans, and a crisp green salad. In a restaurant, thought Lizzie, this meal would have been a credit to any chef. Gemma Caton certainly knew how to cook.

'You know the thing about the salmon?' Caton had at last sat down. 'It's energy incarnate. We eat the salmon and the energy passes to us. It's like a spirit. It's immortal. It goes on and on, different shapes, different forms.'

'That's what these people thought?' Lizzie gestured at the photos on the wall.

'Sure. And it's what we happen to think too.'

'We?'

'Me. And Michala here.'

'And Alois?'

'Sure, Alois is a believer. The Indians had it right. They knew the salmon. They respected the salmon. They worshipped the salmon. It gave them everything they needed. Fresh food in the summer. Cured food the rest of the year. Clothing from the skins. Look at the kids up there. Skinny, sure. But never undernourished.'

Lizzie was beginning to wonder what any of this had to do with global warming. She put the question to Michala, who glanced first at Caton before answering. She needs permission to speak, thought Lizzie. This woman dominates everything.

'The salmon made the coastal Indians their own people,' she said. 'Like Gemma says, they didn't need anyone else. As long as the salmon returned, they had no need to trade or look elsewhere for a living. That's why it was so important that the salmon always came back.'

'But aren't they programmed that way? Isn't it a genetic thing?'

'That's what we think.' Caton this time. 'And I guess that's where the trouble starts. Science has its blessings, but the truth is we've lost touch with everything that matters.'

'We're still talking salmon?'

'Sure we are. It's a respect thing. It's knowing your place in the world. We think the world revolves around us. Which is one of the reasons we're about to destroy it.'

Caton nodded up at the photos again. The hearts of the first salmon were kept and cherished by the tribe, she said. And if a spear fisherman killed two salmon with a single thrust he was forbidden to celebrate in case the salmon already hanging on the drying racks climbed down and returned to the sea.

'Respect,' she said. 'It's about respect. In the developed world we've lost that. And once it's gone, all that's left is what we take from nature. Take, take, take. The spirits have a loaded gun to our heads. And you know what? We're so dumb we can't even feel it. In fact we don't even know it's there. I guess that's the sadness. Disaster stares us in the face and we're looking the other way.'

Lizzie wanted to know more about the salmon she was eating. Where did it come from?

'The Fraser River. I had it shipped over last year. Been on ice ever since.'

'So this is some kind of special occasion?'

'Sure.'

'Why?'

Gemma and Michala swapped glances. Unbidden, Michala left the room. When she came back, she was carrying a tray with three glasses. Beside the glasses was a jug.

'We toast the salmon,' said Gemma. 'Just the way they used to.'

Michala was filling the glasses from the jug. The liquid was cloudy, a lightish green in colour.

'What is it?'

'Salmon broth and aquavit. Herbs too. This year the salmon are late. But show a little respect and they'll definitely make it back.'

Michala handed the glasses around. To Lizzie's surprise they were warm. Gemma was on her feet again, her glass held high, gesturing for Lizzie to get up. Then came that same prayer, her body swaying back and forth. Through the open French windows Lizzie could no longer hear the kids out on the river. The race is over, she thought. They've gone.

'Drink.' It was an order.

Lizzie put the glass to her lips, tipped it slowly, let the warmth trickle down her throat. It wasn't unpleasant. On the contrary, she could taste the fish, the spikes of fennel and rosemary. Then came the hit of the aquavit. She blinked, feeling her balance go, reaching for the edge of the table.

The glass empty, she sat down again, aware of the two women watching her. She had more questions about the salmon, about the research this woman must have done out among the old Indian sites, about the lessons these ancient societies could still teach us and most of all about Alois Bentner. Did he too eat a salmon? Intone the prayer? Raise his glass to the watching spirits? She gestured at the fish, aware of Gemma's eyes locked on hers.

'Why so many questions, my child?' Caton asked. 'And why Alois?'

'I'm just curious.'

'Sure. But curiosity always has a purpose, right? That's all we need here, just a clue. Alois is a neighbour of mine, and a friend, a colleague, a fellow traveller I deeply respect. It happens he's not here right now, but that's another conversation.'

Lizzie nodded. The aquavit had made her braver.

'Fellow soul?' she asked. 'Would that be closer?'

'For sure. You meet people in life, and the spark is there, the *connection*. No obvious reason. No rationale. It just happens because the spirits choose it to be that way. No one interferes with the spirits. Not if they want to make any kind of life for themselves.'

'And Alois?'

'We were close from the start. The spirits brought us together, and we were both aware of that. Never argue. Never question. Simply accept.'

'And rejoice?'

'Of course.'

'Still?'

'Always.' Lizzie was aware of Michala with the jug at her elbow. Another shot of aquavit.

'You like my Michala?' The gleam was back in Gemma's eyes.

'I hardly know her.'

'That's not the issue. You're in tune with each other. I can sense it. This is a spirit thing. Relax. Listen to what's happening inside. Same question, I guess. You like Michala? She speaks to you?'

Lizzie swallowed hard. She realised this conversation came with strings.

'I don't know what you mean,' she said.

'But you do, my child, you do. That's the whole point. That's where we've arrived. That's where we are. Trust yourself. Listen. Sense. *Become who you really are.*'

'You're asking me whether I want Michala? Is that the question?'

'I'm asking you whether she speaks to you. Look at her. Has

she become part of my life? The answer's yes. Might we find a place for you? Here and now? This evening? I guess we might. Except it needs an act of surrender. From all three of us.'

Lizzie was losing her bearings. This conversation was beginning to frighten her. Back in the car beside the towpath, when they'd first met, she'd detected Michala's interest. If playing along bought her the rest of the evening in Gemma Caton's company then she might unlock some more clues that Jimmy had so far missed. But she was fast recognising that there were limits. Did this investigation of hers justify sleeping with Michala? No way. Tread carefully, she told herself. So far and no further.

'Tell me about prayer flags.' Lizzie was looking at Caton.

'Why?'

'Because they interest me.'

'Why?'

'Because Michala mentioned them. And you're right about the spark, about the surrender.' Lizzie threw Michala a look. 'Nice tattoo as well. Beautiful. Intriguing.' She warmed the compliment with a smile, but Michala turned her head away. For reasons Lizzie didn't understand, the spell had been broken.

Gemma was suddenly busy with the slice. 'You want more salmon?'

'I'd like to use the loo.'

'Upstairs, my child. End of the corridor.'

Lizzie left the room, closing the door behind her. She hesitated a moment, aware of the murmur of conversation behind her, then she headed for the stairs. On the top floor there were three doors off the tiny landing. The first opened on to a bedroom. The river lay beyond the window, and the scatter of oversize clothes told Lizzie the room belonged to Gemma.

Next along was a much smaller room. Lizzie pushed open the door. The curtains were half-closed, and the setting sun threw a rich yellow stripe across the unmade bed. Beside the bed, propped on a table, was a photograph, its aluminium frame gleaming in the golden light. Lizzie stepped in for a closer look. A woman in her thirties was posing on a beach. She was wearing a wetsuit and some kind of harness. A couple of surfing kites lay on the beach behind her, but what drew Lizzie's eye back to her face was the woman's lips. She was blowing the camera a kiss. And she was grinning.

Lizzie had her mobile. She took two shots of the photo before slipping the phone into the pocket of her jeans and turning back towards the door. She hadn't heard Caton come upstairs. She stood in the corridor, a strange smile on her face, and beckoned Lizzie closer. When Lizzie didn't move, she stepped into the room. She was very close now, her sheer bulk masking the open door. She nodded towards the unmade bed.

'You wanna piece of my little girl? No problem. We can fix that. All of us. That OK with you?'

Lizzie didn't move. She knew she was trapped. She could smell the aquavit on Caton's breath, and she felt a sense of overpowering menace. Caton repeated the invitation, her huge hands reaching to cup Lizzie's face. Lizzie shuddered under her touch. Caton frowned, took a tiny step back and jerked her head towards the corridor.

'You found the closet OK?'

'No problem.'

'So what did you think of my soapstone carvings?'

'Great.' Lizzie tried to ease around her. 'Really interesting.'

'You mean that?' Caton's eyes were huge behind her glasses. The aquavit again. Stronger than ever.

'I do.' Lizzie finally managed to squeeze past. 'Would it be rude to tell you I've just been sick?'

Suttle was eating alone in the flat on the Beacon when he took the call. Lizzie sounded like a stranger. She'd never scared easily, but he could sense the fear in her voice. Something had happened. She needed his help. Like now.

'Where are you?'

'Lympstone.'

'Why?'

'I've just been to see Gemma Caton.'

'*Caton?*'

'Yes. Just come, my love. I'm in the Swan. Just be here for me.'

The phone went dead. Suttle abandoned his pasta and clattered down the stairs. Lympstone was ten minutes away. He did it in five.

The Swan lay at the heart of the village, a pub popular with locals and visitors alike. Tonight it was packed. Suttle spotted Lizzie as soon as he walked in. The moment she saw him she got to her feet.

'Give me a hug,' she said. 'Get me out of this place.'

'The pub?'

'Lympstone.'

He took her back to his car. Only when they were inside with the doors locked did she tell him what had happened. Caton was a bull dyke and God knows what else. She gave houseroom to a waif of a girl she seemed to view as some kind of possession. Half an hour ago Lizzie had been in danger of joining this weird ménage.

'She came on to you?'

'Big time. She's full of shit. Loads of stuff about the spirits and the fucking salmon, but what it boils down to is control. She knows what she wants and she gets it. Poor bloody woman.'

'Caton?' Suttle was confused.

'Michala. Her bitch.' Lizzie was crying now, her head buried in Suttle's chest.

Suttle said nothing, holding her tight. Part of him wanted to find out a great deal more. The rest of him knew this wasn't the time or the place.

'You came by car?' he said at last.

'I did, but I'm pissed, my love, so just take me home, yeah?'

They drove back to Exeter. In the gathering darkness Lizzie dropped her keys in the tangle of weeds beside the doorstep. Suttle retrieved them.

'You want me to come in?'

'I do.'

Suttle made her coffee, ran a bath, found a bottle of Radox, then perched himself beside the basin as she sank beneath the bubbles. He waited until she surfaced again and handed her a flannel.

'I need to know what you were doing there,' he said. 'At Caton's place.'

'Why?'

'Because she's a person of interest to us. And I'm guessing that's why you went.'

She eyed him for a moment. Then nodded. 'You guess right. Does that make me an honorary cop? Or just a nuisance?'

'Neither. What did she have to say about Bentner?'

'They're soul mates. He's someone else she needs to own. Sole rights? Soul rites? Fuck knows. I'm being kind, Jimmy. Weird doesn't do her justice.'

'Are they in touch?'

'That's the impression she wanted to give me.'

Suttle held her gaze.

'And you?' he said finally. 'Where are you in all this? Why the cop thing?'

'You don't think I'm being helpful?'

'I think you're putting lots on the line. I think you're taking risks you shouldn't. I also know you're giving me a great deal of grief.'

'Professionally?'

'Sure. And in other ways.'

'Meaning Oona?'

'Of course. Straight question. Do you mind?'

'Not at all.'

'Why did you come to the concert the other night? Since when did you ever like Irish folk music?'

Lizzie gave the question some thought. Then she splashed her face and shrugged. 'I needed to see her,' she said softly. 'I couldn't help myself, and that's the truth.'

'And what did you think?'

'I thought she was beautiful. I can see exactly what she's done to you.'

'And?'

'It made me jealous.'

'Why?' Jimmy was sitting on the edge of the bath now. 'Should I be flattered? Frightened? Or what?'

'I don't know. And that's the truth again.'

'But is that why you're getting involved with all this shit? Harriet Reilly? Gemma Caton? Are you trying to prove something? That you're maybe better at digging out all this stuff than we are?'

Another silence. Then Lizzie nodded. 'Yeah. That comes close.'

'But why? Just tell me that. Just give me a clue.'

Lizzie looked at him for a long moment. Then she stood up, the water sluicing down her body, and put her arms round him.

'Maybe I still need you.' She tried to smile. 'Is that a bad thing to say?'

Suttle didn't reply. With a tenderness that took him by surprise, he shepherded her into bed and – at her request – made a brief tour of the house, making sure all the windows were secured. Returning to the bedroom, he bent to her face on the pillow and gave her a kiss. She had his mobile number. Should anything happen, all she had to do was bell him.

'I'm not ill,' she said. 'And I'm not a child.'

'I know. But you've had a shock.'

'That's what my mother would have said.'

Suttle smiled. He still had the wet imprint of her body on his shirt. Lizzie was looking at the window. 'She knows where I live,' she said.

'Who?'

'Gemma Caton. She was here yesterday. You think she'll come looking for me?'

'Why would she do that?'

'I don't know. But I think she's crazy enough to do anything.'

Suttle gazed down at her. The hot bath had brought colour to her face. She'd always been someone who rationed the truth, he thought. Someone who carefully parcelled out bits of the story, leaving the best until last. Maybe it was a journalist thing. Cops did it too.

'What haven't you told me?'

She smiled up at him, amusement in her eyes, and he caught a brief glimpse of the stranger who'd so recently taken him to bed. Then she looked towards the door.

'On your way, Mr Policeman,' she said. 'I'll try not to bother you again.'

Twenty-Eight

DI Houghton was already at her desk when Suttle got to the Major Incident Room next morning. To his surprise, he'd slept well. Time to come clean, he'd told himself, drifting off to sleep.

'Your wife is the source, is that what you're telling me?' Houghton had the Dean Russell file open on her desk.

'Yes, boss. She told me about Russell, about Frances Bevan, and now it turns out she's in the shit with Gemma Caton.' He described what had happened last night.

'You're telling me Caton's been in touch with Bentner?' Houghton asked.

'Yes. Lizzie can't prove it, but that's the impression she got.'

'Anything else?'

'Not really. Except the woman wanted to get into her knickers.'

'So why did she go in the first place? And why is she bothering with all this?' Her hand settled briefly on the Dean Russell file.

'She's a journalist, boss. She asks questions for a living. It becomes a habit.'

'But why didn't you tell us earlier?'

Suttle had anticipated the question. He said he didn't know. He admitted it had been a mistake and offered an apology, but said that all this stuff was far too close to home, part of a different agenda.

'Whose?'

'Hers. Lizzie's.'

'What does she want?'

'Me, boss. I think.'

'Are you sure?'

'No, but these things form a pattern. Maybe things aren't working out in her life. Maybe she wants to turn the clock back, have another go.'

Houghton was eyeing him carefully. Suttle had rarely met such a shrewd detective. She could tease the truth from the merest scatter of clues. He felt deeply uncomfortable.

'You're still with Oona?'

'Yes, boss.'

'Happy?'

'Very.'

'Then I suggest you sort the situation out. I liked her when we met. Sane woman. Don't fuck her around. Does that sound reasonable?'

'Yes.'

'Good. Because we've found our Mr Bentner.' The smile was glacial. 'Or rather, he's found us.'

She said that Alois Bentner was currently occupying Room 115 at the Exeter Arms across the road from police headquarters. He'd booked in late last night under his own name and phoned first thing to offer his services. Just now he was being babysat by a uniformed PC. The last Houghton had heard, he'd declined breakfast and was reading a paperback called *The First Circle*.

'We're looking for a full account, Jimmy.' She could hear Nandy out in the corridor. 'Yours, I think. Take the bloody man to Heavitree.'

The news that *Buzzard*'s elusive prime suspect had chosen to break cover galvanised the MIR. Detectives sat at their desks, their PCs abandoned, trading thoughts about his motivation. The younger ones thought he had balls. Evading capture for more than a week when your face was all over the media was itself close to impossible. To then make your way back to a hotel a stone's throw from police headquarters – still incognito – was deeply cool. It spoke not of surrender but of something else, something closer to a taunt. The guy had outmanoeuvred them. He'd been streets ahead from the start. And now he was taking the piss. Older heads in the room weren't so sure. Maybe he was simply knackered. Maybe his time on the run had brought him to the point of confession. Maybe this – at last – was endgame.

Suttle wanted no part of this debate. He read carefully through the notes from the Scenes of Crime team responsible for boshing Bentner's house, reminding himself of how little forensic evidence they had to go on. There was nothing that directly tied the man in Room 115 to the butchered body in his bedroom. As ever, it would be a question of the timeline and the painstaking assembly of every particle of evidence gathered to date. That, plus whatever leverage he could conjure from establishing the right relationship. Everything he'd learned about Alois Bentner put this man a little further out of reach. Bridging that gap wouldn't be easy.

He phoned the Custody Sergeant at Heavitree police station and briefed him on the situation. The news that Bentner had kipped across the road from police headquarters drew a soft chuckle.

'Serious player, eh? Can't wait to meet the gentleman.'

Bentner had yet to be formally arrested. Suttle would only do that after he'd conferred with Houghton and Nandy. The later they left the arrest, the more time they'd give themselves in the interview room. No way was Bentner leaving the hotel until *Buzzard* was ready.

Twenty-Nine

Lizzie had been awake since dawn. Since the moment she moved in, The Plantation had been her sanctuary, the key to a new door in her life. Now it felt like a prison cell. Gemma Caton, Lizzie thought, wasn't a woman who left business unfinished. She knew where Lizzie lived. By now she may have sussed that this nosy journalist had more than a passing interest in Alois Bentner. And so, sooner rather than later, she'd come calling. Before that happened, Lizzie told herself, she had – somehow – to snatch another little piece of Operation *Buzzard* and bring this story to an end.

Downstairs in the kitchen Lizzie studied the photo she'd taken in Michala's bedroom last night. All she knew for sure was that the woman in the wetsuit must have played a part in Michala's life. Maybe they had been lovers. Maybe this hunky kitesurfer was yet another courtier in Gemma Caton's waterside ménage, a splash of rich colour after the pale delights of her Danish waif. Either way, Lizzie had to find out more. She recognised Exmouth beach from her days in the rowing club. The moment the wind blew, the place was thick with kitesurfers. She'd go down there later, make an enquiry or two, see if the face on her mobile drew a nod of recognition.

In the meantime she needed to know a lot more about Gemma Caton. She fetched her laptop from the living room and settled down again at the kitchen table. A couple of keystrokes took her to Amazon. She typed 'Native Indian Rituals on the Pacific

Coast' into the search box. The book was only available from a single supplier in Seattle, and even express international delivery would take three days. She frowned, moving the cursor across the screen. By then, she thought, I may have found the mystery kitesurfer. The cursor settled on Buy.

Done.

Jimmy Suttle drove Alois Bentner to Heavitree police station. To Suttle's surprise, the pavement outside the nick was swarming with media, TV crews as well as photographers. Bentner was a big man, sturdy, with a tumble of greying curls that lapped the collar of his shirt. He wore glasses and a full beard. According to the PC at the hotel, he'd already admitted to sleeping rough, but eight days of life in the wild appeared to have done him no harm at all. On the contrary, for an alleged recluse he appeared to be getting a kick out of all the attention. As he pushed through the scrum of bodies, a shout came from a reporter at the back.

'Did you kill her, Mr Bentner?'

The bluntness of the question stopped him in his tracks. He turned towards the reporter and looked him in the eye. He was taking his time. From where Suttle was standing, he seemed to appreciate that his answer would be all over the rolling news channels within minutes.

'There are life and death issues here we ought to be discussing,' he growled. 'Whether I killed my partner isn't one of them.'

The crowd parted. Suttle shepherded Bentner through the doors of the police station, and led him through to the Custody Suite. This time, arrested on suspicion of murder, he had nothing to say.

Lizzie was in Exmouth by mid-morning. To her relief a brisk wind had brought half a dozen kitesurfers to the crescent of beach that fronted the dunes towards Orcombe Point. Four of them were already on the water, criss-crossing the offshore chop, using the bigger waves to launch themselves into spectacular jumps. One of them soared higher, buoyed aloft by the huge sail. Lizzie caught his wild yelp, pure exaltation, then watched as he got the landing wrong and ended in a tangle of arms and legs. *That's me*, Lizzie thought, *if I'm not careful*.

The first guy she approached had already been out on the water. Carefully folding his sail, he spared the time to look at Lizzie's mobile. Then came a shake of the head and the news that he was new to the area. He'd heard about the beach from mates, checked out the forecast and driven down from Bristol that very morning. He was due back at work in the early afternoon. When Lizzie asked what he did for a living he pulled a face.

'I'm a copper,' he said. 'For my sins.'

The other surfer on the beach was a woman. This time it was more promising. She lived locally and thought she recognised the face in the photo from a while back but couldn't be sure. Best to ask at the kite shop, she said, nodding back towards the marina.

The shop was empty when Lizzie arrived. She looked around then spotted the bell on the counter. A couple of rings brought a youth clattering down the stairs. With his shorts and his tan he might have stepped off the beach.

Lizzie introduced herself. She said she was a freelance journalist working on a story about Exmouth. She wanted to put a name to a photo she'd acquired. She showed him her mobile.

'That's Kelly,' he said at once.

Lizzie heard the door to the street open behind her. She turned to find herself looking at a woman in her forties. She had a sheepdog on a lead. She called the boy Marcus. There was a delivery expected. Had it arrived?

Lizzie looked from one face to the other. There was a definite likeness: the same blue eyes, the same blond curls, the same hint of determination in the strength of the jawline.

'Where did you get that?' The woman was staring at the photo.

'A friend gave it to me.'

'Like who?'

Lizzie didn't answer. Instead she asked about Kelly. Was she still kitesurfing? Did she live locally? If so, where might Lizzie find her?

'*Find* her?' The woman sounded incredulous. 'You're telling me you don't know what happened?'

A five-minute drive took Lizzie to an area of grassland over-looking the estuary. The water was protected here, and there were more kitesurfers, less accomplished, trying to master their rigs. Lizzie sat behind the wheel of her Audi, wondering whether Michala too had fallen in love with the sport. Was this how she'd come to meet Kelly? And find a space for her on her bedside table?

Lizzie's iPad was in her bag. She fired it up and tapped in a Google enquiry: 'Kelly kitesurf Exmouth'. Within seconds she found herself looking at a list of entries. One of them took her to the Exmouth *Journal*, the town's local paper. The article was headed WINDSURFER TRAGEDY AT SEA. Accompanying it was the face on her mobile, another grin for the camera but this time no kiss.

Quickly Lizzie scanned the text. Kelly Willmott, thirty-one, had been posted missing after failing to turn up for a drink with a friend. The friend, unnamed, knew she'd been planning to windsurf earlier. She'd waited and waited, made a few check calls and then dialled 999. A joint police and coastguard search had located Kelly's car on Exmouth seafront. Her rig and wetsuit were missing. A helicopter was scrambled and joined the local lifeboat for a search but neither found any trace of Kelly. Three days later, in a separate story, a trawler picked up a kitesurf sail identified as Kelly's. The date on the story was 21 December last year. Kelly's body, it appeared, was never found.

Never found? Lizzie looked up for a moment, wishing she knew somebody who could put all this information in context, somebody who understood about wind direction and tidal flows, someone – in short – who could give her some idea how to navigate the no man's land between a simple accident and something more sinister. Jimmy, she knew, would be useless. He'd never expressed the least interest in anything to do with watersports.

Briefly she toyed with trying to contact some of the people she'd rowed with. A handful had become mates at the time, but her memories of that period of her life were ugly, all the more so because they led to a man called Tom Pendrick. He too had disappeared at sea, only to reappear on her mobile phone months later, texting from a beach in Thailand. Jimmy, she knew, still blamed him for the collapse of their marriage, and God knows he might be right. No way did she want to revisit any of that.

Which left Michala. She'd obviously known Kelly Willmott. And just now, if Lizzie was to find out the truth about Alois Bentner, that relationship might offer crucial evidence. Last night Gemma Caton had seriously frightened her. That she'd played some role in Bentner's disappearance, maybe even Harriet Reilly's death, seemed more and more likely. Michala might therefore turn out to be the key to this puzzle. And given the choice between talking to the *Buzzard* squad or to her guest from last night, Lizzie suspected she'd choose the latter.

Michala's number was still on Lizzie's directory. She answered on the third ring.

'It's me, Lizzie Hodson. I think we ought to meet.'

The first interview session with Alois Bentner began after lunch. He'd conferred with his solicitor, who'd brought sandwiches from the nearby Waitrose, washed down with coffee from the machine in the corridor. Bentner's solicitor was a partner in an Exeter practice Suttle knew well, a waspish thirty-something single mother with a reputation for plain speaking. Suttle asked Golding to handle disclosure, something of a formality because *Buzzard* had so little in the way of hard evidence. When he returned, minutes later, Golding was looking glum.

'She's saying this is a waste of time, skip. Hers and ours.'

'And Bentner?'

'I showed him the scene photos. He refused to look at the shots of the victim. He's not a happy man.'

Golding was right. The formalities over, Suttle opened the interview by asking Bentner to describe the exact nature of his relationship with Harriet Reilly.

'We were together,' he said. 'You'd know that. You'll have checked. Her place sometimes. Other times mine.'

'You saw a lot of each other?'

'Yes.'

'You described her as your partner outside.'

'That's right. She was.'

'Close, then.'

'Of course. In every sense.'

He confirmed they went away together whenever the opportunity arose. Brazil. The States. Europe. The odd expedition up to Scotland.

'Why there? Why Scotland?'

'Because it's one of the few wild places left. That's where you go when you want to turn your back on all this shit.' He gestured up at the window, at the incessant roar of traffic grinding up the hill from the city centre.

'As a matter of interest, who tipped the media off?' This from Golding.

'I did. Last night. From the hotel. It's easy. It's like everything else these days. You phone a number. You give them a name. You tell them you're giving yourself up next morning, and if there's money in it they'll all appear. Everything's for sale. Including me. And you know what? It's because I'm the bad guy. You've done a great job already. That passport photo you used? Doctor Death? A hundred years ago that would have had me hanging from a lamp post. Life's all assumptions, because people love the easy life. Except one morning we're all going to wake up dead.'

Suttle assumed the latter comment was an invitation to discuss global warming. He ignored it.

'You think we've been prejudicial?'

'I think you've made your minds up.'

'Just as well you're here then.'

'Sure. Why else would I have come?'

Touché. Suttle was beginning to warm to this man. Nothing in his manner betrayed a scintilla of anxiety or self-doubt. He didn't really need the services of his solicitor. He was here to correct a misconception or two. In the first place about Harriet Reilly. And afterwards, if there was the time and the opportunity, about one or two other issues.

Suttle wanted to stick with Reilly.

'She was pregnant,' he pointed out.

'That's true.'

'Would you like to tell us more?'

For the first time he glanced at his solicitor, but when she shook her head he chose to ignore her.

'Harriet wanted a child. I said yes.'

'It was that way round?'

'Yes.'

'But it wasn't her child, was it?'

'No. She couldn't have children of her own.'

'Because she wouldn't try?' Suttle remembered Tony Velder on the phone from Australia.

'Because she had a problem conceiving. Trying was never an issue. Not for either of us.'

'She liked sex?'

'She loved sex. It came late to her. Maybe I was able to help in that respect.'

Suttle nodded and made a note. He wanted to know more about the pregnancy.

'Where did the egg come from?'

'From my first wife. She had cancer. We had the eggs harvested and frozen when we knew she wouldn't make it. And thank God we did.'

Suttle checked the date. March 1999. Bentner nodded in agreement. They were in Boulder, Colorado. A fine place to end your days.

'She died soon afterwards?'

'Yes.' Bentner's face was a mask. 'A difficult time for both of us.'

'Her especially.'

'Of course. And me too. Commitment's tough. You have to mean it. Commit, and you lose a little piece of yourself. Commit to someone who dies and you lose everything. It's hard to imagine something like that until it happens to you ...' He nodded, fell silent, sat back, gazed at his hands.

'And it's now happened twice? Is that what you're saying?'

'Yes, that's exactly what I'm saying. Twice in a lifetime. After that you're nothing. It's all meaningless. I used to think we were just animals. How wrong can a man be?'

Suttle was watching him carefully, trying to decide whether there was any element of performance in his account, but the closer he looked, the more genuine Bentner appeared to be. He missed both women, and their absence first bewildered then diminished him. For a man so short of social graces he had the rare knack of being able to voice his grief.

'We understand your partner Harriet miscarried a couple of times?'

'She did. This was our last shot.'

'You must have been delighted.'

'We were. We had plans for afterwards.'

'Afterwards?'

'After the baby arrived. There's an island in the Outer Hebrides. North Uist. Just over a thousand people. Perfect if you happened to be us.'

'You'd found somewhere?'

'A little croft. No one for miles.'

'You can prove this?'

'Prove that we'd had enough?' For the first time Bentner laughed. 'Prove that we wanted out? Clean air? Our own company? Somewhere for the baby to become a real child?'

'We need details, Mr Bentner. Evidence that you were serious.'

Bentner nodded. Said it would be a pleasure. He borrowed a

sheet of paper from his solicitor and wrote a line or two before he passed it across to Suttle.

'Dearcadh is the croft we were bidding on. MacDonald and Co. is the estate agent handling the sale. If you want more I'll have to have my phone back.'

Bentner's phone had been seized by the Custody Sergeant. Golding went to the Custody Suite to get it back. When he returned, Bentner scrolled through a collection of photos. Seconds later Suttle found himself looking at a sturdy stone-built cottage with a rusting tin roof and two milk churns by the front door.

'This is where you've been hiding out?' Suttle had spotted the date on the image: 13/6/2014.

'Of course. I'm surprised you never turned up.'

'Our mistake, Mr Bentner. Shit happens.'

'You're forgiven, my friend. A man can disappear in a landscape like that. The nearest human being? Two miles away. And he's normally too drunk to remember anything.'

Suttle wondered whether this was true. More likely Bentner already had friends up there, locals who'd be attracted by this bearded creature, half scientist, half prophet, who so wanted to turn his back on the madness of the world. A man like this, he thought, would seal lips island-wide.

'We need to talk about the weekend before last,' he said.

'Down here, you mean?'

'Yes.'

Bentner nodded. In essence, he said, it was simple. From time to time he felt the need to get away. Harriet understood this. It was one of the reasons they worked so well as a couple. She was a bit of a solitary herself. And after an especially brutal month at the centre he was ready for a change of scene, something very different.

'So what did you do?'

'I drove down to Exmouth on the Saturday afternoon. There's a guy I know down there, fascinating man, a rough sleeper.'

'What's his name?'

'Geordie John.' He paused. 'You know him?'

'Go on.'

'He's a great guy, ex-army, a good man, educated, right attitude. We've always talked. He's one of the few human beings I can relate to.'

'A drinker?'

'Of course. It goes with the territory. But this guy is wise. Wise in ways most of the world never understands. He had money once, gave it all away. He even had a house and a mortgage. Living rough is a conscious choice. He thinks the world is teetering on the edge and he wants to be there when we all fall off. Good man.'

'So what happened?'

'He lives out on the cliffs. I spent the night there.'

Suttle nodded. Glanced at Golding. Made another note.

'We believe you took a call that evening,' he said. 'At 23.47 to be precise.'

'That's right.'

'Who was it from?'

'Harriet.'

'What did she say?'

'She asked me how things were going. I told her they were going fine.'

'How did she sound?'

'Fine. Normal.'

'The call lasted less than a minute. Was that usual for the pair of you?'

'Yes. She said she was very tired. I told her to go to bed.'

'Told?'

'Suggested.'

'What about the next day? Did you phone her? Check she was OK?'

'No.'

'Why not?'

'I might have woken her up. In any case I'd be seeing her later. There'd be no point.'

'You had a tent?'

'I always have a tent. Back of the car.'

'And next morning?'

'I stayed there. Lovely weather. I walked along the beach to the end and then went on to Budleigh. Bought some supplies for Geordie John.'

'Food?'

'Drink. Dropped them off on the way back.'

'And then what?'

'I went home.'

'And what did you find?'

'You know what I found. She was dead. Beaten. Hacked about. Marianne all over again. Except worse.'

'So why didn't you phone us?'

'Is that a serious question?'

'Of course it is. She's dead. This wasn't an accident.'

'But you're telling me a call to you lot can bring her back?'

'Of course it wouldn't. But that's not the point. Someone had killed her. That has consequences.'

'For whom?'

'For everyone. There's someone out there. It happens once. It can happen again.'

'A serial killer, you mean? A serial disemboweller?'

Suttle shrugged. He wasn't quite sure where this conversation was going. In some respects it was like talking to a child. Time to move on.

'So you left her there?'

'Yes.'

'For someone else to find?'

'Obviously.'

'So where did you go?'

'Dartmoor. I know it well. Not as remote as Uist but not bad if you need to keep your head down.'

'And then what?'

'I saw a paper. By Tuesday my face was all over everywhere, and it was obvious you'd made your minds up. I didn't want any of that. I dumped the Skoda. Bought an old van from a

Polish guy. Cash. Five hundred quid. I could sleep in the back. It did the job.'

'You were carrying that much money?'

'More. Lots more. Banks are a conspiracy to rip you off, always have been, but it's much worse these days. Harriet felt the same. We had thousands between us. Primitive, I know, but it works.'

He said he'd driven north, into Scotland. Then the west coast. Then the ferry out to the Hebrides.

'That was Thursday night. I spent the weekend in the croft – broke in, kipped on the floor. I started south again on Sunday night. Twenty-seven hours. Door to door.'

'But why? Why did you come back?'

'Because you're right.'

'About what?'

'I need to know who did it. I need to know who killed her. She's never coming back. And neither is Marianne. And neither will that poor bloody baby. I need to mark their passing.' He offered Suttle a thin smile. 'Life is an act of separation, my friend. It happens to everyone.'

Thirty

Lizzie had suggested a café beside Exeter Central station for the meet with Michala. She wanted somewhere public where she'd feel safe. Michala, when they'd talked on the phone, was at the university. Early afternoon she'd be taking the train back to Lympstone. The Fountain Café? Perfect.

She was already there when Lizzie turned up, tucked behind a corner table next to the window. She was wearing tight jeans and a white vest with a scoop neck. A tiny silver fish hung on a silver chain around her neck.

Lizzie reached across the table and touched it. 'That's really pretty,' she said. 'Really unusual.'

'It's a salmon,' Michala said. 'I had it made. There's a silver-smith in Totnes. It was a present from Gemma. She's got one too.'

Lizzie nodded. Michala was nervous, which came as no surprise, and Lizzie wondered whether she'd shared the fact of this rendezvous with Caton.

'You've been together long? You and Gemma?'

'Nearly three years.'

A waitress was hovering. Lizzie ordered a latte. So far Michala hadn't asked why they were meeting like this and Lizzie was happy to take her time. Play the innocent, she told herself. Build the rapport. Try and gloss over what had happened down in Lympstone.

Michala wanted to know whether Lizzie was in a relationship.

227

'No. But I used to be married.'

'Me too.'

This came as a surprise. *More*, Lizzie thought. *I need to know more*.

'This was in Denmark? Back home?'

'Yes. Years back. It feels like another life.'

It turned out that Michala was older than she looked. She'd married a Norwegian guy when she was nineteen. They'd travelled a lot and ended up in Canada. She'd worked for a time in Montreal, and then she and her husband had taken a bus across the prairies to Calgary.

She bent into the conversation, suddenly animated. This was a story she wanted to share. Ludvik, she said, was ten years her senior. He was a geologist. He was taking time off from his job in the oil industry. At his insistence, they'd gone up to the Athabasca tar sands. She'd never seen anywhere more ruined in her life. Ruined wasn't a word that Ludvik recognised. He knew the stats by heart. Price per tonne for extraction. Price per tonne on the open market. The tar sands had transformed the prospects of millions of people around Calgary and Edmonton. Even the Inuit in the high Arctic had got a little richer. Cheap energy. Fat profits. Win-win.

'In the end I didn't even argue with him,' she said. 'One look at that place and you knew it was wrong, but what can you do?'

They'd taken another bus through the Rockies to the west coast, then crossed the border into the US. In a tiny village on the Snake River below Shoshone Falls she'd met Gemma Caton.

'She was just finishing the research for her book. She'd been all over the area, making contact with survivors from the old tribes. She was a woman you could listen to for ever.'

Michala said she'd stayed in the village for nearly a month. After the first couple of days, bored, Ludvik took a bus down the valley towards the coast. Michala stayed on, helping Gemma with her research.

'I had a laptop. I was happy to type out her notes every night. The people we were meeting were amazing. Two tribes. The

Nez Perce and the Shoshone. They lived on the salmon for more than ten thousand years. They worshipped the fish. Then the Europeans came, two explorers, Lewis and Clark. Then more explorers, and fur trappers, and timber people. They saw a sign for the river that the Shoshones had made. It was really a salmon but they thought it was a snake. That's how the river got its name.'

One hand strayed to the silver fish. Lizzie asked about Ludvik.

'I never saw him again.'

'So where did he go?'

'I've no idea.'

In the nineteenth century, she said, the pioneers arrived, leaving the Oregon Trail and plunging into the backwoods. Then came steamboats and railroads, and soon they were building dams for irrigation and hydroelectric power, transforming the lower river, and soon the salmon didn't come any more.

'That's when the old ways began to die. Ten thousand years. Gone. In less than a century.'

It was Gemma, she said, who had made her understand the real implications of everything she was seeing around her. The arrival of a market economy. Processed food. Pickup trucks. Tourism. Nails in the coffin of a world that had disappeared.

'She was a fine teacher. She still is. You should come and hear one of her lectures. She'd like that.'

Lizzie nodded. Going anywhere near Gemma Caton was the last thing on her agenda.

'You became lovers?' she asked. 'You and Gemma?'

'Of course. I knew what she wanted. She made me very happy.'

'And now?'

'She still makes me very happy.'

'And last night?'

'Last night was a shame.' She looked Lizzie in the eye. 'You weren't really sick, were you?'

'No.' Lizzie ducked her head and then looked up again. 'How did you know?'

'Because there aren't any soapstone carvings in the lavatory. That made Gemma laugh.'

'Because I was lying?'

'Because you were frightened. There's no need. We like you.' Her hand closed over Lizzie's.

Lizzie nodded, said nothing. She realised she was backing herself up the same cul-de-sac. How far was she prepared to take this thing? She didn't know.

'I need a favour,' she said. 'Which is why I wanted to meet.'

'What is it?'

'There's a woman called Kelly Willmott. I think you probably know her.'

'Kelly?' Michala's eyes were wide. 'You knew Kelly?'

'Yes.'

'How well?'

'Very well.'

'She never mentioned you.'

'I'm sure she didn't.'

'You're a kitesurfer?'

'No way. I was a friend. In the end we had a big row. It was horrible. But before that we were very close.'

Michala nodded. Lizzie could see she was trying to absorb the news. Then she looked up. 'You know what happened to her?'

'I know she was lost at sea. That's pretty much it. I was living away last year. I only got back a couple of months ago.'

Michala glanced at her watch. She said her train was due in ten minutes but there'd be another one.

'You want me to tell you the way it was?' she said. 'At the end?'

Suttle and Luke Golding drove across to Middlemoor to conference with Nandy and Houghton before starting the next interview with Alois Bentner. Suttle listed points in Bentner's account that *Buzzard* needed to check: was it true that he was intending to buy the property on Uist? Were negotiations in hand? And if so, were there any indications that both Bentner and Harriet Reilly were actively preparing to turn their backs on their careers and journey north with the new baby?

Houghton left the office to talk to the D/S in charge of Outside Enquiries. She had the name of the estate agent in the Western Isles and she'd raise another action to dispatch *Buzzard* DCs to the Hadley Centre and to Reilly's Exeter practice. The ticking of the PACE clock would be driving the next twenty-four hours. Before Suttle and Golding tackled the challenge phase of the interviews with Bentner, they needed every shred of evidence they could muster.

Houghton had briefed Nandy on Suttle's use of the leads raised by his ex-wife. Now the Det-Supt wanted an explanation.

'I haven't really got one, sir. Losing our daughter has changed her. And so has success. She's wealthy now. She's become a bit of a star. There are bits of her I don't recognise any more.'

To Suttle's surprise, Nandy didn't contest the point. Instead he wanted to know why she'd got herself involved with *Buzzard* in the first place. This, Suttle knew, was delicate territory.

'She runs a website, sir. It's always been a bit of a dream, and now she has the money to make it happen.'

'What sort of website?' This was news to Nandy.

'It's an investigative thing. She looks for local stories. Dirt, basically. Then starts digging.'

'You mean interfering.'

'Yes, sir. But she was the one who took us to Maguire and Russell.'

'Which went nowhere.'

'Sure. But we didn't know that at the time.'

'That's irrelevant, son. The real question is this: what the fuck is she up to? Getting in our way? In my book that's perverting the course of justice.'

'To be fair, sir—'

'To be fair, bollocks. There are procedures here. If she wants to become an informant, then she has to be registered, she has to be handled. You know that.'

'That's not her way.'

'Too fucking bad. You're still on talking terms?'

'Yes, sir.'

'Then phone her. Get her back in line. Tell her she either behaves herself or she's on a nicking. Do I make myself clear?'

'Yes, sir.'

'Good.'

Nandy was beginning to calm down. It was a question, he said, of aligning Lizzie's interests with those of the investigation. *Buzzard* would obviously welcome any help on offer, but it had to be done properly. Otherwise they'd end up with a pile of evidence that would never make it to court.

'And another thing, son, while we're talking of her interests.'

'Sir?'

'Might they include you?'

Michala and Lizzie were on their second coffee. Michala was talking about Kelly Willmott. She said they'd met last year at a barbecue in Exmouth. Gemma had contacts at the sailing club where the party was taking place and insisted on Michala coming along. A brilliant evening in late spring, she said. Home-made burgers and good beer, and dancing on the sandbank once the tide had gone out.

'And Kelly?'

'She was the centre of everything. She'd just come back from some championship where she'd won a medal, and she was wearing it around her neck. She was a wild woman. She danced like a native. Gemma loved that.'

Afterwards, she said, they'd all gone back to Lympstone. Drunk, Kelly had stayed the night. Within weeks she and Michala had become lovers.

'Gemma didn't mind?'

'Not at all. She loves having people around her. She says it makes her feel alive.'

'You mean the right people.'

'Of course. That's why I asked her to invite you over. And I was right. She likes you very much.'

232

'That's good to know.' Lizzie ducked her head and did her best to mask a smile. Was this woman some kind of pimp? Scouring East Devon for offerings to lay at Gemma Caton's door?

She nudged the conversation back to last year. Did Kelly move in?

'Yes, more or less. Then she got ill. After that she was with us all the time.'

'Ill?'

'Skin cancer. She had a little mole on her ankle. It was a tiny thing at first. She showed me when it started to bleed. I told her that she should get herself checked out but she was always too busy. By the time she finally got to the doctor it was too late.'

The melanoma, she said, had spread. First to her lymph nodes, then to her liver. She lost weight. Thin didn't suit her. Then, always tired, she started sleeping a lot. Michala watched the life draining out of her and knew something had to be done.

'Kelly agreed. She had no choice. She was in pain most of the time and her doctor was talking about getting her into a hospice when things got really bad. She hated the thought. She didn't want that and she didn't want the pain either. She knew that her life was over but she wanted to leave it on her own terms.'

On her own terms. Lizzie nodded. She sensed exactly where this story was heading. First Jeff Okenek's gay lover. Then Julia Woodman. Then Betty Russell. And now Exmouth's kitesurfing queen. Lizzie had never met her, had never even heard of her, but there was no way Michala would ever know that.

'Kelly was always a fighter,' Lizzie said softly. 'I can imagine exactly the way it must have been.'

'It was terrible. She was such a beautiful person. She was so strong, so full of life.' Michala's eyes were glassy. Lizzie reached for her hand.

'Where was Gemma in all this?'

'She was away a lot. She does lecture tours. But we talked on the phone every day. She knew Alois really well. His partner was a GP – Harriet Reilly.'

233

'This was the woman who was murdered?' Lizzie did her best to feign ignorance.

'Yes.' Michala flinched slightly. 'That was horrible too.'

She'd been to see Alois, Michala said. They'd talked a couple of times over the garden wall and she took the chance to explain about Kelly.

'Alois was really good, really kind.' She was staring out of the window. 'He said there were ways you could plan to end your life. Good ways. Ways without pain.'

'And Harriet would make that possible?'

'Yes. She came round one night and sat with Kelly. I was there too. Harriet took lots of notes and in the end she agreed to help Kelly die.'

'How?'

'With an injection. No pain. Just a drifting away. Kelly was really pleased, really grateful. She wanted it to happen while she was still able to enjoy life. Does that sound strange?'

'Not at all. Kelly was always like that. She needed to be in charge.'

'She did. You're right. But there was a problem.'

Harriet, she said, insisted that Kelly would have to be buried. Michala never understood why, but it seemed to be a legal thing. Either way, Kelly couldn't bear the thought of ending up in a grave. She had a fear of being in the darkness with the silence and the worms. She wanted to be cremated. She wanted her ashes scattered on the estuary.

'Sunset on one of those cloudless winter days.' Michala was smiling now. 'She'd worked it all out. She couldn't predict the weather but she'd looked at the tide tables and come up with a list of dates. It had to be a big tide. And it had to be going out. A big tide and maybe some wind as well.'

'But Harriet said no?'

'Exactly.' Michala nodded. 'She said it was burial or nothing. Kelly was hurt. And then she was angry.'

'With Harriet?'

'With everything. The cancer. The doctors. God. But especially

Harriet. It was like she'd spoiled Kelly's party. You only get one chance to die. That woman could have made it so sweet.'

Lizzie said she understood. She could hear the bitterness in Michala's voice. Harriet Reilly had made enemies of these women. Not just Kelly but Michala too.

She asked what had happened next. By now, said Michala, it was December. Kelly had been working in the kite shop down on Exmouth marina, but even this was getting beyond her. Then one morning she woke up with a smile on her face.

'It was a week before Christmas,' Michala said. 'For once she'd had a good night. No pain. No nightmares. No sweats. She asked me to come with her down to Exmouth. We put her kite and all the other stuff in her car. She said she'd checked the forecast and the wind was perfect. Then she asked me to leave her alone for a couple of minutes.'

'Why?'

'It turned out she wanted to write me a note. I didn't find it until the weekend.'

'But did you know what she was doing? Why you were both going down there?'

'I think I'd guessed.'

'And?'

'I didn't try and argue her out of it. A diagnosis like that? I'd probably do the same thing.'

She said they didn't get down to the beach until early afternoon. It was a beautiful sunny day and there was just enough wind for her to cope with.

'I helped her blow the kite wing up. She was pretty weak by now but she told me she'd saved up the strength for this one last trip. That was the word she used. Trip. She'd borrowed a weight belt from a diver friend and she made me fit it around her waist. In a way it was a cruel thing to do, but I knew it was what she wanted. We hugged and kissed there on the beach, and then she was in the water, sorting out the rig.'

'You never saw her again?'

'Only in the distance. Smaller and smaller. Then she was gone.'

Gone.

Lizzie sat back, trying to imagine the scene on the beach. The winter sun beginning to dip towards the horizon. The long tongues of bubbly white spume reaching up the beach. And way out on the horizon a single sail. There were worse ways to go, she thought.

'And afterwards?'

'I waited until it got dark. After a while I phoned the police and pretended we had a date for a drink and that Kelly had never turned up.'

'You'd discussed all this? With Kelly?'

'Yes. She told me what to do on the beach. They never found her, of course. Which is exactly what she wanted.'

'She just sank? And then drowned?'

'Yes. She told me it would be painless. In December the water's so cold. She said she'd end up with the fishes. They were welcome to what was left of her.'

'And the letter?'

'I found it in the bedroom. She said she loved me. She said she'd wanted my face to be the last thing she saw on earth before she drifted away, and she blamed Harriet for that never happening. Saying goodbye on the beach was close but it wasn't the same.'

Michala was crying now, the tears pouring down her face. Lizzie found a tissue and passed it across. Michala ducked her head and blew her nose. Then her fingertips found the tattoo above the pulse point on the thinness of her wrist.

'There was two hundred pounds with the letter,' she said. 'I gave some to the diver for the belt and spent the rest on this.'

'The wind horse? Peace? Harmony?'

'Sure.' Michala sniffed. 'And a prayer for a good death.'

Thirty-One

Suttle launched the next interview with the knife retrieved from Bentner's bedroom. It was a Kitchen Devil with a black handle and a serrated blade. Bentner studied it through the clear poly-thene evidence bag, balanced it in his hand, then tried a sawing motion back and forth. Suttle wondered what he was thinking, but Bentner's face gave nothing away.

'This is yours, Mr Bentner?'

'I have one, certainly.'

'We couldn't find one like it in the kitchen.'

'Then it must be mine.'

'Good. Because it probably has your fingerprints on it.'

Suttle briefly explained the fingerprints the SOC team had re-trieved from all over the house. They were on the knife too, and the assumption was that they belonged to Bentner. He'd only been fingerprinted a couple of hours ago down in the Custody Centre, and these prints had yet to be forensically matched against the prints from the house and the knife, but either way Bentner seemed unmoved.

'It's my knife,' he said. 'I use it daily. I cook. I chop. I carve. No wonder my prints are all over it. If you're asking me whether I used this on Harriet, the answer has to be no.'

Suttle made a note. Golding asked him about his next-door neighbour. How well did he know Gemma Caton?

'Well. Like you say, we're neighbours. I'm lucky in that respect. She's an intelligent woman. We have similar interests. She's an

237

anthropologist. I'm assuming you know that. Anthropologists are keepers of the ancient wisdom. From where people like me sit, that can be interesting.'

Keepers of the ancient wisdom. Suttle, thinking of Lizzie, wanted to know more.

'Gemma has built a career on the study of Native American tribes on the Pacific Northwest coast. She's published a number of papers plus a book. It's a fine book. If you want to know where the madness comes from, you should read it.'

'The madness?'

'Ours. The Indians Gemma studied were self-sufficient. They lived off the pelt of the planet. They put back what they took out. They maintained a balance. All that's gone. This was a culture, a way of life, based on hunger, on improvisation and on the kind of in-tuneness that's gone. These people were never greedy. They had respect.'

Respect. That word again.

'You see eye to eye? You and Gemma?'

'Completely. I'm a numbers guy. I crunch the data, turn it into lines on a graph. That's my job. I sit down for weeks on end and I extrapolate conclusions – likelihoods – from all this stuff. That's looking forward. Gemma does the reverse. She looks back. That's her skill, her calling. She sieves all the folklore from the Indian tribes and she figures out what made them so success-ful, and so *content*. But you know something? There's a point of fusion between us, and that's now, right here and now. We sat together during the winter, during the storms. There were nights when we thought the river was coming in the house, nights when we sat watching the news, seeing the damage along the coast, the breach in the railway line over in Dawlish, all that stuff, and it's at those moments when you realise how little time we've got. That change in the name I gave my house?'

'Two Degrees? Five Degrees?'

'Sure. That was Gemma's idea. Except I'm gonna have to change it again. Five degrees is way too high. Four will do it.'

'Do what?'

'End it all. Do you mind being frightened? You two gentle-men? We up the temperature by four degrees and you know what happens? What *has* to happen? We lose the Greenland ice sheet, and probably the Western Antarctic sheet as well. That raises sea levels by thirty feet. Which will put two thirds of the world's cities under water. Forget everything else. Forget extreme weather events – droughts in Africa, bush fires in Oz, anomalies in the jet stream, heatwaves in summer, constant winter storms. Forget crop failures and water shortages and re-source wars. Just do the math. Sixty years. Thirty feet. London gone. New York gone. Melbourne. Amsterdam. Hamburg. All under water. All those poor bastards will still be streaming out of Africa and the Middle East and God knows where else, but you know something? They'll be in the same boat as the rest of us. They'll have nowhere to go.'

Suttle didn't know quite what to make of the small, tight smile on Bentner's face. Did he get pleasure from predictions like these? Was there an ounce or two of satisfaction in pushing his graph lines ever further north? Did he and his neighbour raise their glasses to the end of the world?

'Sixty years is a single lifetime,' Suttle pointed out.

'You're right.'

'So why bring a baby into the world?'

'Because it needn't be this way. Even now we can still turn the thermostat down. Just.'

Luke Golding shook his head, his notepad abandoned. 'But realistically?' he said. 'Knowing what you know? And know-ing what Gemma knows? How greedy we are? How we take everything for granted? How billions of Chinese can't wait to get two cars in the garage?'

Bentner sat back. He'd moved the interview onto his own turf. He was enjoying this.

'The difference between two and four degrees,' he said, 'is human civilisation, everything we've built over the millennia. That's where you start. You know something? I used to work out in Boulder, Colorado. A fine institution called NCAR. If anyone should know about where we're headed, it's the folks in Colorado. They're canny, they understand the science and they want to make a difference, many of them, yet you know how many fracking operations are going on in that state? Fifty thousand. *Fifty thousand.* Anyone tells you fracking is a free ride, they're lying. All kinds of bad things happen down the line. Yet on it goes. More and more wells. More and more extraction. However hard the folks who live there protest. So I guess this is the heart of the problem. On the one hand democracy, which is a fine idea. On the other hand money, and big business, and politicians who never get elected without big business paying their campaign bills. Neat, eh? And probably terminal.'

'So why have a baby?'

'Because I'm as human as the next guy. We're at the mercy of our genes, gentlemen. And those genes are heading for the next generation, and the one after that. That's the way it works. That's the way we're programmed.'

'But you don't *have* to have a baby. You could just say no.'

'Sure. But what if my baby, our baby, turns out to be the one who makes a difference? What then? Life's a lottery. Always has been since way back. Just talk to Gemma. The fact is we've loaded the odds against ourselves in ways the Indians would consider deeply foolish. We have to get back to that kind of wisdom. Else we're fucked.'

'So be honest. What's the likeliest outcome?'

'We're fucked.'

Suttle nodded. Bentner's world, he realised, had already become uninhabitable. 'Gemma agrees with all this?'

'Broadly, yes. She's spunkier than me. She has energy to burn. Hook that woman up to the national grid and we could do without power stations. I always tell her she'd have made a fine general. Maybe the American Civil War. Or maybe Napoleon. *On s'engage. Et puis on voit.* First you get stuck in. Then you see what happens. You're looking at a woman who can think on her feet. She's tough, she's fearless, and she doesn't care who she hurts. Thank Christ she's on our side.'

'Our side?'

'Me, and her ... and Harriet.'

'Harriet knew her too?'

'Of course.'

'They got on?'

'Sure. Gemma likes women with opinions.'

'I get the impression she likes women full stop.'

'You're telling me you think she's a lesbian?'

'Yes.'

'You're right. Men don't do it for Gemma. In that respect I'm an honorary female.'

'Meaning?'

'We like each other's company, do each other favours, look out for each other. I guess it's a neighbourly thing. Maybe more than that.'

'How much more?'

'I dunno. It can be tough living in a small village. Folks who've been there for generations are fine. Gemma calls them the Native Indians. The blow-ins, people like us, can be a problem. Work, work, work. Spend, spend, spend. Hamsters on the wheel. I guess that's the problem. No time to look up and sniff the wind. You tell them sixty years, and they roll their eyes. They think sixty years doesn't matter because we'll all be dead. Yeah. True. Except they're more right than they know.'

Suttle bent to his briefcase and produced another evidence bag. The sight of Harriet Reilly's travel diary caught Bentner's attention. Suttle slipped it out. He'd already bookmarked the relevant pages.

'Harriet sometimes wrote about someone she called ND.' He bent to the diary. '"A. bad this morning. D & V plus a determination not to talk to me any more. As a doctor, not good. As his mate and favourite bedfellow, deeply worrying. Am I right about ND? Is she as mad as I think she is?"' He looked up. 'A. would be you. Am I right?'

'I guess so. And D & V is diarrhoea and vomiting. We were in the jungle. I wasn't at my best. She misinterpreted the signs,

241

the symptoms. A fine doctor, Harriet, but sometimes she got it wrong.'

'And ND?'

'I haven't got a clue.'

'But she's talking about a specific person, isn't she? Someone you'd both know?'

'No idea. The heat? The humidity? A climate like that can get to you.'

'You're suggesting she was the mad one?'

'I'm saying it was somewhat hot out there. Makes it hard to think straight sometimes.'

Suttle nodded, said nothing. Then he turned the page.

'You're in Oregon this time. It's earlier this year. March. Harriet has just discovered she's pregnant. She writes this: "A. over the moon. Me, too. ND? Who fucking cares?"' He looked up. 'ND again?'

'Pass. I've just told you.'

Suttle glanced at Golding.

'We think it may mean next door,' Golding said.

'Like a code?'

'Yes.'

'Sweet. Meaning Gemma?'

'Yes.'

'Meaning Harriet thought Gemma was some kind of threat?'

'Yes.'

'How?'

'You tell us.'

'Emotionally? Sexually? This woman is a thousand-per-cent lesbian. Other women? She eats them for breakfast. No way would she ever bother with me.'

'So maybe we're not talking sex.' Suttle this time. 'Maybe it's more complex than that. Gemma is a powerful woman. Plus she's a kind of soul mate when it comes to all the stuff you have in common. That can be a threat. First of all to Harriet. And maybe to Gemma too.'

'You think so?'

'It's a suggestion. I'm asking.'

Bentner frowned, gave the proposition some thought. Then the huge head came up.

'Harriet was a tough woman. She was very sure of herself.'

'It doesn't sound that way. Not in the diaries.'

'That was a tricky time in her life. Her guard was down. She was talking to herself.'

'So she must have meant it, mustn't she? About ND?'

Bentner shrugged. Said he didn't know. Then he asked about the other half of the proposition. Gemma and threat, two words that didn't belong in the same sentence.

'How come she could ever feel threatened?'

'Because she maybe wants all of you.'

Bentner didn't respond. He ducked his head. Golding said he was sorry about what had happened to Harriet. You wouldn't wish a scene like that on anyone.

Bentner nodded. Agreed. Studied his hands. Suttle was watching him carefully.

'Harriet took a holiday recently,' he said.

'That's right. Tenerife.'

'And you didn't go. Why was that?'

'I couldn't. I had commitments.'

'Did she want you to go?'

'Of course. Why on earth wouldn't she?'

'I've no idea. I just find it odd that you couldn't find the time to join her. She's pregnant. She's carrying your baby. I guess the word that comes to mind is support.'

'Harriet looked after herself.' The smile was cold. 'Always.'

There was a long silence. Out in the corridor someone was cursing the drinks dispenser.

'So what happens next?' Golding asked. 'Once everything's resolved?'

'To me, you mean?'

'Yes. Will you still bail out of the Hadley Centre? Bin the job? Go up to Scotland?'

Bentner studied him for a moment then shook his head. 'No

way. That was always for the three of us.'

'So you'll stay in Lympstone? Next door to Gemma?'

'Yes.' He nodded, that same chilly smile, recognising the trap Golding had sprung. 'But don't read too much into it, my friend. There's lots to be done.'

Thirty-Two

Luke Golding turned up at Lizzie's place in the early evening. Michala had just gone. She and Lizzie had walked the half-mile from the café beside the station and spent the rest of the afternoon at The Plantation. Revisiting Kelly's death had shaken Michala to the core, and she'd been grateful for the chance to share more about the good times they'd had. Lizzie, trapped in a lie of her own making, had done little more than listen, but she felt genuinely sorry for the depth of Michala's loss. Kelly had meant everything to her. And now she was gone.

Luke Golding was standing in the rain. Was it OK to come in?

'Of course.' Lizzie was curious. 'Is this business?'

'Sort of.'

'Do I need a lawyer?'

'No. I'm here to mark your card. Think Citizens' Advice. Never fails.'

They sat in the big living room. Looking around, Golding was seriously impressed. *No wonder Suttle's in the shit*, he thought. A house like this, with all its potential, could send any marriage back to the mender's.

'So what's all this about?' Lizzie enquired.

Golding took his time. He said the situation was difficult. He said he was piggy in the middle. And then he said that his bosses were less than comfortable with the way Lizzie had been interfering in stuff that belonged to *Buzzard*. There was a feeling that homicide was a CID responsibility, not the business of any passing journalist. If Lizzie wanted to register as an informant, no problem. He'd even brought a set of forms.

'You're here on a mission? Is that it?'

'Kind of.'

'You mean they haven't got the bottle to tell me themselves?'

'That'll never happen. They'll have you nicked first.'

'You're serious?'

'Always. I know these people. They think journalists are a joke. And not in a good way.'

The word joke did it for Lizzie. Earlier she'd been tempted to pick up the phone and share what she knew about Harriet and Kelly with Jimmy. If the *Buzzard* squad were looking for fresh leads then surely the passing of Kelly Willmott was a prime contender. Now, though, she found herself in a different place.

'So what are they really saying? These bosses of yours?'

'They're telling you to back off.' He frowned. 'And there's something else too. I know your private life is none of my business ...'

'You're right. It's not.'

'Sure. But I get the feeling you might be making some kind of play for Jimmy.'

'Have your bosses told you to ask that too?'

'No. This is me talking. No one else.'

'I don't believe you. Everything in your world has to do with your fucking bosses.'

'Wrong again. All I'm saying is that Jimmy is really happy just now, really sorted, and you're talking to someone who knows.'

'How come?'

'Because he nicked my woman. Her name's Oona, and she's seriously bonkers about him, which is nice to see, and the really great thing is he feels exactly the same way.'

'Is that right?'

'Yes.'

'So why has he been sleeping with me?'

'You *what*?'

246

'He was here earlier in the week. I was down at his place a couple of nights ago. Crap wallpaper and a nice view? Ring any bells?'

Golding was still staring at her.

'Men are stupid,' he said at last. 'They let their dicks do the thinking. Don't tell me you haven't noticed.'

'So what would Oona say?'

'You wouldn't.'

'How do you know?'

'Because you care about Jimmy, about that head of his. Because you're brighter than we are. You've got a lovely house. Loads of profile. You could have anyone you wanted. You're on a roll. A woman in your position shouldn't be going backwards.'

'Meaning Jimmy?'

'Of course. We're cops. We're rough as fuck, and some women love that, but I'm betting you're not one of them.'

Lizzie didn't answer. She wanted Golding gone. She wanted to pick up where she'd left off. She wanted to be a proper journalist again.

'Tell Jimmy no hard feelings, yeah?' She nodded at the door. 'And tell him thank you for last night.'

Suttle was contemplating another Stella when Golding rang.

'I'm outside, skip. Let me in?'

Suttle went downstairs. Golding was trying to shelter from the rain driving in from the sea. Suttle led him back upstairs, fetched two tinnies from the fridge.

Golding pulled the tab on the Stella, avoiding Suttle's gaze.

'Tell me about Lizzie, skip.'

'You sound like a cop.'

'Don't fuck around. Just tell me.' At last he looked up. 'You've been giving her one. Am I right?'

'Who told you that?'

'She did.'

'When?'

'This evening. Is it true?'

'It is. And it's two, if she's counting.'

'Whose idea?'

'Hers to begin with. Then ...' he shrugged '... mine.'

'So why did you do it?'

'Fuck knows. It seemed right at the time.'

'*Right*? Her name's Oona, skip, if you've forgotten.'

'I know, I know.' Suttle tried to calm him down. He didn't want this. 'You know someone for that length of time, you don't see them for a while, then – bang – they're suddenly back in your face. We're paid to be curious, right? We're paid to be nosy, to find out stuff. That's the way it was.'

'You're telling me this was some kind of fishing expedition? You're telling me it was *job-related*?'

'That's the way it felt. She came on to me. She gave me some good intel, stuff that checked out, and then she suggested we went back to her place. What's a bloke supposed to do? You want the truth? It was like fucking a stranger.'

'That makes it worse. Why fuck a stranger when you've got a woman like Oona?'

'This is you asking? Golden Bollocks? Shagmeister extra-ordinaire?'

'Yeah but I'm brain-dead and selfish and never see further than the end of my dick. Ask Oona.'

'I have.'

'And?'

'She agreed.'

'Does she miss me at all?'

'Yeah, big time. Some nights she was convinced you'd been shagging two women. Different clubs. Different flats. Other nights she wondered why you bothered to come home at all. Plus you never even bothered to cover your arse.'

'You're right. I didn't. And that's why she was right to kick me out. You're not like that, skip. This thing's eating you up. I can tell. You've had a dip or two with your ex-missus, and something tells me she's clever enough to have kept you on the line.'

'There is no line. It's finished. It's over.'

'Wrong. She wants more.'

'Who says?'

'Me.'

'How come?'

'Because she loves you.'

Suttle got up. Rain was lashing at the window, the trees beyond the fence groaning in the wind. Suttle wanted Golding to promise that none of this would ever get back to Oona but he was too proud to ask. He needed a change of subject. Fast.

'So what do you think?' He turned back into the room.

'I think you've been a twat.'

'I meant about Bentner.'

'You're changing the subject.'

'I am. Do you mind?'

Golding shrugged and then gave the question some thought. Late afternoon, with the rain setting in, DI Houghton had dispatched *Buzzard* DCs to statement the rough sleepers on the cliff top. All three of them had separately confirmed that Bentner had spent most of the weekend on the cliffs. Generous guy. Good company. Proper thirst on him. They said that Geordie John had bailed out of Exmouth for the time being and was rumoured to have moved down the coast to Dawlish. There was good safe camping in some of the tiny coves beside the railway line. Tomorrow more DCs would nail him down, but already Golding guessed that he'd confirm what they knew already. That Alois Bentner hadn't been anywhere near Lympstone when Harriet Reilly met her death.

'Well?' Suttle was still waiting for an answer.

'I think it's unlikely, skip.'

'Unlikely doesn't cut it. Yes or no.'

'No.'

'Excellent.' Suttle grinned and extended a hand. 'You owe me twenty quid.'

Thirty-Three

It was Luke Golding who got finally got through to Gemma Caton's London friend.

'Michala Haas?'

Golding introduced himself. He said he'd been trying to make contact for days. He understood Ms Haas had been away.

'That's true.'

'We believe you're a friend of Gemma Caton.'

'I am.'

'We need to talk. Are you back in London?'

'No. I'm in Exeter.'

Golding laughed. Wednesdays, for whatever reason, were normally crap. Nice to have an interview fall into his lap. The voice sounded light, perfect English but definitely a foreign accent. He visualised Gemma Caton, a mountain of a woman, the way she'd burst into the Custody Suite at Heavitree. This, he sensed, would be someone similar. Maybe they had a relationship.

'You know Heavitree police station?'

'I can find it.'

'Two o'clock this afternoon? Is that good for you?'

Lizzie was at the kitchen table, gazing at her laptop, reviewing her options. Her investigative website didn't belong to the world of deadlines. Working in the print media, she'd always been aware of the ticking clock, of the gun to her head, of the presses downstairs waiting for her to reach for her keyboard and fire off yet more copy. *Bespoken* wasn't like that. Working in the virtual world, she could take her time, gather her material, choose her moment and only upload to the Internet when the time felt exactly right.

But how did what she'd found out relate to *Buzzard*? To the corpse of a GP who may have paid for the deaths of others with her own life? Who'd been brave enough to risk her job and maybe even a prison sentence in the name of compassion? So far, to the irritation of her ex-husband and his superiors, Lizzie had somehow stolen a march on the official inquiry. But where, exactly, had that taken her? And what on earth was she supposed to do next?

Yesterday's conversation with Michala had taken the story a great deal further. In Jimmy's shoes she'd now be looking hard at the tangle of relationships in the adjoining waterfront houses. Bentner and Harriet. Bentner and Gemma Caton. And now Michala and Kelly Willmott and a death withheld that might have proved Harriet Reilly's undoing. Lizzie would never have imagined someone sane being able to commit so savage a murder. But now she'd spent time with Gemma Caton, seen the woman in action, she sensed she was probably capable of anything.

She bent to her laptop, played with an idea or two, tried to get a fresh fix on the material she'd acquired, the interviews she'd done, the lives she'd tapped into. Then she was struck by another thought, on reflection all too obvious. No way was she a detective. Neither was she some half-arsed PI. What she was looking at was a story. And to do it justice she had to rely on a different set of talents.

She reached for her mobile and checked the time. Mid-morning was normally perfect for a lengthy chat to her agent but when she got through Muriel said she was up to her eyes.

'Anything urgent?' she asked.

'Nothing that can't wait. I'll try again later.'

*

Suttle took the call from Exmouth police station. It was Kenny, the DC who'd arrested Dean Russell in the Powder Monkey and delivered him to *Buzzard*. He had another Exmouth regular waiting in the interview room down the corridor.

'Like who?'

'His name's Clark. You won't know him. Serial burglar. Specialises in country properties. Not bad when the mood takes him. He wants a word.'

'With us?'

'Yeah.'

'Why?'

Kenny explained the guy had been following the Bentner saga. He'd turned over Reilly's cottage a while back and returned for second helpings about ten days ago. One o'clock in the morning.

'And?'

'You'd better come and talk to him. I can't do it justice.'

Suttle was in Exmouth within the hour. *Buzzard*'s hold on Bentner was about to expire, but Suttle managed to convince Houghton to apply for a twelve-hour extension. When she enquired what kind of case she was supposed to make to the duty superintendent, Suttle said they were looking at new evidence.

'So what's the strength?'

'I dunno, boss. Just trust me?'

Trevor Clark turned out to be a thin fifty-something with nicotine fingers and a deeply retro affection for greasy denim jackets. His runners were brand new – Nike Air – but his jeans had seen better days. He refused Suttle's proffered hand and said he wanted another coffee. Kenny went outside to the machine. Suttle took the chair across the table.

'You're here voluntarily, right?'

'Yeah.'

'So what's this about?'

Clark said he badly needed a smoke. He had three roll-ups in a neat line on the table. Suttle told him to forget it. Interview first. Then they might stop for a break.

Clark shrugged. Suttle waited. Then Clark leaned forward over the table. He said he lived in Exeter, made a living doing bad things, famous for it.

'I know,' Suttle said. 'I checked.'

'It's tough just now. Hard. Harder than you guys would ever believe.'

'So what happened? Just tell me.'

'I was out and about a couple of weeks back. Just minding my own business. Nothing heavy.'

'And?'

'There's a field behind the cottage where that doctor lives. The one who got killed. I'd screwed her place before, done time for it, but there was another one down the lane. Easy.'

This property was a bungalow. Suttle asked for a description. It matched the Weatheralls' place perfectly. Greenhouse in the back garden. Extension around the side. Gnomes in the gloom.

'Any good?'

'Crap. Yappy dog. Fucking nightmare.'

Fleur, thought Suttle, remembering the spaniel nestling in Weatherall's lap.

'So what did you do?'

'I climbed back out. Back into the field. Because I was there I thought I'd take a look at the cottage, Reilly's place. The lights were still on downstairs, but these days that means nothing. People go away and leave the lights on a time switch. Radios too. When there's no cars out front that can be a giveaway.'

'The place was empty?'

'No way. She was there. The doctor.'

'How did you know it was her?'

'I saw her in court when I went down. She gave evidence against me.'

'It was definitely the same woman?'

'Yeah, for sure.'

'And?'

'There was a bloke there too. His photo's been in the *Echo* since, on telly, everywhere. The one who works at the Met Office.

There was a huge fight. The man was pissed, falling around, pathetic. He was throwing stuff at her – glasses, a bottle, whatever he could find. He never hit her. She wasn't, like, in any danger.'

'How close were you?'

'Close enough.'

'Could you hear what they were saying?'

'Yeah. More or less.'

'What does that mean?'

'It means I got the drift. She'd been away somewhere, maybe on holiday. The way he saw it she'd been with some other fella. He said she was a slag. He was crazy. He was out of his head.'

'And what was she saying?'

'She wasn't having it. She just turned it round on him. Told him it was all his fault. Told him to fuck off back to wherever he lived. Told him he had to make his mind up.'

'Make his mind up how?'

'I dunno. I got the impression this was a relationship thing.'

'You mean someone else was involved?'

'Might have been. I dunno. She wasn't pissed at all. Just really upset.'

'So how did it end?'

'It didn't. I left them to it.'

'Why?'

'It turned out there were horses in the field. I'm a city boy. Horses scare me shitless.'

'But they were still fighting when you left?'

'Yeah.'

Suttle nodded. This explained the broken glass and the wine stains, he thought, barely concealed evidence of a ruck that had got out of hand. He checked the exact date with Clark and warned him that he'd need a formal statement plus a positive ID on Alois Bentner.

'Is that his name?'

'Yes.' Suttle was struck by another thought. 'Why have you come forward like this? Why bother?'

Clark was reaching for one of the roll-ups. He had a lighter in his other hand.

'That lady was a doctor,' he said. 'She looked after my mum when she was really poorly. Did a fantastic job.'

'Your mum's better now?'

'No chance. She had cancer. Sweet it was. She was at home. Lovely death, according to my dad. She just drifted away.'

Thirty-Four

Michala was late turning up at Heavitree police station. Golding was about to phone her when the Custody Sergeant put his head around the door of the interview room.

'Danish lady? Name of Haas?'

'The very same.'

'Lucky you.'

Moments later the door opened properly. Expecting a continental version of Gemma Caton, Golding found himself looking at a waif-like blonde. Tight jeans. Tense smile. Extremely pretty.

He asked her to sit down, offered his warrant card. She said no to coffee. Why had she been asked to attend?

Golding briefly explained about *Buzzard*. The word murder didn't appear to come as a surprise.

'You were there?' Golding asked. 'Next door? That night?'

'No.'

'So where were you?'

'I have a flat in London. You know Streatham Hill?'

'Never had the pleasure.'

'That's where we were.'

'We?'

'Myself and Gemma. She's my landlady in Lympstone. She owns the house next to Mr Bentner. The house where I live. We were up in Streatham all weekend.'

Golding nodded. He wanted to know whether anyone else had been at the flat.

'No. Just us.'

'And when did you come back?'

'On Tuesday.'

'By car?'

'Yes.'

'Whose car?'

'Gemma's. Parking is very expensive in London but I know a German guy around the corner. We left the car in his drive.'

'All weekend?'

'Yes.'

'You have his name? This German guy?'

'Of course.'

He passed her his pad. She scribbled a name: Gunther Schmidt, 34 Meredith Avenue.

'And the registration number of the car?'

She didn't have it. Golding would have to ask Gemma. The car was yellow. That's all she knew.

Golding nodded. He'd met Gemma Caton. He needed to know more about this relationship.

'You spend a lot of time with Ms Caton?'

'Yes.'

'Are you partners?'

'Yes.'

She held Golding's gaze. Suttle had briefed him about Lizzie's visit to the house. *What a waste*, he thought.

'And the man next door? Down in Lympstone? Alois Bentner? You know him too?'

'Of course. Not well. Not as well as Gemma.'

'They're close?'

'They're friends. They talk a lot.'

'And Harriet? Harriet Reilly? You knew her too?'

'Not so well.'

'How did you find out about what happened?'

'You mean the murder?'

'Yes.'

'We were coming back in the car. It was on the radio.'

'And Gemma?'

'She couldn't believe it. Neither could I. Some stranger in that house? Doing what he did? That could have been us. That could have been me. I'm often alone in the house. Sometimes the door is unlocked. You never like to think so, but things like this can happen. You think you're safe. You're not.'

'Why do you think Mr Bentner disappeared?'

'I don't know. He's a strange man. Maybe he drinks too much.'

'You don't think he might have had some hand in what happened?'

'I don't know. Sometimes he can be very gentle. I've watched him with her. It was nice to see.'

'Her?'

'The doctor. Harriet.'

Golding looked at her for a long moment. She ticked all the right boxes. She was troubled, maybe even shocked. Very bad things had happened. Evil had stepped into her life. The notion of a stranger was very persuasive. A madman was on the loose. Help me. Help us all.

Golding smiled. Time to ask the harder questions.

'You had a little party the night before last,' he said.

'Where? Who?' Her surprise was unfeigned. There was something close to panic in her eyes.

'You and Gemma. In Lympstone.' The smile widened. 'There was another woman there. Why don't we talk about her?'

Lizzie spent nearly an hour on the phone to her agent. Step by step, she walked Muriel through the investigation she'd mounted around Harriet Reilly. This was a woman, she said, who'd won the trust and eternal thanks of the terminally ill. In Lizzie's view her private crusade had taken her close to sainthood, yet somewhere along the way she'd made an enemy ruthless and desperate enough to have killed her. Lizzie offered descriptions of Jeff Okenek. Of Ralph Woodman. Of Frances Bevan. And now of Michala. All of them, she said, had been supplicants. All of them had begged Harriet Reilly to put their loved ones out of their misery. In only one case had she refused. And now she herself was dead.

Muriel was impressed. She said it sounded an extraordinary story, all the more so because it still lacked a resolution. Who had killed Harriet Reilly? And how – exactly – had that happened? Only by staying close to the investigation would Lizzie be able to do the story justice.

'Is your husband part of the squad?'

'Yes.'

'Are you still on speaking terms?'

'Just. But it's complicated.'

'Everything's complicated, my darling. That's how people like us make a living.'

Lizzie still needed an answer. 'You think I should use the website? Or write a book?'

'Both. I'm a fan of the website. You know I am. It's liberated you. It's set you free. I can feel it.'

'Sure. But it's not the same, is it? Not the same as a book?'

'That doesn't matter. It's a first draft. It'll send a message. It'll get people thinking. These people are potential readers. You need to juice them. You need to make them ask for more. And that's when we move on the book. Do I smell an auction in the offing? I do.'

Lizzie nodded. She thought she understood.

Then came another question. Muriel had a gift for scenting other people's weakness. 'You say this Danish woman came on to you?'

'Yes.'

'Then stay close to her. She's our best chance.'

'Of what?'

'Of taking you where you deserve to be.' Lizzie heard a throaty cackle of laughter. 'Do I hear a yes?'

The conversation came to an end. Muriel wished her good luck and hung up.

Lizzie stared at the window for a long moment and then

reached for her mobile. When there was no answer, she sent Michala a text: 'We need to talk. Plse ring me.'

Luke Golding called a break in his interview with Michala Haas. Challenged about the dinner party hosted by Gemma Caton down at her waterside house, she'd said very little. Michala had met Lizzie Hodson last week. She was a journalist. She was doing a thing about wind power. She was an interesting person, a nice person, and she wanted to meet Gemma. Michala had been happy to pass on the invitation and they'd all had a good time. When Golding asked her about what else might have happened, she'd looked blank.

'Like what?'

'Like you making a pass.'

'I don't understand.'

'You wanted to sleep with her.'

'That's right. I did.'

'So what happened?'

'She said she was ill. She left.'

'Have you seen her since?'

'Yes.'

'Do you still want to sleep with her?'

'Yes.'

'And Lizzie? She feels the same way?'

'I don't know. I hope so.'

These questions brought the interview to a temporary end. When Michala said she had to go, Golding said he'd prefer she stayed. He had to make some calls, have a conversation or two. Then they'd talk some more. When she said that might be difficult, that she had things to do, Golding told her she had no choice. Either she agreed to stay or he'd arrest her. The word arrest brought something new to her eyes, something Golding recognised at once. Fear.

He left Heavitree and drove back to the MIR and conferred with the CSM in charge of the forensic file. Suttle had just emerged from a meeting with DI Houghton. He took Golding aside and told him about his expedition down to Exmouth. A serial housebreaker had witnessed Alois Bentner at full throttle. The difference between small and large acts of violence could be marginal.

'We believe this guy?'

'I can't see why he'd be making it up.'

'So Bentner's back in the frame?'

'Has to be.'

The thought that he might get his twenty quid back put a smile on Golding's face. He told Suttle about the interview with Michala Haas.

'She's trying to bed your missus, skip. And she thinks she might be pushing at an open door.'

Suttle stared at him, then agreed to accompany Golding back to Heavitree. In the younger man's opinion, the resumed interview might yield a surprise or two. All he needed was a little leverage.

'Like what?'

Golding was carrying an A4 Manila envelope. The young lady was waiting, he said. Best to put her out of her misery.

Michala was talking to a WPC when Suttle and Golding got back to Heavitree police station. She'd finished one coffee, asked for another. The WPC said no problem.

'This is a colleague of mine, Michala.' Golding nodded at Suttle. 'He's working on the murder as well.'

In the car Suttle had wondered about the wisdom of offering Michala the services of a lawyer but agreed that it wasn't strictly necessary. She'd volunteered for the interview in the first place. In Golding's phrase, what happened next was strictly a punt.

Golding took Michala back to her relationship with Gemma Caton.

'Would you describe it as a marriage? You and Gemma?'

'Not at all. Why do you ask?'

'Because we need to know whether you find room for other partners.'

'You mean sex? You're talking about sex?'

'Yes.'

'Of course.'

'Of course what?'

'Of course I have sex with other people.'

'Men? Women?'

'Both. But mainly women.'

'And Lizzie? Lizzie Hodson? The journalist you met? Did you have sex with her?'

'When?'

'That night? After dinner.'

'No. She got sick. I told you.'

'Have you had sex with her at all?'

'No. Not yet.'

'But soon? You think?'

'I hope so, yes.'

Golding reached for his pad, made a note. Suttle was studying his hands. He'd been right. His ex-wife had become someone else.

Golding pushed the envelope across the table and asked her to open it. Michala slid the contents onto the table. They were the Scenes of Crime photos from Bentner's bedroom, the mutilated body of Harriet Reilly sprawled on the bed.

'Look at them all, Michala. Take your time.'

She was staring at the top photo. She swallowed hard, turned away, shook her head.

Golding found a close-up of the slashed belly, the glistening loops of intestine, the ruined womb. And then came an even tighter shot of the remains of the fetus. He laid them carefully side by side. A tadpole without a head.

'Please take a look,' he said softly.

Against her will, Michala did his bidding. At the sight of the fetus, she closed her eyes. 'Why are you doing this? Why are you showing me these pictures?'

'Because you're lying. Because you have lots more to tell us. And because you need to know why we're asking all these questions.'

'You think I did that?' She was looking at the baby.

'I think you may know who did.'

'How? How would I know that?'

Golding didn't answer the question. Instead he glanced at Suttle.

'Skip?'

Suttle shook his head. He had lots of questions of his own but only one seemed to matter just now.

'This journalist ... Lizzie Hodson ...'

'Yes?'

'You say you're seeing her again?'

'Yes.'

'When?'

'I don't know.' She risked a smile. 'Soon, I hope.'

Thirty-Five

Golding drove Suttle back to the MIR. DI Houghton had just returned from a snatched lunch in the canteen, where she'd run into the Deputy SIO on the Barnstaple job. A keen young DI, he'd been only too pleased to share one or two highlights from the inquiry that had nailed the two Romanians who'd done the elderly couple. How he'd acted on an early hunch. How most of his investigative gambles had paid off. And how delighted Nandy had been to have the job sorted within a couple of days. None of this made for easy listening, and Houghton, only too aware of the car crash that was Operation *Buzzard*, was glad to get back to her office.

She listened to Golding's account of the interviews with Michala Haas. She agreed the woman might know a great deal more than she was letting on. And she decided it was time to put her account to a sterner test.

'Check out the London alibi,' she said. 'Talk to the German guy about the car. Make sure it really was on his driveway all weekend. Talk to the girl's neighbours, as well. Saturday night's the key to everything. If we can break the alibi, if we can put them both back in Lympstone, then we're getting close to a result.'

Suttle wanted to know about Bentner. Time was running out. They still hadn't confronted him with the evidence from the burglar, Trevor Clark. It might be nice to back it up with something else.

Houghton agreed. The row at Harriet Reilly's cottage suggested the relationship between Bentner and Reilly was in deep trouble. If a third party was involved, logic suggested it had to be Gemma Caton. Think about it from Reilly's point of view. She was already carrying Bentner's child. She probably felt vulnerable on that score alone. The fact that his neighbour was playing way too large a part in his private life – the huddles over global warming, their sunset tête-à-têtes in Bentner's waterside garden – would simply make things worse. No wonder she'd taken herself off for a holiday.

Golding departed to drive to London. He'd check out the parking alibi and talk to Michala Haas's neighbours and report back.

Houghton asked Suttle to stay. 'We just had another conversation with your mate,' she said.

'Mate?'

'Geordie John. That was his word, not mine. I think he took a shine to you, Jimmy. He thinks you're OK.'

'So what's he saying?'

'Nothing. Yet. He'll only talk to you.'

'Where is he?'

'Dawlish. There's a tiny beach. Horse Cove. He's been living rough there for a while. Go and talk to him, Jimmy. Nandy wants to monitor the final session with Bentner. You'll be partnered with Rosie. We're thinking six o'clock.'

Lizzie was about to go out when she heard the *tap-tap* at the front door. She had a date with Anton at the Costa in Waterstones. He was promising more news about Gemma Caton.

It was Michala. Lizzie knew at once that she'd been crying. She shepherded her inside and shut the door. When she gave her a hug, Michala began to sob uncontrollably. Lizzie led her through to the living room, sat her down on the sofa, suggested tea or something stronger.

'Hold me. Please. Tell me I'm not evil.'

Lizzie took her in her arms, letting the storm blow out. At length she asked what on earth had happened.

Michala wouldn't tell her. Not yet. Something terrible, she said. Something she couldn't even describe.

'This is about Gemma?'

'Yes.'

'And Harriet Reilly?'

'Yes.'

'So what is it? What do you want to tell me?'

Michala gazed up through a shine of tears. 'Nothing. I can't. I won't.' She looked around. 'Can I stay here? With you?'

'Of course.'

'You're sure?'

'Yes.'

'And no one else will know?'

'No one. Just you and me.' She gave her another hug, fetched a box of tissues, dried her tears. 'You're safe, Michala. I promise you. Give me a minute? I have to make a call.'

Lizzie went through to the kitchen. She sensed that this story of hers was coming to the boil. In some ways it was crazy to let Michala so close because she would – in the end – bring Gemma Caton to the door. But what choice did she have? If she really wanted to see this thing through?

Still in the kitchen, she phoned Anton. He was on his way to Waterstones for the meet. She apologised for the glitch but told him something had come up. What was the news about Gemma Caton?

'She's cancelled all her lectures, all her supervisions, everything.'

'How do you know?'

'I was talking to the secretary. It seems she has unfinished business elsewhere.'

Suttle was in Dawlish by mid-afternoon. He'd downloaded an Ordnance Survey map of the area and located a footpath he thought might lead to Horse Cove. Parking in a bay off the main road, he headed off through a thicket of brambles, hunting for the top of the cliff. He found it minutes later. Steadying

266

himself against the updraught from the cove below, he noticed his leg was no longer giving him any pain.

The drop from the edge of the cliff was dizzying, and there were signs of recent slippage. The wounds on the cliff face were raw, a rich ochre bareness where plants and grasses had yet to reseed. The winter storms, Suttle thought, shading his eyes against the afternoon glare, wondering what it must be like to live in one of the properties further along the cliff. Every time another gale arrived you'd worry about the rest of your garden sliding into oblivion. Could you insure against the near-certainty of disasters like these? And was global warming the reason for all those sleepless nights?

The footpath no longer existed, another of winter's casualties. Instead, Suttle had to make his way back along the cliff top until he found an access track the railway engineers working below must be using. They were netting this stretch of cliff face against further falls. Below him lay the dull metal threads of the line, the south-west's only link to the rest of the network. February's breach in the sea wall had now been repaired, but the locals believed it was only a matter of time before nature came calling again.

Suttle, who loathed heights and mistrusted gravity, made his way carefully down the zigzag path. By now he'd spotted a blue tent on the patch of scrub between the railway line and the beach. It was low tide, the wind pleating the water offshore, tiny waves lapping at the shininess of the pebbles. The cove had turned its back on the land, a tiny crescent of privacy hemmed in by the jut of the cliffs left and right, each headland penetrated by a railway tunnel. If you enjoyed your own company and didn't mind trains, this would be a perfect spot to call home.

Geordie John thought so. He was asleep in his tent when Suttle finally made it down to the beach. His flysheet was pegged open, and he was lying naked in the hot sunshine, his eyes closed. Suttle gazed down at him. In the absence of a bell or a knocker, he poked a grubby big toe with his foot. The puppies were in the tent too. They barked. Geordie John stirred, opened one eye.

Suttle's face was black against the brightness of the light.

'Who the fuck are you?'

Suttle squatted beside the tent. Nice place. Real find. What happened when the wind got up?

'You button up. Hunker down. A good book does it. And maybe a candle.'

He was struggling into an ancient pair of Calvin Kleins. The puppies were all over him. He hadn't expected Suttle so soon. In fact he hadn't expected Suttle at all.

'Why not?'

'Expectation's second cousin to disappointment, my friend. If you're wise, you kick the habit. Don't get me wrong. People can be lovely. You learn that, living the way I do. They give you money, food, clothing, whatever it takes. But that's where it ends. A decent conversation? Forget it. It's all arm's length these days, and you know why? You're carrying the virus. You make your own decisions. You live like this.' He gave the nearest puppy a pat. It licked his face.

Suttle wanted to know more about the virus. What was it?

'It's the freedom virus. It scares most people to death.'

Suttle wondered whether he was drunk. On balance, he decided not. Solitude made you value conversation. Obvious, really.

'I'm here for a chat,' Suttle said. 'It's your lucky day.'

'Yeah? And maybe yours too. Fancy a brew?'

Suttle said no. Time was tight. He didn't want to bore Geordie John with the real world but he had less than an hour. Absolute max.

'An hour is an eternity, my friend. An hour can cement a friendship for life. You take sugar?'

It turned out he had the tea already brewed in a Thermos, one of a number of early-morning chores. Life, he said, was for sharing.

'Milk? Powdered, I'm afraid.'

Suttle took the tea, tasted it. Yuk. Geordie John watched him, amused.

'You want to talk about the scientist fella, am I right?'

'Bentner? Yes.'

'Because you think he killed that woman? Or am I wrong?'

'You may be. At this point we don't know. You're aware he's in custody?'

'I am. Your mates told me. So what's he saying?'

'He's saying he was with you.'

'On that Saturday night?'

'Yes.'

'That's true. He was.'

'I'll need a statement to that effect.'

'I'm sure you will. Biscuit?' He rummaged at the back of the tent and produced a tin of assorted shortbread. It seemed that Sainsbury's offered the best pickings in Dawlish. Nice people. Generous. Loved small dogs.

'Tell me about Bentner.'

'The guy's bright. Really bright. Also damaged. Much like the rest of us but probably worse. His drinking puts us to shame. Serious thirst on the man.'

'Damaged how?'

'He's delusional. Some days when I was working the precinct in Exmouth he'd settle down for a chat and be Mr Sanity. Other times he'd rock up, totally wasted, and give me all the people on his death list. I thought he was taking the piss at first but it turned out he was serious.'

'Was a woman called Harriet Reilly on that list?'

'No way. I met her too. She used to come down to Exmouth with him. She'd give me little presents. Freebie drugs, mainly analgesics. I'd share them with my wilder brethren. Lifesavers if you're not taking care of yourself.'

'They were tight? The two of them?'

'Like that.' He crossed two fingers. 'Soul mates.'

'So who did he want to kill?'

'The list writes itself. He always said he was spoiled for choice. Big business, shitbag scientists they've hoisted on board, piss-poor politicians – take your choice. There's no way he'd ever get to these people, but he'd never admit it. Delusional, like I say.'

Suttle let the tea cool in the Oxfam mug. The sun was hot on the back of his neck.

'That Saturday night,' he said. 'You talked?'

'Yeah, and drank.'

'He took a call. Near midnight. Were you with him then?'

'I was. He went over into the trees.'

'The call didn't last long,' Suttle said. 'About a minute, tops.'

'That's right. And he was a different man when he came back.'

'Different how?'

'Sober for starters. Which I guess was just as well.'

'Why?'

'Because he left us for a while.'

'How long?'

'Ten minutes? Fifteen? Something like that.'

'Right.' Suttle didn't bother to hide his disappointment. No way could Bentner have made it to Lympstone and back in fifteen minutes. 'What then?' he asked. 'After he came back?

'He'd found them.'

'Found what?'

'His car keys.'

Thirty-Six

Lizzie brooded about Gemma Caton's sudden disappearance while she did her best to sort out Michala Haas. Her front door was secured with two bolts and an ancient Yale lock. She asked Michala about the car Gemma was driving and then went out into the street to check for something small and yellow. Nothing. Back in the house, she secured the front of the property and then locked the door in the kitchen that offered access to the garden at the back.

Already she felt under siege. Now, with Michala under her protection, she had a double responsibility. This evening, she told herself, she'd get to the bottom of what had really happened to Harriet Reilly. In the meantime it might be wise to hedge her bets.

Michala was in bed, evidently asleep. Lizzie closed the bedroom door and went downstairs to the kitchen. She kept the text to Jimmy as brief as she could. 'Gemma Caton might be a flight risk,' she wrote. 'Surveillance?'

Suttle showed the text to Carole Houghton. The two of them were about to drive over to Heavitree for the third interview with Alois Bentner.

'Why is she telling us, Jimmy?'

'I've no idea, boss.'

'Do you think it's true? About Caton?'

'It is. I just checked with her department at the university. She has some kind of crisis in her personal life. Needs to sort it out.'

'And you think that might involve Lizzie?'

'I don't know, but my guess is Lizzie's frightened. Surveillance would give her a bit of cover.'

'You mean reassurance.'

'Yes.'

'So how do you feel about all this?'

'All what, boss?'

'Lizzie and Michala. You must have a view, surely?' Golding had shared the morning's interviews with Houghton. In Michala's view, she and Lizzie were on the verge of an affair.

They were driving down the Heavitree Road. A couple of minutes and they'd be at the nick. The fact that Houghton was also lesbian, tucked up in a long-term relationship with a high-flying London lawyer, had never been a secret.

'I don't really have a view, boss. Maybe Lizzie's playing games with the woman. Maybe she really fancies her. You want the truth? Nothing she does any more will ever surprise me.'

'But you must care about her? No?'

'Of course. I care about the woman she was. What's been happening lately is beyond me. She's lost her bearings, she's lost her judgement. Success and money and all the rest of it have turned her into someone else.'

Houghton nodded. She seemed to understand.

'Lost is an important word, Jimmy. Maybe we should bear that in mind.'

Rosie Tremayne and Det-Supt Nandy were waiting for them at the Custody Centre. Nandy had organised an office for a pre-interview meet. Bentner was still in one of the cells downstairs. According to the turnkey, he'd nearly finished *The First Circle*.

Suttle briefed them both on what he'd learned from Geordie John.

'You can trust his account? You statemented him?' This from Nandy.

'I did, sir. I think he's kosher.'

'And he's telling us that Bentner was away for a while? That Saturday night?'

'Yes. He's already admitted finding the body on the Sunday, but he never mentioned leaving the camp on the Saturday night.'

'How long was he away? Exactly?'

'At least an hour. He had to find his car keys first. After that Geordie John went for a kip. When he woke up, Bentner was back in his tent.'

'Did he ask him where he'd been?'

'Yes.'

'And what did he say?'

'He said he'd been to check on the family.'

'Interesting phrase, son. Nothing else?'

Suttle shook his head. He told Rosie Tremayne about the recent domestic – Bentner and Harriet Reilly, witnessed by her former burglar. Tremayne wanted to know how much importance she should place on this account.

'It might be key, Rosie.' This from Houghton. 'We have to shake the man up. I doubt we're anywhere near a confession, but if it turns out we need a further extension we have to have more shots in our locker. He may let something slip. Good hunting, eh?'

The interview began at 18.42. Bentner's solicitor had arrived forty minutes earlier and had spent longer than Suttle had expected with her client. Was this some kind of clue to what might lie ahead? Suttle didn't know.

Bentner, as expected, was the soul of composure. If nothing else, Suttle thought, we must be doing wonders for his liver.

'I want to take you back a couple of weeks,' Suttle began. 'Harriet has been away on holiday. She's been to Tenerife. She comes back. How did she feel?'

'Rested.'

'And you?'

'I was glad to have her back. As I explained earlier, I'd have gone with her but it was a last-minute thing on her part, and I couldn't get the time off.'

'Why so last minute?'

'I don't know.'

'Was she especially stressed?'

'She was pregnant. And that had never happened before.'

'She was relaxed about having the baby?'

'She thought she'd carry it to term. That isn't necessarily the same thing.'

'So she wasn't happy about having it? Is that what you're telling me?'

'She was cautious, wary.'

'And you? Was she happy about you?'

'I don't understand the question.'

'I get the impression she may have been under some stress. Might you have added to that?'

'How?'

'I don't know. It's a question.'

'Then the answer's no. She knew I cared about her. She trusted me. Why do you ask the question?'

'Because we think you had a major row. Thursday, 5 June. One o'clock in the morning. At her cottage. Does any of that ring a bell with you, Mr Bentner?'

His gaze went from one face to the other, then settled on Suttle again. *We've shaken him*, Suttle thought.

'We had words,' Bentner admitted.

'It was worse than that, much worse. You attacked her. You threw things at her. You were screaming at her. Or have we got that wrong?'

Bentner said nothing. His solicitor wanted to know where these allegations had come from and why they hadn't been disclosed before the interview began.

Suttle explained about the witness in the field behind the cottage. The solicitor wanted to know the witness's name.

'Trevor Clark.'

'Clark?' Bentner had come to life again. 'The man's a thief.

He's a criminal. I was there in court. All this stuff comes from him?'

'It does, Mr Bentner. Are you denying it?'

'Absolutely.'

'Then how do you explain the broken glass we found in Harriet's living room? The wine stains? There's a pattern here. We call it corroboration.'

'Call it what you like. I'm a scientist. I deal in certainties. What's certain is you can't trust a man like Clark. He has an agenda. It's obvious. Harriet helped put him in jail. Low life like Clark never forget something like that.'

Suttle leaned back, shot a glance at Rosie Tremayne.

'Harriet was worried about you seeing someone else,' she said. 'We have that from her travel diaries and now Mr Clark's telling us the same thing. Who might that someone be?'

Bentner shook his head, refused to answer. His solicitor beckoned him closer. A murmured conversation.

Bentner turned back to Rosie. 'No comment.'

'Might she have had grounds for being worried?'

'No comment.'

'Gemma Caton was a good friend of yours.'

'Is. Not was.'

'*Is* a good friend of yours. How far does that friendship go, Mr Bentner?'

Bentner threw his head back and barked with laughter. 'The woman's a dyke. I thought I told you that.'

'You did.'

'Then why would I have sex with a lesbian? Or she with me?'

'It doesn't have to be sex, Mr Bentner. Betrayal is rarely as simple as that. We're putting it to you that Harriet was jealous about your relationship with Gemma Caton. That she felt excluded by that relationship. That she mistrusted the woman. And that she may even have been frightened by her.'

'Nothing frightened Harriet. Ever.'

'I don't believe that. I think she was frightened of losing you.'

'I'm flattered. It's a generous thought but it happens to be wrong. We understood each other, Harriet and I.'

'Just like you understand Gemma?'

'Exactly.'

'And you saw no contradiction between the two? Two special people in your life? Two special relationships? Most people can only handle one. So maybe that takes us back to Harriet.'

Pause. A lengthening silence. Nandy, watching in the room next door, couldn't tear his eyes from the screen. He had a smile on his face.

Suttle took up the running again. 'We put it to you, Mr Bentner, that your private life had got out of control. That you had to choose between two women.'

'One I was fucking and one I wasn't? What kind of choice was that?'

'Just answer the question.'

'You're saying I killed her? Harriet? To make everything nice and tidy? Is that what you're saying?'

'We're asking, Mr Bentner.' It was Tremayne again. 'We're making a suggestion. Life is always more complex than you might expect. And you're talking to a couple of experts.'

Bentner was shaking his head. He didn't have to put up with this bullshit. He really didn't. The world was coming apart at the seams. Nowhere in the last six months were the symptoms more obvious than down here in the south-west. The coast had been eaten alive. Half of Somerset was underwater. Yet here he was banged up with a couple of lunatic policemen determined to take a scalp or two.

'You people are off the planet,' he added. 'Which I guess makes you lucky.'

Suttle acknowledged the comment with a smile. Not beaten yet. Not quite. 'Let's talk about that Saturday night,' he said. 'It was only two days after the fight you had with Harriet. You left her at your house and went off camping.'

'That's right.'

'You know a man called Geordie John. A rough sleeper.'

'Yes.'

'You sat up with him and a couple of other guys out on the cliffs there.'

'Yes.'

'Just before midnight you took a call.'

'Yes.'

'Do you remember that call?'

'Yes.'

'Who made it?'

'Harriet.'

'Why?'

'I think I told you. She wanted to know about my day. She was tired. She was about to go to bed.'

'Shortly afterwards you went to your car.'

'Did I?'

'Yes, according to Geordie John. Where did you go?'

A moment's hesitation. Then that same tight smile.

'Tesco. On the Salterton Road. They're open twenty-four hours.'

'Why?'

'I needed to buy more drink.'

'Did you pay by card?'

'No. Cash. Always cash.'

'Did you keep the receipt?'

'Of course not. We drink the stuff. We never take it back.'

'You're aware they have CCTV at Tesco?'

'No. Is that relevant?'

'It might well be, Mr Bentner. What time are we talking? Roughly?'

'Maybe one in the morning. I can't remember.'

'Fine.' It was Suttle's turn to smile. 'We'll check it out.' He paused. 'What did you do afterwards?'

'I drove back to the cliff top. Orcombe Point. Everyone seemed to be asleep.'

'I see.' Suttle sat back, abandoned his pen and pad. 'Do you have anything else to add? Anything you'd like to share with us?'

Bentner stared at Suttle, then shook his head. 'No.'

Suttle held his gaze. 'Geordie John was awake when you got back, wasn't he?'

'He may have been. I can't remember.'

'He says he was. Do you remember what you told him? When you got back?'

'No.'

'You said you'd been to visit the family. What exactly did that mean?'

Bentner blinked, then settled back in the chair.

'No comment,' he muttered.

Minutes later, after Suttle called a halt to the interview, Nandy was punching the air. A result at last. He'd already dispatched Carole Houghton to the duty magistrate for a custody extension. First thing tomorrow detectives would be crawling all over Tesco's CCTV footage. *Buzzard*, he said, had blown a huge hole in Bentner's account, and the next twenty-four hours would see him charged.

'With what, sir?' Suttle wasn't convinced.

'He killed her. He solved his problem. Sober the man's probably a genius. Pissed he can do anything. There were two women in his life. He settled for the one next door. God knows why but he did. Genius, son.'

'Whose?'

'Yours.'

Thirty-Seven

Michala spent the evening huddled on the sofa. She was wearing a dressing gown of Lizzie's, a size too big for her. It was red silk, a present Lizzie had bought for herself on publication day, and it enveloped Michala's thin frame. This was like looking after a sick child, Lizzie thought. Lots of tea. Lots of physical contact. Lots of reassurance.

It was gone nine. They were watching television. Australia v. the Netherlands. Wall-to-wall football.

Lizzie took her hand. It was cold. She wouldn't look Lizzie in the eye. Didn't want to talk. It had been this way all evening.

'You have to tell me,' Lizzie said again.

'Tell you what?'

'Why you're so frightened. What's been going on.'

'I can't.'

'You mean you won't.'

'That's right.' Her eyes were still glued to the screen. 'I won't.'

'You think you're protecting me in some way? You think it's better – safer – if I don't know?'

'Yes.'

'You think I wouldn't be able to handle it? Whatever it is?'

'Yes.'

'Then you're wrong.' Lizzie cupped Michala's face in her hands. 'I'm a big girl. A lot's happened in my life.'

She held Michala's gaze. She had to level with this woman. They had to become allies in the same war. She told her about losing Grace, about hitting rock bottom, about wondering whether she should follow her daughter to wherever she'd gone. Some nights, she said, ending it all would have been a release. But you soldier on. You battle through. Because the alternative is infinitely worse.

Michala seemed to understand. She nodded. Then her eyes strayed back to the TV. The Dutch were attacking, swarms of attackers punishing the Australian defence.

'I saw the poster in the kitchen,' she said at last. 'I want to read that book.'

'I'll give you a copy.'

'Is it about your daughter?'

'Sort of.'

'What else is it about?'

'It's about the woman who killed her.'

'She was crazy, this woman?'

'She was damaged.'

Michala nodded, pulling the dressing gown a little tighter around herself.

'I want you to write in it.' She glanced at Lizzie. 'Please.'

'You mean a dedication?'

'Yes.'

Lizzie studied her a moment, then got up and left the room. She kept hardback copies of *Mine* in a box in one of the spare bedrooms. She found a pen and wrote a brief message.

Back on the sofa she gave Michala the book.

'So soon. So quickly.' Michala opened the book, looking for the dedication, and tried to make sense of Lizzie's scrawl.

'What does it say?'

'It says you're a lovely person. It says you don't deserve any of this. And it says take care.'

'You mind if I start it now? You mind if I go back to bed?'

Michala was already on her feet. Lizzie reached up to her, squeezed her hand, settled down again, her eyes returning to the TV. *Let her take her time*, she told herself. *She needs to trust me.*

A little later, the game over, Lizzie abandoned the post-match analysis and went upstairs. The bedroom door was half open and the light still on but Michala appeared to be asleep. The book, unopened, lay on the duvet beside her.

Suttle spent the evening in his Exmouth flat with Oona. She'd driven straight from work, pausing in town to pick up a takeout. She'd copped Australia in the prize draw at work and no way was she going to miss the game. Suttle had already invested in another bottle of Rioja and was on his second tinnie by the time she arrived.

The game was a classic, the best of the tournament so far. The Dutch were on a roll after demolishing the Spanish, yet – to Oona's delight – the Socceroos matched them goal for goal. At the final whistle, with the Dutch 3–2 ahead, the crowd rose to salute both teams, little consolation for Oona, who was close to tears.

'But they were so *good*,' she wailed. 'How come they lost?'

Suttle was still reliving Arjen Robben's opening goal. The lightning breakaway down the wing. The way he left his marker for dead on the halfway line. The sheer power of the man as he raced towards goal. And the teasing angle of the final shot. Far corner. Goalie? No chance. No wonder Robben got Man of the Match.

Oona wanted to know whether Suttle also had a prize draw at work.

'Yeah.'

'And?'

'Algeria. If they get through the group stages they'll be play-ing Germany next.'

'Shit.' Oona pulled a face.

'Exactly.'

'And Golden Bollocks?'

'Guess.'

'Germany.' Oona shook her head. 'I don't believe you. That man was born lucky.'

'You think so?' Suttle rolled over on the carpet and reached for her. Three Stellas and the sheer quality of the game had left him nicely mellow.

'Tell me you love me, big man.' Oona was straddling him.

'I love you, big man.'

'Right answer, Man of the Match. What can a girl do for you?'

'Somewhere in the kitchen. Maybe top of the fridge. I can't remember.'

'What am I looking for?'

'A DVD. The Spain–Netherlands game. A mate recorded it for me. I still haven't see it.'

'More Arjen Robben? He of the haircut and the nice legs?'

She disappeared into the kitchen. Suttle yelled for another tinnie. No answer. He turned back to the TV. The pundits were previewing tomorrow's England game against Uruguay. Luis Suarez, he thought. His heart sank.

Oona was back. No DVD. No tinnie. Just a single question.

'How come you've been seeing your ex-wife?'

Suttle stared up at her. Caught offside. Big time.

'Seeing?'

'You're telling me she hasn't been here?'

She was holding a small leather-bound address book. She threw it at Suttle.

He picked it up. 'Where did you find this?'

'Up on the shelf where you keep those recipe books. You're telling me you didn't know it was there?'

Suttle had opened the book. On the first page all the clues Oona would ever want. Lizzie Hodson. Contact details. Address. The lot. Not just the earrings, he thought.

'She called round,' he said.

'When?'

'The other day.'

'Day? Like when you were at work? You think I'm stupid? It was that evening, wasn't it? The day you got bitten, that fucking dog. I should have come down. I bloody knew it. Eejit, me.

Totally brain-dead. You needed someone.' She paused. 'Well, big man?'

'You're right.'

'And she stayed?'

'Yes.'

'You knew she was coming? When we were talking on the phone? That was all arranged? That's why you put me off?'

'Yes.'

'So what's she got? Apart from a trillion pounds in the bank? I thought this thing was supposed to be over. That's the way you sold yourself, my lovely. Divorce in the offing. All over bar the paperwork. Good, was she? Good as ever?'

Suttle didn't answer, mostly because he didn't know what to say. Maybe he should ask for a lawyer. Maybe he should go No Comment. Or maybe he should find the DVD, settle Oona down and let the storm blow out. Having Lizzie here had been a huge mistake. In the end, come what may, life always finds you out.

'I'm sorry,' he muttered.

'Sorry doesn't cut it, my lovely. We had a good thing going. A great thing going. I was right about Golden Bollocks. Wrong about you. I thought you were better than this. I truly did. And you know what that makes me? One sad fuck. Believe the worst and you won't be disappointed. Give me that, will you?'

She nodded at the address book. Suttle handed it over.

'What are you going to do now?'

'What am I going to do now?' She was staring down at him. 'Like I'd tell you? Like I'd trust you? Like you'd be the slightest bit interested?' Her eyes were moist. 'If I had a pound for every time you said you loved me, I'd be a rich woman. But you know the truth? What I am just now? Totally skint.'

Her anorak was on the back of the chair. She put it on and headed for the door. Then she stopped and looked back at him.

'Fuck you, Jimmy Suttle.' She was on the edge of tears. 'You know something? You deserve the bitch.'

*

Lizzie was drifting into sleep under a blanket on the sofa when she heard the banging at the front door. She got up on one elbow, wondering if it had been part of a dream. More bangs, even louder.

She got off the sofa, her heart racing, and went through to the hall. The previous owner had fitted a security spyhole in the front door. The outside light didn't work but Lizzie still peered through. Oona.

She unbolted the door, took the Yale off the latch. Suddenly Oona was inches away, one foot inside the house. She was taller than Lizzie and she'd definitely been drinking.

'Father Christmas,' she said. 'Come with a wee present.'

She thrust something into Lizzie's hand. Lizzie found herself looking at her own address book.

'You meant me to find this? Was that your game?'

'I don't know what you're talking about.'

'You don't?' Oona was looking past her. Through the open door, she could see the shadowed spaces of the living room. 'Nice place. Did you fuck him here too?'

'We're talking Jimmy? He's my husband, in case you'd forgotten.'

'That wasn't my question. I asked you whether you fucked him here as well.'

'Then the answer's yes.'

'Like where? In there?' She nodded at the open door. 'On the carpet? On the sofa? Or did you take your time? Old habits die hard. I expect you took him to bed.'

She pushed past Lizzie, heading down the hall, then started making her way upstairs, looking for the bedroom. Lizzie tried to stop her, but it was hopeless. She was fit as well as drunk, and the anger was boiling out of her.

She'd found the bedroom. She pushed the door open. Michala was standing on the other side of the bed, her toes curling on the bare floorboards. She'd taken off the dressing gown and was trying to get into her thong. Naked, she stared at this stranger.

Oona returned the stare and then began to laugh.

'You two are a couple? I'm interrupting something?'

'You're interrupting nothing. I'm downstairs on the sofa.'

'Yeah? Really?' Oona shook her head in disbelief. 'My poor bloody man,' she whispered. 'What the fuck have you done to him?'

Thirty-Eight

Lizzie woke to the sound of Michala being sick. Oona had come and gone. There'd been a scuffle at the door, nothing serious, and Lizzie had managed to survive the encounter intact. She'd ducked the half-hearted headbutt and bolted the front door just in case. Now Lizzie made her way upstairs to the bathroom, where Michala was bent over the toilet bowl.

'I'm sorry ...' She wiped her mouth. 'I'm really, really sorry.'

'It's nothing. Don't worry. Something you've eaten?'

'I expect so.'

'Like what?'

Michala didn't know, couldn't say. Lizzie asked whether it had happened before. The way she shook her head, immediately emphatic, told Lizzie she was lying.

'It happens a lot, yes?'

'Sometimes.'

'For no apparent reason?'

'Excuse me.'

She threw up again, gesturing blindly for Lizzie to leave her alone. Lizzie went back to the bedroom. Michala had arrived with a daysack, nothing else. It lay on the carpet beside the bed.

Lizzie went through it. Beneath a couple of paperbacks and a handful of spare underwear she found a car rental form. Curious, she unfolded it. The local branch of Budget had premises on the Marsh Barton Industrial Estate, to the south of the city centre. On Friday 6 June, at 12.00, Michala had picked up a Ford Focus diesel. The three-day rental had cost her £89.87. The car was returned, with a full tank of fuel, at 11.06 on Monday. Under payment options the Budget clerk had ringed 'Cash'.

Lizzie glanced at the open door. There was no sign of Michala. Lizzie's printer lay beside her laptop on the table downstairs in the living room. She took a photocopy of the car rental form and then went back upstairs and returned it to Michala's bag. At the very bottom of the bag she found another item, a knitted wristband still in its wrapping. The trademark was Sea-Band. She made a mental note, then left Michala's bag where she'd found it. The flushing of the loo brought Michala back to the bedroom. She looked terrible.

'Tea?'

'Water, please.'

Lizzie obliged, fetching a glass of water from the bathroom. Only when Michala was asleep again, curled beneath the duvet, did she return to her laptop. Googling Sea-Band took seconds. According to the website, their wrist bands were medical aids against nausea and vomiting caused by travel. And by pregnancy.

A phone call from DI Carole Houghton cleared the way for a *Buzzard* detective to descend on the Exmouth branch of Tesco. The store manager provided a back office and a PC to review the CCTV disc. The officer involved happened to be Colin Myers, the youngster in the squad. An hour and a half shuttling back and forth between midnight and five in the morning on Sunday 8 June produced no sightings of the man whose mug-shot adorned the Major Incident Room. Unless he'd disguised himself as the furtive shoplifter in Aisle 3 or one of the noisy lads who'd swaggered into the store at just gone midnight, Alois Bentner was lying.

Nandy was unsurprised by the news. The duty magistrate had given *Buzzard* another thirty-six hours to charge or release its prime suspect. What Nandy wanted – needed – now was a full confession.

He'd summoned a mid-morning meet in the MIR, principals

only. Suttle, who'd pulled together the intel file, offered an overview of the case against Bentner. As far as motive was concerned, he said, the jury was out. There was every indication that Bentner's affection for Harriet Reilly was real. They'd spent a lot of time together. They were fellow solitaries, both a little obsessed, she with a cascade of issues around euthanasia, he with the death of the entire human race. But they were also a jealous couple, sternly possessive of each other. Add Bentner's drinking, a level of consumption that put him deep into alcoholism, and it was conceivable – just – that he'd been driven to do something physically extreme.

Nandy wanted to know about opportunity. Suttle said that wouldn't have been a problem. They could now prove that he'd been away from the rough sleepers on the Saturday night for at least an hour. His alibi didn't stand up. Harriet was asleep in Bentner's house and he obviously had a key. He could have arrived, slipped into the house, killed her and then left again. The pathologist had drawn a six-hour window around the time of her death. It all fitted perfectly.

'You don't sound convinced, Jimmy.' This was Houghton.

'I'm not, boss. OK, I can see him assaulting her, beating her around the head and face, maybe even suffocating her. He'd be remorseful afterwards, but he'd have meant it at the time. What doesn't work for me is the rest of it.' He gestured down at his belly. 'Especially the baby. That's bizarre. We're into serious weirdness.'

'Gemma Caton?'

'Exactly.'

Heads nodded around the table. Luke Golding had been in touch within the last hour. He'd managed to interview the German guy around the corner from Michala's London flat, and he'd confirmed that Caton's yellow Nissan Micra had sat in his driveway all weekend. The neighbours in the apartment block were telling a similar story. Two of them had seen Michala and Caton on the Saturday afternoon and stopped for a chat.

The next-door flat belonged to a young Indian IT worker.

He'd returned from an evening out on the Saturday night to find a light under Michala's door, and the sound of the TV on low. His girlfriend, he said, had woken up at dawn. The TV next door had still been on, but by the time she got back to sleep someone had turned it off. The TV was evidently brand new, a Samsung 32-inch. The Indian guy had helped Michala set it up.

Suttle, who'd taken the call from Golding, had made a note. Now Nandy wanted his take on Gemma Caton's involvement.

'For me, sir, she's the key to all this. If we're talking obsession, she's way out front. This is a woman who doesn't take prisoners. What she wants, she gets – and it has to be on her own terms. For me Bentner is on that list, whether he knows it or not. So is the Danish girl. And so, I suspect, is my ex-wife.'

'You think this is a sexual thing?' Nandy asked.

'Not necessarily, sir. Rosie nailed it last night when she was in with Bentner. With Caton it's more primitive than sex. Think dog. This is a woman who lives in a world of lamp posts.'

'And Bentner?'

'A lamp post. Definitely. She wants to own him. To leave her smell on him. Caton's not a woman for sharing. It's a territorial thing. I'm not sure we've got a form for it.'

'And that's enough to explain Reilly? The state of her?'

'More than enough. With Reilly, remember, it's not just one body, but two. Caton wanted them both out of her way, both mother and fetus.'

'So she killed Reilly? Is that what you're saying?'

'She may have done. It's a possibility.'

'But she's in London. So how does that work?'

'It doesn't. Not yet.'

'So what next? We pull her in?'

'We put her under surveillance.'

'Like your missus suggested?'

'Yes, sir. I'm afraid so.'

Nandy nodded, glanced at Houghton. Everyone in the room understood the budgetary implications.

'Let's do it, Carole. I'm not sure we have a choice.'

Easier said than done. Suttle conferred with the D/S in charge of the force Surveillance Unit by phone. He had an address for the target and a workplace contact number but little else. Golding was scouring the Internet for more details. Caton's Facebook account offered a gallery of photos, many of them recent, and some remarkably candid hints about the developing shit storm that was her private life.

'Serious grief on the home front,' she'd posted yesterday. 'Bummer.' What hundreds of disappointed students were to make of this self-confessional moment was anyone's guess, but Suttle emailed the best of the photos to the Surveillance Unit and left them to make their plans. Early afternoon the surveillance D/S came back to him by email. 'Can't find her anywhere,' he'd written. 'Any clues?'

Sadly not. Suttle went back to her Facebook page, staring at the photos on his PC. Caton grandstanding behind a lectern, presumably in a lecture hall at the university. Caton in the student union bar, mobbed by adoring students. Caton knee-deep in water at a bird reserve on the Exe estuary, stooping to collect an armful of eel grass. In every shot the expression on her face was virtually the same: gleeful, slightly manic, untroubled by restraint or anything as worrisome as self-doubt.

The threads which tied these images together were spelled out in accompanying posts. Nature is giving up on mankind. The Anglo-Saxon model of capitalism has hollowed out the world we once knew. Only democratic protest on a vast scale offers any real hope. We have to be stronger than them, cleverer than them, less greedy than the guys with the boardrooms and the chauffeurs and the shareholders and all the other goodies of an economic system that is cooking us slowly to death. Turn down the gas. Cap the oil wells. Seal the coal mines. Give your kids, and your kids' kids, a fighting chance.

Did Suttle sign up to any of this stuff? He wasn't sure. Like most of the rest of the human race he told himself he was too busy – too stretched – to give it the attention it deserved. Deep down he suspected that the Catons and the Bentners of this world were probably right, that all of us were pedalling fast towards disaster, but whenever he gave it a moment's proper thought he asked himself what he could really do to make a difference. Take the train instead of the car? Give up meat? Live on lentils and soy milk? None of it was especially appealing, and lentils definitely made him fart, but a couple of months ago – on a snatched holiday on the Costa del Sol – he and Oona had discussed the madness of the world one night in a bar near Marbella.

Everything around them, for miles and miles, seemed less than a decade old. In certain lights – especially at dawn or at sunset – the effect could be spectacular, but even where the developers hadn't run out of money, the results looked fake. Fake Moorish arches. Fake marble walkways. Fake haciendas. Inland, beyond the sprawl of developments that would never be finished, lay the golf courses. Keeping these playgrounds green was emptying the aquifers and sucking the rivers dry. The price of cucumbers in the mountain villages was soaring so rich men could make it to the eighteenth tee. Where was the logic in that? How long before the people began to march off the mountains? Camp on all those manicured greens? And chase all the bloodsucking foreigners back to where they belonged? Suttle didn't know, but the memories of that evening were achingly sweet.

He'd been thinking of Oona all day. They were in a new place, a bad place, and that had never happened before. He'd wanted to talk to her, somehow to get in touch, but he didn't know what to say. She was right. An apology would be pathetic. The word sorry would bounce off her.

He eyed Golding for a moment. His desk was on the other side of the MIR. He was on the phone to someone and he was laughing. Probably a new woman, Suttle thought. *How come he gets away with it time after time?* He bent to his keyboard, opened an email to Oona. 'If I was Arjen Robben,' he wrote, 'would it make any difference?' He sent the email and sat back, wondering if it had been such a great idea. Within minutes came the reply. 'If you were Arjen Robben, I'd be learning Dutch. *Waar en wanneer?*'

Waar en wanneer? Sensing a chink of light, Suttle fed the phrase into an Internet translation website. Easy. *Where and when?* He smiled. He grinned. The website was still open. The website obliged with an answer. He keyed his reply: 'De Engel, 19.00.'

Lizzie had spent the afternoon working on her laptop while Michala stayed in bed and read *Mine*. Around six in the evening she appeared in the living room. She'd read more than half the book and said she was proud. Proud, to Lizzie, seemed an odd reaction. Shocked, she could cope with. Moved would be fine. But *proud*?

'I'm proud to know you. Proud to be your friend. So much. You went through so much. Not once but twice. That makes you strong. No wonder ...'

'No wonder what?'

'No wonder Gemma thinks so much of you. In Denmark we have a saying. Two herrings in the same tin.'

'You mean we're similar? Peas in a pod?'

'*Ja.*' She nodded. 'Two peas exactly the same.'

Lizzie didn't know how to take this. What little she'd seen of Gemma Caton had first alarmed and then frightened her. The woman was a force of nature fuelled by an ego the size of the planet, and the more she imagined what might have happened in Lympstone had she stayed that night, the more she wanted to keep her at arm's length.

'You worship her, don't you?'

'Who?'

'Gemma. She looks after you. I understand that. She protects you. I understand that too. But in return she needs all of you.'

'You think so?'

'Yes.' Lizzie nodded. At last she thought she understood. 'So are you her friend? Her lover? Her companion? Or something else?'

'Like what?'

Lizzie didn't want to use the word. It was too blunt. Too crude. Then came the inner shrug. What the hell. 'Slave?'

Suttle had been in the pub a couple of minutes when Oona walked in. The Angel again. Across from Exeter Central station.

'What have you done to your hair?'

'Change of image, my lovely. Buy me a drink.' She sank into the leather sofa under the window.

Suttle fetched a couple of large glasses and a bottle of Côtes-du-Rhône from the bar. Oona nodded in approval. *Good start*, Suttle thought.

'God says we should let this breathe.' She nodded at the bottle. 'God's wrong. You pour.'

Suttle was still looking at her hair. Green tints among the auburn curls. He reached for the bottle.

'Why green?' he asked.

'I'm jealous as fuck. I'm also really angry. Tell me about that wife of yours.'

'What do you want to know?'

'Two things. How long has she been screwing women? And how come you're still in the queue?'

'Screwing women? You can prove that?'

'Sure I can. You want the details?' She described what she'd seen in Lizzie's bedroom. 'She was pretty too. I'll give her marks for good taste.'

Suttle laughed. He'd spent the last couple of hours wondering how difficult this was going to be. When he was living with Lizzie, he'd got used to endless silences, tiny spasms of reproachful point-scoring, an unvoiced bitterness that could last for weeks. Not this woman. Not Oona.

'Three things,' he replied. 'Number one, I haven't a clue. Number two, because I was a twat. And number three, it will never happen again.'

'Says you.'

'Says me.'

'You never knew she fancied women?'

'Never. Big surprise.'

'But you're a detective. You're supposed to spot these things. No clues at all?'

'None. She was always hetero. Ambitious? Yes. Clever? Definitely. A turn-on? I'm afraid so. But lesbian? No way.'

'So what's changed?'

'I just told you. I haven't the faintest. She got into trouble the other night. She's after a story. She's been playing the cop. Do that and you sometimes need back-up. My ex-wife doesn't do back-up.'

'That's because she's got you.'

'Wrong. I'm part of the furniture as far as she's concerned, and that's fine by me.'

'What sort of trouble?'

Suttle hesitated. The last thing he wanted to do was let this conversation stray onto Job turf. He'd let that happen with Lizzie, and he was still living with the consequences.

'She's a journalist,' he said. 'Once a journalist, always a journalist.'

'You mean people don't change?'

'Not in her case.'

'And in yours? Were you always a two-faced serial shagger?'

'No. As it happens.'

'Why should I believe you?'

'Because you're here. Because you answered my email. In Dutch. Lovely touch.'

'Gold star? You approve?'

'I'm very glad you came.' He paused. 'Are you?'

She wouldn't answer. She reached for her glass. In the light from the window Suttle watched her take a sip, then another. He'd never realised what a strong face she had. Oona, to his certain knowledge, always favoured the boldest line through life's trickier corners. Where might this one lead?

She returned the glass to the table. Then she took his hand and kissed it.

'Where I come from you always get two goes,' she said. 'After that, you're history.'

294

Thirty-Nine

Mid-evening, the D/S in charge of the Surveillance Unit briefly conferenced with Carole Houghton on her mobile. Despite exhaustive covert checks around the university, plus a number of inputs from other sources, his guys had failed to locate Ms Caton. Two of them had plotted up her Lympstone house in case she came back. Another team had driven to London to sit on her partner's Streatham flat. For the time being, she'd simply vanished.

Houghton wanted to know about Michala Haas. She knew that Suttle had provided photos lifted from Caton's Facebook page that included them both. A sighting of one might lead to the other.

'This is the pretty woman? Younger? Blonde hair? Slight?'

'Yes.'

'You want us to expand the search? Budget-wise that could be tricky.'

Houghton thought about the question. She knew that Nandy regarded *Buzzard* as home and dry. Bentner was squarely in the frame. Why spend another couple of grand on walk-on parts when the lead player was under lock and key?

'No,' she said at last. 'Just find me Caton.'

Lizzie sat up late after Michala had gone back upstairs to finish *Mine*. Despite repeated attempts to trap or seduce Michala into revealing what had brought her to The Plantation, she'd got nowhere. She tried to fathom what Michala really felt about Gemma Caton but without success. Whether this reticence was due to fear or loyalty wasn't clear. But whenever Lizzie even mentioned her name, Michala's head would go down and the conversation was over. Finally, with the nearby church bell striking ten o'clock, she determined on one last attempt.

Michala appeared to be asleep. The book lay beside her, evidently finished. Lizzie perched on the bed, stroked her hand. Michala stirred and rolled over, and Lizzie rearranged her pillow to make her more comfortable. Under the pillow was Michala's phone.

Lizzie toyed with slipping it out and taking it downstairs, but Michala was awake now, rubbing her eyes. She sat up in the bed.

'You finished the book?'

'Yes.'

'And?'

'I liked it. Very much.'

She said it was sad at the end. She'd nearly cried.

'Sad for who?'

'For all of you. Grace. You. And Claire as well. It was a good thing to do.'

'Kill my daughter?'

'Write the book.'

Lizzie nodded. There was an opening here. She had to take it. Tomorrow morning Michala might decide to leave.

'You're pregnant, aren't you?'

Michala was staring at her. 'How do you know?'

'I had a daughter. There are some things you don't forget.' She smiled. 'Like morning sickness.'

Michala said nothing. Lizzie took her silence for a yes.

'How many months?'

'Ten weeks.'

'Does Gemma know?'

'Of course.'

'Who's the father?'

Another silence. Longer this time. Then Michala turned into her. She wanted to be held. She wanted comfort. She wanted these incessant questions to end.

'Are you frightened about having the baby?'

'Of course I am.'

'Why?'

She shook her head, wriggled free and burrowed down under the duvet. Lizzie could hear her sobbing.

After a while Lizzie lifted the duvet. 'I'm your friend,' she said. 'Trust me.'

'That's what Gemma says.'

'Do you believe her?'

'Yes. I have to believe her. She knows everything.'

'You mean she's wise?'

'She knows everything.'

'What does that mean?'

Michala was staring up at her. Her eyes were glassy. She shook her head. No way.

'Maybe you should go,' she said at last. 'Leave this place. Go somewhere else.'

'Why would I want to do that?'

Another shake of the head. Lizzie gazed at her for a long moment and then stripped off and slipped into the bed. Michala's thin body was trembling. Her flesh was cold to the touch. Lizzie held her again, trying to offer comfort. This, she told herself, was her last and only opportunity to tease out the truth.

'You're frightened, aren't you?'

Michala looked at her and nodded. 'Yes.'

Suttle was alone in his flat. It was nearly midnight. He'd done his best to persuade Oona to come down to Exmouth with him but she wasn't having it. She meant it about a second chance, but there was no way she was sharing a bed with him for a while. They were starting all over. When it happened, it happened. But not tonight.

They'd parted friends. She'd disappeared to find her car with most of the bottle undrunk, asking him to phone her.

'Tonight? Tomorrow?'

'When it feels right.'

'It always feels right.'

'Bullshit. You want to watch the football. My best to Mr Rooney. Sleep well, my angel.'

She was right about the football. Back home in Exmouth he settled down to watch the England–Uruguay match and then caught a highlights round-up of the day's other games. He was wondering what he'd do if he found himself in Roy Hodgson's shoes when his mobile buzzed with an incoming text. He checked caller ID. Lizzie.

His heart sank. After meeting Oona again, the last thing he needed was another knock on his door. He studied the phone for a moment or two, then put it to one side. Whatever it was could wait. For now, thanks to Luis Suarez, Mr Hodgson had a real problem.

Lizzie, still downstairs, waited for Suttle to respond. She'd sent him a one-line text – 'Check out Budget Rent-a-Car Exeter booking in the name of Haas' – and thought at the very least she deserved an acknowledgement. She'd no idea where this tiny piece of intelligence lay within the bigger picture but imagined him alone in his flat, bewildered by developments in his private life, nailed by the address book she'd left. Neediness like that had consequences. There was no way she'd make it to Exmouth tonight, but over the weeks to come she could visualise all kinds of possibilities. He still belonged to her. And she could still make it happen for him.

She went back upstairs. Michala was fast asleep. For the first time since she'd turned up on the doorstep there was a smile on her face. Lizzie slipped under the duvet, checked her watch – nearly midnight – and drifted off. Tomorrow morning, first thing, she'd have it out with Michala. The woman knew exactly what had happened to Harriet Reilly. Hence the state of her.

Lizzie woke hours later. She'd no idea what time it was. She lay absolutely still for a moment, listening to the wind in the eaves. She had a roof full of loose slates, and their rattling sometimes woke her up. But then came another noise, a whispered conversation, very close. She rolled over, reaching for Michala, wanting to warn her, but the bed was empty. She struggled upright. A creaking floorboard on the bareness of the landing. She called Michala's name. Nothing. Then came more whispers. Her blood turned to ice. Intruders, she thought. Definitely.

Her mobile was on the floor beside the bed. Waiting for a response from Jimmy, it was still switched on. She rang his number. Then, in the darkness, she felt a presence in the open doorway. She abandoned the phone and reached for the bedside lamp. At first, semi-blinded by the light, she couldn't make out the looming figure above her. Then she felt hands around her throat, big hands, strong hands, squeezing and squeezing. Gemma Caton, she thought.

She was struggling now, fighting back, trying to wriggle free, but Caton's weight was on her chest, another pressure, forcing the air from her lungs. The huge face was inches from hers, eyes glittering behind the rimless glasses.

Then came a question, gravel-voiced, American accent: 'You gonna tell me?'

Somebody was at the foot of the bed, hands working under the duvet. Lizzie felt the bite of something sharp around her ankles. She tried to kick free again, couldn't. The hands had tightened on her throat. Colour drained from the room and a greyness fogged what little she could still see until darkness stole into the room again. *Help me*, she thought dimly. *Please God, someone help me.*

Jimmy Suttle woke to the sound of an incoming call on his mobile. He groped for it in the darkness. Lizzie. It was 03.21. Oona had told him about the visit she'd paid to Lizzie's house, about the woman in her bedroom upstairs, about the admission she'd wrung from Jimmy's so-called ex-wife. Sure, she'd spent the night down in Exmouth. And guess what? She'd happily do it again.

He put the phone to his ear, angered by yet another intrusion. When would this bloody woman leave him alone?

About to tell her to stop ringing, he froze. It was an American voice: forceful, terse, commanding, unmistakable. Gemma Caton.

'You know about Kelly, right? Because Michala told you, yes? So what else did she say?'

Suttle strained to catch a reply but heard nothing. Then came a groan and the faintest attempt at a question.

'What are you doing? Leave me alone.'

Lizzie. Definitely Lizzie.

Suttle was out of bed now. He had two mobiles, one a work phone, one for personal use. The work phone was in the kitchen. Still monitoring the conversation, he fired up the work phone and dialled Houghton's number. The number answered within seconds. He was about to speak when he realised the open line would carry his conversation. He wrapped the personal phone in a tea towel.

Houghton sounded wide awake. Night owl. No wonder she always looked so knackered.

'We've got a situation, boss. Caton's with Lizzie. My guess is we're talking serious violence.'

'Where?'

'Either Caton's house or Lizzie's. God knows which.' He was trying to remember exactly where Lizzie lived. Then the name of the property came back to him. 'The Plantation, boss. St Leonard's. Off the Topsham Road.'

'I'll get someone there.'

Suttle grunted, asked her to hang on. The phone wedged against his ear, he was pulling on a pair of trackie bottoms and wondering what he'd done with his car keys. Then he was back on the phone.

'I've got an open line, boss. She must have left her mobile on. I'll come straight in. Get me a contact number for whoever responds. Have them wait outside. Nothing happens until I give the word. We need to let Caton talk herself out. Yeah?'

'So you're going where?'

'St Leonard's. The Plantation.'

Houghton rang off. Suttle, back in the kitchen, retrieved the other phone. Then he headed for the door.

Trussed hand and foot with cable ties, Lizzie lay naked on the bed. Michala had pulled the curtains across the window. The nearest neighbours were way beyond screaming range. Thank God no one had spotted the live phone.

Gemma Caton was sitting on the bed. She was wearing an army surplus camo top over an oversize pair of jeans, her big hands crammed into a pair of tight-fitting black leather gloves. She wanted to know what Lizzie had done with the information about Kelly Willmott. Lizzie said she didn't know what she was talking about.

'You've been to the police, right?'

'No.'

'So why did they pull Michala in?'

'I don't know.'

'You do, my child. You do. And soon you're going to tell me.'

She leaned forward, her huge face inches away. Lizzie could smell spearmint on her breath again. Then she felt the big hands closing around her neck, squeezing and squeezing. She tried to scream. Nothing happened. Then the pressure suddenly relaxed.

'You wanna tell me now? Do yourself a favour?'

Lizzie nodded. Keep her talking, she thought. Just keep her talking. Play the journalist. Pretend you're not looking at madness. More questions. String this out.

'What does Michala say?' She was staring up at Caton. 'What did she tell them?'

'Nothing. And my beautiful girl never lies.'

'So why do you think I've been to the police?'

'Because you played games with us. Your little trick with the closet? The soapstone carvings? You're denying any of that?'

301

Lizzie shook her head. Michala had edged closer. Her eyes were wide in the paleness of her face. Lizzie stared up at her. She realised at last that she'd got this woman badly wrong. She was the cuckoo in the nest. She'd rung Caton, probably opened the front door to her.

'I was right all the time, wasn't I?' Her eyes strayed towards Caton. 'You're her slave.'

The blow caught Lizzie by surprise, smack in her mouth. She screamed with the pain, felt her eyes watering.

Caton's face hung over her again.'We're talking choice here,' she said. 'Don't ever call me unreasonable.'

'Choice?' Lizzie forced the word out. Her lips felt like rubber, swelling already under the force of the blow.

Caton had bent even closer. She was chewing gum.

'Number one, you tell us how much the police know. Or number two, we burn your house down … with you inside it.'

Suttle was already on the long hill climbing out of Exmouth. The road was empty. He was driving flat out, the crest of the hill approaching. Then came a call on his work phone. He'd anticipated this. He hauled the car to a stop in the forecourt of a fuel station. Covered the live phone with a cushion. Answered the call.

'PC Billington,' a voice said. 'We're in position outside your missus' property. Light in the top window. Await your call. Out.'

Suttle pulled out onto the road again, trying to visualise exactly what had happened to Lizzie. Assuming she was at The Plantation had been a punt but a good one. A prisoner in her own bedroom, at the mercy of someone as deranged as Caton, she'd somehow mustered the presence of mind, the sheer balls, to play the scene for all she was worth. Suttle knew exactly what she was doing and he wondered whether – in the same situation – he'd be performing as well. *Fair play*, he thought, removing the cushion from the phone. *Keep talking*.

*

Caton, to Lizzie's horror, was serious about burning the house down. She'd dispatched Michala downstairs to look for cardboard, old newspapers, anything to start a fire. She'd noticed logs and kindling in a big basket beside the open fireplace. An old place like this, she was assuring Lizzie, would go up in minutes. Windows open downstairs for a draught. Bedroom door open to funnel air upstairs. Bedding loosened, the sheets and the duvet trailing into the flames. Lower the big sash window and the fire would take care of itself.

She said she was sorry about smacking Lizzie in the mouth. She'd been a little wound up. A little provoked. Needn't have happened. A misunderstanding on both parts. Not a classy thing to do.

She reached down and touched Lizzie lightly on the cheek. Lizzie turned her face away. She felt numb with shock. She was going to die in her own bedroom. Burned alive like some heretic witch.

Caton, as ever, was ahead of the game, taking a visible pleasure in spelling out what Lizzie might like to anticipate.

'Think Viking funeral, baby. Think Hindus beside the Ganges. Think *purification*.'

'Purification? What have I done?'

'You played us for fools. No one does that.'

'I asked some questions. That's all I did.'

'Sure. And what will you do with the answers? You think we can take a risk like that? Think again ...'

She got off the bed and left the room. Moments later she was back with a leather bag. She produced something the size of a smallish torch, wrapped in tissue paper. Inside was a carving. She held it in front of Lizzie's face. There were tiny primitive marks on the carving, maybe a face at the top.

'Soapstone.' Caton was stroking it. She named an American Indian tribe. 'Headwaters of the Fraser River. They carved these like they carved totem poles. They were talking to the spirits, to the gods of the river. They gave them to the women. The women used them whichever way they wanted. If you made love to the soapstone, the tribe won the blessing of the spirits. That way the tribe got through another winter.'

'Why do I need this?'

'Because you need to make friends with it. That way it will keep you safe on the journey.'

'You're crazy. This is crazy talk.'

'You think so?'

Caton made a space on the bedside table for the carving. Erect in front of Lizzie's pile of paperbacks, she could almost believe it had a presence. She closed her eyes. Naked in the draught from the door, she was trembling with fear and with cold. This wasn't happening, she told herself. *Please God, someone help me.*

Suttle was on the edges of Exeter within ten minutes. Aside from a near-collision with a van delivering milk, a flash of white in the darkness, the road had been empty. St Leonard's lay on the southern edges of the city centre. Busting through a series of red traffic lights, Suttle slowed for the turn that would take him off the main road and into the cul-de-sac that led to Lizzie's property. Already he could see a couple of marked cars parked up in the looming shadow of a hedge, invisible from the house. Top work, he thought.

His personal phone pressed to his ear, he slipped out of the car. A uniformed PC met him beneath the hedge. They talked in whispers. He had two guys around the back of the premises. Another had tested the front door and confirmed it was open. What now?

Suttle was still listening to the phone. He made a tiny gesture with his other hand. Wait.

Michala was back in the bedroom, her arms full of twists of newsprint. Watching Caton scatter the newspaper around the bed, Lizzie cursed her habit of keeping back numbers of the *Express and Echo*. She'd always told herself that – over time – these would serve as an archive for stories that might find their way onto her website. Now they were going to cook her alive. Caton's mention of Hindu funerals beside the Ganges had nailed itself to the inside of her head. She'd watched footage of these rituals of passage. The images were all too graphic. The body's fat fuelled the leaping flames. First you charred. Then you caught fire. Then you melted.

'Logs, angel?'

Michala departed. Caton was back beside the bed. Lizzie had run out of questions. She was terrified.

Caton was looking down at her. She'd pulled the duvet up, tucking the top around Lizzie's neck, apologising for the cold. She might have been a care attendant at one of the dodgier nursing homes: roughly solicitous, keen to keep the patient in the picture. Information is power, honey. You better believe it.

'You want to know what we do next? We let you say goodbye. We light the fire. We make sure the spirits feed the flames. And then we leave.' Caton smiled in the semi-darkness. 'They'll find your little bedside lamp on the floor. Crap electrics. A lesson for us all.'

'Say goodbye?' Lizzie managed.

'To the spirits.' Caton's gloved hand had descended on the soapstone carving. 'You want to kiss him? Just gimme the word. Only time's running out, sweetie, and there's no way we're leaving him here.'

Lizzie shook her head. Michala was back with a huge armful of logs and kindling. She was much stronger than she looked. Caton watched her building the fire, then turned back.

Lizzie stared up at her. What the hell. 'You killed her, didn't you?'

'Killed who?'

'The doctor. Harriet.'

'Not me, angel.'

'Then who?'

'The spirits. We're nothing on this earth. We're empty. We're the empty urn. Tap us on the outside and what do you get? An

305

echo. The echo of emptiness. When the spirits will it, when the time is right, we do their bidding. And the urn fills up.'

'And they told you to kill Harriet?'

'They told me the salmon were lost. They told me the salmon were waiting.'

'So you killed her?'

'I listened. I acted. Ask Alois. He knows.'

'And afterwards? After this …? ' Lizzie nodded towards Michala. More logs. More kindling.

'We go to Scotland. All three of us.'

'But Alois is under arrest. They'll charge him. He'll go down.'

'All three of us,' she repeated. 'Me, Michala, the baby. It helps in life to count.'

Lizzie was beyond counting. She stared up at Caton. The scene had become surreal. She was looking at her own death, her own mad funeral, her own disappearance. Just ashes, she thought. And a pile of bones. Did burning hurt? Did the pain get worse and worse until all your fuses blew and you melted away into unconsciousness? Was that why fire and brimstone had tormented the conscience of the guilty? Was this God's final judgement on her for losing Grace and haunting Jimmy? Was this the real meaning of wrath?

'A favour?' Lizzie's voice was no more than a whisper. 'Please?'

'Anything.'

'Can you kill me first? Suffocate me? Strangle me? Whatever?'

Caton thought about the proposition for a moment, then turned to Michala. Michala nodded, turned her head away. She had a lighter in her hand. She was kneeling at the foot of the bed, in the teeth of the draught from the open door.

'The window,' Caton said. 'Open the bloody window.'

The rumble of the sash window carried on the night wind. The PC heard it. Suttle too. The phone still to his ear, he'd lost the final part of the conversation. The voices were too low, the words indistinguishable. All he knew was that Lizzie was still alive, still conscious. Evidentially, he thought, they'd reached the end of the line.

The PC had heard enough to understand what lay in wait. Already, with Suttle's blessing, he'd alerted the fire brigade and an ambulance. Twice he'd suggested intervening, and twice Suttle had shaken his head. We need more, he'd said. We need the whole story.

Now the PC was close to making his own decision. Suttle gazed across at him. He still had the phone to his ear. He was still listening.

'Give me another minute,' he said. 'Leave this to me.'

Lizzie had resigned herself to whatever happened next. Fear had numbed her, stealing her wits, and now terror had robbed her of everything else. She could scarcely think properly. Her life, all too literally, was in the hands of a mad woman – the second one she'd encountered – and now she couldn't take her eyes off the black leather gloves. At the end of it all, she dimly realised, death is pitiless, a sequence of actions with only one end. Thick black fingers, flexing in front of her face. A pair of eyes from a horror movie. The shadow of Michala in the background, her lighter ready, a wraith at the foot of the bed.

Her turn next, Lizzie thought. Should I warn her? Should I tell her to get out of here, to leave this woman, to squirm free of the force field? Or should I take advantage of the open window – one last chance – and just scream?

The latter was all she had left. She opened her mouth, filled her lungs, but Caton had read her mind again, clamping her swollen lips with one huge hand, pressing down and down, the other hand circling her throat, squeezing harder and harder. Once again Lizzie fought for her life, trying to loosen the cable ties, trying to wriggle free beneath the crushing weight of Caton, but her strength had gone, and her resolve with it, and in the end she just relaxed, an act of acceptance, the feeblest gesture in the face of what was to come. The flames, she thought, licking around the bed. The roar as the fire took hold. Please let me die before I burn.

Suttle pocketed the phone. The PC had two officers from the other car staking out the back garden. They could smell smoke.

'Go,' Suttle said.

He and the PC burst through the garden gate and ran along the trail of paving stones towards the front door. The PC's oppo had already kicked it open. The smoke was thicker now, coiling out of the upstairs window. Suttle plunged into the darkness of the hall, trying to remember where he'd find the stairs, aware of the crackle of flames above his head. Lizzie's bedroom had been last on the left along the landing at the top. The door was wide open, the fire sucking the draught up the stairs. The lights were out, but the flames were reaching for the bed, the room full of smoke, the small shape of Lizzie motionless beneath the duvet. Of Caton and Michala there was no sign.

Suttle took one last suck of clean air and stepped across to the bed. Adrenalin scalded his veins. He'd carried Lizzie a million times before. She weighed nothing. Her wrists and ankles were bound with cable ties. He scooped her up from the bed and backed out of the bedroom, then turned and ran along the corridor. The other two officers were at the foot of the stairs. The air here was still clean. Suttle followed him out of the house, laid Lizzie gently down.

'Get rid of the ties,' he said.

One of the officers ran to his car for a knife while the other watched Suttle giving Lizzie mouth to mouth. He could find no pulse, no sign of life.

Suttle nodded at Lizzie's chest.

'CPR.'

Already kneeling beside Lizzie's body, the officer began a series of compressions, both hands flat on her chest, forcing blood around her body.

'Where's the fucking ambulance?'

'Coming.'

Suttle bent to Lizzie's face again. Her lips were swollen. He put his cheek to her mouth, desperate for signs of life. Nothing.

The fire had taken hold now, and a glance up at the window told Suttle they'd barely intervened in time. Long fingers of flame were reaching out through the window, eating the curtains, showering sparks into the darkness of the night air. Then, suddenly close, came the wail of sirens, at least two, and Suttle bent to Lizzie again, trying to will her back to life.

'Please,' he implored her. 'Please. Just for me.'

Forty

Gemma Caton and Michala Haas were arrested for breaking and entering in the back garden of Lizzie's house. Caton tried to attack one of the two arresting officers with a half-brick from a spoil heap beside the garage but was restrained without difficulty. Pressed for an account of what they'd been up to inside the property, she'd said nothing. When Michala showed signs of wanting to help, Caton had silenced her with a single look.

Driven to Heavitree police station, they were booked into the Custody Centre and lodged in overnight cells. The custody sergeant took the precaution of keeping the cells a distance apart.

D/S Jimmy Suttle arrived from the hospital an hour and a half later. He stank of smoke and didn't say very much. Having checked that Caton and Haas would be available for interview first thing, he left the police station and drove to the Major Incident Room at Middlemoor. It was nearly seven o'clock in the morning, the first trickle of rush-hour traffic heading in towards the city centre. Suttle drove past the line of cars waiting at the lights on the roundabout. Life had become abruptly unreal. He was totally spaced out. Did they have commuters on Mars?

DI Carole Houghton was waiting for him in her office at the MIR. She gave him a hug and said she was surprised he wasn't still up at the hospital.

'They're doing what they can,' Suttle said. 'It's fifty-fifty.'

'You should be there with her.'

'I know. And I'm not.'

He gave Houghton his personal phone and explained how he'd eavesdropped on the bedside conversations before Caton had done her best to kill his ex-wife.

'I'm thinking Haas jumped the gun, boss. Lizzie wasn't quite dead when she set fire to the place. They were out of there before Caton had the chance to finish her off.'

'Thank God for that.'

'Too right.' Suttle shook his head.

At the hospital they'd taken him aside with a warning that if Lizzie survived he might have to expect brain damage. CPR had kept her blood circulating until the ambulance had arrived but there were no guarantees. Her heart had stopped working and a full twenty minutes had elapsed before the paramedics got the defibrillator on her and shocked her heart back into life.

'You're telling me you waited a while before going into the property?'

'I did, boss.'

'Why?'

'Because Lizzie was doing a number on the woman. She knew the phone was still live. She knew I was probably listening. She was after an account. That's the way she works.'

'And you, Jimmy? Is that the way you work?'

'I knew it was what she wanted.'

'At the price of her life?'

'Hopefully not.'

Houghton nodded in mute agreement. This was way beyond any call of duty, she seemed to be implying. No matter how difficult their relationship, Lizzie was still a human being.

'It's not about the relationship, boss. It's about Lizzie. She put herself in this position. She needed to see it through.'

'That's harsh.'

'You're right, boss, but I got her out of there, didn't I? That was me in the bedroom, me carrying her downstairs, me giving her mouth-to-mouth.'

'And this is me suggesting you left it very late. Not on the record, Jimmy. This goes no further. But sometimes there are steps we shouldn't take, risks we shouldn't run. She may yet die. That would be a very great shame, as I'm sure you'd agree.'

'Of course, boss. Do me for negligence. Do me for whatever you like. I did what I did. And the way I'm looking at it, once she comes round, she'll say thank you.'

'Let's hope so.'

They gazed at each other. Then came the inevitable question.

'So what *did* she say? Caton?'

'She killed Reilly. She admitted it. There's lots of bollocks about the spirits and Caton acting as some kind of agent, but that's the drift. We were right first time, boss. It was a ritual killing. It's all there.' He nodded at his phone. 'I wrote down as much as I could remember after the ambulance took Lizzie away. Contemporaneous notes. Best I could do.'

Houghton was looking at the phone while Suttle sorted through his notes. They had the whole morning to prepare for the interviews with Caton and Haas. Given Lizzie's involvement, there was no way Suttle should be part of these interviews, but she wanted him to brief Myers and Rosie Tremayne.

'What about Bentner, boss?'

'We talk to him first. Hope he sees it our way. Let me go through those notes before we put Bentner in the interview room. You'll be watching the video feed. We'll shoot for a twelve o'clock start. Get some sleep. I'll brief Nandy myself.'

It was a colleague in A & E who broke the news to Oona about the overnight admission to the ICU. He was Irish too, an acting registrar from County Carlow.

'Woman called Lizzie Hodson. Thought you ought to know.'

Oona was preparing a line of trolleys. She toyed with a box of scalpels.

'What's the matter with her?'

'Heart failure after suffocation.'

'Shit. And you're telling me she's still alive?'

'Just. The cop may have got to her in time. The jury's out.'

312

'Cop? You got a name by any chance?'

'Afraid not. Either way, he's probably down for a medal. Just thought you'd like to know.'

'Great.' Oona forced a smile. 'Thanks.'

Suttle got his head down in one of the rooms at headquarters reserved for overnight visitors. He slept fitfully, waking from time to time to try and still the voices in his head. It was Caton, always Caton. Sometimes she was dressed as a squaw. Other times she was stark naked, plodding heavily after him, her head down, a bent, menacing figure growing slowly bigger. It was the worst kind of nightmare, denied any kind of resolution, and when he finally surfaced it was to find Luke Golding at the door.

He knew what had happened. Houghton had given him the gist.

'You should have phoned me, boss.'

'Bollocks. It was three in the morning.'

'I meant afterwards.'

'Why?'

'It can't have been ...' he shrugged '... a riot of laughs.'

'It wasn't.'

'Anything I can do?'

'Yeah.' Suttle was rubbing his eyes. 'Give Oona a bell. Tell her I did my best.'

'What does that mean?'

'Just tell her. See what she makes of it.'

Houghton had scheduled the next Bentner interview for midday. Suttle washed and shaved with one of the overnight kits before phoning Lizzie's mother in Portsmouth. He briefly explained what had happened and gave her contact details at the hospital. If she wanted to come down to be with her daughter, she was welcome to stay at his flat in Exmouth. She was shocked. She'd be down as soon as possible. She said she'd find somewhere closer to the hospital to stay.

Suttle drove across to Heavitree. Rosie Tremayne and Colin

Myers were waiting for him in an office off the Custody Suite. Houghton had already briefed them about events overnight.

Rosie had just finished reading the notes Suttle had made.

'That must have been a tough thing to do.'

'It was. Tougher for Lizzie, though.'

Rosie nodded, held his gaze, said nothing. She thinks I played God, Suttle thought. And she's probably right.

The interview started early. Suttle had given Bentner's solicitor partial disclosure. He'd taken a call from Lizzie. She had intruders in the house. One of them had been Gemma Caton. The phone had stayed on. He'd monitored what followed while he raced into Exeter. Mercifully, he'd been able to intervene in time to get his ex-wife out of the burning bedroom. God willing, she'd be up for a full recovery.

The solicitor made some notes and then enquired what charges these women would now be facing.

'They were arrested for breaking and entering,' Suttle said, 'but I imagine it'll go a lot further than that. They tried to burn her alive. That's arson and attempted murder in my book.'

Bentner was waiting in the interview room when Tremayne and Myers arrived. Ten minutes with his solicitor appeared to have changed him. He seemed less defensive. Some of the wariness, the gloom, appeared to have lifted. Suttle was monitoring the interview on a video feed, curious about this change of mood.

Bentner wanted to know more about the events of last night. Tremayne filled in the gaps in the account Bentner had got from his solicitor. A fellow officer had been in the happy position of eavesdropping on more or less everything. Ms Caton, it seemed, had been agitated about a woman called Kelly Willmott. She believed Lizzie had learned information from Michala Haas that would have been valuable to the police. Hence the need to silence her.

Bentner said nothing. Then he wanted to know more about Lizzie Hodson.

314

'I understand she's some kind of journalist. Am I right?'

'Yes.'

'And you're telling me she knew Michala?'

'Yes. She had dinner with Michala and Ms Caton earlier this week.'

Mention of Michala Haas won Bentner's total attention. It appeared to be news that she too had been at Lizzie's house last night.

'What was she doing there?'

'We don't know yet. It appears that she may have been in the property before Ms Caton arrived.'

'Staying, you mean?'

'Yes.'

'And you're telling me she's here? In a cell? Arrested?'

'Yes.'

'Have you talked to her yet?'

'No. We have that pleasure to come.' Tremayne leaned forward over the desk. 'You know we had an opportunity to listen to the conversation last night. Mainly between Caton and Lizzie. That conversation throws a great deal of light on what happened to your partner, Harriet. Before we go any further, Mr Bentner, we'd like to give you the opportunity of sharing your version of events.'

'I've already told you.'

'You told us you went to Tesco in the middle of the night. We checked. That turned out to be a lie. You were never in the store. You also told us that you got a call just before midnight. Which was when you decided to go shopping. You said the call was from Harriet. It certainly came from her phone, but we suspect it might not have been her.' She softened the suggestion with a smile. 'Can you help us here?'

Bentner thought hard about the question. Then he asked about Michala. What had she said last night?

'Very little.'

'But she's charged too?'

'We think she laid the fire. Then lit it. Watched what happened

315

afterwards. That's certainly arson. It may also turn out to be murder.' Tremayne paused. 'Why Michala? Why is she implicated?'

Bentner shook his head, refused to comment. He seemed to be back in a world of his own, but Tremayne had definitely touched a nerve. *Michala*, Suttle thought. *It's all about Michala*.

Tremayne, it turned out, shared exactly the same thought. Without binding *Buzzard* to any definite offer, she hinted that a full account from Bentner might help Michala's defence in court. Evidentially, she hadn't got a prayer. Arson alone was an extremely serious offence. At the very least she could be looking at four years behind bars.

'A full account?'

'What actually happened down in Lympstone. Before and afterwards. Given what we know, what we can prove, we think we can make a decent case for you killing Harriet Reilly. That may not be true. Only you know.' She shrugged, smiled again, then settled back in the chair, her arms folded over her chest. Over to you.

Bentner was conferring with his solicitor. Suttle, watching the feed from an office down the corridor, caught the tiny nods, hers first, then his. He turned back to Tremayne. He looked, if anything, relieved.

'You're right about the call I took that Saturday night,' he said. 'It was on Harriet's phone but it came from Gemma.'

'What did she say?'

'She said for me to come at once.'

'Why?'

'I'd no idea. That's all she said. Come at once.'

'And?'

'I drove over there.'

'Where?'

'To Lympstone.'

'What did you find?'

'I found Harriet upstairs. She'd been butchered. Torn apart. You've seen the photos. That's the way she was.'

'And Gemma?'

'She wasn't around. She'd gone.'

'Michala?'

'I've no idea about Michala. She wasn't there either.'

'So why didn't you phone us? Why didn't you get in touch?'

'Because life is never as simple as that.'

'You're telling me this thing was planned? That you knew it was going to happen?'

'I knew it was possible. Not the way she did it. Not like that. But I knew the way Gemma thought about –' he shrugged, '– us.'

'Us?'

'Myself and Harriet. Jealous is too small a word. It wasn't that. It was to do with possession. Gemma has to own things. They have to be hers. Exclusively. She owns Michala, for instance.'

'And you?'

'Yes.'

'Yes what?'

'She owned me. Or wanted to.'

'There's a difference, Mr Bentner. Did she own you? Or did she not?'

Bentner nodded, acknowledging the distinction.

'Yes, in a way she did. She's a powerful woman. I've no idea whether you've met her or not, but she has a presence – more than a presence, an aura, maybe even more than that. She's one of those people you meet once in a lifetime. She's committed. She's a superb anthropologist. Most of her, including her heart, *absolutely* including her heart, is in the right place. We talked constantly. She never bored me, never irritated me, always left me wanting more. Her take on where we're going and why was exemplary. I've never heard it better expressed. She'd penetrated the core of the problem and made it hers.'

'Just like everything else?'

'Indeed. That can be compelling. I'm a climate scientist. I can reduce catastrophe to hard facts, to lines on a graph, to the certainty of what's going to happen. But Gemma is so much better than that. She has the gift of tongues. She can make the language dance. I've seen her with a hall full of students. They're captivated. She's got them here.' His right hand settled softly on his heart. 'She's utterly compelling. An hour with Gemma, and you become someone else. It's remarkable to watch. But it has consequences.'

He talked of moths around a flame. Far away you remained in the darkness. Too close and you risked immolation.

'That was Harriet's fate?'

'Not at all. Harriet couldn't stand her. Harriet thought she was a phoney. Harriet was never one of the converted, and Gemma knew that.'

'But Harriet ...?'

'Knew I was one of the converted.'

'Hence the fights? The diary entries?'

'Of course.'

'So why didn't you defend her? And why did you become complicit in her death?'

Another silence. Suttle sensed this was new territory, even for Bentner's solicitor. She was doodling circles on her pad. Frowning.

'What did it for Gemma was the baby,' Bentner said at last. 'You didn't want to be around when she found out Harriet was pregnant.'

'Harriet told her?'

'Harriet told her nothing. I told her. Gemma was like a child herself. It was like she'd been deprived. I'd betrayed her. Worse still, I'd betrayed what we had in common.'

'Which was?'

'The cause. Fighting the opposition. Fighting apathy. Fighting ignorance. Trying to get the world to wake up. Gemma has a way of making you feel that small ...' He narrowed his fore-finger against his thumb. 'I felt even smaller. Then she said there was a way we could still be friends, still make it work, still carry the struggle forward. I thought it was crazy to begin with, but then she explained properly and I said yes.'

'To what?'

'Sleeping with Michala. Making her pregnant. Giving her a baby.'

'You did that?'

'Yes.'

'She's carrying your child?'

'Yes. We must have fucked twice. That's all it took.' There was a hint of pride in the half-smile.

'And afterwards? Once the baby had been born? What then?'

'It would become Gemma and Michala's child, their baby. As far as everyone else was concerned, she'd bought sperm from a donor bank. Mr Nobody.'

'But it's going to be yours.'

'I know. Because that's the way Gemma wanted it. She likes me. She may even love me. She certainly loves my genes. There was no way she could ever have me properly, and she knew that. Harriet and I and our own baby were off to Scotland, and she knew that too. That's why giving a baby to Michala was such a neat solution.'

'And Harriet?'

'She knew nothing. Obviously. I thought that was for the best. In fact I thought everything was for the best. Gemma was off my back. She and Michala had the baby they wanted. Harriet and I were off to Uist. Win-win. Easy.'

Win-win? Easy?

Rosie Tremayne was playing a blinder, Suttle thought. She could have been a therapist, a counsellor, teasing out the knots in this man, paving the way for the full confession. Most of it was there now. All Suttle wanted was some hint of regret, of contrition, even of anger. To date, as far as Harriet was concerned, Bentner had displayed indifference to the pain she must have suffered. At work, according to Sheila Forshaw, there were certain colleagues who put Bentner high on the autism scale. Maybe they were right. Maybe, on an ever-warmer planet, he remained ice-cold inside.

Tremayne, yet again, didn't disappoint.

'Win-win is wrong, Mr Bentner.' Her voice was soft. 'You're

telling us Gemma killed your partner. Tore her belly apart. Mutilated the child she was carrying. Yet you never lifted the phone. I find that inexplicable.'

'Me too.' He nodded. 'We talked afterwards on the phone. Gemma knew about Scotland. She knew I wanted to put money down on the property. She wanted us all to go up there. That's why I went last week. To check the place out. To try and visualise what it might be like.'

'You mean the croft?'

'Yes.'

'That's why you broke in? Stayed over?'

'Yes.'

'And?'

'Hopeless. Being out there on the edge of things gives you perspective. The world is crazy. So is Gemma. No way would it ever have worked. That's why I came back, booked into that pub across the road, gave myself up.' He sat back, his story over, that same hint of relief on his face. 'So here we are. Here we have it. Beware of Gemma. Be gentle with Michala. None of this is down to her.'

Afterwards

Gemma Caton and Michala Haas were interviewed later that same day. After consulting with the duty solicitor, who'd earlier conferred with Rosie Tremayne, Michala read a prepared statement admitting her role in the events of the previous evening. She'd used her phone to talk to Gemma while staying with Lizzie. She'd opened the door to her while Lizzie was asleep in bed. She'd done Gemma's bidding, fetched the paper and the wood, and set fire to the bedroom. Asked why she hadn't intervened when Gemma tried to kill Lizzie, she refused to comment.

Finally, Tremayne asked about the hire car from Budget. Michala admitted that she'd hired the Ford Focus to use at the weekend. She'd taken it to London and then driven Gemma back down on the Saturday evening. After Gemma killed Harriet Reilly, they'd both returned to London, their alibi intact. On the Monday Michala and the hire car were back in Exeter.

Gemma Caton did her best to browbeat both Tremayne and Myers. This was yet another show that belonged exclusively to her. She happily confirmed that she'd done her best to kill Lizzie. She suspected that Michala had told Lizzie everything. By getting so close to Michala, she had sealed her own fate. Agreeing to suffocate her before the fire took hold was an act of mercy. For that, Gemma insisted, she deserved nothing but thanks.

Tremayne ignored the suggestion. When she put it to Caton that she'd killed Harriet Reilly, she simply nodded. Asked to explain why, she said that Reilly had made Michala deeply unhappy by denying Kelly a pain-free death. Worse still, by getting herself pregnant she'd come to stand between herself and Alois

Bentner. In the world that she and Alois shared, there was no room for another. Harriet Reilly was a trespasser and had paid the price. Caton had no remorse, no shame, no guilt. It was, she said, simply an overdue adjustment to the order of things.

Rosie Tremayne wanted to know where she and Michala would have headed next. The croft in Scotland was no longer a possibility. With Lizzie dead, the victim of a presumed accident, the pair of them would have been home free. But where was home?

Caton had seemed indifferent. The world was a big place. She'd already seen most of it. Bhutan? Laos? Certain parts of the Mongolian steppe? They were all possibilities. Michala would love it because all three of them would be together, far from the madness of the rest of the world.

'Three?'

'Me. Michala. And the little one.'

From Gemma Caton, to Nandy's delight, *Buzzard* was thus looking at a full confession: not to one murder but possibly two. The news from the ICU was far from conclusive. Lizzie was still breathing with the aid of a machine, and there were hopeful signs that she might surface over the coming days, but the uncertainty about brain damage remained. Either way, in the opinion of the consultant in charge, she'd had a remarkable escape from what would otherwise have been certain death.

Golding thought the same. He and Suttle had driven over to St Leonard's. The fire brigade had saved most of the lower half of the property, but the house that Suttle had so briefly known was a ruin. The roof had gone, charred rafters against the summer sky, and swallows dived and soared through the smoke still curling from the wreckage inside.

Suttle went to the front door. A fireman was standing guard. Forensic investigators were busy inside, combing through the debris to establish the seat of the fire. Within the hour they'd be joined by a Scenes of Crime team, but for the time being even Suttle's warrant card couldn't gain him entry.

'Take this, though, buddy? Delivered this morning.' The fire-man gave Suttle a parcel. It was book shaped.

Suttle returned to the car. They both got in.

'Oona?' They were driving back to the MIR.

'Talked to her about an hour ago, skip.'

'And?'

'She thinks you must be in a state.'

'She's right.'

'She says to give her a ring when you're ready. Not before.'

'Good or bad?'

'You're asking me?'

'I am.'

Golding nodded. Stared out of the window. 'Houghton told me the way you played it last night,' he said at last. 'You pushed it to the limit. I thought that was gutsy.'

'And Oona?'

'She thought the same.'

Suttle spent the evening alone. He bought himself a bottle of wine from the Co-op in town, returning to the shelf from the queue at the cash desk to make it two. He had no appetite for either food or football, preferring to sit at his window and watch the sun expire over the smoky ridge lines of the Haldon Hills. It was a beautiful evening, more swallows against the last of the light, and after darkness had fallen he fetched the parcel from the kitchen.

It was from Amazon. It was addressed to Lizzie. It had a return address in Seattle. He unwrapped it. Dr Gemma Caton, *Native Indian Rituals on the Pacific Coast*. He opened the book, looked at a photo or two and poured himself another glass of wine. The writing was brighter and more fluent than he'd anticipated. This woman could compel attention on paper as well as in the flesh. She had the knack of recreating an entire way of life, of taking you there, of making you aware of just how precious, and just how precarious, life in the wild could be.

Then salmon leaped into the story. How important they were.

How they held the promise of survival. And how the elders of the tribe awaited the moment when they appeared offshore, nosed up the river and began the last stage of their journey to their spawning grounds. On a bad year they were late. Once, on the Fraser River in the 1840s, they didn't come at all. The elders conferred. It was, they concluded, a question of propitiation. The spirits were troubled. The spirits demanded a sacrifice. And so they found the most pregnant woman in the tribe. Killed her. Opened her belly. And offered the child's head to the river. The salmon, wrote Caton, appeared next morning. And there was much rejoicing.

Three days later, with Lizzie still unconscious in hospital, Suttle phoned Oona and asked her to come down for the evening. Her car was in for servicing, so she took the train. Suttle met her at the station. She gave him a hug and then another, and linked her arm through his. En route home, a detour took them to a pub called the Bicton Arms. Suttle had used it a couple of times and knew the landlord was a fishing fanatic.

Oona, intrigued by the place, perched herself on a stool while Suttle waited for the landlord to appear. There were a couple of trophy specimens in glass cases behind the bar. When the landlord finally arrived, Suttle asked him about current prospects on the river. The landlord said the fishing was good. Promising bass. Plenty of mackerel. Even a decent show of pollock.

'And the salmon?'

'Came late this year. Unheard of.'

'And now?'

'Back. Loads of them. Strange, eh?'

Acknowledgements

I owe this book to a series of storms that hit the West Country just after the Christmas before last. Neither Lin nor I – both connoisseurs of extreme weather – had ever seen anything like it. The force of the wind was beyond belief. The sea wanted to eat you alive. On a couple of wild nights the highest of tides exploded over the promenade and threatened to flood whole areas of the town. Scary.

A couple of months later I was talking to a friend, Mark Martineau, who knows the Exe estuary intimately. For the first time in living memory, he said, the salmon had failed to show. This phenomenon, in some respects, was as alarming as the weather. Might there be some link between the two? Did the salmon know something we didn't? Thus does a book like this begin to shape itself.

Speculation, though, is barely a start. For a hard-core brief on the study of climate change I had to turn to experts in the field and happily the Met Office was just down the road in Exeter. Dr Debbie Hemming and Phil Bentley gave me an extensive tour, answered endless questions, and set me on the road to Chapter One. From the moment I stepped out of the building, I knew exactly where the book would lead.

Other contributors to this wild adventure? To Dr Amy Todd I owe a big thank you for sharing some of the secrets of the world of the GP. To Amy's dad, Peter Todd, an equally warm round of applause for introducing me to the Fureys. An unforgettable evening. My eldest son, Tom, happens to be a gifted – and fear-less – photographer. He lives round the corner and whenever my memory of those winter storms became a little hazy he'd send me a video or two he'd managed to shoot as the ocean came roaring out of the darkness.

This book was finally completed in the depths of rural France and I owe Marie-Josephe Tolufu and Florence Fremont a warm *merci beaucoup* for plugging the edited manuscript back into the world of Internet connections and e-mail in time to meet the publishing deadlines.

Finally, a well-earned thank you to Oli Munson, my indefatigable agent, to Laura Gerrard, who kept a firm hand on the editorial tiller, and to Hugh Davis, who copy-edited with his usual attention to the rogue commas. Jenny Page steadied the ship when it mattered most and Diana Franklin worked her usual magic with the proofs.

Lastly, my wife Lin. We've both fallen in love with the Touraine. The weather is superb. Cloudless skies. Constant sunshine. Barely a whisper of wind. Don't be fooled, I tell her. Just you wait …

Civray-sur-Evres
June, 2015